MW00450939

Kidnapped from the Caribbean

Kidnapped from the Caribbean

A Cannon and Sparks Adventure Novel

by

Todd Duff

Tablet Publications

TABLET PUBLICATIONS • COCOA BEACH, FLORIDA

Kidnapped from the Caribbean
A Cannon and Sparks Adventure Novel

Copyright © 2017 by Todd Duff

Published in the USA by:
Tablet Publications
2023 N. Atlantic Ave., Unit #226
Cocoa Beach, Florida 32931
Phone 321-610-3634
Email orders@tabletpublications.com
www.tabletpublications.com

All rights reserved. No part of this book may be reproduced, stored in a retrieval system, or transmitted in any form or by any means, electronic, mechanical, photocopying, recording, or by any storage and retrieval system without permission in writing from the Publisher. All photography in this book is by the author, unless otherwise noted.

Tablet Publications is an imprint of Seaworthy Publications, Inc.

Library of Congress Cataloging-in-Publication Data

Names: Duff, Todd, 1955- author.
Title: Kidnapped from the Caribbean / Todd Duff.
Description: Cocoa Beach, Florida : Tablet Publications, [2017] | Series: A
   Cannon and Sparks adventure novel.
Identifiers: LCCN 2017025183 (print) | LCCN 2017032593 (ebook) | ISBN
   9781892399953 (Kindle edition) | ISBN 1892399954 (Kindle edition) | ISBN
   9781892399946 (softcover : acid-free paper)
Subjects: LCSH: Private investigators--Fiction. | Missing
   persons--Investigation--Fiction. | GSAFD: Adventure fiction. | Mystery
   fiction.
Classification: LCC PR9275.B743 (ebook) | LCC PR9275.B743 D845 2017 (print) |
   DDC 813/.6--dc23
LC record available at https://lccn.loc.gov/2017025183

Dedication

This book is dedicated first of all to my mother, Mary Lou, who always encouraged me in my many varied pursuits, to my mate Gayle who has so graciously supported my efforts and to my family and all my friends and most of all to my fellow sailors who have provided many of the inspirations for the actual events woven into this tale.

To all of you, as you turn these pages; bon voyage and I hope you enjoy the story!

One

My name's Brice Cannon and my partner is Juliet Sparks. We're marine insurance investigators which means we're sort of like private eyes, but we mostly work along the waterfronts of the world, dealing with lost or stolen boats and the sometimes dubious circumstances that occasionally surround insurance claims on yachts. We deal with insurance losses on yachts in almost every remote corner of the globe and although we do get a lot of routine assignments, once in a while something out of the ordinary comes up that takes us out of our comfort zone. And when business is slow, we have been known to deliver people's boats from point A to point B, almost anywhere in the world - mostly sailboats, but sometimes power boats too. Not like we do it all that often, and we don't usually do normal deliveries; taking people's boats back and forth from the Caribbean or Mediterranean, or up and down some coast. When we get called for a job, it's usually a repo; someone who has run off with a boat and the bank wants it back -or stolen boats. We get called in for a few of those from time to time and there have been times when our job has gotten quite interesting. Sometimes even dangerous.

We both grew up in and around the water — surfing, scuba diving, sailing and so, many years back our love of the ocean and sailing brought us to the decision to buy a sailboat, live on it, and sail it around the world's oceans in search of exotic places. We travel seeking the exquisite solitude and the natural beauty of remote lands and sometimes we find it. We also crave excitement and adventure, and sometimes we get more than our fair share of that too.

When I was young I worked for a boat builder and eventually became the yard foreman; after that I became a marine surveyor which means people paid me to look their boats over and tell them what was wrong and needed fixing so that they could get insurance, and then sometimes people would not fix things I had told them about and later lie to their insurance company about it when there was a loss. I'm pretty detail oriented and can find out in most cases the real reason why an accident has happened. Because we're both divers, sometimes we've found boats that were reported lost and had in fact been scuttled by their owners so they could collect on the insurance policy. We get a lot of insurance work. Juliet is an artist, and not much into the mechanical aspects of boats, but is also a licensed captain and is more fearless and far more optimistic than I am. We make a great team.

It was a beautiful clear and breezy late-October morning and we were at one of the remote little windswept outer islands of the Bahamas where we had been diving and beachcombing. Our boat was anchored in one of our favorite 'secret' anchorages, a tiny pocket in the reef that can only be reached by threading your way carefully through dangerous coral formations which the charts showed as impassable, but which we had found our way into years back and revisited whenever we were down this way. We were taking a break from our busy life and looking forward to a few more weeks of solitude before we would sail back down to our home waters of the Virgin Islands later in the season.

That morning an email came in over our shortwave SSB radio which was to change our plans in a bad way over the coming months. If only I had known then what we were getting involved in, I would have deleted that email and gone back out spear fishing.

But the mail was from a good friend; an insurance investigator named Rudy Bellows, and it was short and to the point. *Hope you two are well. There was a yacht loss reported off Panama. Looks suspicious to me and wonder if you could nip down there and investigate it for me?*

Nip down, yeah, right. Rudy is British and has a tendency to understate things. Panama was over a thousand miles away across the windiest part of the Caribbean and it was now one of the stormiest parts of the year. But never the less, I emailed back. *Tell us more. Call us on the sat phone any time later today.*

Rudy is a short, stocky, balding, and sometimes rather intense man who was born and raised in the UK, but has lived in the British Virgin Islands, usually referred to as the BVI, for over thirty years. That is when he isn't in London, Berlin, or New York in board meetings with underwriters and agency heads. Usually the meetings were routine but sometimes a claim would come up that needed looking into. If he can, Rudy often hires a local to check things out for him, but in this case, whatever was going on was important enough that he felt it necessary to elicit our assistance.

"This must be a big one," I said to Jules. Just then the sat phone rang. It was Rudy's number. "Jeez, he must have been online already, watching for our response," I said as I picked up the Iridium satellite telephone on the chart table and punched 'talk'. Rudy's deep sounding voice came on the line.

"Good morning, Brice! Thanks for the quick response. We've got some real trouble here, and feel free to say no if you don't like the sound of it, but it looks like this is right up your alley." What he was probably referring to is that it could be daring and risky, and if we hadn't had some real close calls which had come out OK, we wouldn't have gotten the reputation of being big risk takers. I don't like having that reputation, but it's there.

"So what's this all about, Rudy?" I asked, realizing that I probably sounded weary and impatient. It had only been a few weeks since our last assignment, which had turned out to be a somewhat dicey repo of a large motor yacht that had been 'stashed' up a river on the south coast of the Dominican Republic. But which we had located fairly easily; sneaking in past the sleeping security guards at the private residence where the yacht was docked and just hopped aboard one night, untied the dock lines and made a beeline for the States. The fact that we had left the river under a hail of gunfire and that we'd had engine problems the whole way to Miami had us looking forward to a month or two of peace and quiet.

Sitting up at the chart table, I looked over at Juliet with a slight grimace on my face. I was, quite frankly, rather annoyed at this intrusion into our quiet time. You can't have everything.

"An ex charter boat, an old Beneteau 44 sloop, was stolen from a marina in the BVI almost a year ago. We didn't find out till a couple of days after it went missing. Clever devils who nicked it must have had a local connection. The boat had been phased out of one of the charter fleets and was already sold, awaiting its new owners' arrival. Some men showed up, according to a few people in the marina, late on a Friday. Colombian or maybe Venezuelan, one person said. Anyway, they convinced the few people who talked to them that they were the new owners. Provisioned the boat in one day and left the next night. No-one thought anything of it until the broker who had sold it went over on Monday morning to see about a few questions the new absentee owners had, and the boat was gone. Anyway, the long and short of that part of the story is that we've never had a trace of the boat or the men since."

I thought a few seconds and replied, "So how does this come up now, so many months later?"

Rudy went on. "OK, the boat may have been found wrecked on a reef in Panama a few weeks ago. We're not positive yet. It's not on the surface, maybe even too deep to dive, but if it's the boat, then we need to know."

"Rudy." I was irritated at this point. "Why don't you just hire a local to dive it? What makes one old stolen charter boat so important? It's gone. Maybe it's your boat or maybe not, but why send us all the way across the Caribbean to find out? I don't get it."

There was a long pause on the line and I heard Rudy as he inhaled before he went on in a bit of a lowered voice.

"Brice, this isn't an isolated incident. We've lost four other boats in the Caribbean in the last eight months and it's my gut feeling that the others may be somehow tied into this one. We need someone we can trust to find out what's going on. Maybe go down there 'under cover' and try to suss out what's happening. It may be that the other boats are being used by the same people and we need to know. A couple of them were fairly big catamarans and are worth three quarters of a million dollars each."

Now I understood. I looked up at Juliet, who was standing in the galley next to the chart table, trying to follow the conversation as well as she could but clearly concerned by my wrinkled brow and the look in my eyes. We've been in dangerous situations a few other times and I don't really like the idea of intentionally going into one if I can avoid it. But at the same time Rudy's a good friend, and we are after all, in the business of reclaiming lost or stolen property. I had to go forward.

"OK, Rudy, I think I have an inkling of what you're talking about now, but let me get this straight; You think that the boats that have been stolen have all been taken by the same people and that the trail begins in Panama? You also think that there is a good chance we can find out who's behind this and possibly intervene, and want to have us snoop around so the boats aren't scuttled or taken somewhere else if they feel like there is someone on to them?" Rudy murmured an affirmation and I went on, "What makes you so sure this boat on the reef in Panama is related, or that it's even the boat from the BVI at all?" Rudy was ready for this question and I could almost imagine him leaning forward in his big leather chair for the next exchange. I was also sitting up straight now, very interested in what he might have to say.

"Apparently one of the passengers thought he could see an old boat name painted over. The name he thought he saw was the same as what was on the missing boat... and Brice, there's been a murder."

"Where?" I cut in, and he quickly added.

"Where this boat was lost, it was carrying backpackers and from the reports we've gotten from some of the passengers, they had a South American guy on board who was their captain, more or less, who apparently got drunk. The boat came into the San Blas Islands at night and the captain was possibly asleep, or passed out, and hit a reef. All the backpackers and the captain made it to shore through the surf and a few of the cruisers on other boats had heard the whole thing happening because one of the backpackers got on the boat's VHF radio and was calling Mayday, so a few of the crews of some of the other cruising yachts anchored nearby came to help out. Apparently, at first they thought that it was just an innocent backpacker run gone wrong. You know, there are a lot of boats that make that run back and forth from Panama to Colombia with young backpackers off on an adventure. There must be close to a hundred boats in that trade in the peak season. Anyway, these backpackers all talked about how the captain was kind of a scary guy and one of the crew saw some packs of something stored under the cockpit that might have been drugs."

I scooted over at the chart table seat and motioned to Juliet to come sit down, adjusting the phone better so that she could also hear and as Jules gave me a look of concern, Rudy went on.

"There's a lot of speculation that some people are using backpacker boats as a cover for drug smuggling, and bringing them into the San Blas Islands where there are hardly any patrols. So these kids thought that the captain had drugs on board maybe. This is where the story gets really interesting." By now Jules had scrunched in next to me and had her head pressed close to the phone so she could hear what was being said. Rudy went on, "In any case, the next morning one of the cruising boats was gone from the anchorage and the South American captain was gone too. The other cruisers all thought it was strange because the boat that was missing was owned by an old guy, an American, who hardly ever went anywhere and certainly not at night in an area choked with so many reefs and shoals." Rudy paused for a few seconds and finished up, "The boat was found two days later up the coast about fifty miles near a town called Linton, stashed in the mangroves, and the old man had been shot in the head. Blood everywhere." Juliet and I looked at each other as he continued, "A real mess, Brice. The Panamanian national police were all over this at first, but there's no trace of the captain and after a few weeks now, the Panamanians have stopped looking."

Two

Juliet's not the early riser. I am. In the early morning twilight, I looked over at her lying next to me in our big double berth in the aft cabin, her auburn hair in disarray all over her pillow and a peaceful smile on her lips. I felt remorse that I might, once again, be putting her in harm's way. *This time I'll be much more careful*, I thought to myself as I quietly slipped out of bed and padded down the passageway into the main cabin and to the galley to make coffee. Juliet is late thirties, slender and covered in freckles when she's exposed to too much sun, which is most of the time. With green eyes, long wavy hair and her stunning figure, she usually attracted attention wherever she went. She is a relaxed and calm person, the opposite of how I am sometimes, is a wonderful cook, a careful and competent captain and can sing and play guitar too. I'm a very lucky man. I am medium build, forty-five years old and about five foot eleven on a good morning. Never had a problem with weight, but sometimes wish I had a bit more beef on me; particularly when I find myself in a dicey situation with thugs. But with my sandy hair and nice smile, and blessed with a quick wit, I can often talk myself out of having to use force when things go bad.

After our conversation with Rudy the day before, we decided to leave for Panama the next morning and spent the afternoon preparing the boat for a rough passage across the Caribbean Sea. We had checked the weather on our laptop computer using the GRIB files - long range weather forecasts transmitted by our SSB radio mail service - and decided that it was better to leave sooner as opposed to later, and that the best route south would be to go west of Jamaica after transiting the Windward Passage between Cuba and Haiti as this looked like the less boisterous, less windy way to go.

"Just think of how much fun it will be to see our old friends down that way!" I had said to her in an effort to make it sound like we had planned on going that way all along, but our conversation was somewhat reserved all that afternoon and evening and we both slept fitfully, thinking of what we might be getting into down in Panama. *I'll be really careful and we'll bail if it looks too dangerous*, I promised myself and had said to Jules,

"Don't worry, we won't stay if it gets too dangerous, OK?" To which she had just looked at me without any response.

Finally, she had said, "It's OK, Brice, we're well paid and if there really is an organization behind this, we'll find them and turn them in. I have faith in us and I'm sure it will be OK."

I love this woman, was all that came to mind.

As the dawn arrived I brought Juliet her coffee back in the aft cabin and then went up on deck to start taking the anchor in. After starting the engine to let it warm up, I looked out at the reef opening. Breakers were well defined on either side of the deep water of the narrow channel and we had dived on the pass many times, so I had no concerns about leaving in the strengthening predawn light. But something was bothering me and I went about the business of taking the anchor in with some misgivings. *It's only the usual pre-passage butterflies*, I said to myself as I went back to the mast and began to raise the mainsail. It was normal to feel unsettled before heading out on a long offshore sail and most long distance sailors admit to experiencing apprehension before leaving. But this time it somehow felt different. Bigger.

By now Juliet had come up into the cockpit and assumed her normal position at the wheel, ready to motor forward when it was time to finish taking in the anchor chain and get underway. I had tied in a reef in the mainsail, to make the sail area smaller because of the strong winds we were expecting offshore and so I soon had the mainsail raised and cleated off and scrambled back up forward to finish taking in the anchor. Juliet motored forward as we came over the top of the anchor and we broke the 'hook' out of the clean white sand easily. She swung the wheel to port, bearing off towards the pass in the reef while I secured the anchor in its roller for the passage offshore.

Soon we had the engine off and were surging through the waves under the shortened mainsail and our high cut Yankee jib on what is referred to as a close reach, sailing fairly close to the wind to allow us to clear the end of the island. Within a few hours we made the turn downwind and had left the palm and casuarina trees of the little island far below the horizon. We made our course for the middle of the Windward Passage between Cuba and Haiti. Six to eight foot seas and twenty knots of wind had us going along at a good clip and by the evening of the third day out we were nearly halfway to the Panamanian coast.

We had received a series of calls on our satellite telephone from the insurance agency and they had filled us in with some additional information which they hoped would be of some help. They had also promised to supply some photos of the missing boats by email on our regular Gmail account for when we got to Panama, but because of the 'party line' aspect of Sailmail, which was our shortwave SSB radio email provider, nothing more in writing had come over – just in case someone might overhear. We did send out a few emails to friends telling them that we had decided to go to Panama for a few months, and so no-one would be surprised when we turned up in Portobelo in a few days' time. We even went so far as to email an old friend who owned a backpacker bar in Portobelo and knew the waterfront scene well to tell him that we were coming down that way and that we might be interested in getting some work doing a few backpacker runs. Never hurts to stir the pot a little before you taste it.

The weather was actually glorious. Other than being a bit on the windy side, the sunshine was warm and the air felt fresh and clean. Flying fish scudded out of our bow wake and on the morning of the fifth day out I heard Juliet scrambling around on deck and shouting to me below in the cabin where I was plotting our course at the chart table. When I came on deck I saw her up on the bow watching hundreds of spinner dolphins putting on a fantastic show all around our boat. At times like this it's like Juliet is a child. Her excitement was contagious and soon I was up with her on the deck whistling and shouting to the sleek mammals, trying to communicate in some crude fashion. Just as we were both in the middle of a chorus of out-of-tune whistles, four spinners jumped at once right off the windward bow and drenched us both in a shower of spray. Laughing, we both hugged each other and I kissed her, looking into the laughing green eyes of the woman I loved with my entire soul.

"I'm glad we took this job, Brice. Just think, if we hadn't come this way, we would never have seen this," she said as her arm swept out across the sparkling windswept sea foaming with the antics of the dolphins all around us. "This is a good omen, I know we'll be successful and find the bad guys," she added and went back to whistling to the dolphins as they started to move off en masse towards the horizon.

That evening, as the nearly full moon rose and the sun was almost setting, we sat quietly in the cockpit of our floating home while we sped across the darkening lumpy seas. We both felt more at ease with the decision we had made which I mused to myself was good, since we had decided to play the 'eager but low on cash cruisers' who needed to earn money, and to try to elbow our way into the clique of captains and crew who are involved in the backpacker trade of Panama.

A lot of long distance sailors, most commonly referred to as 'cruisers', operate on a shoestring budget, sailing from country to country and stopping to work at whatever jobs they can find to avoid running out of money. In the Panama area, new people were always coming and going in the backpacker business. The typical scenario was to pick up six or eight young backpackers, and charge them each about five hundred dollars to deliver them from Cartagena, Colombia to Portobelo, Panama, or vice versa. Some captains just did a few runs to bring in some extra cash before heading on across the sea while others had been doing it for years.

Our boat is a Kelly Peterson 44, built in Taiwan back in what I like to call the 'Golden Age of Fiberglass Boatbuilding', the 1970s. We call her 'Mahalo' which means 'thank you' in Hawaiian and although she is about forty years old, her previous owners had spent a lot of money on her and we have managed to keep her up in good shape. She is a center cockpit cutter which means she has a single mast but two sails up front and a main sail on the boom. She has a nice aft cabin in the back part of the boat, and room for five or six more people to sleep in varying degrees of comfort in the middle and forward parts of the boat, so it would be a plausible boat in which to attempt to be doing backpacker runs. Although many of the boats doing the human cargo trade, as some people jokingly called it, were larger and had multiple sleeping cabins, the boat that had been stolen and which our friends at the insurance company believed was sunk on the reef in the San Blas Islands was also by coincidence forty-four feet, so we felt pretty sure no-one would think twice about our sincerity in wanting to do some backpacker runs with our boat, especially if we dressed down a bit and adopted a more laissez faire attitude in public. We had even gotten an email back from our friend in Portobelo saying that business was good and that he thought he could help us fill up our boat for our first run to Cartagena, and had enquired about when we might be ready to start.

In order to understand the whole concept of a backpacker boat, a little background is necessary and a quick look back in history will put things in perspective. Panama used to be a part of Colombia. In 1903, with the help of the US military and a few crooked politicians, a group of greedy businessmen and power-hungry civil servants overthrew the legitimate government of the state of Panama and ceded from Colombia. At that time, there was a primitive road from the main part of Colombia through the mountains to Panama. But this was quickly destroyed in order to assure isolation from her former masters and with the help of the US, which had immediately recognized the new government and had sent navy ships to protect the harbors, Panama set off on her own as an independent country. Now, over a century later, there are still no roads linking the two neighboring and mutually distrusting countries and so, for the ever increasing numbers of young, enthusiastic backpackers who are out 'seeing the world' on their gap year from college, or just twenty-somethings who have taken on traveling the world as a way of life, these adventurers are finding themselves bumming and hitching, riding trains or buses all the way down to Panama or up from Brazil or Bolivia to Colombia, only to learn that there is no road linking the two countries, and that an airplane ride costs many hundreds of dollars. So, a few enterprising captains of small yachts began offering rides between the two countries for the same price as, or less than, a plane, promoting the romance of a sailing adventure and five days of exploring through the pristine San Blas Islands of Panama.

That this route traverses what are some of the most navigably dangerous and primitive areas in the western hemisphere is not mentioned in any of the websites or posters advertising this adventure. Each year boats are lost on this run but nevertheless, a seemingly endless tide of young people come along and decide to take life by the horns and join a boat going one way or another. Soon word got out of this new trade and more and more boats began doing it. It was written up in *Lonely Planet* and other travel guides, and in a few years had developed to the point that in peak season, over a hundred boats were engaged in the trade.

On all but a few boats, things like life rafts, EPIRPS (emergency radio beacons) or even life jackets were of secondary concerns to the greedy, usually unlicensed captains who often would overload boats with these naive young people and were literally 'cleaning up' on the runs. They would even typically make it a requirement that the passengers, made up of the young adventurers, participate in cooking, cleaning and running the boats. A recipe for disaster? Yes, sometimes. Each year a boat or two was lost, and on each side the governments responded by gradually tightening regulations. A few of the bigger boats actually complied with the new rules. This never seemed to stop the fly-by-night small operators who would simply bypass the law, offering rides to Colombia or back to Panama for less money, slipping out of port at night or from a coastal town down the way from the main clearance ports. With money changing hands under the table on each side of the border, the trade went on with little interference from officialdom. Coming to Panama from Colombia, once safely in the San Blas Islands, the myriad reefs and small islets, most of which are improperly or not even charted at all offered virtual immunity from patrols.

All of this is interesting and academic in the big picture, but was not our concern as we approached the Panamanian coast on day seven. Winds had lightened up and we were enjoying our last dinner at sea when we got a call from Rudy Bellows.

"Brice?" He practically shouted in Jule's ear before she could even say hello.

"It's Juliet, I'll get Brice. He's up on deck."

Hearing the phone, I had started down the companionway, the entry area to the main cabin where the chart table and galley were and where we kept the sat phone.

Juliet handed me the iridium telephone and I looked at the caller ID before saying "Rudy? What in the hell time is it in the BVI? It's 8 p.m.! Why are you still in the office? What's going on?"

"There's been another boat theft, Brice. A Lagoon 62 from right here on Tortola!"

Lagoon 62s are very expensive, sumptuously appointed and luxurious yachts — probably two million dollars new and are one of the premier big catamarans out in the Caribbean charter trade.

"What happened, Rudy? What's the story?"

He went on, "A family from Ecuador rented it. Said they were meeting friends who were coming in from St Barts for a week of sun and fun. No big deal. Happens all the time. Well, after a week, they never showed up back at the charter base. At first the charter company thought maybe they were just late, and after a few more days thought maybe they had been sunk or pirated or something, but then the bank called and told them that the funds for the charter had bounced. It had been a cashiers' check and whoever had issued it knew how to pull a scam. That much I can tell you." He took a breath before going on. "The boat is missing, and they've had ten days' head start on us. We have no idea of where to even start looking!"

By now the last glimmer of the orange sunset had faded in front of us and the bright waxing moon was sparkling off the waves to the east, illuminating our wake. A magic carpet of stars above us and the consistent and gentle breeze had me in a calm and clear thinking mood.

"Rudy, I hear what you're saying. I agree, this could be more of the same group, or it could be an isolated incident, but in any case, we'll certainly add that one to the growing list. Obviously you've notified the coast guards of the various countries on the way north and south, and have called all the customs offices within two thousand miles, right?"

"Yes of course. I just wanted you to stew on that tonight, Brice. You have a nose for things like this. If you think of anything, call me right away. The underwriters are unbelievably upset with me. I need to give them something soon!" He then lowered his voice and became very serious. "There's one more thing, Brice. They had a captain and cook aboard. Both in their early twenties. Captain was a Brit; the cook was an American girl. And it turns out her father is a US Senator. I don't need to tell you that this incident has taken on a very serious tone."

I said nothing for a moment. I had to think. If this really was a related incident, now there could be kidnapping involved... or maybe the kids were somehow involved too? Nothing surprises me anymore. "I'll give this all some thought, Rudy, and I'll let you know if I see or hear anything."

After a few pleasantries, we signed off. Looking over at Jules perched casually in the downwind cockpit seat, I brought her up to speed on the latest developments.

"Doesn't seem likely they would bring a boat like that down here to the Southwest Caribbean," she said and went on, "It would stand out like a sore thumb here. They'd be caught in a few days."

She was right. All that night while on my watches, as we closed the coast of Panama and made our final approach towards the old Spanish treasure harbor of Portobelo, I thought about it. There was no way these big charter catamarans could be anywhere near the typical yachting centers, or even be sold on the black market. They were too rare, too big and too obvious. What in the world whoever stole these boats could have been thinking was completely beyond me. The smaller monohull boats that had been taken were more common and would be easy to disguise. One was a Beneteau 47 which is almost as common in the sailing world as Toyota Camrys are on the roads of America. And the other was a Jeanneau, a similar generic looking fiberglass sloop. These boats could easily be repainted, their names changed and have their canvas work like sail covers and spray dodger colors switched; No-one would ever guess they were stolen. But these big catamarans? I was stumped...

Dawn had us only ten miles off the harbor and by 8 a.m. we were at anchor in the old seaport of Portobelo. It was originally chosen by the Spanish because of its excellent protection from the easterly trade winds behind low hills, and because it offered ships an easy escape should a marauder arrive. Seven hilltop fortresses surrounding the harbor had protected Portobelo, and its strategic location had made this the primary trans-shipment point for the plundered gold stolen from the Inca Empire during the early 1500s through the late 1600s. Despite the formidable defenses, Portobelo had been sacked on numerous occasions and it always brought me back in time to look up at the brooding, overgrown fortification in the surrounding mist-enshrouded hills while thinking of the absolute unabashed balls it took for a bunch of half-starved and ill-trained soldier/sailors to sail in on a cumbersome square rigged ship, bombard the town, take the forts and steal what they could, escaping before the rest of the Spanish fleet could arrive, once messengers who would have been dispatched the moment the marauders had arrived had been sent by horseback to alert their commanders. Even today, that 'beyond the law' attitude and general feeling of lawlessness is easy to adopt in a place that is so far beyond the normal boundaries of first world civilization. That the backpacker trade was running without proper safety gear, or even any government regulations beyond simple immigration and customs check-ins, was evidence that it was more than likely that some amount of money was changing hands under the table, so to speak, in both countries. And it didn't take much of a leap of the imagination to conceive that combining these seemingly innocent backpacker runs with a bit of drug smuggling would be a natural progression, and a whole lot more lucrative for the captains, and anyone in the respective governments that might have their hand in the pot, to please excuse the pun. And of course, it was more than likely that cocaine, being smaller and easier to transport than marijuana, would be the cargo of choice; stuffed in the bowels of a boat already crammed with backpacks, sleeping bags and guitars; who would notice a few extra bags? It was also more than likely that a lot of the captains and crews of the backpacker boats were good and honest people, and might be either unaware, or in denial about the true color of the business going on right under their own noses.

Three

It was very dark and stuffy. She struggled with the tight bindings around her hands behind her back and pushed herself to a semi sitting position with her head hitting what she guessed was the underside of the deck. It was night and the boat was sailing fast through the water. She could hear the pounding of the waves against the hull just outside and she realized she was on a canvas bunk up in one of the bow storage sections, all the way up front in the boat. These lockers were normally for storing sails and water toys, and sometimes extra crew slept in the two makeshift berths up there. Gradually her eyes adjusted and she could make out dim shapes in the starlight.

Jenny Tatterson was slightly built and attractive with straight shoulder-length white blonde hair, an even, mellow tan, blue eyes and a big smile. With her sailing background, growing up around the yacht club and junior sailing programs in Annapolis, Maryland she had gained an edge when after college, rather than pursuing a 'normal' career like her parents had wanted her to, she instead decided to try her luck in the charter sailing business in the Caribbean. She was bright and had become a good cook in her four years at college, and was strong and independent.

She had done one whole season as a freelance cook on various charter yachts out of St Thomas and Tortola and, after a too brief visit back home that summer, had just gotten back in the islands and signed on with one of the big charter companies when she got the assignment to 'Lady of the Woods', the Lagoon 62 that her friend Toby Myers was skippering. She had met Toby a few times over the previous season and he seemed like a great guy; Never came on to her and was always pretty reserved around her, but had a nice smile and a funny sense of humor. She had imagined what it might be like if he did make a pass. Would she refuse?

Toby was tall, with short dark wavy hair and a fairly sturdy build. A pretty strong sailor type, could have been a rugby player, she had thought. With his dark complexion and somewhat curly hair she'd at first guessed he was part Hispanic, although he had a normal British accent as far as she could tell. When he had seen her on the docks in Tortola the week before, he had been instrumental in getting the charter company to take her on.

"Where's Toby?" She wondered.

Thinking back, the last thing she could remember was being anchored in the Bight at Norman's Island, a big bay at the southern end of the British Virgin Island chain and a very popular anchorage with the hundreds of charter yachts that cruised the local islands during the high season. The Ecuadoran family they had aboard seemed very nice. The mother and father had introduced themselves as Anita and Carlos Valdencia, and their two boys Diego and Santiago seemed like nice polite guys and looked like they were in their early twenties. The family insisted on a dinner ashore that first night which they said was "To save you the trouble of cooking" and then after they arrived back around 10 p.m., the parents went to bed right away. Jenny had thought to herself how easy this charter was shaping up to be. She and Toby had sat up for a couple of hours and, Jenny realized, she probably had too much to drink. In fact, she didn't remember at all how she had gotten into the locker and couldn't imagine why she was tied up. It was all very confusing and very scary. Had the boat been pirated? What had happened to the family? She hoped they were OK.

"Can't you go any faster?" the woman snapped. Toby had been at the helm, the steering position on the catamaran, all night and with the boat overpowered in the strong trade winds, he had been 'on his toes', making sure nothing broke or went wrong. He had more at stake in this than they did, he thought to himself. And he looked back at the woman he knew as Anita and scowled.

"I'm sailing this tub as fast as it will go. Nobody will think anything of us unless we *break* something and have to call for help. Lots of boats are moving all over the Caribbean this time of year. I already told you this. They won't miss us for at least a week and by then we'll be off Suriname, or maybe even Brazil if these winds hold, so give me a break." He paused and then added, "And how about seeing if the American bitch is awake so she can make us some fucking food? I'm starving!" he spat back.

"Get her yourself, *Capitan*, and remember who you are talking to. Keep your manners!" and she turned and went down the steps and disappeared into the interior of the yacht. Toby set the autopilot and started to make his way towards the makeshift holding cell the Valdencia boys had set up in the crew quarters.

The Lagoon 62s can make better than ten knots in moderate winds and they had at times been hitting twelve knots, so by sunrise they had covered almost a hundred miles – more than a quarter of the way to the relative safety of the open Atlantic. The trick was going to be getting through one of the passages to the Atlantic between the Lesser Antilles islands without being seen, and the best chance of that was to time it so that they would slip between islands in the night. Toby had already done what he had thought was a very clever thing. All the big charter catamarans had AIS transceivers, which stands for "Automated Identification System." When he had explained this to Carlos and his 'boys' he had told them, "It sends out a constant identification signal to other vessels with AIS receivers giving a speed and course." The charter base also had an AIS receiver on top of a nearby mountain so it could keep track of all its boats in the island group. This saved a lot of time when confused charterers sometimes called in for help and a chase boat was dispatched to find them. "We can't disable it or the charter company will try to contact us to see what's wrong, and we can't just turn it off for more than a short while for the same reason. So we need to put it on another boat." They had scoped out the various boats that had left the charter base that day and one, thankfully, had picked up a mooring close to them that evening. A group of college kids from some Midwestern US fraternity were aboard and by sunset they had all disappeared off to the Willy T, a famous floating bar which was in fact an old Baltic trading vessel converted to a restaurant and that had been anchored in the bight for more than three decades. The parties aboard the Willy T were legendary and so when the 'family' had gone off for dinner ashore, a stop back at the fraternity brothers' boat for an hour while he installed the AIS behind the main electrical panel had gone unnoticed. Charterers never had a clue about what sophisticated electronics were onboard their boats, so the unit would never be discovered until the boat returned to the charter base. Later, after the drugged American girl cook had been deposited in the starboard crew cabin up front, the Valdencia 'boys' had gone back over to the Willy T and had bought a round of drinks for the fraternity brothers, learning that they had booked a ten-day charter and were hoping to get all the way around the whole island chain in that time, hitting every beach bar in the BVI so that they could write about it on their fraternity web blog.

Perfect.

Jenny had dozed off finally and was jolted awake by a shower of spray as someone opened the deck hatch above her, drenching her with salt water. "Rise and shine, sweetheart," she heard in Toby's familiar British accent. "Don't act so surprised, princess. We need our cook back. Time for breakfast," he spat out in a strong Latin American accent as he grabbed her arm and jerked her to her feet into the bright morning sunlight, just in time to receive another face full of spray. "Let's get the fuck off the bow, bitch," Toby shouted with his head facing back toward the main cabin where the two Valdencia boys were watching from the shelter of the cockpit, and he dragged her all the way out on deck, slamming the hatch shut behind her. He then moved her roughly back along the pitching boat to the relative comfort of the cockpit and took out a long hunting knife from somewhere on his waist.

Jenny stiffened as he moved towards her but then he reached behind her and cut the ropes binding her wrists. Pain shot through her hands as blood rushed back into her palms and fingers and then he grabbed her long blonde hair, giving it a hard tug. He placed the knife at her throat and whispered softly in her ear, "Play along with me if you want to stay alive," and then added loudly, gradually raising his voice until he was nearly shouting, "I'm going to cut off your gag, but if you do one single thing wrong, if you fail to do exactly as I ask, and if you don't act like the perfect little princess that I know you were brought up to be, I'll cut your throat and throw you to the sharks! Understand?" He once again pulled sharply back on her hair, causing her to emit a gasp, despite her gag. "Si, yes?" he said, jerking her hair again. Jenny nodded her head quickly in tiny jerks with her hair still being nearly yanked out of her head. He threw her down on the cockpit deck and stood over her while she slowly looked back up at him, terror in her eyes.

"That's better," he said as he reached down and cut the gag off her mouth. Once again he dragged her roughly to her feet and sliding the door to the main cabin open, he pushed her heavily into the main cabin saying in his strong Spanish accent, "Get some food on and if you want to live, make it be good!" Laughing, he slammed the door shut and turned back and climbed the stairs back up to the helm.

Jenny turned around to see the two Valdencia boys who had been watching everything, leering at her, and so she quickly made her way to the galley and began noisily going about getting a meal started so that she could buy herself some time and figure out what to do.

Days went by in a blur. Jenny was either making food or sitting quietly, trying to be as small and inconspicuous as she could be. Oddly enough, although at first she had expected to be raped at any minute, or at least beaten, she was allowed to walk about freely during the days, if she dared. Occasionally Toby or Carlos, the father, would warn her not to try anything stupid, but beyond that she was left to wander freely about down below decks on the boat as she made up bedding, did laundry and cleaned up after her messy crew.

What in the world is going on? she wondered. *Where are we going?*

She had noticed once when she had been allowed a brief visit to the upper cockpit where the steering station was located to do some cleaning that the boat was on a SSE heading, which meant they were going possibly to South America. Beyond that, she had no idea. Each night, she was locked back in her bow cabin and warned not to try to escape. Where in the world would she go anyway? The handles that allowed the hatch to be opened from the inside had been broken off. They had seen no land now for several days and after a week, she began to realize that they were no longer in the Caribbean Sea. The swells were much bigger and the wave period, the time between the waves, was much longer. They were also sailing very close to the wind, meaning that the wind was coming from up in front. With winds in this area of the world coming from the east most of the time, that meant that the boat was still heading in a southeasterly direction. She knew enough of the geography of the area to realize that they were probably somewhere off the northeastern coast of South America. It didn't take a lot of guesswork to imagine that they were probably heading to Brazil or Suriname.

Oh great, she thought. *There is so much wilderness. The eastern part of Brazil alone is as big as the whole of the US. They'll never find us.* Jenny began to slip into a deep despair.

Four

Roger Tatterson's phone jolted him out of his deep thought. Sitting in his office at the Maryland Statehouse, he had a view of the Chesapeake Bay through a break in the trees and from what he could see, the early November day was promising to be rainy and cold. "Tatterson," he answered and a British man responded.

"Senator Tatterson? You don't know me but my name is Rudolph Bellows and I'm with Ainsley and Dunbar Ltd. out of London, the insurance underwriters. I'm actually their agent in the Caribbean and am based in the British Virgin Islands where I'm calling from today. I have been told to get in contact with you regarding your daughter's disappearance."

Roger Tatterson sat up straight in his chair and responded, "What have you heard? Have you found her?"

"I'm afraid not, Senator. My call is just to find out if you had heard anything, and to ask you a few questions that might help our investigators. Your wife gave me this number. I got your home number from the charter company that had hired your daughter. By the way, Interpol may be getting in contact with you shortly if they haven't already, but we really want to get a jump on things if at all possible. Sometimes bureaucracy moves a bit too slowly in my way of thinking, if you'll forgive any implication of offence, sir."

"No, I haven't heard a thing. I only just heard the boat was missing a few hours ago. What can you tell me? Wasn't my daughter's boat based out of the BVI?"

"Yes, Senator, the charter company is doing all they can and have authorities from all of the Caribbean countries on the lookout for the vessel. If it turns up somewhere, we'll know right away." Roger slumped back in his chair and ran his wrinkled hand through his thinning gray hair.

"What can I do to help?" he asked. "I used to be involved with the CIA and still have some connections there. What have you got so far?" he demanded.

"Well," Rudy began and he filled in the distraught senator with the details the charter base had given him, along with what was looking more and more like fictitious names and passport numbers on the charter guests and the information about the bounced cashier's check.

"How in the world could a big charter company accept a bogus check? I just can't imagine how that would happen."

"The check appeared good, and had appeared to have cleared immediately at the local BVI bank. It was only after the bank of origin had the actual check in hand that the forgery became apparent, and by then the boat had been reported overdue. When the bank had called to tell the charter company that the check had turned out to be no good, the charter company put two and two together and they called me. The banking system here is less than first world, and quite frankly, the charter company should have known better than to accept a cashier's check, but they explained that the charterers were from Ecuador and it was a last-minute charter, and they told us that the check was drawn on a well-known Cayman bank. They thought it was OK. And on top of it, it's a big charter boat that rents out for a lot of money. I'd guess the charter company was a bit too eager."

"I'd say so!" Roger nearly shouted, and after a few seconds passed he calmed himself and continued, "What do we have on the captain? He was British, right?"

"Yes," Rudy answered and went on, "Turns out he is a naturalized Brit originally from Colombia. We've asked Interpol to check on him now. We're not sure if he's involved or not but I'm sorry, Senator, I have to ask you a few delicate questions." A moment's silence followed and Rudy started in; "Senator, are you on good terms with your daughter?"

"What in the hell are you getting at Bellows?" the senator shouted as he stood up, clutching the phone in his trembling hand. "How dare you ask that?"

"Please forgive me, Senator. We just need to try to get a profile of your daughter, and try to see what we can learn about her. Can you describe what brought her to the Caribbean and why you think she was on that boat?"

The Senator exhaled heavily and sat back down in his heavily padded leather chair and began to fill Rudy in with what appeared to be a very normal profile; good student, graduated with honors from the University of Maryland and a collegiate sailor, even competing in the US Nationals on two occasions sailing International 420 sloops, a small one design sailboat used by most colleges and high schools in the States. Nothing seemed out of place. But just before he signed off the Senator added,

"I'm not sure if this matters or not, but the year before I went into politics, after I had sold my law practice... The kids were in their early teens. We took a year off to sail, took our 42' ketch and went all the way around the whole Caribbean. I think that might have spoiled Jennifer from wanting to work in the real world. She learned a lot that year and if it's of any use knowing, she is fluent in Spanish. After the trip, she took Spanish and Portuguese as well as French in high school and then again in college. Befuddled me how she could keep track of so many similar languages, but she has a knack for that sort of thing. I always thought she should go to work for the State Department. Maybe she will someday if..." His voice trailed off and then he hastily added, "Not sure if that helps at all."

Rudy thanked him and signed off with the Senator, promising to fill him in with any additional details as they came to light, and eliciting a promise of the same from Senator Tatterson.

Tatterson paced the office for a few minutes while he rubbed his chin and then he sat back down heavily at his desk and picked up the phone.

He punched the intercom for his secretary. "Marion, get me Andy Winters at CIA. His number is in section three in our secured files." He hung up again, sitting back in his chair, deep in thought. Minutes later his phone rang and he picked up.

"Roger? How in the hell are you? Long time! How are June and the kids?" Winters said cheerfully; "What brings you to be calling me, buddy?" The Senator started in by explaining as best he could what he had learned from the insurance man he had just spoken to.

"And the thing that bothers me most," Tatterson added, "Is that I just don't know where to start!"

The CIA man thought for a second and responded. "Well, it could just be that the charterers are late, and that the check thing is a mistake. Don't get yourself all worked up just yet, Roger. This could all be for nothing."

"I don't think so, Andy," the senator went on. "That insurance guy thought this was a boat theft and he seemed pretty sure. I'm really worried! Is there any way you can get someone to look around on some of the satellite images of the area to see if you can spot the boat?"

Andy breathed out heavily and said, "Roger, listen. From what you've told me, the boat could be anywhere by now within a fifteen hundred-mile radius. It would be like looking for a needle in a haystack and to top it off, we have no probable cause to even *think* about reallocating assets to search for someone who may not even be lost at all and quite frankly, Rog, this is just not up our alley. Maybe try contacting one of the private firms to see if you can get some help, but unless you come up with more to work with, I just don't see how we can help. I'm really sorry, Roger. My hands are tied."

After they had hung up, Tatterson picked up his phone again and asked Marion to place a call to the charter agency in Tortola. After a few minutes he was speaking with the base manager John Johnson and had managed to get him to promise to send a scan of the passports of the captain and family who had chartered the boat and a copy of the charter agreement. That was something anyway.

◆◆◆

After clearing in with the Panamanian Customs and Immigrations it was nearly lunch time by the time Juliet and I had made our way up the hill to Captain Mack's Bar overlooking Portobelo Harbor.

"Great to see you, Brice!" Mack said as he pulled off his apron and the tall, muscular man in his sixties came out from behind the bar to give me a firm handshake and Juliet a long hug and a kiss. "She's as beautiful as ever. God only knows why she hangs around the likes of you!" he said to me with a wink to Juliet and then he said, "Lunch is on me. You two must be hungry for some fresh food after that passage. How about some nice local salad, Panamanian beef and a cold cerveza? And sit down and tell me what in the heck brings you two back to Panama? Where have you been the last couple of years?"

I held both hands up in front of me as if fending off and answered. "Whoa, Mack. One question at a time! Yes. Food sounds great, and free sounds even better! Juliet and I are really glad to see you too! Looks like business has been good." I said as I looked around the full bar and admired the eclectic décor that Mack had always claimed evolved on its own, rather than by design.

We had met Captain Mack a few years previously in the Caribbean when he was just finishing up a circumnavigation on his Island Trader 51 ketch he had named "Infamous", because he was in fact a former 1970s rock star lead singer from the heavy rock band "Desperados'. We had become fast friends over the next few months as we island hopped north and west through the Lesser Antilles and the Bahamas, until he went back down to Colombia before going on to Panama and we went north for the summer into New England. That next winter we sailed down to Panama on our way through the Panama Canal and to Hawaii. Just before we went through the canal we had stopped into Portobelo, which had been one of our favorite ports of call for years.

Mack had just bought the property there back then and had only recently opened his bar and youth hostel a few weeks before. By the looks of things, business had been good since our last visit. Our evenings together back in the Eastern Caribbean were often full of sharing stories of our own world travels and listening to his never-ending stories of misadventure, intrigue and sometime dubious exploits that had led him to Colombia originally where he married a beautiful Colombian girl thirty years his junior. His adventures had taken him on around the world, and ultimately back to Portobelo and to the idea of starting up in the backpacking trade himself. Now he had a captain running his boat for him while he lived ashore and his business included booking charters and backpacker runs for about two dozen boats. His bar had a clientele of some locals, but mostly ex-pat sailors, cruisers who were sailing around the world or just hanging out in Panama for a season or two, and some captains that were always making runs back and forth between Cartagena and San Blas or Portobelo with backpackers aboard.

It sounded like the backpacker business was booming and so we started in on our prearranged story. Juliet and I had agreed that although we hated to lie to our good friend, in order to learn what we needed to know, we couldn't dare involve anyone else and also, we felt like anyone overhearing might be a potential enemy. Also, having our story out in the open would only help us to maybe get closer to the real people who were operating in the background of the less than up and up part of the backpacker boat business. Whether our friend Mack knew much about this part of the trade, or if he might even be involved himself in some small way was difficult to guess, so our lies were told earnestly and with our best acting thrown in for free.

I lowered my voice a bit but spoke loudly enough that I could still be heard if someone wanted to eavesdrop and said, "Mack, Juliet and I are in a bit of a bind. We had an accident back about a year ago in an anchorage. We dragged anchor down on a mega-yacht and scratched their hull. Well, we had let our insurance lapse, and the people sued us and won. We owe them over a hundred thousand dollars to repaint their stupid boat. Can you imagine that? Jesus, we're in a bind, They've placed a lien on our boat and we've got to pay them off, so we need as many jobs as you can throw us, and if there are any other ways to make some extra money, any way really, we'd be interested. If we can't come up with the money within a hundred and twenty days, they're going to have our boat seized and then the next time we check in anywhere in the US, our boat will be gone and I could go to jail."

Captain Mack frowned at us and wrinkled his forehead as he looked right straight into my eyes and said very quietly so that only we could hear, "That's the biggest crock of shit I've ever heard in my life, Brice." And he leaned closer and said loudly enough so that he could be overheard, "Come back to my office where we can really talk." I looked over at Juliet as Mack added, "You too, Julie," as he got up and motioned with his thumb towards the back room as if he were a principal in a school, ushering disobedient students into detention. "Let's go, you two."

As we followed Mack's bulky shape across the room and through the swinging doors to the kitchen, I looked back and saw two well-dressed Latino men who had been at a table nearby watching us closely. We followed Mack past the kitchen to his small office, he let us pass and closed the door. He offered us the only two extra chairs which were near the wall next to his messy desk covered with food order forms and receipts. Up on the back wall of his office was a chalkboard with about thirty boat names and a calendar of weeks with most of the blanks filled in. He was a busy man from what I could see.

"Now suppose you tell me what's really going on, Brice," and he looked over at Juliet and said, "What's this big idiot gotten you involved in now?" Mack was smiling, but in a serious way. I thought about it for a few seconds and then began.

"Mack, I know this sounds out of character, and reckless of us, but we really are in a bind here. It's more than just the boat accident." I was making it up as I went by now, and as I continued I noticed Jules looking at me with her mouth half open in surprise. "I got in an argument with the captain of the megayacht and pushed him off our boat. He had come over and climbed aboard screaming at me and what a little prick he was. A twenty-something know-it-all, and I just got tired of listening to him and pushed him over the side. Thing is, he hit his head and almost drowned. We got him out of the water and I did CPR, but he has permanent brain damage. In addition to the insurance suit, we're being sued for a million dollars. We've hired a big-time Miami lawyer to help us, but the defense alone will cost at least a hundred grand. I'm in a real bind here, Mack, that's why we came down here. I thought I could make some quick money and I also thought, well, maybe...

maybe I could find a way to make more than just what we'd get from doing backpacker runs."

Mack scowled at me and put both his massive hands on his face, burying his face for a few seconds before he looked up at me and said, "Good fucking God, Brice. That's quite a story and I'm not saying I believe any of it either, but obviously, you need to raise some money. I get that." He looked at me for a few more seconds and then over at Juliet, obviously thinking carefully about what he was going to say next.

"Look, Brice, Juliet, I've known you both for years, and thought I knew you pretty well. I really don't think you're telling me the whole story or maybe even anything close to the actual story of what you're down here for, but I'm going to do at least some of what you want. Look, I have nothing whatsoever to do with what you're talking about. Drugs, to me, are the poison of our society. More good people are killed over drug deals gone bad in my wife's country than from cancer even. I hate it and don't have anything to do with it. But I also know that there are people involved in the trade here - not people I book for, but some people - and they do this thing you're talking about. All I can tell you is that I'll play along with what you want me to be doing, but I can't be involved. I've made a good life for myself here and I want to live to be old and gray with great-grandchildren bouncing on my knees. So, here's what I'll do: we're going to walk back out there. I'm going to say, just loud enough to be overhead, that I'm sorry but that I can't help you with what you're looking to do, and that I don't want you two to get into any trouble. I'm going to say you two need to stay away from this business and that you should go away soon, then I'll walk away. You should hang out at the bar and tell some more of the great lies you just told me, and then-"

I broke in. "Mack!" He held his hand up to stop me.

"Brice, I get it, You've got to lie to me for some reason, I don't know what it is or why, but I'm saying I'll play along... but some time you'll have to tell me what this is really all about. Now let's get on with this before I change my mind," and he got up, opening the door for us and ushered us out of his office and back into the busy bar. The two Latino guys were still in their same corner and noticed us right away.

"Listen," Mack said loudly enough for anyone to hear. "You two are asking me for things I can't do. I suggest you should leave here and take this idea somewhere else. Maybe go to Colombia and look around there. I know nothing of that sort of stuff and don't *want* to know," and with that Captain Mack turned around and pushed his way back through the double saloon doors to the kitchen and his massive six foot six height disappeared from sight.

We returned to our table and to our now cold food and sat down to eat. As I pulled up my chair I said loudly to Juliet, "Well, he was no help, but at least we got some free food from the old codger." We began speaking quietly with each other, and had just finished our food when one of the Latino guys sat down in the chair that Mack had been using and spoke to us in good English.

"Hello, my friends, mind if I join you? I couldn't help but overhear what you all were talking about."

I looked him in the eye and said, "Yeah. My bad, I guess I should be a bit more discreet," and took a long drag on my half-empty mug of beer. The man smiled and chuckled to himself.

"Not to worry. This place has seen worse. Lots of things go on here that the owner knows nothing about. He is an old fool, but he leaves us alone, and we leave him alone — it is a nice arrangement, si?"

The man sitting across from us introduced himself as Ramon, and said he was from Cartagena. He also said he had noticed our boat come into the harbor earlier and noticed our eight scuba tanks secured on the stern rail of our boat. "You two are divers, yes?"

"Yeah, we're divers. Why?" I said.

"I also understand that you two are looking to earn some money, and it doesn't sound like you will be getting any backpackers from our amigo Mack any time soon. Am I right?" he said with a twinkle in his eye and a slight, sneering smile. His eyes were very dark and his short cropped curly hair and dark skin, combined with his large bulk, gave me the impression he was some sort of enforcer in a criminal organization. I am usually right about those quick assessments, by the way.

"Yeah, we could use some work. But we're thinking about heading over to Cartagena right away, so if you need something done on your boat, it better be today. I don't really do underwater boat repairs much anymore, but we do need the cash. What's wrong with your boat and which one is it?" I said, playing the desperately poor, short on cash cruiser.

"My friend," he responded, "What I am proposing is not a boat repair and this job I am speaking of, it is actually on the way to Colombia. It is in the San Blas Islands."

I sneaked a quick eye contact with Juliet who was also leaning forward and she joined in on the conversation with, "What do you have in mind, Señor? What kind of diving do you need?"

"Ah." He sat up straighter and motioned to the waitress to bring a round of drinks and then went on. "I work for a charter company in Colombia. We are in the backpacker trade and we also ship some...eh, 'cargo', at times. We had a boat which was lost in the San Blas about a month ago and the Capitan, well, he has 'disappeared'. He was a bad navigator and wrecked a boat that belonged to my company. Personally, I don't think he will ever be found." He let that sink in for moment so we would get his true meaning. Just then the waitress arrived with our drinks and after she left, he went on, "This man, he lost not just our valuable boat, which I expect is a total loss and not worth raising, but he also lost some very valuable cargo." Taking half his mixed drink in one gulp, he blotted his mouth with his sleeve and went on. "My proposal to you is to dive on this wreck and retrieve what belongs to my employers, and to return it to us in Cartagena. If you are successful in that, then we will have more work for you — less dangerous, and not diving, but you can earn good money and maybe this is what you need, yes?"

Juliet and I both looked at each other and I tried to remain calm. Either we were having very good fortune to have happened on this man on the first day of our arrival, or maybe we were being set up. But in any case, I felt like we could proceed, at least for the moment, with agreeing, and so I looked back at him and said, "Exactly how much do you propose that this will pay, and supposing we succeed in retrieving your cargo, how will I contact you once we are in Cartagena?"

He smiled and sat back in his chair, folding his hands over his chest in the self-satisfaction of having snared me so easily. "Come over to our boat this evening after dark. Alone, my friend." Looking only at me he went on, "If you can succeed in this, you will be well rewarded," and with that he downed the remainder of his drink, put a hundred-dollar bill on the table, got up and walked over to his waiting friend who was now by the stairs, and they both departed.

A short time later we too were walking down the stairs and back down to our dinghy which we had tied up behind a small music school that offered dinghy tie ups for a dollar, with 'security' in the form of one small eight-year-old boy who spoke three words of English. There was a note inside which I picked up and read:

It was nice meeting with you Señor. We will see you at around 7 p.m. on 'Inca Gold', the motor cruiser behind your boat, two boats back. See you then my friend. - Ramon

After we got back to our boat, we both slept for a couple hours and then set about getting the boat cleaned from our wet passage. We then had dinner and a drink as the sun set over the verdant green hills behind Portobelo Harbor and chatted quietly about what this new connection we had made might be all about.

It was fully dark by the time I arrived over at the Inca Gold. I rowed our inflatable dinghy over rather than running the outboard motor, partly to make my approach slowly and partly to see if I could overhear anything as I made my way towards the back of the yacht. All was quiet aboard though and as I circled around to the open stern cockpit I saw that Ramon and his partner were sitting casually with two good-looking Latino women at a varnished teak table. The yacht was very beautiful and in this setting, the men looked much less menacing.

"Welcome, Señor Capitan Brice. Come aboard, come aboard!" Ramon said as I rounded the stern of the yacht and, motioning me to the boarding platform and taking my dinghy's bow line, he expertly tied up the dinghy and opened the transom door as I scrambled aboard. "Welcome to Inca Gold. The only classic wooden Trumpy out of South America. She was built in 1929 and was the pride of my father's fleet and is the last of her kind in our waters. May I offer you a drink?"

I looked around the cockpit at the glistening teak caprails and rich furnishings and said, "She is a beautiful vessel, Señor and yes, a rum drink if you have it, or anything else if you don't. I'm not picky." Ramon motioned me to sit down at the round table in the center of the large cockpit and looked over at the tall slender woman across from me whose high cheekbones, long dark hair, perfect olive complexion and aristocratic poise suggested a woman who was used to being waited on, not the other way around.

But he said, "Please, my dear, get the Capitan his drink will you, Frederica?" and the woman got up and gracefully left. "Now, if you will excuse me, my dear," and the other woman got up and left too. There was a pause for a minute while the two men spoke in Spanish and then just as my drink arrived the other man got up, nodded slightly to me, and he and Frederica left us alone. Turning towards me as I lifted my glass, Ramon raised his and said, "To a long and fruitful relationship, my friend," and clinked my glass with his. We toasted and I sat my glass back down. "Now, you have probably been thinking more about what we spoke of in that dive of a restaurant earlier, si? Let me fill you in on a bit more of what is really at stake here." He settled back in his chair as the door to the cabin was discreetly shut by his partner.

We both gazed out across the calm harbor at the dozens of anchor lights of the various yachts twinkling in the foreground with the shadows of the hills above us and he looked over at me and said, "Capitan Brice, my father was a very powerful man in Colombia. Until he died six years ago, he oversaw one of the largest fortunes in our country. What he had in wealth though, it is not easy to measure in traditional terms. Although my family had many millions of dollars in cash assets, and many properties, the real wealth my father had accumulated was in some of the lost antiquities of my ancestors, the Incas." He let this sink in for a moment and my mind began to reel. *What on earth had I gotten myself into now?*

Ramon went on. "Six years ago, my father was involved in a very big business transaction. The American government had run a sting operation in conjunction with certain people in our own government and well, my father was killed and most of his assets were stolen from us by enemies in our government." He let this settle in for a moment while he took a sip of his drink. I followed suit.

"I managed to save a few things of my fathers'," he said as he waved his arm to emphasize the boat, and he continued in a more melancholy tone. "Although almost all the money was gone, one thing though that I did save, was my father's secret. He knew of a previously unknown stash of Inca treasures from ancient times. Things the Spaniards," he turned his head and spat overboard, "Never found." It is this treasure that I have been moving from our country to here, and then shipping to Europe through a friend who handles international container shipments in Colon. I am selling these to choice collectors and this is helping me to rebuild my father's empire. What I am doing is technically not legal and my government of course would claim all the treasure for themselves if they could find it, or catch me moving any of it. And yet it was my father's ancestors who kept this secret for so many hundreds of years, so I have no intention of sharing this with anyone else. I am trying to rebuild my father's wealth, and no, I don't work for anyone, Capitan Brice. I work for myself."

"I, I don't know what to say, Ramon. How can I respond to this?"

"It is alright, my friend; what I have told you is not such a big secret really. Many people know that I am secretly smuggling these things away from Colombia, but no-one has yet discovered how I have been doing this."

I thought for a moment and said, "Ramon, if you are taking these things that you can argue as being rightfully yours, then why not just get a lawyer and try to cut a deal with the government? Why not work something out and then you could retain at least part of it and not break any laws?"

Ramon slammed his drink down on the table and stood up while he became very angry. His nostrils flared as he spoke. "You are a stupid gringo to think like this. This is not the United States. There are many factions in our government and there are many enemies of my family. What I have been doing would gain me a firing squad, and I will not let them have that satisfaction." He sat back heavily again in his chair and after a pause while he regained his composure, said in a more controlled manner, "I am asking you to dive on this boat of mine that has been lost. There will be some packages onboard that are wrapped in tight bundles. Eight in total. They are green. Find these for me and bring them back to me in Cartagena unopened and unharmed and I will pay you twenty thousand dollars cash. Do this for me and I will ask you to do other things to help me regain the power that was stolen from my family."

I looked at him and slowly raised my glass to his. "To our success, my leader," I said, and toasted him once again.

We went on to discuss the possible whereabouts of the sailboat, and what he was describing to me sounded exactly like the boat I was trying to locate for Rudy Bellows. The hairs were standing up on my arms when my perceptive host said to me, "What is the matter, Capitan? Are you afraid of this dive, or is there something else concerning you perhaps?" I told him that it was only the unknown depth that was of concern to me and assured him that if the wreck was not deeper than a hundred and twenty feet, I would do as he asked. He filled me in with a few more details and about how we would rendezvous in Cartagena and then just as I was leaving he said, "Oh, and Capitan Brice, just to make sure that all goes as I wish, I will be sending my partner Javier with you. When do you wish him to be aboard tomorrow?" to which I replied, trying not to sound too startled.

"We'll leave at 8 a.m. See him then." And I climbed down off the Inca Gold and shoved off in my dinghy.

Rowing back to the Mahalo, I realized I had been totally sucked into a very dangerous situation. Whatever my new friend Ramon was, it wasn't just an antiquities smuggler. There was a lot more at stake and now with his partner aboard our own boat, I realized that from now on out, we would be swimming in very dangerous waters.

Five

"He what?" Rudy Bellows shouted to his secretary Fiona.

"Sorry, Mr. Bellows. He called last night and left a message, and sounded rushed. He just said to tell you verbatim: '*Please check out a man named Ramon who owns a classic old Trumpy motor yacht named Inca Gold out of Colombia. Has a friend named Javier that will be aboard with us starting 8 Am and so DO NOT CALL.*' He asked me to capitalize those words. Sorry, boss."

Rudy ran his hand through his nearly non-existent hair and stormed into his office, plopping his ample bottom down into his heavily padded leather chair and picked up the phone. He quickly dialed a familiar number in England and a few moments later his old friend came on the line.

"To what do I owe this special pleasure, guvnor?" Clifford Gaines said in his clipped Yorkshire accent which had been refined and smoothed from his years in London. Clifford was an agent at Interpol whose specialty was the West Indies and South American region.

"Cliff, old boy, we've got a situation here and I need your help as soon as possible. One of my men is involved in something that may have gotten a bit dangerous. Knowing a few things might help him for when, or if he calls me back."

"Hmm," Clifford said. "How can I help?" Rudy started in by explaining what he knew so far, and added in the fact that there was now this South American connection and the two first names and a boat name. "Not much to go on, you know, Bellows," Clifford said but added, "I'll see what we can turn up and will let you know. Say. You think this might be a bad spell for your man on the ground then?"

"Yes, afraid so, and he's got his wife with him too," Rudy answered. "Please do what you can."

"Good God, Bellows. Well, I'll see what I can do and will call once I have anything to go on. Oh and Rudy, do you know where they're headed by chance?" Bellows said he didn't know but that he suspected that Cartagena might be a possible destination. "Well then, we might just be in luck. I believe we might have a source there that could be of some help. A woman who has been working undercover as I recall. Can't remember all the details. It's not my case, but I'll check into that too and let you know what I learn." The two men then hung up.

◆◆◆

My depth gauge read a hundred and ten feet before I saw the wreck. Jules and I had been diving the reef outside the Hollandes Cays, a small island group in the northern San Blas Islands, for almost a week before we finally found the boat. The boat was on her side on the edge of a drop-off about twenty feet below me and looked to be precariously balanced.

Great, I thought to myself when I considered the dangers involved in going inside a wreck that might tumble off into the depths at the slightest shift in weight, and I signaled to Jules for us to surface. We'd already been down below a hundred feet for twenty minutes and so a decompression stop was mandatory. Ten minutes later we were back in our dinghy which we had anchored nearby. We marked the spot on our handheld GPS. I started the dinghy and we went on two more dives nearby to other spots and stayed just under the surface; mainly to throw off anyone who might be watching and curious, and we then made our plan to return the following day to try to retrieve the 'property'.

Back aboard Mahalo, Javier was sleeping in the cockpit as usual with a spilled drink nearby. He had been virtually useless since the day he came aboard, and the only good thing was that he rarely spoke to us, instead spending his time reading porn magazines of which he seemed to have an endless supply, and eating, which was his only other diversion it seemed. The few times I had tried to engage him in conversation he only gave short answers and showed no interest in learning about what we were doing, beyond asking me each day, "When are you going to find this boat, amigo?"

The next two days were spent in covering tracks. It had taken us only two dives to retrieve the eight bundles and we had towed them back to the boat immediately, keeping them below the surface so as not to be observed and put them aboard while it was still early morning, returning to other nearby sites later in the day in order to create the impression that we had been unsuccessful. We then did a few more dives a mile away the next morning and finally picked up anchor and left. Ramon had been quite impatient with us, but had at last agreed to our logic that it was wise to throw off any possible observers among the twenty or so other boats anchored near Mahalo into thinking that we had not achieved whatever goal they might have imagined we had.

I did manage to get a photo of the hull ID number on the transom of the boat with my Go-Pro digital camera and discreetly confirmed that the boat we had been diving on was indeed the vessel that had been stolen from the BVI nearly a year before. Bingo.

As the sun set we hauled our anchor up and headed out the northern pass, heading towards Colon. Again we were thinking of how to throw off any pursuers. We had seen nothing unusual really, but you can never be too careful. Shortly after darkness we altered course for Cartagena and began the two-hundred-mile sail to windward. The motion of the boat was quite short and uncomfortable and Javier immediately fell ill with seasickness. I discreetly smiled to Juliet as I suggested that he move up to the forward cabin where he might be more comfortable, knowing that the front of the boat was the worst possible place to be and that he would almost certainly be nearly incapacitated by seasickness by the time morning came...

◆◆◆

It had been ten days since Jenny had been abducted, and food and water were running low. As she went about preparing the evening meal from the dwindling supplies, she overheard Carlos and Anita arguing with Toby up in the cockpit. She couldn't make out all the details, but she sensed it was very bad. Her Spanish was good enough to understand that they were arguing about whether to put into a port or to continue under strict rationing.

"You were stupid to fail to place enough food aboard when you knew how long this trip could take," she heard Carlos say to Toby who responded,

"If I had put too much food aboard, they would have suspected something. We will just have to stop in a port."

"No!" Anita snapped." "It is too dangerous. We will just continue on."

And Carlos added, "How much longer to our first re-provisioning port up the river? How much longer until we can stop for food?"

Toby lowered his voice so Jenny was not able to hear, but Anita shouted, "Six more days? That is too long! We need to stop another boat and take what they have. The fishing boats we have seen, they will have fish and fuel, yes?"

Carlos answered, "Yes, we will do that, we will take a fishing boat and kill them, and take their fish and fuel." Toby muttered something about how the fishing boats would only have gasoline and that they needed diesel. He slid the door open and entered the main cabin near the galley. From the look in his eyes, Jenny could see that he was afraid. Toby suddenly remembered the two big packages that had been delivered aboard by a shady-looking Rasta fellow just before they had left the dock at Tortola, and wondered if they had been full of weapons.

The evening and night passed without further incident but in the early morning, before Jenny had been released from her locker up forward, she heard the boat slow and felt it change course. A short while later she heard running on deck and several gunshots. Then the boat stopped and she felt something slam into the side.

A moment later what sounded like a small machine gun opened up and a bullet punched through the hull right next to her head. She crouched down and held her breath, expecting the worst, and heard several more gunshots and then shouting.

She recognized the voices of the Valdencia boys as they said in Spanish something like, 'Don't shoot the girl, she is valuable'. Several more gunshots exploded nearby and then there was only shouting and the scrambling of feet. Several minutes of relative silence followed and then suddenly her hatch opened up and a body was thrown below, then the hatch slammed shut again and was once again latched from the outside.

In the gradually brightening daylight filtering in from the hatch lens, Jenny could make out a crumpled figure of a girl about her own age lying on her side facing her. She had medium length brown hair and was slim and tan. She also appeared to have been sprayed with blood and just as Jenny reached over to touch her, the girl gasped and pulled away in fright.

Eyes wide in terror, the girl whispered, "Where are we? Who are you?" in French. Jenny quietly answered her in somewhat rudimentary, halting French that her name was Jennifer and that she had been a prisoner on the boat for ten days. The girl said her name was Bridget and that she was crew onboard a French sailboat with a man, a single-handed sailor that she had met in the Canary Islands, and that they had been heading for the Amazon to explore the mightiest of all rivers. Jenny reached out again and put her hand on Bridget's arm and tried to comfort her as Bridget started to sob.

Just then there were footsteps again on the deck above their heads and the hatch was opened. It was Diego, the younger of the two brothers, who said to her in his poor English, "Come now and clean mess. We have food, you need work." He reached down and grabbed Jenny's arm to force her to hurry and after she was on deck, he looked down at the terrified French girl with a leering smile and slammed the hatch shut again.

As they dragged Jenny back along the side decks she saw the sailboat they had pirated beginning to burn a hundred or so feet away off the stern while the catamaran once again got moving. They had been tied alongside the smaller boat for almost two hours in the calm seas and during that time the brothers and Toby and Carlos had taken all of the food and most of the fuel off the boat and had then, just before casting it free, set it on fire. As she went below to start putting the new provisions away, she nearly gagged at the blood on some of the canned food cases. Choking back her tears, she got to work and overheard the father Carlos talking with Toby in Spanish. Thankfully they were in the same cabin and still had no idea that she understood Spanish. She had been very careful to act as if she understood nothing; even when the 'boys' would make lewd comments about her body and suggest awful things to her, she had carefully ignored it all.

The conversation in rapid-fire Spanish was heated. Toby was very angry and was nearly shouting, saying that he hadn't signed up for murder, and wanted nothing to do with this plan any more. He was threatening to turn the boat around, head to a port and surrender. Carlos simply reached into his pocket, pulled out a 9mm pistol and shot Toby in the lower leg. The bullet had gone straight through and tore a hole in the deck under the salon floor above the waterline and Toby crumbled and screamed in pain. Carlos reached down and placed the pistol to Toby's head and said, "You will pilot this boat to our destination or you will die. Do this and I will spare your life and pay you as we agreed, and your sister will live, but one more outburst, one more act of defiance and I will shoot you in the head. Do you understand?"

Toby trembled as he nodded his head, fighting back the shock that was beginning to take over his body. For reasons she couldn't say, Jenny ran across the cabin and crouched down to try to help Toby up and get him away from Carlos, who was still fuming, veins bulging on his forehead.

What was that about Toby's sister? she thought to herself.

"Make sure we stay on a course of a hundred and sixty-five degrees for the next hour at least," Toby said to Carlos as he dragged himself with Jenny's help to the salon table and placed his bloody leg up on the table to slow the bleeding. Thankfully he had been barefoot and was wearing shorts, she thought. She wouldn't have wanted to try to take pants off a leg that looked like this. The bullet had pierced the fleshy part of the lower leg and it didn't appear to have broken any bone from what she could tell. Her first thought was only to stop the bleeding and she was thankful that now that the leg was elevated, there didn't seem to be any pulsing, so the bullet probably hadn't pierced an artery or any major blood vessels. Still, it was a mess and it took her almost an hour to get it cleaned up and tightly bandaged. She was surprised that Toby hardly made a sound as she swabbed the wound with iodine and wrapped it with gauze from the first aid kit, even though she could see by the way he tensed his muscles that the pain was excruciating. She didn't have any needle or thread or she would have tried to stitch it up, but all she could do was to wrap it tightly and tell him to keep it elevated. Just as she was finishing, Carlos and Santiago, the older brother, came back in the cabin from the cockpit and ordered Toby to go to the helm and adjust the course. Still shaking, Toby grimaced as he got up and made his way outside and up to the helm seat and propped his foot back up, his bandage already soaked with fresh blood.

"If you don't want him to die," Jenny said defiantly while she stood up directly in front of Carols, fists clenched at her sides, "You're going to have to let his wound clot up before you try to make him move around anymore!" She found herself shaking as she quickly lowered her eyes from Carlos who was looking at her in amazement.

This was the first time she had spoken directly to him since that first night. Carlos reached out and grabbed her chin, jerking up it so their eyes met and then, looking her directly in her eyes, he slapped her hard across her face with his other hand, drawing blood on her upper lip and nose as he growled, "Shut up and clean up this mess and make some food. And never speak to me like this again!" He stormed out to the cockpit to attend to the sails for the course change that was coming up as the boat slowly came about to make its final approach to the entrance to the mouth of the mighty Amazon.

Back in the galley as she began storing the stolen food away, Jenny wondered why she had rushed to help Toby. He had kidnapped her and made her work like a slave and yet, she had sensed in that moment before he was shot that there was more to his story than she had guessed, and that a change had come over him. Maybe he wasn't all bad after all. Maybe there was still a glint of hope that she might survive this nightmare...

Six

As the lights of Cartagena began to appear on the horizon three days after leaving the San Blas, the seas and winds finally began to ease and by mid-morning the Mahalo passed the breakwater, entering the relative calm of Cartagena Harbor. We had sailed the whole way, beating against the strong winds so that the motion of the boat had been terrible at times and our progress had been slow, at best.

Now that we were in calmer waters, Javier had finally reappeared from his self-imposed isolation in the forward cabin. He had not been out of his cabin except to go to the toilet since the boat had left San Blas and I had used the time to discreetly make a few calls to Rudy and to my brother back in St. Thomas to try to get a little more information to work with. I had been careful to clear the call log after each call, just in case our satellite phone was found. But it appeared that he had no idea that we had a sat phone on board.

Rudy wasn't surprised that the sunken boat was the one that had been stolen from the BVI, but he had expressed concern about the revelation about the artifacts and possible drug smuggling, and was still convinced that there was a connection between the stolen boat we had located and some of the other missing boats.

"So, you want me to continue to pursue this then, Rudy?" I had asked and Rudy had told me that it was up to me, but that if I could at least stick with it for a few more days to see if there was a link to any of the other stolen boats, that it would be much appreciated.

The night before we were to make landfall, while we were sure our 'guest' was sound asleep below, Juliet and I had discussed whether we should continue with this investigation or just deliver the packages and quit right on the spot. We agreed that if there was even the remote chance that there could be a connection between Ramon and the missing crew of the big catamaran from Tortola that we had to try to find out more.

On my final conversation with Rudy he had told me that there was an undercover Interpol agent working in Cartagena and that he was working on getting me a name, but that there was some problem with clearances. His friend in England who was the Caribbean chief officer was being road-blocked from higher up, and was in quite a snit over it, but had promised Rudy that he would bulldoze his way through to the truth. Rudy said he would get me some information as soon as he could — but that he still didn't have a name.

No sooner had we entered the inner harbor than we were met by Ramon in a beautiful classic wooden runabout and were led to a dock a short way from the main mooring and marina area. We had not flown a Q flag as is normal protocol for a newly arrived vessel from a foreign port as this would have attracted undue attention to ourselves. As we dropped our bow anchor and backed down on to a broken down old pier, several men in coveralls appeared on the dock to help us with our lines. Within minutes Ramon was alongside in his runabout. He scrambled aboard and was directing the unloading of his packages and ten minutes later we were left alone, watching the V of the wake of the runabout as it sped away across the harbor with the rumpled figure of our passenger of the last two weeks, Javier, sitting hunched over in the back.

Just before the runabout had untied, Ramon had looked back at us and said, "Thank you, my friends, there is a package for you on your bed down below. And come over to see me tomorrow evening after you have finished clearing in. I will send my car by for you at 6 p.m. I will treat you to a fine dinner."

Down below was a small metal suitcase. I opened it up and neatly packed inside was what appeared to be a very large sum of money. Juliet looked over at me and said, "Well, here's evidence that crime does pay."

◆◆◆

Fifteen hundred miles away and two hundred miles inside the entrance of the Amazon River, the weather had turned nasty. Torrential rains in the interior were the result of massive thunderstorms. Nearly gale force winds were funneling into the mouth of the river and causing short, confused seas with overfalls and whirlpools, but the fair wind had the big catamaran crashing along at nearly twelve knots, despite the outgoing current. Toby wondered how much he dared to push the boat, but felt that the sooner he got her into the upper stretches of the river, the better off they all would be.

It was the second day of the trip upriver since the catamaran had left the Atlantic and so far, progress had been good. The river here was still over forty miles across though, and the catamaran, despite her size, was having a tough time of it.

Up in their prison in the bow, Jenny and Bridget held each other in utter despair. Terrified that at any moment the seemingly paper-thin hull could be breached by a floating log or that they might hit a sandbar or one of the legendary floating islands in the pitch-dark night. The two women had found each other in the darkness and held each other tight. Constant flashes of lightning and the incessant crashing of waves over the bows made sleep impossible. Any moment might be their last.

"Thank you for bringing me fresh clothes and a clean cloth," Bridget said. Jenny began to cry and Bridget held her tighter.

The night passed this way and miraculously, dawn came and they were still alive. The boat's canvas cockpit enclosure had been torn and the small exposed sections of jib sail sun cover that had been left unrolled had been ripped to shreds, but overall the boat was still doing well, with the wind now down to twenty-five knots and coming across the boat more on the beam, blowing from the side. The big catamaran had all her sail up and was making nearly fifteen knots counting the boost of the incoming tide. It was hard to believe that the Amazon was tidal for almost a thousand miles inland, Jenny thought to herself as she was putting together a breakfast. Poor Bridget had still not been allowed to leave the forward storage cabin yet, but thankfully, because it had been originally set up to be a possible crew quarters of sorts, at least there was a toilet and two cramped cots up there. Jenny had just brought her some food and she had seemed to be in much better spirits, considering the circumstances.

Back in the galley, Jenny saw Anita coming up from the port hull and overheard her asking Carlos how much longer until they got to the first refueling spot.

Carlos had responded, "Ask your useless captain, if he manages to get us there at all, especially if we have another night like last night, it will be a miracle." Toby's condition had deteriorated since the gunshot incident. Without antibiotics or any new bandages after the ones in the first aid kit had been exhausted, he had developed an infection and Jenny heard Diego tell Santiago that Toby had spent half the night semi delirious, nodding out on watch, and had nearly gone over the side at one point while trying to reef the mainsail to make it smaller, barely able to keep his balance with his badly injured leg.

Anita answered, "If we don't make port soon, he'll be dead anyway. Just make sure you know where to go before he gets too sick to drive." And she turned around and went back to her cabin.

"May I take Toby some food?" Jenny asked Santiago.

"Ah, yes, after he is gone, there will be no-one to protect you, and then I'll have you for my own my little *chiquita*," and he laughed and walked away. Pushing her way past Diego who was smiling, amused by the last exchange and partially blocking the passage to the cockpit, Jenny forced her way out and up to the helm area to Toby who was propped up at the helm with some cushions, slumped part way over and not looking well at all.

"How are you feeling?" she asked and Toby looked up at her with a half-smile.

"After all I've done to you, you actually care? Well, I'm not doing too well at all, thank you very much," he answered in his well-rehearsed British accent. And he went on "I'm really sorry about this. I thought I was a bad-ass enough guy to get away with it, but now I realize I made a huge mistake. I should never have agreed to go when they said they wanted you. I should have backed out." Jenny opened her mouth to speak and Toby raised his hand to stop her before going on. "I was supposed to get fifty thousand dollars and a flight to anywhere I wanted. I was going to go to Australia and start over... but then they saw you and wanted you aboard and then after I realized what they had planned..." His voice trailed off

"Wha-what plan? What are they going to do with me?" Jenny asked.

Just then the door slid open and Santiago appeared at the bottom of the stairs and began walking up to the upper cockpit, leering. "So, Capitan Toby, you talking to my baby, huh? Pretty soon you not going to be able to keep her all for yourself, you know. Pretty soon you gonna be dead by the look of things." And with that he grabbed Jenny by her arm and shoved her down the stairs and pushed her out on the side deck. "Go back to your French lesbian bitch and stay there till we need you again," he said, and he followed her back up the side deck, locking her down below.

Carlos then entered the cockpit and came to Toby up at the helm. "What is the distance to our first refueling port?" Toby bent over to punch some numbers into the GPS.

"About twenty-six more hours if we can keep up this speed, we've been going much faster than I had hoped. Maybe a bit longer though if the winds lay down." Carlos paused and then turned his back, whipping out a sat phone that Toby had not up until now seen and as Carlos punched the numbers in, Toby grimaced with pain, readjusting himself in the helm seat and stared ahead, watching for logs or other debris that would surely cause damage if they struck one at this speed. They had to pass by the major cities along the lower river at night and the refueling ports Toby had been told to use looked isolated and remote. Carlos began talking rapidly in Spanish. Toby's Spanish was very good but he only got the gist of things because of the sound from the strong winds, and with Carlos on the other side of the cockpit he was only able to hear parts of the one-sided conversation. The best he could understand was that Carlos was asking for a replacement captain and that he planned to put Toby ashore for medical help. *That's encouraging*, Toby thought and then Carlos finished his call and turned to Toby.

"We will bring a doctor to you at our first refueling port. And when we get to my country, I will put you ashore at our last refueling port and you can seek help for your leg. I will not pay you the full amount as you have failed to get us to our destination, but I will give you some of the money, and we will honor our agreement with your sister. But always remember, if you ever breathe a word of this to anyone, your sister will be killed. That much I can assure you. If I find that you have betrayed us in any way, both the girls here will be shot and you will be found, no matter where you are, and will be brought to us to watch them die and then you will be cut to pieces. Do you understand?"

Toby swallowed hard and looked Carlos in the eye and nodded, then answered, "I'm as deep in this as you are, Carlos. I'll never speak of any of this to anyone, ever." Carlos stared at him for a moment and then brushed past and returned to the lower cockpit to go below to give the news to Anita and the brothers.

Just as he was about to leave the lower cockpit Toby spoke to him again from the head of the stairs and speaking more loudly said, "Carlos, I am sorry for my outburst and maybe I deserved what you did to me. I was just surprised and afraid after we took that sailboat and killed the man. But now I understand things better and I will obey you now, and at any time in the future, no questions asked, should you require my services again... Please forgive me for my moment of indiscretion." Carlos paused and appeared to be somewhat mollified and with a small nod of his head, slid open the companionway door and went inside.

The boat continued upriver for the next ten days, making two stops for fuel. Both times it was at a small, remote pier and done under cover of darkness. Twice Toby thought about jumping over the side and swimming away, but then he remembered his sister and thought about her being held hostage somewhere up river. He had to go on.

The doctor came aboard at the first refueling stop. He was a dirty, balding, overweight man who smelled of alcohol and marijuana, and he barely looked at Toby's leg, but gave him an antibiotic and for a few days it seemed to help. But then by day seven, his condition began to once again deteriorate.

In order to keep the boat moving day and night, Toby had the Valdencia boys switching off steering with him every three hours, standing 'watch on watch', so he was growing increasingly tired and had to remain ever watchful as they approached the upper reaches of the river and made their turn to the branch that would lead them up into Colombia. Finally, on day nine, still a day and a half short of the beginning of the Río Ica which would lead them to the Putumayo River, he passed out at the helm and only because Jenny happened to be bringing him some coffee did he keep from falling off the helm seat and injuring himself more, and perhaps running the boat aground.

◆◆◆

As promised, precisely at 6 p.m., a black Mercedes sedan rolled up outside the doors of the Club Nautico where Juliet and I had tied up the Mahalo. The driver got out and went around to open our door and as we slid into the luxurious black leather back seat, a man in front of me turned and smiled. It was Javier, looking much better now, and he politely welcomed us to Cartagena. Driving through the old city and into the new section, we made a series of bewildering turns before arriving at a large set of heavy wooden doors off a small side street. The doors swung open inwards and the sedan entered a large courtyard with several cars parked surrounded by extensive gardens. The heavy main doors to the house were next to us and were promptly swung open by a man who appeared to be a butler, as Ramon and the woman I recognized as Frederica from the yacht in Portobelo came out to greet us.

"Welcome, Señor Capitan Brice and good evening to you, Señora Juliet," Ramon said as he gestured with his arm for them to enter the house. The large double doors entered into a foyer area with a guard post and a second set of heavy doors beyond. Looking up I saw small windows above which doubtlessly had at times been manned by sentries. The days of lawlessness in Cartagena were not such a distant memory, and wealthy people had to maintain security at all times. *Especially criminals*, I thought to myself.

"This place is absolutely stunningly beautiful, Ramon," Juliet said as she gazed upon the intricate stonework of the entryway and elaborate tile work of the floors and surrounding walls and he replied,

"I am very flattered by your appreciation. This place was built by my father's grandfather back when this was on the edge of the city. Now, as you see, we are surrounded by buildings. But once we close the doors, it is easy to think back to simpler times."

As he ushered us into the large central hallway, we were awed by the sweeping staircase and intricate carving of the banisters which led to a second story. Off to our right was a parlor and to our left a large living room with another room beyond, probably the dining area. To the left of the staircase was a hallway which led to the kitchens by my guess, as we saw activity through the partially closed door and the smell of food wafted out to us in the main area.

"Please, come in and have a seat," Ramon requested and the butler led the way into the larger living area. We both took our places on one of the couches and Ramon and Frederica sat opposite in two ornate chairs. We chatted a bit of small talk and shortly a young female servant came in and asked us what we would like to drink.

I answered "I'll have a scotch on the rocks, and Juliet?"

She replied, "White wine if you don't mind, a chardonnay preferably."

Frederica interjected as she leaned forward in her chair,

"Perhaps you would like to try Ramon's family's private label chardonnay. It is exquisite," to which Juliet immediately responded,

"That sounds wonderful!"

"You see, Capitan Brice," Ramon started in shortly after the drinks had arrived and the servant and butler had left the room. "This dinner is in appreciation of the fine service you have provided me, and also to offer you a small additional job which I certainly hope you will strongly consider taking on. It is a simple thing really." I sat up a bit straighter in my seat and Juliet put down her glass of wine and looked first at Frederica, to me and then over to Ramon. He went on. "I have a new boat being delivered to me that has had a problem. The Capitan of that boat has fallen ill and I need a good Capitan to finish moving this boat to its new home."

"Where is the boat now?" I asked as I tried to cover my surprise and interest in this new development.

"The boat is up a large river, and needs to come to my own country where I am doing some work. It is to be my 'home away for home' while we are completing a project there. My guess is it will take you about a week and I will pay you another ten thousand dollars for this. Would that be agreeable?"

I blurted out, "But that's way too much for such a simple job! Surely you could find someone who would move a boat for a lot less than that, Ramon. Not that I don't appreciate your generous offer, but I think the pay is too high!" Already I was thinking that surely this must be the missing catamaran but I waited for his response before continuing on.

"Capitan Brice, you have already proven yourself to me to be a trustworthy man, and I require just such a man for this delivery. The pay is commensurate with the level of secrecy which must be maintained in this. And I am sure you can understand the value of such discretion."

"I am flattered by your offer," I said and as Ramon stood up to usher us to dinner, he said,

"You and I will discuss the details after dinner in private while the women talk." And we all stood and entered the elaborately decorated dining room.

Like stepping into another century, the exquisite décor and tasteful furnishings belied the present. We sat down at the huge carved mahogany table to a very good four course meal and afterwards, as Ramon had suggested, he and I retired through a small door to a room beyond the dining room which seemed to be an office of sorts and the ladies went over to the smaller of the two living rooms to the right of the main hallway. Ramon closed the heavy door and, as we sat down in large comfortable armchairs, he offered me a cigar which I declined, instead taking out a pack of cigarettes I had brought with me.

Shrugging, he lit up and told me, "These are the finest Cuban cigars, Capitan, and it is a shame you have no appreciation for such fine things," and then he went on. "Capitan Brice, this boat I am speaking of I have recently purchased, it is a large catamaran and although I probably paid too much for it, I believe that it is in good condition. I am not really much of a sailor, but the accommodations are as I like them and so from this man I know, who sometimes has such boats for sale, I bought it and it is already well up the Amazon River. What I need you to do is to fly in and take this boat the rest of the way to my country for me."

I interjected, "Excuse me, Ramon, but can you actually get to Colombia from the Amazon? Or do you want me to sail it around to Cartagena for you because if that's what you want me to do, I will need a good crew and it will probably take about three or four weeks."

Holding up his hand while he took a long drag on his cigar, he let out the smoke slowly and went on. "There is in fact a river that is navigable all the way into my country and it is up this river that I have some land where I wish the boat to be brought." He continued; "Capitan Brice, this man I purchased the boat from, he is not a hundred percent honest and the boat may have in fact have been a stolen boat, but I only found this out after I paid good money for it, and I cannot afford to lose what I have paid. And besides, I am sure this boat was insured, so no-one is getting hurt here, except for me if I do not get to keep this boat that I have already paid for." With this he paused, sitting back in the big chair and looking at me closely to see what my reaction would be. A man like Ramon did not get as far as he had in a life of crime by a failure to read people, so my response was going to have to be carefully thought out.

"Ramon," I started in, "I think I understand your dilemma. While I'm not sure why you can't just ask for your money back if you truly believe this boat was stolen, I might be able to help you out, but I need to know a few things first." He stopped puffing on his cigar and sat up a little in his chair, shifting his crossed legs, waiting my next words. "If I do this for you, I need to know what the dangers are. Who is involved that I need to watch out for and if it is dangerous? And I will need a weapon to protect myself and Juliet."

He paused for a moment and responded, "This is not a dangerous situation, Capitan. The transaction was completed weeks ago and the boat is already in the hands of my brother. There is no danger to you other than the sandbars or floating islands!' He laughed and ashed his cigar. Looking back up he added, "This is a straightforward delivery of a boat in good condition. I am not worried for your safety and neither should you be. But still, I think it will be best for your wife to stay here in Cartagena – to guard your boat and your cash that I hope you have secreted away. Cartagena is not a good place to leave a boat unattended. And there is no need to bring her along as my brother, he has his family aboard to help; two strong boys, his wife and a cook, plus an extra crew. This will be an easy trip for you, and you will have a week or so to relax before you have to leave. So what do you say, Capitan? Are you willing to help me in this?"

I smiled my best actor's smile and stood up, advancing towards him with outstretched arm, and shook his hand to seal the bargain.

◆◆◆

It was 11 p.m. when Carlos had come up on deck to speak on his satellite phone again. He then climbed the stairs up to the helm. Carlos had allowed the American girl to assist Toby in keeping watch and so when he saw that Toby was sleeping in the seat in the upper cockpit and that she was at the helm, he was at first angry. But then he thought about it for a moment and realized that this was probably a good thing. The river was still wide here and the winds were down to less than fifteen knots. The boat was still moving well and there were fewer and fewer floating logs and weeds to dodge, so for the time being he decided not to send the captain back to the helm and instead shook him lightly to awaken him.

"Capitan Toby," he said as Toby opened his eyes with a start. "No, no, it is OK, I see that you are very tired and you will need the rest because tomorrow, when we get to our refueling stop, there will be a new Capitan to take over for you. So, rest and be ready for entering the side river as we have discussed." Toby slumped back down and secretly hoped that this was not to be his last day on earth. Although since his apology to Carlos he had been treated better, he had begun to hold little hope for his own, or the girls' survival.

After Carlos left the helm and returned below Jenny bent over Toby and spoke to him softly. "What do you think our chances are for escaping when we dock the boat?"

Toby looked at her with utter lack of hope in his eyes responding, "No better than the last two stops we made." She thought back to the two brief fuels stops they had made. She had been locked below decks for both of them and there hadn't been a hint of a chance to get away. He went on, "I'd be surprised if an opportunity presented itself. It's even worse here. We're a thousand miles from anywhere, with dense jungle all around. There is more lawlessness here than in the Wild West a hundred fifty years ago. I think our best bet is for you to play along as long as you can, and for me to get out and get to help somehow. If I make a mistake, I could get you both killed." He strained a bit to change position and added, "I'm so sorry for all of this." Jenny smiled at him thinly, placing her left hand on his cheek briefly before returning her attention to the helm just as the sliding door below them opened and in a moment Santiago appeared up at the helm.

"I've been sent to keep an eye on you two. So, no funny business and NO talking," he said brushing his hand over Jenny's bottom, as he pinched her.

She shook him off and uttered "shit" as she abruptly turned the wheel as if avoiding a floating object and this distracted him enough to cause him to go back down to the main cockpit and sit down where he soon dozed off.

With Toby now also dozing off just behind her on the helm seat, Jenny was left alone with her fears and a situation that she barely understood.

Seven

Arriving back at the Yacht Club after 11 p.m., we saw immediately upon going below that someone had been aboard. Despite being on a guarded dock, somehow the boat had been entered and although not ransacked, things were not exactly like they had been left. It looked as if the intruder or intruders meant to be discreet. Juliet started to say something and I put my finger up to my mouth indicating that she should remain quiet. Juliet immediately caught my drift and I said, "Wow, Jules, wasn't that a wonderful evening? I really like Ramon and think our association with him is going to be very worthwhile." To which Juliet responded,

"Frederica is so nice as well. What a lucky break that was — meeting them and you being offered that job. I'm so happy." I rolled my eyes, giving her a look as if that might be laying it on a bit thick, but began to snoop around for any listening devices that may have been left aboard. Meanwhile, Juliet said, "I'm bushed. I'm going to get ready for bed."

But I said, "Oh, c'mon, Jules, it's not even midnight. Let's go up to the club for a nightcap and then we'll call it a night. It sounds like it'll be a busy day tomorrow."

She acquiesced with, "Sure, why not?"

We then both went back up to the cockpit and disembarked, walked past the guard on the finger pier with a nod and moseyed on up towards the clubhouse.

Along the way I said to her, "I think there's a good chance our friend Ramon may have put listening devices aboard and so we'd better play the act while we are aboard." She nodded. "And I still need to find out if he found our sat phone or my personal computer, but my guess is that they didn't. I've got to get a call off to Rudy to get some backup down here if possible. This is turning out to be a real mess."

Juliet looked over at me, stopping me with her arm and as we stood there on the shore side of the pier, the lights of Cartagena shimmering off the tranquil waters of the inner harbor, she put both arms around my tensed shoulders, giving me a deep long kiss and whispered in my ear,

"We'll be fine. I'll be fine. Just be very careful." And we turned and went up to the bar for a drink, eventually returning to the boat after midnight.

◆◆◆

"I think they are just as they say they are," Frederica said as she listened to the recording of the exchange Ramon had gotten from the bug he had one of his people place aboard Mahalo while they were all at dinner. They were both in Ramon's office at the back of the house and she said, "I don't know what you are worried about, my love," as she walked over and wrapped her arms around Ramon's torso and squeezed him.

This distracted him enough and he said, "Perhaps you are right, but it always pays to be careful."

He returned her kiss and squeezed her bum while pressing heavily against her and the two of them then turned and left the room to go to up to bed.

◆◆◆

In the morning, it didn't take me long to find the bug. There only appeared to be one, but nevertheless, we continued to speak as if everything were normal and that we were excited about the 'easy' job and the money.

The next several days went by in a blur with daily sightseeing and shopping outings arranged by our gracious employers, and by day seven we had almost forgotten why we were really there. But then I was summoned by the guard on the dock to come to the parking lot and there I met with Carlos briefly as he filled me in on the developments.

Returning to the boat, I told Juliet what was going on.

"I'm going up to the showers," I said as I carefully removed the sat phone from the secret locker well back and underneath the starboard settee, inside of what appeared to be a water tank. When I had created this secret hiding place it had been mainly a deterrent to theft, but now more than ever it provided the necessary security to keep our true identities secret. To cover up the sounds of me rooting for the phone I was saying, "Where on earth did you put the ketchup, Jules? I want ketchup with my eggs."

To which she replied, "Just dig around over there, you'll find it."

As soon as I had closed up the secret compartment I said, "Got it!" and dropped an actual ketchup bottle down next to the bug which we had found wedged in a crevice in the galley. Never hurts to go for realism.

Leaving the boat with the sat phone and my toiletries wrapped up in a towel, I made my way up to the showers. Once inside one of the private shower rooms, I turned on the shower full blast, stepped back over to the counter next to the sink and quickly dialed Rudy's number in the BVI. After being transferred to Rudy's extension, I heard my old friend come on the line.

"Brice? How the hell are you and is everything alright?"

I spent the next several minutes quietly filling him in with what I knew so far and after a brief silence he said, "There is a development on this side too. It seems that my friend at Interpol has a person inside this Ramon's organization. His source was not at liberty to tell us who just yet, but he assured me that they have been brought up to speed on who you two are and what you are doing there. I have to tell you I'm not happy about you flying off to help move that boat, Brice, but if your judgment says it's the thing to do, by all means go for it. Big question is: Will you be able to bring your sat phone?"

"I doubt it, Rudy," I replied. "If they knew I had this, it could change the whole situation. Like, who am I calling and why do I have it? I'll leave it with Jules and try to make contact in some other way. Meanwhile, if you can do any groundwork on what areas in Colombia can be accessed by a big boat like that catamaran via the Amazon, that might narrow down the possibilities of how to find me should I not check in for a while..." I let this hang and Rudy got my meaning.

"Brice, you're taking a bigger risk than I'm willing to approve. I want you and Juliet out of there now. We can turn the rest over to Interpol at this point and let them deal with it."

But I quickly responded, "Rudy, there is at least one or possibly two hostages here, and a boat worth close to two million dollars. Plus, I want to stop this creep before any more bad things happen. Let me go, and please try to keep an eye on Juliet. And remember, they have our boat bugged, so no direct contact unless you can figure out a way to get her away from the boat and any people who might follow her. I think they trust me for the most part, but they are criminals and well, they don't trust anybody. So we have to be careful! I'll be in contact as soon as I get back and can tell you more and then I *will* get us the heck out, OK?"

To this Rudy agreed and I signed off, quickly wetted down and toweled off and when I opened the door to the shower, there was Javier standing at the entrance to the shower block.

"Ah, Señor Brice, there you are. I have been sent to fetch you, and your lovely wife told me you had come for a shower. I hope you are feeling refreshed and ready for your voyage to begin," he said with no apparent suspicion in his voice and so being careful to make sure my sat phone didn't fall out of my towel roll, I followed him back to the boat and asked him to wait in the cockpit while I packed my bag.

Fifteen minutes later, with the satellite phone stashed in a temporary hiding place, Juliet and I emerged from the cabin; me with my one bag packed and her with a shoulder bag.

"May I accompany him to the airport?" Jules said, but Javier said that would not be possible, but that Frederica would be by soon to keep her company until he, Javier, returned.

Javier then turned to me and said, "Because this is such a dangerous city, Señor Capitan Brice, and at Ramon's insistence, I have personally agreed to stay onboard with your wife during the nights to protect her, and Frederica has volunteered to come check on her every day to see if she needs anything or to take her shopping if she wishes. And we must now move your boat over to raft up next to Ramon's yacht, Inca Gold. Both your wife and your boat will be safest there."

Not seeing how any protests from me would be useful, I nodded my head and said to him, "I will be most gratified if you keep a good watch out for Juliet's safety and will reward you on my own when I return."

To this Javier gave me a queer look before responding, "Of course, she will be perfectly safe, and you will be back in no time at all."

We went about getting Mahalo underway and a short time later arrived next to Inca Gold. After securing the boat alongside, I said my goodbyes to Juliet and stepped off the boat, walked down the docks and exited through the marina gates where Ramon's black Mercedes awaited.

Driving off to the airport I began to feel queasy with apprehension, but did my best to mask this as I carefully made the motions of going through and rechecking the contents of my bag. Javier had insisted on seeing the contents as well and only objected to the emergency radio beacon I had brought along saying, "The boat will have its own so I will return this to your boat. Besides, it is no doubt registered in your name,

Capitan Brice, so it would do you no good on another boat, si?" I gave no argument.

Instead of going to the main airport, we drove to a small regional strip outside the city and within an hour I was aboard a small six-seat airplane, an aging but nicely maintained Cessna 411 with a pilot and co-pilot, Javier and me as the only occupants. As we took off and headed southeast, the city quickly disappeared from sight behind us to be replaced by endless, trackless forest. Three and a half hours later, I spied a huge river on the horizon and within fifteen minutes we had landed on a small grass strip nearby a small village located off a muddy tributary to the main river. I had no idea where I was other than deep in the limitless rain forest and possibly near the Amazon, but was sure that once I was aboard the missing boat, I could get a feel for what was going on and where I would be going from here.

Disembarking from the airplane I was immediately smothered in the oppressive heat and humidity of the jungle. Immense trees encroached on both sides of the airstrip and a flock of parrots flew above the forest canopy towards the edge of the strip. A small partially painted wooden shack with a rusted corrugated metal roof and a fuel drum outside appeared to be the 'terminal' building and next to it a rusty old yellow jeep was parked. As I walked towards the building with my bag, a small dark man in tan pants, a flowered shirt and wearing a Panama hat stepped up to me from where he had apparently been sitting in the shade.

Introducing himself as Tico, he said, "Welcome to Brazil," in fairly good English.

Looking behind me I heard the two pilots already restarting the airplane and watched as Javier disappeared inside the plane and closed the door. The airplane began to taxi out to take off as I was led to the rusty, dilapidated old jeep CJ7 I had seen parked by the terminal. I climbed in the open vehicle, sitting on the torn, broken down passenger seat and as we started to drive away from the airstrip I watched the plane clear the strip and bank out over the dense forest. As we bumped down the ruddy dirt pathway, my new guide began to fill me in about the happenings here.

"The boat you are to take over is overdue, but we hope to see it come in today. In the meantime, I have arranged for you to stay with a local family near a small business next to the wharf. They do not speak English, but I will be staying just a short distance down the street in the business that is also a small bar, and will help you with whatever you need."

We came to a fork in the road, and turned right for the short drive into a very ramshackle village straggling along the riverbank of what I assumed was a tributary of the Amazon. A mixture of mud and grass shacks was interspersed with corrugated steel and pole structures, some with thatched roofs, others with rusty corrugated steel. Dogs, chickens, hogs and a few horses wandered about milling for food. Barely clothed Indians with short spears and bow and arrows were watching me as we drove past, and a mixture of Portuguese and Spanish Mestizos leaned in doorways, eyeing me with benign interest or perhaps suspicion as we lurched down the mucky thoroughfare.

Arriving in front of one of the more substantial structures on the road, I realized we were very close to the village wharf. This rickety structure was lashed together mostly with short to medium length rough cut timbers and stood approximately twenty feet off the water.

"The wharf is sometimes under water in the wet season," Tico informed me. "But now the river is low. Your accommodations are just over here," he said as we pulled in front of an aging Shell Oil sign and parked. Stepping down into the mud I took in the scene around me. Across the street was a small Chinese store and several small houses. Next to this was a clinic with a line of natives and Mestizos lined up outside waiting to be seen. A large aerial was mounted on the back edge of the building, which promised a radio at least, and three buildings down was a small police station.

Following my gaze Tico said, "Do not worry about the local police, Señor. Your presence here is known and they have been well paid. It is no worries for you, OK?" To which I simply nodded my head. The dense jungle encroached all around this tiny village and only the river gave a sense of possible relief from what was otherwise an almost claustrophobic scene.

He led me towards the larger building and we entered what appeared to be a small hostel of sorts. Surrounding the main room were several dilapidated couches and some crude wooden benches. A small stage was off to the right. Perhaps there was live music at times? A pool table off to the left side was in front of a series of rooms that opened right into the main gathering area, but two small hallways were towards the back. I was led down the left hand hallway to a small room with a cot, a single bare light bulb hanging from the ceiling and cracked plaster with a few cockroaches thrown in for good measure. Other than that, it was reasonably clean and I set my bag on the bed.

"This is my room, capitan, but you can leave your bag here safely while we go get something to eat." My new friend immediately produced a key and as soon as we had exited the room, he made a show of locking the door and pressed the key into my palm. "Follow me to the best restaurant in town, Señor!" he said with a smile. As he turned and walked back down the hallway he looked back over his shoulder and added with a chuckle, "And the only restaurant, I might add."

A funny guy. I wondered how much he knew about what I was involved in, or whether he was an innocent simply hired because he was the only man in town who could speak English. I guessed the latter. We walked down the main street a few buildings and entered a small dwelling. He looked over at me and said, "This is the place where you will be staying if your boat arrives late. These people will feed us too."

We went in, and a rather strikingly beautiful young Amazon Indian girl of about eighteen dressed only in a short woven skirt entered the room and spoke to Tico in a dialect I guessed was tribal. She smiled at me and offered us a seat at the only table in the room before disappearing through a curtain to the back of the house.

"She is nice, Señor, no? For a price maybe she will lay with you," he said with an innocent smile.

I ignored the remark and asked him bluntly, "How much do you know about why I am here, Tico?"

He looked up at me and answered, a bit uncertain, "I only know that you are an important man, a sea captain, and that you are here to take over piloting a small ship that is due to arrive. I know nothing about where it is from, or where it is going. I do not wish to know either." And he got up and went into the back room where he could be heard speaking with the Indians before he returned with two warm beers. "I am sorry, Señor, but we have no refrigeration here, but the beer is still good, no?"

To this I raised my bottle and toasted him. "To a fruitful friendship, Tico, may we both live long." We each took a long pull on our bottles just as our meals arrived. The pretty girl set the food in front of us on the roughly finished table and placed some mismatched silverware next to the plates. As she left she looked me in the eyes briefly with what appeared to me to be a mixture of fear and hope.

"This is all there is to order, and it was already made up, so I took the liberty. It is roast chicken and rice, no?" Tico spouted mirthfully. I smiled and we began to eat just as the Indian girl retreated and then peered back at us from behind the curtained doorway.

After our dinner and with evening coming on, we walked back to Tico's hostel and entered to a somewhat different scene. A few locals were lounging about and some Indian girls were sitting on the couches next to them, with two sitting on the lap of one of the men. No-one seemed to give us much notice as we strolled over to what was now a makeshift bar along the back wall, between the two hallways. A small radio was tuned into a distant scratchy station with Latino music playing. The whole scene was out of some adventure novel. I hoped the boat would be here soon as this was a place I didn't care for much.

Sensing my discomfort, Tico said, "This place is also a house of love, as you have probably guessed. But it is owned by the police and so you are quite safe here. As I said, they have been amply paid and will watch out for your comfort." I looked over at him and he went on, "If you would like that Indian girl to come to you and lead you back to your house for tonight, just say the word. And if you want her, I will see what the price is," to which I responded,

"What happens if I don't take her tonight, what will she be doing?"

Tico laughed. "None of these men can afford one like that, she will sleep alone at her house until a prince comes for her."

"I'm a happily married man, Tico, but thanks for thinking of me," I said. He chuckled to himself as he took a long pull on his beer. I stood up and said, "I need to get off to bed, so please take me back to the place I am supposed to be sleeping."

"Certainly, Señor," and he tipped his beer in my direction as I exited to the hallway and unlocked his room to retrieve my bag. Re-entering the main bar area, I saw two fresh cervezas, and an older Indian woman leaving the table and exiting the door. Tico looked up and said, "She is going to get someone to lead you to your place for tonight. I am going to entertain myself here."

Sitting back down at the table I sipped my beer and a few minutes later a small Indian boy quietly entered the room and padded over to our table. Tico spoke to him for a moment and the Indian boy put out his hand for mine. Tico said, "This is Beqa. He will take you to back to your sleeping quarters."

As I stood up and finished my beer I said, "Wake me the minute the boat arrives. I don't care what time it is," and to this Tico, now obviously becoming tipsy, simply smiled and tipped his beer in my direction. No sooner had I left the table with the young boy when two girls came over and sat at Tico's table. *A young man with a pocketful of change,* I thought to myself as I went out into the night.

Beqa led me back down the pitch-dark street, artfully helping me dodge the larger mud puddles, and brought me faithfully back to the doorway of the shack where we had eaten our dinner. Opening the door, I saw that there was a bed made up in one corner with mosquito netting over it. The Indian girl was fussing about trying to make things neat on a small table at the foot of the bed and turned abruptly when I entered the room. With hand motions, she pointed to the bed and I said, "Thank you," to which she smiled. I also motioned for some water and said, "Bottle water, *agua?*" Although I understood that Portuguese was the language here, it seemed to me that a lot of Spanish speaking natives were also around. Tico was certainly Spanish speaking. In any case, she seemed to understand and shuffled out of the room, returning a couple of minutes later with a warm bottle of drinking water. Dasani. Somewhat surprised, I also said, "Where is the bathroom? *Donde está el baño?*" and she reached out her hand. Her small hand felt warm and soft as she closed her fingers around mine. Leading me out the back door to a crude outhouse, she left me there to do my business and I saw her disappear back into the house. Upon my return I was alone and so got partially undressed and climbed into bed, pulled the mosquito netting over me and within a short time was fast asleep.

◆◆◆

How could you make such a mistake!" Carlos was fuming. During the early morning hours when it was very dark, Jenny had inadvertently missed the main channel and was aground on a sandbar. Toby had awoken instantly when they struck and was frantically trying to work the engines to back off.

After a few minutes of fruitless effort, he shut the engines down and said in Spanish, "We are hard aground. We'll need to wait for light to see how we can get off." Carlos struck him in his face with the back of his hand and shoved Jenny unmercifully down the stairs and along the deck towards her dungeon in the bow. Opening the hatch, he practically threw her down, and only Bridget's being there prevented her from hitting the bottom with enough force to injure herself. Slamming the hatch shut, Carlos stormed back up to the cockpit where Toby was now reclined with his foot up.

"What are you doing? You need to get us moving!" Carlos vented, to which Toby said,

"Carlos, running aground on these rivers is not that unusual. This section isn't even on our chart plotter! We will get off, but not in the dark." Toby looked down and saw the two Valdencia brothers eyeing him from the hatchway and switching back to English he said, "Quite honestly, I'm surprised we haven't run aground sooner. This is a treacherous river and you can't expect me to stay on watch twenty-four hours a day. Please, go get some sleep, Carlos, and we'll get ourselves off as soon as it's light enough to see where we actually are, OK?" Toby's unconcerned demeanor somewhat calmed Carlos, and he turned and went down the stairs and pushed his way past his sons who were standing just outside the closed doorway looking out at the black night.

Carlos slid open the hatchway and looking back at them snapped, "We are aground. There's nothing we can do till it's light. Go back to bed." Turning back, he slammed the companionway door shut.

Morning arrived with a heavy rain, but the river had fallen almost a foot overnight and so the catamaran was listing to starboard. The port hull was pinned on the sandbar and until the river rose, or a tow came along, they weren't going anywhere.

As soon as it began to get light outside Carlos had sent for Jenny, who was now below cooking a meal. Toby had come into the main cabin during the wee hours to get a little sleep and had been awakened by Santiago at dawn.

Carlos asked Toby, "How far are we from the landing?"

Toby had calculated the distance during the night and reported, "About seventy miles. If we can't get off before afternoon, I could take the tender up river and see if we can bring help."

Carlos smiled and said, "Wouldn't you like that? Leave us here and disappear up river, never to return." To which Toby replied,

"You have my word and you can send one of your boys with me. And I am not going to let down my sister or give up my money. If we don't get help, we could be here for a week!"

Anita, who was standing behind Carlos, took a deep breath and started to curse. Toby knew this was a lie and that in all likelihood a boat would pass any time before that. This river was a main artery into Southeast Colombia and was known to some as 'The River of Drugs', but this was a chance to get word out of their plight. He had to take a risk, and he hoped that he could get some antibiotics for his leg as well which was getting worse again after a slight improvement a few days back.

"Alright, get the tender ready. Diego will go with you and you will bring help today! Don't wait, I want you to go now!"

◆◆◆

I awoke to a warm hand on my chest. Startled, I sat up quickly and the Indian girl gasped in surprise.

"Breakfast?" she said in heavily accented English. I got my bearings and said,

"Do you speak English?" to which the girl blushed and nodded.

"I speak little English. Learn at missionary school near my village."

Swinging my legs out from the netting I stood up and found my pants neatly folded on a nearby chair. As I pulled these on, the girl handed me my shirt which I slid into and I walked a few steps over to the table that was already set. The smell of eggs and bacon wafted out from the back room. Hot coffee was awaiting me as I sat down at the small table. The old crone I had seen the night before at the nightclub peered out at me from the kitchen and cackled, letting the curtain fall as the girl sat down across from me.

"What is your name?" I asked. The girl hesitated and said,

"Melowa," touching her small brown hand to her bare breast.

"Brice," I responded, making the same motion.

"Brites," she mimicked. I let it slide.

She got up from the table and returned shortly with my food. Eating my breakfast, I quizzed Melowa about where she was from, and how she had ended up at this house in the village. She explained as best she could that her village was many miles away. That the village had been raided one night by an enemy tribe and most of the men were killed. The older women and boys were taken to work as slaves and the younger women were sold. A trader had purchased her and brought her here. She had managed to save her grandmother who was the old woman in the house. All of this had happened several months ago. She told me that she guessed she was to become a prostitute because some of the other girls from her village were already working down the street doing that, and then she began to sob quietly.

I could hardly eat my food, I was so upset. I looked over at her and said, "I will find a way to save you. Do not worry. I will do everything I can to help you." She looked at me with pleading eyes and then quietly got up and left me alone.

"Good morning, Señor Capitan?" I looked up from the table to see Tico entering the house. He looked somewhat disheveled with an untucked, wrinkled shirt and mussed up hair, but also appeared rested. He pulled out a chair and sitting down across from me at the small table he took out a pack of cigarettes and laid them on the table.

"Is there any word about the boat or when they will be in?" I asked, to which he replied,

"No, Señor, but I am sure they will be here soon." And he asked, "Did you sleep well?"

I looked over at him and replied, "Who owns this Indian girl?"

Somewhat surprised by my question he slouched back in his chair, lighting up a cigarette and took a long drag before answering.

"Señor Capitan, this girl is mine at the moment. I paid quite a lot of money for her. But when the boat arrives, I am guessing they will pay me even more and then she will go with you on the boat. So my offer last night was good for one night only," and with this he smiled and took another long drag on his cigarette before going on, "You see, Capitan, I have supplied many girls to your friends to keep their workers happy. This is nothing new. But your bosses are so picky! They only accept the most beautiful ones now. I believe ones like this are for themselves, and the others were just for the workers. So, the police have purchased the other ones you saw last night that are here now. They are still nice though! You should come over this morning and lay with one or two before your boat arrives!" I was stunned but kept my composure. What kind of a monster was this guy?

But I answered, "Tico, what I need now is to finish my breakfast in peace and to get cleaned up. I'll be over in a short while and we can take a look at the dock. I need to see how to get fuel and water, and what provisions might be had at the store across the way."

Tico looked at me intensely for a moment and perceptively said, "Capitan, I am not a bad man. I saved these girls from those savages and now instead of having little savage babies hanging from their tits until they are worked to death at an early age, they can make a little money, and save for a phone, or nice clothes if they want. And they can even earn their freedom if they want to go away. They are not prisoners. I think of it like I saved them from a worse fate and this was the only way I could do it."

What a humanitarian, I thought to myself but said, "I understand, Tico. No worries. What do I care? I'm just here to drive a boat. Give me a few minutes to finish up and I'll be over."

He picked up his cigarettes and put them back in his top pocket before saying, "No problem, Capitan. I will be waiting," and he snubbed out his cigarette as he stood up and left the house.

Thirty minutes later I was walking down the main street towards the pier when I thought I heard an outboard motor in the distance. Picking up my pace, I walked out onto the rickety pier and looked down river. There in the distance was the distinctive form of a high-speed inflatable tender making a V wake towards the town. Others had heard this too and at that moment Tico showed up, as well as one of the policemen who eyed me suspiciously, but kept his distance.

"This may be the tender from the yacht," I said to Tico, who looked over at me and said,

"But why are they coming and not the big boat?'

I didn't answer but instead sat down on the edge of the pier with my legs hanging over the side and took out a cigarette, lighting up while I awaited further developments.

Within a few minutes the inflatable slowed and came alongside the pier, coming to a stop at the base of one of the ladders that descended towards the water. It was obvious that the driver was injured and yet he was the one who was trying to secure the boat to the long pier pilings. I tossed the butt of my cigarette aside and scrambled down to give him a hand. Stepping aboard to grab the stern line I said, "Are you from the yacht?"

At that point the man in the passenger seat spoke up. "Are you our new Capitan? My name is Diego." He stood up and stuck out his hand. I quickly shook it and went back to assisting in securing the tender.

"What happened to you?" I asked the driver who appeared to be a mid-twenties mixed Anglo fellow, and not a local.

"I hurt my leg and need to get to a doctor. The boat's aground on a sandbar about seventy miles downriver. We need to get back to them and try to get some help to get them off." He then attempted to start climbing the ladder but was clearly unable to do so.

"Can you help me, Diego?" I asked and the young Spanish-looking fellow slowly got up and made a halfhearted attempt to get Toby onto the ladder. I ended up telling the young captain, "If you can grab onto my back, I'll give you a piggyback ride up." The young man did as I asked and I made my way, with difficulty, up the poorly made ladder, testing each rung as I climbed. By now quite a crowd had arrived including a man I guessed was the village doctor by his white, blood-stained clothing and the stethoscope hanging around his neck. As I reached the top rung, many hands reached down and thankfully took my load, lifting the injured driver up onto the dock and quickly bearing him off to the clinic across the street. The doctor hurried along behind them, glancing back over his shoulder as they disappeared into the small clinic building. I looked back behind me as I stood up on the pier and saw the man who had called himself Diego climbing slowly up the ladder to the top of the dock. I reached down to help him over the edge and took his hand, hefting him up on the pier and looking him in the eye said, "Why didn't you help me get that man off the boat?" to which he replied,

"That man is a troublemaker. He ran us onto a sandbar and now he is abandoning us. I am glad you are here to help."

We now both walked back towards the clinic and Tico fell in alongside; the policeman a few steps behind said nothing but was watching us closely.

Tico spoke up first, directing his question to the passenger. "When is the big boat coming, Señor?"

Diego looked over at him and said, "Who are you and why do you want to know?"

"My name is Tico and I was hired by a man named Ramon in Cartagena to help you when you arrived."

Diego stopped walking and turned towards the shorter man saying, "I am sorry for my rudeness," and sticking out his hand he added, "My name is Diego and my family is down river. We need to organize a boat to go help tow them off a sandbar so that we can get the boat here for refueling."

Tico smiled and said, "I know just the man to help us with this," and quickly added, "I will go get him now. I will find you at the clinic, or over at the bar." He pointed at the whorehouse across the street from the clinic. And Tico turned and rushed off along a pathway that paralleled the tributary and disappeared from sight.

Diego looked at me and said, "I do not wish to go to the clinic. Please go check on what is happening there and I will be in the bar. Find me when we are ready to leave." And he turned and walked across the street, entering the dilapidated bar through the swinging saloon style doors. The policeman who had overheard all of this shrugged and trudged back towards his office and I was left alone, standing in the middle of the street. I turned and walked down towards the clinic.

Eight

Roger Tatterson slammed the telephone down and bowed his head, fuming in his frustration. After several days of phone call after phone call trying to make some headway as to how he might be able to assist in locating his daughter, he had finally been led, albeit discreetly, to a phone number in the UK where after much pleading and coaxing he had eventually gotten through to a man by the name of Gaines who seemed to actually have a clue as to what was going on. Unfortunately, the call had ended with the man telling him that this was an ongoing operation and that he couldn't tell him anything more at the moment. Roger did, however, elicit a promise that as soon as something came to light that he would call back and give him an update.

The only real revelation that came through, though, was that it appeared that the DEA might somehow be involved, and that Interpol was actively working on whatever this case was as well. Roger picked up the phone again as he exhaled deeply and asked his secretary Marion to get Andy Winters at the CIA on the line.

"Jeez!" Andy said as he came on the line in an agitated voice. "You sure have stirred up a hornets' nest, Rog."

"What in the hell would you do in my situation, Andy? And nice to speak to you too," he answered sarcastically. Tatterson was fuming.

"Calm down, Roger," Winters said and added in a more conciliatory tone, "I've made some progress here, so I'm glad you called." Tatterson sat up as he asked anxiously,

"What have you learned?"

"OK," the CIA man started in. "All your calls have drummed up some activity and I've heard from a source inside the DEA that there is some kind of elaborate sting operation that Interpol has going relating to stolen artifacts and cocaine smuggling that they are pretty well up to their knees in. I got a hint that this may have something to do with the FARC, Colombia's revolutionary army. They've been in an active guerilla war with the central government for over fifty years and apparently hold vast sections in the southern part of the country under their rule. It sounds like a complicated and dangerous situation, but it very well could somehow involve your daughter's captors, if indeed she is in the thick of things."

"How so?" Tatterson asked, and Winters went on,

"Well, funding a revolution is expensive, and for years many of the drug lords paid substantial amounts of money to protect themselves from the legitimate government and to make sure they could operate unmolested. It appears that someone or some organization in Colombia has been smuggling pre-Colombian artifacts out of their country for the last couple of years to channel funds to FARC, and these artifacts have been turning up at some of the more dubious collectors and private galleries in Europe. From what we've been able to ascertain, the stuff appears to be Inca or even pre-Inca in origin and all of it is pretty unique. Stuff no-one has really seen before, so it's attracted undue attention and that's where Interpol got involved. As near as we've been able to tell, whoever has been sending the stuff may be using freight containers out of Panama and moving the artifacts in through the drug lords. These drug lords have a very secret pipeline and so neither the DEA or Interpol have been able to crack exactly how or where they are getting the stuff out, or once it is in Europe, how in the heck they dispose of it to the art dealers. But believe me when I say that Interpol is way on top of this and our own DEA is cooperating with them for reasons of their own."

"So why sell art when selling drugs seems like it would provide plenty of money on its own? How does that tie into what may have happened to Jenny?" Tatterson pleaded.

Winters went on, "Artifacts, Roger, not art. And artifacts are a lot less 'hot' to a crooked customs man than drugs, and easier to pass over. You'd be surprised though, Rog, a small Inca artifact can sell for hundreds of thousands of dollars. Some of the bigger pieces might fetch millions, so this is no little thing. It was your own lead about the insurance guy in the BVI that helped us put two and two together. Seems he has two of his own investigators inside their organization and we've learned that Interpol has someone on the ground there too, so this is complicated."

Andy paused and then added, "we're talking about sending an assault and extraction team down to the area to stand by in case force is needed to recover your daughter, but for the moment, Roger, just stand down and let us see what can be done." The CIA man then went on in a friendly tone, "and I owe you an apology, Roger, for not taking you seriously last week. But believe me when I say that this is a big priority for us now. We just have to be careful not to step on any toes or get in the way of the Interpol operation already underway. There's a lot at stake here and we don't want anyone innocent to get killed, or to destroy all the hard intel work that's already been done. But rest assured that your daughter's life is our most important priority."

Roger exhaled heavily and thanked Andy, signing off with the assurance that he'd be called as soon as any new developments came to light.

◆◆◆

The phone on Rudy Bellows's desk rang and jolted him out of his deep thought. "Bellows here," he wearily answered. He'd been sleeping little over the last few days after all of the calls he had been making and getting — mostly due to the activity that the senator in the states had stirred up.

It was the senator again. "Hello, Mr. Bellows, and I'm sorry to bother you again, but I just had a call that I think is important to tell you about."

Bellows told him that it was no bother and Tatterson went on. "I've just had a call from some people in my government and they are prepared to provide military assistance if it should be needed and are even now moving into position to provide backup if necessary. This is for your ears only but just wanted you to know, and so if anything develops that may be aided by force, please call me straight away, will you?"

Typical American, Rudy thought. *Go in with guns blazing.*

But he thanked the senator and then quickly passed the intel on to his man at Interpol who exclaimed, "Bloody hell. I hope they don't muck the whole thing up. But thanks for the call." Rudy hung up, got up from his chair and wearily left his office.

◆◆◆

He was snoring again. The sound reverberated down the hallway from the forward cabin and Juliet rolled over in bed and put her pillow over her head. It had been only twenty-four hours, but already having Javier aboard was becoming interminable. *Thankfully,* she thought, *today I can go shopping with Frederica and get off the boat for a few hours.*

She'd worried all night already about how it might be going for Brice, and Javier had gotten in well after dark, telling her only that the flight was uneventful and that the boat had not arrived yet.

Dawn was breaking and since it was obvious that she wasn't going to get back to sleep, she decided to get up and get some coffee going.

Creeping quietly down the passageway and through the main cabin, she carefully closed the forward stateroom door, shutting the majority of the snoring noise out and then returned to the galley and began getting the coffee brewing.

With a hot cup of coffee, she sat peacefully at the dinette table and read through some tourist brochures Frederica had given her the day before when she had stopped by to arrange their outing for today. An hour passed and as she began making up some breakfast, Javier nosily came into the main cabin and asked for coffee. She poured him a cup and asked him if he wanted any breakfast.

"No, Señora, I'm fine and I can go to the restaurant at the club. But thank you for asking," he replied.

She'd been surprised by how courteous Javier had been. After the sullen and withdrawn way he had acted on the previous week while they were sailing, she had been prepared for more of the same, but in fact he appeared to have turned over a new leaf — going out of his way to be polite and helpful.

Javier looked at his Rolex watch and said, "In an hour Señora Frederica will be coming by to pick you up. Be sure not to keep her waiting! Perhaps you may want to start getting ready?"

She sensed that this was more of a dismissal than just a gentle nudge and she decided to take the cue. "Of course! I'll get my things together and head up to the showers now. Help yourself to more coffee if you need any," and she went aft to gather up her toiletries, then returned to the main cabin and climbed up the companionway and left the boat. As she was leaving she noticed that Javier had pulled out his iPhone and was making a call.

She took her time in the showers and so forty-five minutes later when she walked back down the dock, she saw that Frederica was already there and that she and Javier were both sitting close to each other in the cockpit of Mahalo, talking with heads bowed, and she sensed an urgency in Frederica's manner.

Frederica looked up as she saw Juliet in her peripheral vision, sat up and gave her a big smile saying, "Good morning, Juliet and I hope you slept well! I hope that you did not worry too much."

"Thank you, Frederica," Juliet said as she stepped aboard. "I'm not worried at all, Brice will get the job done for you and he'll be back here in no time."

Frederica said, "Good, then let's get started. I have a fantastic day planned for us!"

At the parking lot, Frederica stooped down to open the door of an older but nicely maintained white Jaguar XKE 2+2. "I've always loved these old Jaguars," she told Juliet and opened the passenger door for her. Juliet scrambled in and a few moments later Frederica had started the throaty sounding engine and pulled out onto the street. Rolling her window down, Frederica lit up a cigarette and turned towards Juliet, looking at her straight in the eyes and said in an accusing tone in perfect English, "I know who you really are and why you're here."

Nine

Inside the crowded waiting room of the small clinic I eased my way in past screaming infants clutching their mothers' sagging breasts, stepped over one elderly man who had no legs and tried to push past a big foul smelling Mestizo fellow who had his arm in a sling. I could look down the short hallway to where it sounded like there was some activity, but the big man resisted my attempts to get past him in line. The whitewashed plastered walls were cracked and patched and lacking paint in many areas and aside from a few tattered medical posters depicting childbirth, the ear and lungs and a few smaller posters advising celibacy and birth control, the place was sparsely decorated and looked like it hadn't been properly cleaned or painted in many years.

Peering down the hallway I saw a short native Indian looking nurse dressed in a stained white uniform come out of the room at the end of the hall and, seeing me standing there, she motioned me to come down. This seemed to satisfy the thug with the bad arm and he grudgingly let me pass. A few steps down, I entered the examination room where the young crewman I had helped out of the boat was laid out on the table, his lower leg draped in clean but well used cotton sheet, and the doctor was probing the open wound on his leg. The wound looked awful. It had gone gangrenous around the edges and smelled bad. The doctor looked up at me and said in good Brazilian accented English, "Do you know this fellow?"

I could see that the man had either passed out or had been put under and I answered, "I don't know him personally but I know his employer. If you are wondering if he can pay for treatment, rest assured the costs will be covered."

The doctor looked ashamed and said, "It's just that we have so little medicine available, we can't afford to give what we have away to those that can't afford to pay. I'm sure you understand."

I looked down at the young man who I assumed was the captain I had been told about by Rudy Bellows and asked, "He was conscious when you brought him in here five minutes ago. What happened? How long has he been out?"

"He passed out as soon as we put him up on the table. By the look of him I'd say he is extremely exhausted."

"You'll do what you can for him?" I asked and I reached into my pocket and pulled out two US hundred dollar bills and handed them to the nurse. "Just keep track of what I owe and I'll make sure you get paid. But try to get him patched back up as soon as you can, OK?" I asked and the doctor nodded, bending back to his job cleaning the wound. I turned and walked back down the hall, past the gauntlet of damaged humanity and out into the bright morning sunlight. I was already sweating in the oppressive rain forest heat.

I looked up and saw Tico reappear from a pathway off to the right of the wharf and he ran up to me, out of breath.

"I have located the man with the boat who can help us and he is coming to the pier now. He will need to be paid in advance for his services though. Where is the other fellow who came up the river?"

I patted Tico on the shoulder and turned him to walk back down the street toward the wharf saying, "Tico, You're a good man. Don't you worry. I'll take care of things from here on out but I'll still need you to help as an interpreter."

Tico looked up at me and smiled and we both turned our heads to the sound of an approaching boat coming from upstream.

Looming from around the bend, a heavy old forty-foot wooden workboat with what looked like a pair of huge truck engines roaring in the open hold through straight exhausts made a huge sweeping turn and came roughly alongside the pier, narrowly missing the yacht tender. Four scruffy looking indigenous crewmen threw lines on to the dock, tying her off. A moment later a sixty-or-so-year-old gray-haired and weathered European looking fellow with a stubby cigarette in his lips came up the long ladder and stood in front of me. His dirty torn work shirt and stained long pants smelled of oil and fish guts, wood smoke and whisky, but the twinkle in his eyes made me feel at ease, despite the appearances of the boat, crew and captain.

Tico chimed in, "This is Capitan Brice. Capitan Brice, this is Capitan Olivier."

Captain Olivier introduced himself as a former French Merchant Marine sailor who had come up the Amazon while still in his twenties and had liked it so much that when his ship left, he had hidden ashore and has never been back home again. He laughed at himself at this, and went on to tell me that his old boat made regular runs up all the tributaries into Colombia and even as far as Ecuador and Peru on occasion, and that it was the most powerful small workboat on this part of the river. He elaborated saying that his boat had very shallow draft and that he was regularly employed towing large rafts of logs down river to the sawmills to feed the hungry new towns and cities of Brazil.

I asked Tico to go fetch the young fellow who had introduced himself as Diego and went about the job of negotiating a price for the salvage of the stranded catamaran. Olivier also told me this section of the rivers Ica and Putumayo was difficult to navigate, and so I worked up a price to have the captain accompany us as a pilot for the rest of the way to our destination, leading us up river with this powerful tug. A few hundred more dollars one way or another was no big deal to me as long as it made my life a little easier. Added to this was that I was almost totally unprepared to navigate and wasn't even sure, until I could get aboard the catamaran and have a look at the navigation equipment, where I really was in the vast labyrinth of rivers, streams and side channels of the upper Amazon basin. I hadn't really been given much of a clue from Ramon as to where exactly I was supposed to take the boat once I had her back underway, and was only told that his brother was aboard and would fill me in as soon as I arrived.

Going back to the discussion of the stranded catamaran I said, "I don't know how far down river it is, but I am guessing less than a hundred miles, maybe closer to fifty. The yacht tender made it up here in just under three hours."

He squinted at the river and then up at the sun and said, "well, we will need to get moving soon then. My ship can make eighteen knots, but we will be racing daylight."

I immediately set Tico to the job of getting gasoline arranged for the yacht tender and, handing a thousand dollars in cash to Captain Olivier as a deposit, I ran back up the street to the clinic to see if the young captain had awoken.

This time the people in the waiting room allowed me through. Word of my cash donation must have filtered out to the waiting room and when I went into the examination room I was thankful that the patient was awake. He looked over at me and said, "Thanks for arranging to pay for my leg. I guess I just sorta passed out."

I came closer to his bed and asked him point blank in English, "Were you involved in the theft of the boat or were you hijacked?" It was a big risk to take but I could feel time was beginning to run out.

He looked at me, unsure of what to say and finally admitted, "I was involved from the beginning. It was an inside job." I could see that he was afraid. How was he to know if I was there to help or was a henchman for the organization?

So I bent over him and said quietly,

"If you want to save this from becoming a complete disaster, wait for me here and I'll help you when I get here with the boat."

I asked him how to find the boat and he explained that I only had to go down river until I hit the main channel and then it was just a dozen or so miles down from that, well off to the right, out of the main channel.

Walking back out to the street, I saw Tico and Diego come through the saloon doors and I met them in front of the tavern.

"We need to get moving right away," I said to Diego who arrogantly replied,

"Fuck that, man. You go yourself. I only just got here and I've had enough of that stinking boat for a lifetime already. I'll wait for you here. It's not hard to find, just go down the river and make a left. You can't miss it, it's the only big catamaran in Amazonia." He laughed at what he thought was a clever remark and turned and went back inside the whorehouse, the swinging doors squeaking in protest at being thrown open so abruptly.

Tico looked up at me and said, "The little boat should be fueled up by now."

With Diego occupied for the moment, I walked back over to the clinic and pushed my way once again inside to where the young captain was being treated. He was alone now and I grabbed him by his shirt, shaking him and seethed, "Tell me about what's really going on. Is there an American girl onboard named Jenny Tatterson?" He nodded quickly and I added, "Is she OK?"

He told me quickly about the family and the extra crew girl they had taken, but left out how she had gotten aboard. I knew he had no idea if he could trust me and as I turned to leave I said, "There's a local girl here in a house across the street. Her name is Melowa. Have Tico take you to her and she'll take care of you."

I hurried out of the clinic and quickly made a detour to the shack where Melowa was staying. I found her in the back room and told her quickly about the young captain in the clinic, eliciting a promise from her that she would seek him out and look after him. I pressed an American fifty into her hand and closed her fingers over it. She smiled thinly up at me and then, unexpectedly, leaned up and kissed me on my cheek. With that I squeezed her hands and turned and ran down the street towards the wharf.

I saw Tico sitting on the porch of the whorehouse and motioned him to join me and as we walked on I told him, "Go get the other captain out of the clinic and take him to the Indian girl where I stayed last night. She can look after him until the boat arrives and I have already paid her for food and lodging."

Arriving at the pier, I scrambled down into the tender and, checking the fuel tanks, I started it up and untied the lines, coming alongside the old workboat as I was leaving.

Olivier leaned out over the side, a new cigarette dangling from his lips and I told him I was going to go on ahead — that he should follow at best speed and that I'd stand by on the VHF radio on channel 69. I then gunned the throttle, making a sweeping arc as I headed the tender downstream.

The river was as flat as a pond and as the inflatable tenders seventy HP outboard sang at an easy three-quarter throttle, I cut a clean V down mid channel doing close to thirty knots. The river narrowed in places and the incredibly tall trees from the rain forest sometimes nearly met overhead, creating the strange sensation of skimming down a long tunnel. At other times the river opened up and other small tributaries emptied into the river, making it imperceptibly larger as I made my way downstream.

Two hours down river I noticed a visible change in the scenery. I had just gone by a small village. I really wanted to stop and try to find a radio or phone to call in, but I was very unsure of who might be watching, or who was a friend or foe, so I carried on. Besides, I really had no precise idea of where I was and until I could get aboard the yacht and look at her navigation equipment and charts, I'd just be guessing as to our actual location. I was pretty sure we were still in Brazil, and the fact that I speak no Portuguese kept me from thinking of turning back.

A short while later the engine began to miss and I quickly slowed down to idle, switched to the reserve fuel tank and then picked back up to just a little over half-throttle. I now began to become increasingly concerned that I may have missed the catamaran off some side channel or behind one of the small islands that I had begun to see since passing the village.

I decided that I'd give it another half hour and that if I hadn't found the boat by then that I'd return to the village and wait for Captain Olivier.

Not five minute later though I saw the yacht, way off to the right, just as the young captain had described her. I slowed down to just above planing speed and made a wide arc, coming in from astern to see where the channel she had come in on led. I knew the best and surest way to get her back to the main channel would be to retrace the route she had taken into the shallows. Proceeding along the edge of the main channel, sure enough, I saw two big sand bores just under the surface in line with what might have at first seemed like the easiest route out, but I made a circle and found a deeper channel farther on.

All my noise and my wake had brought the crew of the catamaran up on deck, and I counted three people as I slowed to idle and made my final approach to come alongside.

As I came up to the boat I switched the engine off and scrambled up to pass my bow line to the younger man on the side deck. I quickly introduced myself. "I'm Capitan Brice, your relief skipper."

The older man quickly took my hand and helped me aboard, introducing himself and his wife and son.

Instinctively I looked around to assess the situation. The boat looked a bit of a mess. Tattered canvas and a dirty deck along with a cluttered cockpit area told me that these people had had a rough time of it and that they weren't sailors. The older man who had introduced himself as Carlos began again.

"We are very happy to see you, but where is my son Diego?"

I filled him in as best I could on what had happened since I had met his son, and also told him that a tug boat was coming down river within the next two hours that would help us get off the sandbar. Just then the cockpit sliding doors slid open a small way and a gaunt looking blonde girl stuck her head partially out and asked Carlos,

"Would you like me to make dinner early, since we may be getting underway again soon?"

Carlos exploded in anger at her, "I told you to stay inside!"

She recoiled but didn't shut the door and Carlos quickly regained his composure and said, "Yes, yes, make some dinner." And looking over at me said, "I'm sorry for the outburst, we have all been very worried since we went aground last night."

The girl slid the door shut and rather than broaching the obvious question of who she was or who else may be aboard, I asked if I could see the engine rooms and went about checking the systems so that I could ready the boat for the eventual arrival of help.

Looking things over carefully I could see that the boat had been poorly maintained since she had been on this voyage. A quick check on the engines showed the port engine nearly two quarts low on oil and a coolant leak on the starboard engine from a broken hose clamp was causing loss of salt water which had begun to rust some of the bolts nearby, but overall, it looked like I could get things squared away if I could just find the spare fluids and some tools.

I stuck my head up and called for Carlos who was standing nearby, and I asked him where I might find spare oil, coolant and some basic tools. He quickly summoned the man he had introduced as his son, Santiago, and then his son and I went forward to the deck locker and I dropped down inside and began to gather what I would need to get started. I also took a quick look at the generator which clearly needed servicing and asked Santiago if there was a log of any details on when the oil was last changed. He went aft to look and as soon as he left I immediately went up on deck. Wondering where other fluids or tools might be stored I crossed to the foredeck hatch to starboard and opened it. Staring up at me, a slim, dirty and disheveled but unusually attractive looking girl with mid length dark brown hair who appeared to be in her early twenties peered up at me.

Just then I heard Santiago returning and, seeing the foredeck hatch open he shouted, "Hey, Capitan, keep that hatch shut! She is a crazy one and needs to stay there."

I gave the girl a quick reassuring smile and closed the hatch, latching it tightly, as I looked back at Santiago and said, "I was looking for oil and transmission fluid. Where do you keep that?"

Santiago paused for a moment, apparently thinking of what to do and shrugged saying, "I do not know, I do not think it is up in that cabin though. I'll look in the other side," and I went back to the generator locker, dropped in and shouted up to him, "Oh, here it is. Sorry!"

Grabbing three quarts of oil and some rags, I also picked up a small box of tools and handed it up to the young man saying, "We will need to find a small hose clamp. Where would I look for that?"

Over the next hour I worked on getting the main engines ready to go again, and then I went up to the helm area to start figuring out the controls and to look at the navigation equipment. A quick look through the track log on the GPS chart plotter showed me a lot: That the boat had been more or less underway continuously since it was stolen from the BVI nearly three weeks before, and that I was actually on a large tributary of the Amazon, still inside Brazil, but less than a hundred miles from the Colombian border. On a whim, I scrolled over to the waypoints page. I found a set of coordinates for preselected spots along the route chosen and discovered that my hunch was right. There were waypoints selected for each of the fuel stops and a final destination simply labeled 'End'.

Just then Carlos came up to the helm area and, looking at his watch said, "So, Capitan Brice, how much longer do you think it will be until this help arrives?"

I looked at my watch too and did a quick mental calculation answering, "I'd expect to see them anytime within the next half hour." And went on, "I've noticed that the water level has been rising. We aren't heeled over, leaning, as much as we were even two hours ago when I got here."

I went on to tell him about what I had done to get the boat ready to move and expressed concern that the genset, which had been running for who knows how long, more or less continuously, needed to be serviced too and that maybe on the run up river to the refueling spot someone could steer the boat, following the tug, while I could then get the oil changed and service the unit. Carlos seemed to be wary of that idea though. I also asked about whether there was any food I could have. "I am sorry, Capitan Brice; I have forgotten my manners in all the excitement of having you come to our rescue! I will immediately have some food brought to you," and he turned and left, climbing down the steps to the main cockpit and disappeared inside the big cat through the sliding glass doors.

About two minutes later the doors slid open again and the young blonde crew girl came up the steps holding a plate with a sandwich and some chips and a glass of what looked like orange juice for me. I took them and thanked her and she turned to go but then hesitated and turned back, looking me in the eyes and said, "Please don't let them hurt us."

Before I could answer her or ask any further questions, I heard a shout from up in the forward cockpit. It sounded like the younger man and he was saying, "Look, there is a boat coming down the river." The girl smiled imploringly at me and, quickly turning, went back down the steps just as Carlos and his wife came out to the cockpit and scrambled up to the helm area to where they could see up ahead.

About a mile away, the dirty old tug was coming down river making a huge wake as she pushed her displacement hull at well beyond its normal hull speed.

The radio came to life with a call. "Capitan Brice, it is Capitan Olivier, do you copy?"

I picked up the radio mike and answered, "Captain Olivier, I copy you. There is shallow water off our starboard bow. Swing wide and come up on our stern quarter. The deepest water seems to be that way. We are only lightly aground now, so if you can put a heavy hawser off our stern quarter, you should be able to pull us free. Do you copy?"

He came back in his strong French accent with, "Yes. Copy all. Stand by. I'll be there shortly."

The old tug passed by in the main channel, slowing as it made a wide turn. Two of his crew were up on the bow looking into the water ahead and the tug slowed to a crawl as they threaded their way through the intricate maze of side channels leading to where we were stranded.

About five minutes passed before the bow of Captain Olivier's tug nudged up to our starboard stern quarter and one of his crew passed a line to us. I grabbed it and made it fast to the stern mooring cleat and then, as a precaution, tossed one of our own dock lines back to them, securing it to a different cleat so that the load could be shared between two cleats. These big cats were actually pretty lightly built and I didn't want to tear a cleat out. This way I had a better chance of being able to withstand the immense load that would be coming shortly.

"Just a minute. Let me get our engines going," I shouted to the tug. Captain Olivier acknowledged with a small salute from inside the wheelhouse and I ran back up to the bridge, starting both engines before I picked up the radio and said, "All ready, Captain. Please be easy at first. The cleats don't look too strong."

A few seconds later the big diesels belched some black smoke as they roared, and the cat lurched as the slack was taken up and the tug began to strain against the stranded yacht.

"Easy does it," I said to myself and I noticed the blonde girl was now halfway up the steps. I looked over at her and said, "Please be ready to go cast off the tugs line when we come free."

She nodded but stayed where she was. Carlos and his wife were holding onto one of the cockpit hardtop posts, peering intently at the tug and the ropes and only Santiago seemed like he was ready to help if need. Slowly, imperceptibly, the big cat began to slide off the sandbank and a few seconds later, the tugs engine went to idle and the crew of both boats quickly scrambled to undo lines and pull them in so that the tug could get away before we collided or ran aground again in the narrow channel.

The tug backed down and made a tight turn to head back out the way she came in, and I applied forward to the port engine and reverse to the starboard engine to swing the cat around to face the opposite way she had been facing when she ran aground. In a minute we too were heading back downstream and away from the maze of sandbars, heading toward the relatively open water of the main channel.

Swinging in an arc, following the tug, we made our turn to go back upstream in the main part of the river and I radioed the tug to ask them to keep the speed down to about ten knots which seemed to be a good cruising speed for the big cat. We all breathed a sigh of relief and I felt around for a cigarette in my top pocket.

Pulling one out, I looked over at the blonde girl who was now the only person at the helm area and said, "My name's Brice. Brice Cannon," to which she replied,

"Jenny Tatterson, thanks for saving us."

◆ ◆ ◆

Toby began to feel a little better. He was now sharing his room with a young mother who was obviously in the final stages of labor, and he had been given something for pain which seemed to be working. The nurse came in the room and checked on the woman and then came over to Toby, asking him in Portuguese how he felt.

"I'm doing OK," he said in Spanish and she seemed to understand, saying to him in Spanish,

"You can go any time if you wish. There is a girl asking for you and she will take you to a place to rest."

Toby was confused for a moment about who might be asking for him and then remembered the other captain telling him about a local girl who would look after him. He began to get up and the nurse helped him, giving him a pair of old crutches which would need to be adjusted to fit, but which were a huge help. He gathered up his clothes and put on his shirt and pants, struggling with his heavily bandaged lower leg and following the nurse, he made his way down the short hall to the waiting room. Immediately the nurse ushered another patient to the room with the now empty bed Toby had left. As he looked around, a bit bewildered, for a moment until the main door opened. A beautiful young Amazon Indian girl in a simple white dress looked into the dingy waiting room. She spied him right away and entered, crossing the room to offer her hand to help him.

"My name is Melowa," she said in fairly good English and went on, "Capitan Brice say to come help you. Please come with me now."

Toby smiled at her and followed her outside, slowly making his way across the heavily rutted main street, avoiding the drying mud puddles. His leg was throbbing heavily by now, but with effort he arrived at the door of the girl's house and they went inside.

She crossed the room and quickly brought him a chair to sit on. Easing into the chair he asked in Spanish, "Do you live here alone?"

"No, I live here with my grandmother, but this not my house. I only here until I am told to go. I am not free person."

"What do you mean you aren't free? Are you married?" to which she replied,

"I not married. I may never be. I am to be a worker for the people who also hire you. I think I will be slave."

"A slave? But I thought there was no such thing anymore!" Toby said.

"I will be a sex slave I guessing," she said as casually as if she was telling him she would be a dishwasher. "I had little hope of anything better. But Capitan Brice say he help me. Maybe he help you also?" She was looking him in the eyes now and then broke her gaze and abruptly turned and left.

Just who was this Captain Brice and who was he really working for? Toby thought to himself as the girl went about preparing some food. He wondered if he could trust the man or if he should even say anything about what was really going on. A slip of the tongue could cost him and his sister their lives. He had to be very careful about whom he trusted.

Ten

"I'm sorry, I don't know what you mean." Juliet looked truly shocked, and tried to regain her composure as Frederica went on.

"You have no need to worry. I am not who you think I am either," she laughed and ashed her cigarette out the window of the Jaguar as they made their way out onto the main street towards the historic district. Looking over at Juliet she continued, "I don't expect you to believe me without checking, but relax and just know, I am here for other reasons than just as a companion for a criminal drug lord." She let this sink in and Juliet said nothing.

Juliet finally answered, "I don't know what you are talking about, Frederica. I'm sorry but Brice and I are just normal people who need to make some money. We really do appreciate everything you and Ramon have done for us. Believe me when I say this, please."

Frederica studied her face for another moment and laughed saying, "I'm sorry for the little test! I was told to try to see if there was a lie somewhere in your story. But I can see you are just as I thought. So, no worries! Let's go to the first shop!"

She pulled the Jaguar over in front of a very fancy looking boutique and a doorman stepped up to help them out of their car. Going inside, Frederica introduced Juliet to the shopkeeper and they began to look through the selection of clothing. Skirts and dresses for all occasions graced the racks of the small shop and Juliet was told that these were only samples and that if she required something unique, all she had to do was to ask and a seamstress would meet with her to design something special, just for her.

Being a cruiser and careful with her finances, Juliet was always conscious of spending too much money. But on this day she had a lot of trouble not going over her budget. Frederica took her to three other shops and so in the end, Juliet had spent close to five hundred dollars. But what a grand selection of clothes she had gotten! Frederica had clearly enjoyed the experience almost as much as Juliet had and even bought a few things for herself.

They had lunch at a nice outdoor café in the historic district. At one moment Frederica was telling her all about the history of the street and of this part of the city when, seeing two men get up from a nearby table and suddenly leave, Frederica looked over the top of her sunglasses and quietly said "we need to leave here immediately. Come with me." No sooner had she and Frederica gotten up and started to make for the street when a car roared by and two men leaned out the windows with small machine guns and opened fire in their direction.

Frederica grabbed Juliet and pulled her down alongside a small truck parked on the street and reached in her handbag, taking out an ominous looking handgun she jumped up, returning fire at the speeding vehicle. The men quickly withdrew from the windows as the car sped away. She went out in the street and continued firing at the car until the rear window exploded just as the car careened around a corner and was lost from sight.

Running back to Juliet, she saw that she was bleeding. "Oh my God, Juliet, where are you hit?"

Juliet held her arm and looked more closely at her injury. It appeared that a small bit of broken glass from a shattered window had grazed her and Frederica said, "Come on, we need to get out of here before the police arrive."

Already people were starting to get up from where they had thrown themselves to hide from the unknown gunmen. Miraculously, it didn't appear that anyone had been hit. They both got up and ran down the street, down a side street to her car, and got inside. Frederica started it up, burning rubber as she pulled out onto the street. After a few quick turns she got it out onto a main boulevard and so was shortly lost in traffic. Three police cars went tearing by toward the direction of where they had just been, sirens blaring.

Frederica looked over at Juliet and said, "There is much you need to know. Please, stop with the charades. I know you are working for a London insurance agency and I will tell you, I am working for people who are investigating Ramon and his brother Carlos. This is an exceptionally dangerous and complicated situation and you need to get away from Colombia. This is way over your head!"

Juliet was still breathing heavily from the terror and running but said earnestly to Frederica, "How do you know this? What makes you think this?"

Frederica said, "My people have been working on this operation for almost two years. I have been heavily involved now for almost as long. There is much at stake that goes way beyond a few boat thefts!" She was quite agitated as she continued, "As I said, this is a complicated and very dangerous situation." She paused for a moment while Juliet studied her and then asked, "How much do you know about the FARC?"

Juliet looked puzzled for a moment and then answered, "You mean the Colombian Revolutionary army? I thought that kind of thing was over a long time ago."

"No, no, no," Frederica said and added, "The FARC is very much alive and well and in fact, they hold vast sections of this country under their complete control. The entire southeast interior is all FARC governed and Ramon's father that he speaks of? He was a major FARC organizer, but very secret, very underground. A big man in the movement. The government finally figured out that he was behind a lot of things that had been happening and they raided his stronghold in the south years ago to break up his stranglehold on the drug cartels, but this was only like cutting off the head of the hydra." Frederica changed lanes and slowed down, trying to blend in better with the tourist traffic and went on. "Now there are many new cartel heads that have their own independent armies and they sometimes answer to FARC, sometimes not. But the whole country down to the south is a battle zone. Thousands of people die there every year in this conflict. And Ramon is one of their generals. He holds the key to their finances, and raises most of the money for the revolution through the sale of drugs and now also, with the sale of antiquities and also, I'm sorry to say, through the sale of young women."

Juliet was speechless but finally said, "I'm sorry, I had no idea we were involved in such a big operation," to which Frederica shot back,

"Of course not, and you're just a small-time player. But you are in the middle of a very dangerous game and you need to get out. Now!" Then she smoothed her tone and said in a more conciliatory manner, "Don't blame yourself, but we need to figure out a way to get you and your husband out of involvement as soon as possible... if only I knew how."

They continued on through the city and gradually made the way back to the marina when Juliet asked, "Who was it that attacked us today?"

Frederica thought for a second and said, "I am guessing it was a rival drug lord's gang. I'm not sure why they were after me, but I'll certainly find out and I'll let you know what I learn, but in the meantime, start to prepare to leave the moment your husband returns. Even if it is the middle of the night. You need to leave if you want to live and don't want to get other innocent people killed in the process."

Dropping her at the main gates Frederica looked slightly nervous as she said, "Do not breathe a word of what happened today to anyone. Just show Javier the nice clothes you bought. And have a nice night... Ciao!" Frederica sped off and Juliet, legs still shaking slightly from the experience at the restaurant, made her way down the docks to her boat.

◆◆◆

Night was rapidly approaching and I needed to find a place to stop. Even though I understood that the boat had been traveling night and day up river to this point, the sandbar grounding and the fact that we were now on the Colombian and Brazilian frontier made me feel cautious. Captain Olivier agreed and told me of a small village ahead where we could tie up for the night.

"No, we will not tie up, Capitan Brice. This is not a good idea!" Carlos said with agitation. "We may stop if you like, but only to anchor. We cannot tie to the shore. It is too dangerous!"

Rather than argue with him I radioed Olivier and told him that we would instead stop at the closest wide spot and anchor for the night. He told us he was going to go on ahead to the dock, but that he'd come find us in the morning if we hadn't overtaken him by 8 a.m.

A short while later I saw a nice-looking cove off to the right-hand side of the boat and we cautiously edged our way in towards the densely wooded north bank of the river. As I watched the depth sounder, it suddenly began to show that we were now out of the channel and the main part of the current, but still in water sufficiently deep that we could safely anchor without worry of a grounding, even if a strong wind blew us towards the shore. So, I asked Carlos, who was standing nearby on the steps, if he would take the helm while we crawled forward slowly. When he expressed reluctance, I called for Jenny and before he could object, she edged past Carlos, scrambled up into the helm seat and looked at me for directions.

"Put it in neutral when I make this signal." I showed her a hand signal I would use. "And if I point one way or the other, just put the engine that's opposite of where I am pointing in gear, but only at idle, OK?" She nodded and I gave her a brief smile and patted her shoulder and then scrambled down from the helm, running forward to get the anchor ready to go.

A few minutes later I signaled her to put the engines in neutral and felt the big cat lose momentum. Once we had stopped, I lowered the anchor I then signaled the girl to put the engines in reverse and a few moments later, once we were moving slowly backwards, I signaled for her to put them in neutral again and I cinched up the anchor chain clutch. Moments later the boat came to an abrupt halt indicating that we were well anchored to the muddy river bottom. I told the girl to shut both engines down and I walked back to the lower cockpit.

It was now nearly dark and with the boat resting well at anchor, I went inside to the main electrical panel and shut down the generator too. Immediately the sound of the jungle close by on our starboard side encroached and then seemed to envelop us in a cacophony of sounds. Thousands of insects, tree frogs and other indistinct noises blended with the gurgling of the current against the hull, and occasional larger animal noises were sometimes heard off in the darkness; the call of a bird, the howl of a monkey and then the sound of a jungle cat. "How long must we go without the air conditioning, Capitan?" Carlos said as he came up into the main salon, patting his forehead with a small towel.

"I need to change the oil on the generator and service the water pump, so give me about an hour and I should have it back up and running," I said as I got up and prepared to go up forward to the machinery space. Turning back to him I added, "I'll need some help. It's hotter than hell up there and very dirty, thanks to the lousy job of maintenance your last Captain did, so I'll need a hand. Care to help? I just need someone to help me mop up the dirty oil and hand me tools."

As I had hoped, he blanched and suggested, "I will send my son to help you."

But a shout from Santiago who had been listening to us from down the corridor squelched that idea. "No way, man. Get the cook to help him. I'm already sweating just thinking about it."

Carlos thought for a second and then said, "I'll go get the girl and she will assist you, and make it fast. This heat is not nice, si?"

I said, "It's OK, Carlos, I'll get her. It's on the way." I had seen him locking Jenny below up in the bow section shortly after we had gotten finished anchoring the boat.

"As you wish, Capitan," Carlos agreed. Already I could sense that he was relaxing with his trust in me as a captain. After all, I had been sent by his elder brother, so I had already passed his scrutiny. I must be OK.

I turned and left the main cabin and went out and around the side deck to the bow compartment. Opening it, I saw that there was one light on, and the two women were sitting next to each other on the lower berth and stopped whatever they were talking about as soon as the hatch opened above them.

"C'mon, Jenny," I said. "I need your help. And please introduce me to your friend."

Jenny hesitated and then said, "Mr. Cannon, this is Bridget."

I was taken aback by just how beautiful the other woman was. She looked fairly tall although I couldn't tell for sure. But she was slim and had a dark complexion, with long wavy brown hair and what in the dim light looked like almost golden eyes. She was dressed in a dirty tank top and cutoff jean shorts, but still looked absolutely gorgeous. I could see why Carlos was guarding her and keeping her out of sight from other men.

I nodded and said hello and then put my hand out for Jenny. She reluctantly accepted my help and scrambled out on deck while I pretended to lock the hatch behind her and she then followed me across the foredeck to the generator hatch. I opened it and the heat poured out. Reaching inside I switched on the light and jumped down inside. Jenny paused for a second, looking up at the forward windows where she saw Carlos watching and then she followed me down into the cramped compartment.

Already the heat was causing us both to sweat, but I set about immediately with getting the oil pump rigged and asked her to hand me two empty oil jugs I had located earlier so that we could drain the oil into them. Hooking it up in silence, I started the electric pump which noisily began to slowly drain the oil out of the generator's crankcase. The sound was loud enough to mask any quiet talking and so I leaned over to her and said, "I'm here to rescue you. I've been sent by the company that insured this boat. I'm not quite sure how I'm going to do it yet, but somehow, I'll get you out of here." She looked at me with intense blue eyes. Her forehead creased in worry and she reached over and gave my arm a squeeze as I went on, "Please, tell me about Captain Toby? I met him briefly up river and need to know his involvement. Can he be trusted?"

Jenny let this sink in for a minute while I spoke loudly saying, "Hand me those rags, we need to get this oil cleaned up. Jesus, it's hot in here!" I said this loudly enough that I could easily be heard above the sound of the pump and noticed that the first jug was now almost full. I briefly turned the pump off, switched jugs and started the pump up again and then, leaning towards her again whispered, "And tell me about Bridget. What's her story?"

Jenny quickly whispered about how they had attacked the other boat and that Bridget had been taken prisoner and hadn't been out of the forward cabin in almost two weeks, and that she was starting to become very depressed and seemed constantly terrified. She then went on to say that while she had thought that Toby was in on the whole thing from the beginning, she thought he was being blackmailed and spoke briefly about how she had heard something about his sister possibly being held captive. She also told how Toby had resisted cooperating with the attack on the sailboat and how later he had threatened to head to a nearby port and that this was when he had been shot.

I started to say something but heard creaking on the deck and looked up just in time to see Carlos and Santiago come into view above us in the open hatchway. "Ah, Capitan Brice, we came to see if you needed anything and to see how things are going."

I looked up, wiping the heavy sweat off my brow and just then the oil pump began to spit, having emptied the oil pan. I said, "We're getting there, Carlos. I'll need the wrench set though, I think I left it back in the port engine room."

Carlos spoke to Santiago who disappeared from view, heading aft to collect the wrenches. It was clear that Carlos was going to watch what we were doing from up above and I was glad I had gotten to communicate with the girl a little at least.

Over the next ten minutes, while Jenny poured the new oil into the genset and wiped up the oil that had accumulated around the generator, I went about changing out the impeller on the raw water pump. Santiago had returned after a few minutes with the wrenches and I had started checking the bolts on various fittings, mainly for show. Carlos and Santiago withdrew a few feet, speaking to each other, and I whispered quickly to Jenny, "Tell Bridget that she should stay ready to go from now on. You should too. I don't know when it will be, but sleep fully dressed and have whatever you will want to bring with you nearby. At least make sure you get three bottles of water. When our chance comes, we probably won't have any time to prepare. We'll just have to make a break for it."

She looked me in the eyes with a grim expression on her lips and a slightly wrinkled brow and whispered, "What's your plan?"

But just then Santiago stuck his head into view and asked us, "What's the holdup, my mother wants to know. How much longer until we can have our air conditioning back on?"

I told him we were almost done and also told him that I was done with the girl. He motioned her out of the compartment, commenting in Spanish on the fact that she was drenched in sweat and that he could see her nipples under her wet shirt. Pinching her on her backside as he escorted her over to the bow compartment, he opened the hatch to lock her down below. "Hey! This forward hatch isn't locked!" He quickly threw it open and scanned the interior of the makeshift cell. He looked visibly relieved when he saw the French girl still sitting on her bunk, and put the blonde down into the locker, closing it tightly. "You didn't lock the hatch, Capitan! What is the matter with you?" he shouted.

I apologized. "Sorry, Santiago, I was distracted. I'm really sorry!" He still looked angry and so I continued. "Where are either of them going to go? Relax. It was an honest mistake, and there's no way they could try to escape here. They wouldn't last half the night in that jungle." I said, motioning towards the dark bank and then added in a friendly tone, "C'mon, I'll make us both a drink and let's get the AC going again, shall we?"

My smile was disarming, and he relaxed and followed me down the side deck to the cockpit and we went inside.

I crossed the cabin to the main electrical panel and started the generator, checked the gauges and made another trip up forward to check over the unit to make sure the new filter wasn't leaking oil and, returning to the main salon, restarted the air conditioning units. I then went over to the wet bar and made up two gin and tonics and handed one to Santiago, slapping him lightly on the shoulder as I turned and went back outside.

Just as I was climbing up to the bridge deck I heard a rumbling sound in the darkness and then a bright spotlight illuminated our boat. Carlos came thundering up the steps and, shielding his eyes with his arm, peered over at what sounded like a patrol boat.

"Let me handle this," he said just as a voice boomed over across the water, thin and tinny sounding, and likely emanating from a poor quality megaphone.

The voice said in Spanish, "Prepare to be boarded."

Why were we being hailed in Spanish? I wondered since from what I had calculated, we were still at least forty miles inside Brazilian waters.

Carlos and Santiago went down into the cockpit just as a rusty gray steel workboat with what looked like a dozen armed men came heavily alongside, smearing black tire marks on our shiny topsides as they quickly secured their dirty ropes to the catamaran. Four men armed with AK 47 submachine guns and dressed in jungle camouflage hopped aboard and confronted Carlos and Santiago, who had come over to the port side deck and, wisely, were unarmed. I noticed one of the men on the other boat was aiming a more sophisticated looking rifle at me, so I stepped back into the shadows of the bridge deck and waited to see what was unfolding.

I couldn't hear everything but after a minute or so of rapid, agitated conversation, I heard laughing and more conversational, normal sounding tones and so I peeked back over the edge in time to see Carlos and the leader shaking hands and patting each other on the back. The gunman who had been pointing his rifle at me had disappeared and Carlos was motioning me to come down, saying in English, "Capitan Brice, these are some of my brother's people. They patrol the river to keep it safe, and they had been told to keep a lookout for us! Come and meet them!"

Coming down the stairs I encountered Santiago who grabbed me and spoke quietly and quickly in my ear in English. "Do not mention the girls or any details of where we are going. Just act as if you can speak no Spanish, si? These are very dangerous men."

I walked over to the side deck and shook hands with the leader saying. "Howdy! *Lo siento, me no habla español!*" Smiling as big as I could, I acted like the big dumb American and shoved my hands in my pockets as I went to stand off to the side, behind Carlos. About this time, I noticed that Frederica was also coming out to the side deck and after Carlos had introduced her and a few pleasantries had been exchanged, she spoke rapidly in Spanish to the leader. The gist of it was that they very much appreciated seeing them, but that they were very tired and had a long way yet to go, so if it was OK, they should go on about their patrol and just radio if anything came up.

The leader clearly was unsure and told her he was going to radio his base to see what should be done. A few minutes later the leader returned, and by then Santiago was holding the attention of several of the men with his story of sailing the boat down from the Caribbean, pirating a sailboat for fuel and food and of course omitting any references to the young women or their plans. Carlos jumped in and said to the leader, "We are expected at my brother's land in a week, so we have only stopped this once to rest. It has been a very trying voyage."

The leader answered, "I have spoken to our commander and he wishes you Godspeed. We will be leaving you now and will alert you on the VHF radio channel 72 if there is any other river traffic. But for now, consider your way ahead to the border to be safe."

He quickly gathered his men and untied from our boat, returned aboard and then they motored off into the darkness.

◆◆◆

Ramon slammed the phone down, seething. The veins bulged out on his forehead and his hands were visibly shaking as he stood up in his small, palatial office.

It had grown dark outside and he had been wondering where Frederica had been all day. She had told him of her shopping trip earlier in the day, but had omitted any reference to what she had been doing the rest of the time. Although he had thought nothing of it then, he was now running all the possibilities through his mind.

The call he had just gotten was from the head of another cartel in the western part of the country. A man he seldom spoke to, but whom he trusted. This man had been one of his father's most faithful friends and was one of the few older cartel leaders still alive and operating after the purging of the last several years.

The cartel leader had spoken of an Interpol investigation that he had gotten wind of after his people had abducted and tortured a British official who was beginning to cause problems for his organization.

The admission that there was another ongoing investigation had made several of the other cartel leaders step up security and when the dying man had mentioned specifically that Ramon's cartel had been infiltrated, out of courtesy for his late friend, he had called his deceased friend's son Ramon to tell him what he knew.

"This man who we questioned said that someone very close to you and high up in your organization was an Interpol agent," the caller had said and had gone on to add, "We could not find out who it was before he finally died, but we believe he was being truthful. He was begging for mercy and one of my men finally gave it to him in the form of a slit throat. We are very upset with you, Ramon, for putting us all in danger. Some of the cartel leaders suggested closing you down, but I pointed out that without the financial assistance that you are supplying to the FARC, that they would soon be without an army to resist the government troops. Of course you know that many of our colleagues now have their own private armies and so from these ones you might expect some trouble, which is the reason for my call."

Ramon had thanked him and tried to assure him that this was just not possible. He couldn't imagine who would betray him. He knew everyone in his inner circle so well!

The man had gone on to say, "Ramon, my people will wait to see what comes of this, but some of the other cartels leaders may not be so willing to sit idly by when they see a threat."

Ramon bowed his head, putting his hands on his antique desk as he thought hard about who this threat to his organization could be. He ran all the possibilities through his mind. Could it be his dear friend from childhood, Javier, whom he trusted with his life? Or maybe the operations manager in the south, Manuel? He had known him as well for twenty years. Or maybe Frederica? No, it could not be her. She was so faithful! And then suddenly he groaned loudly and laughed out loud, realizing his blindness and stupidity. "Of course! It is the American Capitan and his wife! These ones I hardly know. It has to be them!" he exclaimed to the empty room.

"Are you OK, my dear?" Frederica asked as she knocked on the heavy wooden door to his study.

"Yes, yes, Frederica. Come in," he said as he unlatched the lock to his private study and swung the heavy wooden door open. Frederica peered inside first, wondering if there was another person in the room and then, seeing that he was alone, came inside and sat down. Ramon closed the door and went over to her, sitting down opposite her at his desk and looked her straight in the eyes.

"Have you noticed anything unusual in the behavior of your guest today?"

Frederica's mind raced for a moment wondering what this could be about and then said, "No, she seemed very happy to get off the boat, and to do some shopping. Why?"

"I had a call from an old friend of the family. You have never met him but he is a man to be trusted. He told me that there is an undercover agent who has penetrated our organization." He stopped and studied her face. Ramon had gotten far in life largely because of his ability to read people and their body language. He did this out of habit, not for any particular reason and so was a bit surprised when, for a fraction of a second he saw Frederica flush and her pupils dilate imperceptibly.

But she quickly rallied and told him of the day's events including the attack on them at the café. She added at the end of her recounting of the drive-by shooting, "You know, at first I wondered why I was being targeted, but what you have told me makes me realize that you are probably right. It could be her they were after and maybe someone must have found out about her! I wish I had been able to identify the gunmen in the car!"

Carlos thought for a moment, chewing his forefinger nail as he did sometimes when deep in thought. Of course, the drive-by gunman had unnerved Frederica and she had not told him about it right away. She was like that sometimes. She had acted very strong and unafraid many other times which was one of the reasons why he loved her. So, this had to be the reason why she had looked surprised when he brought up the allegations of the other cartel leader.

He looked up and said, "Or they could have been after you because they are angry with me." He got up from his chair and began to pace as he said, "But just to be safe, and to cover ourselves, we need to keep your new friend under twenty-four-hour a day observation, and I will put one of my bodyguards with you as well, Frederica. I would never forgive myself if anything happened to you! I'll also step up security here at the house. This could be the beginning of an orchestrated attack on my cartel. And the whole thing about being infiltrated? It could just be a ruse meant to undermine my power! Since I have raised so much money for our rebel army, there are some cartel leaders who believe I am making a bid for even greater influence." He chuckled to himself and added, "And of course, they would be right. But we will step up our own security and then, just to be safe, let's look into who else might be a possible threat within our own organization. I'll call my brother Carlos and alert him to this as well to make sure he keeps a very close eye on our friend Capitan Brice, and you keep a close leash on our pretty Señora Juliet."

He softened his speech and reached out to Frederica who came to him, and he kissed her and said, "I am sorry for this thing that happened today. We will make sure you are well looked after so this cannot happen again."

Eleven

Dawn was approaching quickly and Toby winced at the pain in his stitched-up leg as he shifted his position to his side and began to sit up in the bed.

Melowa had fed him a nice meal while they had chatted and gotten to know each other a little and, exhausted from the last several weeks of ordeal, he had gone straight to bed after eating. He had woken only once briefly during the night when he heard Diego talking to the Indian girl in Spanish. But that was hours ago.

It was now light enough to see. He looked around for Diego and, seeing no-one, said, "Hola? Como estás?"

Melowa came out from the back room and crossed to where Toby was now sitting up on the side of the bed and offered her hand as he stood up and limped over to the table.

"When did Diego leave?" he asked.

"It was after midnight. He was very drunk. He try to take me with him back to the brothel, but I tell him I on my moon time. I do not expect him to be up early this day," she said with a slight smile.

Suddenly, Toby had an idea. "Is there a telephone in this village?"

She nodded her head in acknowledgment but added, "Only at the police station and at the clinic."

She got up from the table and asked him, "You ready for some breakfast?" Toby smiled and said, "Yes please! And tell me, Melowa. Do you know the doctor? Would he let me make a call? I could pay him well."

She shook her head no, but added, "I do know his nurse though, not very well. But she seem nice and she one of my people, and maybe she let you use phone." She looked away and wrinkled her brow, lost in thought for a moment and then looked back at him and said, "I think we must go now. She come there every day very early to clean and prepare for day, so she probably there alone right now. The doctor do not often come in until eight, and I sure that man Diego, he will sleep for some time yet."

Forgetting all about breakfast, she got up and grabbed Toby's crutches from where they were leaning against the wall and handed them to the tall, attractive man. She then went to the door and opened it and held it for him.

He made his way down the muddy street in the early morning light with the tiny Indian girl at his side. The jungle, which came right up to the backs of the shops and houses in places, seemed bright and beautiful in this shimmering early sunlight and suddenly Toby began to feel more optimistic — more than he had since the whole nightmare had begun. He felt like there might just be a way to save this situation yet!

Before they came to the clinic though, Melowa tugged at his elbow and said, "Come this way. There is back door."

Working their way around between two dilapidated buildings they came up behind the clinic to a dirty white door which had probably not been painted in a decade, and she knocked softly. When nothing happened, she knocked again and suddenly the door swung open.

The nurse stood in front of them, surprised, and Melowa quickly asked a question in a dialect that Toby guessed was one of the native languages. The nurse said something and Melowa answered her and then turned towards Toby and said, "As I say, she is of my people and of course, she will help. And she ask how your leg is doing."

"Tell her thank you and that I am guessing it's OK, but it does seem to still be bleeding and hurts a fair bit."

The nurse ushered them inside and, looking both ways out the back of the door to make sure no-one had seen them, closed and locked it.

Once inside he saw that they were in a different room than the one he had been in before and that there was a desk and a radiotelephone on a small table off to the side. A book case full of medical books and directories filled one wall and a chair and reading light were in one corner next to the small table with the radio. This was obviously the doctor's office.

"This is a radio, not a phone," Toby said in English and the Indian girl translated to the nurse, who looked confused. "I don't know how to make a telephone call with this. Ask her if she does," he added.

The Indian women talked for a moment and then Melowa looked back at him and said, "She does not know exactly. I am sorry, Toby," and laid her small warm hand on his arm.

Suddenly, Toby got an idea. He looked at his watch and noted that it was 5:55 a.m. He quickly sat down at the radio and turned it on. It was an older Yaesu ham radio and he quickly noted the frequency it was tuned to before saying to Melowa, "I'm going to try to call a radio net in the Caribbean. No telling if I'll be able to get through from so far inland, but there's just a chance! I have to try!"

Melowa looked bewildered. She didn't understand all of what he had said but looked at him hopefully and backed up, leaning against the doctor's desk as he turned his attention to the old radio on the table. The young man was clearly excited about something.

Before spinning the dial, he grabbed a pen and a scrap of paper and jotted down the frequency the radio was on and then checked to make sure it was in the correct mode, USB, and quickly dialed in 8137.0, the frequency of a popular weather radio net used by yachts in the Caribbean. He hit the 'tune' button and listened while the automatic tuner, located probably somewhere outside the building, tuned the aerial on top of the building. A moment later, loud static came on and he turned the unit down a bit and picked up the mike. "Mayday, Mayday, Mayday," he said three times clearly and listened. Nothing. He thought for a moment that maybe there was something barely distinguishable in the background noise before he repeated, "Mayday, Mayday, Mayday. This is the vessel Lady of the Woods. Please come in."

A few more seconds went by and then he heard, faintly, "Vessel calling Mayday, this is net controller, Clint Barker. Please come back with the nature of your distress and position? Over."

Toby quickly spoke into the mike. "This is sailing vessel Lady of the Woods, I repeat, Lady of the Woods. Our position is zero three degrees south, sixty-eight point five west. I repeat zero three degrees south, sixty-eight point five west. Please confirm copy."

After a few seconds the net controller came back on saying, "That position is in the middle of a land mass. Please repeat position."

Toby winced inwardly and then repeated. "Affirmative, Position zero three degree south, sixty-eight point five west. We have been hijacked, I repeat, hijacked. Dire emergency, Three prisoners onboard. Please confirm."

The radio boomed, "I have turned my directional antennae towards your position. Confirmed. Position zero three degree south, sixty-eight point five west. Hijacked, three prisoners. Is this affirmative?"

"Affirmative!" Toby spoke loudly and then calmed himself before going on. "Must sign off. Great danger. I repeat. Great danger. Do not call us back. Repeat, do not call back. Contact Sunshine Charters, Tortola, BVI. Repeat, Sunshine Charters. Out."

The nurse had just come back into the room and looked extremely upset. She spoke in hurried words to Melowa who looked suddenly alarmed and said, "Toby! Turn the radio off! The police are outside in the street and coming in this direction!"

Toby quickly switched the radio back to its original frequency and the mode back to LSB, and turned the unit off. He and Melowa got up from the small table and quickly crossed to the examination room. "Get up on table, Toby. Quickly!" she said as the nurse reached down and tore open his bandage and then, suddenly getting an idea, grabbed a vial and a syringe and pulled several Cs of a drug back with the plunger.

She looked at Melowa and said something hurriedly, and Melowa grabbed Toby's hand and put her face very close to his saying, "She must make you sleep, Now! It is only safe thing to do!"

Toby looked nervously at the two women and then offered his arm, understanding what they were doing, but afraid of being put out suddenly with danger so nearby. Before he could have second thoughts, the nurse plunged the needle into his vein and within seconds, he was feeling dizzy. The last thing he remembered was a banging on the main door.

The police barged into the empty waiting room the moment Melowa opened the door. Somewhat surprised at seeing her there, they demanded, "Where is the nurse?"

"She is trying to reach the hospital down the river on the radio," Melowa said in Portuguese, repeating the lie the nurse had told her to say.

The two police men roughly pushed her aside and went down the short corridor, stopping briefly to open the doors to the two examinations rooms. When they saw the young British captain lying on the table the older officer demanded, "Why is he here and where is the nurse?"

Just then they heard a voice in the room at the end of the hall and they quickly stepped over and opened the door. There at the radio was the nurse making what sounded like an urgent call. "Itza Hospital, please come in, this is Putumayo River Clinic. Please come in. Please come in!" Then, acting surprised, she looked up and put down the microphone and got up, crossing the room to where the two policemen stood. "What can

I do for you, officers?" she asked in her best, official voice and then she added, "I am sorry, but this is a private office. Please go back to the waiting room and as soon as I have completed my call I will be right out to help you."

She knew this was wishful thinking, but she was acting her part as the helpful, professional nurse.

"Who are you calling on that radio? It was knocking out our music station! It is normally the doctor who makes the calls. When did he teach you to use the radio?" The older officer was quite agitated.

"The British Capitan came here a short while ago with the help of this woman," she said. "He was delirious! I am not sure what has happened to him and the doctor is out in the villages today. I am afraid the man may be dying."

At that, both officers turned and went back into the examination room where Toby lay unconscious on the table. "How long has he been like this?" the older policeman demanded, reaching down and feeling for his pulse, and then he slapped Toby solidly across the face twice. There was no response.

Melowa had been standing behind them in the hallway and spoke up in Portuguese. "He was delirious most of the night. I brought him here hoping he could be helped. I wish I had asked for your help. He is heavy and I had to practically carry him part of the way."

The two policemen looked at each other and retreated to the hallway, conferring in hushed tones before the younger officer returned to the room saying, "You may keep trying to reach the hospital down river. Call us if you need anything." And the two men left, slamming the outside door behind them.

The two Indian girls sagged against each other once the men had left and Melowa thanked the nurse, hugging her and said in her own dialect, "I do not know you well, but you have proven yourself to me as a lifelong friend. Thank you!"

The clever young nurse said, "Those are evil men. And the men they work for are worse. I will always be here to help you if you need it."

Melowa asked the nurse how long Toby would remain unconscious just as they heard a moan emanating from the room behind them. They both opened the door and went inside. Toby was rolling back and forth on his back with his forearm arm across his forehead moaning, "Oh, my aching head. Ohhh. Why is my face so sore? Ohhh."

◆◆◆

It was midmorning when the phone on Rudy Bellows's desk rang. It was his secretary telling him that there was a weatherman from Florida on the line. "What on earth?" Rudy said aloud as he punched the line and answered, "Bellows here."

"Hello, Mr. Bellows. My name is Clint Barker. I'm a weather router for yachts and I'm based in Florida. I just got off the phone with Sunshine Yacht Charters. The Tortola outfit? And they suggested I call you in person rather than having them relay the information. Apparently, we may have located a missing yacht you have been searching for."

Rudy practically knocked his chair over standing up and asked, "What have you got? Did you say Mr. Parker?

"Barker," the mild-mannered man corrected him. "Clinton Barker. I run an SSB radio weather net and communicate with many of the yachts that sail throughout the Caribbean Basin."

"Oh yes," Bellows interjected, "I believe I've heard of you. So what's this about a missing yacht? Please go on."

Bellows sat back down and listened intently as the weatherman told him in detail of the entire conversation before Rudy said, "That's got to be our boat. I can't tell you how much I appreciate this!"

Barker went on to say he had a recording of the whole conversation and that he could email it to me if it would be helpful. Rudy quickly acknowledged that indeed it would be extremely helpful, and gave the caller his private email address before signing off with a promise from the man that if anything more was heard on the radio that he would call Rudy to fill him in.

Hanging up from the call from Florida, Bellows immediately got his secretary to connect him with Clifford Gaines in London.

"How are you today, my good friend?" the Interpol man said as Rudy's call was put through. "I'm afraid I haven't got anything new for you, old chum. Terribly sorry."

Rudy cut in, "Cliff, old boy, it is me who has some information for you! We may have located our missing boat, or at least found where it has been recently. Seems the boat is up a river in western Brazil, about fifty miles from the Colombian border. And it sounds like this is a hostage situation for sure. Worst fears. And I need to know if you want me to pass this on to the Americans or to hold tight?"

Gaines asked him to fill him in completely and after Bellows was finished, elicited a promise to forward the email voice recording. He also asked Bellows to hold off on passing the intel on to the Americans until he had spoken to his superiors.

Bellows warned him, "Remember, Clifford, it was through the charter agency that I learned of this new development, and they are, firstly, responsible to the parents of the missing girl. So I doubt this will be much of a secret for long."

Gaines thanked him and, after some polite anecdotes, hung up.

"Yes!" Senator Tatterson practically shouted out loud after he had hung up with a Mr. Johnson, the head of the BVI charter company. This was the first real breakthrough in the three weeks since this whole nightmare had begun and, sitting back down quickly, he keyed his intercom, calling his secretary into his office.

As soon as she had entered the office, Tatterson said, "Marion, they've located Jenny's boat, and it sounds like she's still alive!"

"That's wonderful, Senator. Do you want to make some calls?"

"Yes of course! First, let's get Andy Winters on the phone over at CIA."

After a few minutes the senator's old friend came on the line. "Roger! How have you been holding up? Sorry to say we haven't learned anything new, but you know I would have called you right away if we had. How's June holding up?"

Roger began by telling him about the call he'd just gotten from the charter company, and the CIA man asked him to hold on for a moment while he got out of the wind. Apparently, Tatterson had caught him away from the office and the senator's secretary had managed to track him down. *Gotta remember to give that woman a raise*, Tatterson thought, and then Winters came back on the line.

"OK, Roger, give me those coordinates again, and the number for the charter agent. I know I have that at the office, but I want to call him right now."

Roger explained, "It was the head of the charter company that called me. His name is Johnson. John Johnson, and he'll be very helpful." Tatterson paused, then went on, "Andy, it sounded to me like the boat was still on the move. Why not send in a team of Marines and try to extract Jenny? And from what it sounds like, there are at least two other prisoners. God! I have no idea what else to do!"

Winters paused for a second before responding. "Roger, I'll pass this on to my superiors. You know this is a high priority to us, but from what you've told me there are still too many unknowns. We can't just drop a bunch of Marines in there! It's the freaking Amazon jungle, for crying out loud. And you don't even know that the boat is even there, or even if this is a legitimate call. It could be a ruse, meant to send us off the real track." Tatterson blanched. He hadn't thought of that possibility. Winters went on, "Look, we'll get right on this and I'll let you know what we find out, and I'll even tell you when and if we are moving in, but for now? Just calm down and let me handle this."

Tatterson didn't like to admit it but his friend was right. Barging into a situation they didn't even know the dynamics of, even if they did manage to actually locate the boat, would only endanger Jenny's life, and the lives of the other hostages. And maybe it was just a ruse. He hoped not.

He thanked his friend and hung up, slumping over in his chair. Then he picked up the phone and dialed his wife to fill her in on the latest development.

◆◆◆

The sky was just beginning to lighten when I got up for the fourth time to walk around the deck and check on our anchor. We'd had a squall during the night, but the anchor had held and the cooling rain had helped to wash the boat. The patrol boat's crew had left the side deck in a mess with dirty, oily footprints and I had even noticed a few cigarette butts that had been snuffed out on the fiberglass deck. I could just imagine what this yacht would look like after a few years of that kind of abuse. At least the rain had washed the worst of it over the side.

I went into the galley and started the coffee maker which I had loaded the night before. In a few minutes the aroma of Colombian coffee wafted through the main cabin. "At least there are some things Colombian that I like," I chuckled to myself as I poured a cup of the hearty brew.

A few minutes later I heard stirring from the main guest cabin and shortly after, Carlos came up the steps, exchanging nods with me as he reached for a cup and filled it with coffee. He then said, "I'll go get the cook and get her started on some food. We should get moving as soon as possible."

I agreed with him and said, "Maybe before you get the girl cooking you two could help me get us underway. I can eat on the fly."

Carlos nodded and went forward to fetch the blonde while I went outside, climbed up to the bridge deck and went about prepping the boat for starting engines and getting underway. Turning on the GPS and depth sounder and then the VHF radio, I had just started both engines when Carlos and Jenny appeared on the foredeck and looked up at me.

"Once I give the signal," I said "I want you two to start bringing the anchor in." I looked over at the man and said, "Carlos, there's a hose there in the locker. She can show you. I've turned the wash-down pump on so once you start seeing muddy chain, wash it off with the hose." Looking back at the girl I said, "You keep bringing the chain in, and point to which way I should be driving. I can't see the chain from up here. Oh, and tell me when I'm on top of it. I don't want to drive over the top of it and risk getting it caught in one of our props or snagged on something on the bottom."

I then put both engines in forward and at idle. Soon I felt the boat start to move slowly forward. There wasn't much current off to the side of the river, and within a minute the anchor clattered into its roller. Jenny looked up at me and I gave her an OK sign along with a questioning shrug. She acknowledged with an OK signal and I eased the big cat out of the shallows and out into the main channel of the river.

By now it was fully light but the sun had not yet risen. I ignored the GPS chart plotter which showed us about a half a mile inland and concentrated instead on reading the signs of the river. How they'd been able to come so far up river with, I was told, only one grounding was a feat which I considered amazing. But then I remember that they had only been on this narrow tributary for a couple of days. The much wider Amazon must have been a little easier to negotiate. Still, I smiled inwardly at what I thought was pretty good seamanship. The young captain might have been proud of himself for making this voyage so quickly and with so few problems, had this not been part of an act of piracy, a multiple kidnapping and murder!

Thirty minutes after leaving our anchorage, Jenny brought me some food and a new cup of coffee. She offered to take the helm while I ate and slid in easily behind the large carbon fiber wheel.

About this time Santiago came up and joined us. We all sat in silence while I finished my food and when I offered to take the dirty dishes below with the excuse that, "I need to take a leak," Santiago didn't object.

"Just stay in the middle and when we get up to that bend ahead, stay to the outside. That's where the deeper water will be."

The girl smiled and looked up at me and said, "I know."

Santiago then slipped in beside her on the helm seat and I could see her stiffen as he put his hand on her leg and whispered something into her ear.

"I'll be right back," I said and went down below. I needed to try to figure out some way to get a signal off about our plight. I realized that no-one had any idea where we were and the need to get word out was urgent in my mind.

Seeing Carlos sitting at the dining table with his wife Anita, I asked, "Is there a way for me to call or radio my wife? She must be worried, not having heard from me." I realized this was a lame excuse. How could I have expected to make a call from the deepest part of the Amazon rain forest?

But Carlos said, "As a matter of fact, I need to turn the satellite phone on and call my brother. I have not checked in since you arrived. I will do that now and ask him to tell your wife that all is well."

Carlos got up from the table and Anita gathered the dishes, taking them over to the double sinks. He went back to his cabin and then reemerged, slid open the door to the cockpit and got a small Iridium phone out of his pocket. Holding it up while he turned it on, a minute later he said, "Ahh, three bars. This should be good enough," and he punched in a set of numbers on the tiny keypad.

Moments later he began speaking, smiling in my direction at first and then suddenly turning away and clutching the mouthpiece as if to keep sound from escaping. He looked back at me suspiciously and told me, "You go back to the helm. I will tell my brother to contact your wife."

Being dismissed so coldly made me begin to worry and as I climbed the steps to the bridge deck, I looked back one time to see Carlos still talking on the phone, but staring at me as I retreated.

Up on the bridge I could see that things had deteriorated. Jenny was struggling with Santiago who was trying to force his hand between her legs. She was trying to keep steering but fight him off at the same time and the young man was smiling, saying something to her that I couldn't hear.

"Is everything OK up here?" I said loudly, which shook the man up enough that he guiltily stood up, releasing his grip on the girl.

He smiled at me saying, "I was having some fun with our cook."

But before he could go on I said, "She needs to concentrate on the river. You'll have plenty of time for fun when we get to where we're going. There's no time for that now and for sure no room for any more running aground! So, let's keep our minds on the job we've been given, shall we?"

Santiago seemed chastened and looked down, then moved off and went down the stairs.

"Thank you," Jenny said and added, "I can usually handle him, but without his brother or Toby to keep him in check, he's been coming on really strong."

We had been sitting for a few minutes in silence when I saw something out of the corner of my eye and turned just as Carlos was coming up the steps. He had a gun in his hand! Santiago was behind him and he also had a gun. Something had happened on that phone call and suddenly I became more than a little worried.

"Capitan Brice. You need to come with me. We need to have a little talk," he said, motioning me with his gun. He looked over at Jenny and said, "Keep the boat moving and no mistakes! I will shoot him and your French friend if you run aground again!"

He was practically shouting now. Whatever he had been speaking about on the phone had changed things for the worse, quickly.

I went down the stairs to the cockpit and turned around to confront my angry adversary. "What's going on, Carlos?" I said in as innocent and surprised a tone as I could muster while I looked around for something with which to defend myself. But, seeing nothing, I slumped my shoulders and said, "What in the heck is all this about? I'm not your enemy!"

"Really!" Carlos fumed. "My brother tells me you may be an Interpol agent and that I should be watching you very carefully."

"Interpol?" I laughed out loud, although it was difficult to act that way at the moment. I had to regain his trust. "Where in the hell would he get a crazy idea like that?"

"This is not a laughing matter," Carlos said with exasperation. "There has been an informer within your embassy who has paid with his life telling us about being infiltrated. My brother believes it must be you who has done this."

I thought for a second before responding as earnestly as I could. "My embassy? Look, Carlos. That's absolutely ridiculous. Interpol is a European agency and I've never even been to Europe! I couldn't tell you what an Interpol agent even looks like, much less be one! I'm an American, not a Brit! This is a big mistake! You have to believe me! If I was an agent, then why in the heck would I have risked my life to help your brother save some of his stuff from that sunken boat in Panama, and why would I have volunteered to come here? I'm just a man who needs some work and appreciated the opportunity. Carlos. I can be trusted. Test me any way you want, but my allegiance is with you, and with Ramon."

I looked him straight in the eyes and I could see doubt cross his face. Then he said, "It is true. He told me to watch you, not that you were guilty. But just know that I will be watching you carefully. If you make one mistake or betray us in any way, I will not hesitate to kill you."

"Carlos," I answered "I'm your man. I am here to help you!" I stepped over to him and offered him my hand. After a brief moment of hesitation, he put his gun back in his pocket and shook my hand, and we both relaxed. Santiago, who had been watching us closely from a few feet away, also relaxed but kept the gun in his hand by his side as I followed his father up the steps to the bridge deck again.

We had rounded a sharp bend in the river and there, off to our left, was the small town I had passed earlier on my trip downriver with Captain Olivier's tug tied up to the wharf. A shrill whistle issued from the tug which told us that we had been seen, and shortly after, his familiar French accent came over the radio. "Capitan Brice, this is Capitan Olivier. Come in."

I picked up the mike and said hello and he asked how our night had been. I told him briefly about the gunboat and he said he had indeed seen it go by, but hadn't been sure who it was.

Carlos had also asked his brother about this Capitan Olivier and if there was any chance that he was somehow a danger. Ramon had actually laughed saying "That man? He is a drunk and is of no consequence. He has worked for me on occasion, carrying cargo for us, but he can be unreliable. Our father even knew him. He is no danger."

As we neared the next bend in the winding river the tug pulled away from the dock and started moving in our direction. Soon after, the tug passed us close by on the port side and I waved as they went on ahead, showing us the deepest part of the narrow channel. I hugged their stern a few hundred feet back and we settled in for the long ride upstream to the small settlement where I had left the other captain and Diego.

Jenny had just returned to the bridge, after having gone up forward with Carlos and given some food to the French girl Bridget, when the small settlement finally hove into view. I told her to go down and get the fenders and dock lines ready, and so she quickly returned to the deck level and rounded up the rest of the crew to help dock the boat.

It was now early December and the rainy season, which seemed to be late in coming this year, was only just starting - so the river was still fairly low. I slowed down and cautiously eased over towards the edge of the bank. Captain Olivier had already secured alongside the dilapidated wharf and as Carlos, Santiago and Jenny quickly tied fenders and dock-lines on, I eased the catamaran alongside the pier and by then, Captain Olivier's men were there to take our lines. I was surprised to see the river bed clearly, only a few feet inside the first set of pilings, but miraculously, we didn't touch the bottom.

As soon as the boat was secure, Carlos hurried Jenny back to the bow compartment and locked her below just as the police and a small crowd of locals came up onto the pier to see what all the excitement as about. No-one there had probably ever seen such a large and fancy yacht before and the towering mast, along with the palatial look of the cockpit and bridge deck held them in awe. Clearly, this was a very expensive boat... a billionaire's yacht!

Tico and Diego pushed their way through the small crowd and, because the catamaran's bridge was so high off the water it was almost level with the top of the pier. Tico looked over at me and asked, "How was your little trip, Capitan? We are glad to see you!"

I shut down the engines and walked across to the railing to chat with the man. "It was a fine trip, Tico. How was your night and how has the young Capitan been doing?

Tico answered, "I just saw him a short while ago and he seems fine. As you had asked, he was staying at the same house I took you to."

I looked over to the right and saw that Santiago and Carlos had gotten off the boat and were in a discussion with Diego, who looked decidedly scruffy. I chuckled to myself as I guessed what kind of night he must have had.

"What is so funny, Capitan?" I looked behind me and saw that Anita had come up onto the bridge while I was talking to Tico, who had now walked over and joined in speaking with the other men.

"I was just thinking about how Carlos thought I was a British secret agent. Sorry, that's just really amusing. Me, James Bond. That's so far from reality that it makes me chuckle just thinking about it."

My quickly thought out reply sank in for a moment and then Anita replied, "I was thinking the same thing, Capitan Brice. You do not seem nearly bright enough to be a secret agent." She smiled at her jab and added, "Maybe it is the other Capitan, or even that man Tico. Or maybe it is all a bunch of crap. That is what I think about it." And she wheeled around and went back down below.

Following Anita down I said, "I need to go ashore and find out about refueling and getting some provisions. Have you made up a list of what we need?"

"The girl has this list made up. I will find it," she said and shortly after, she returned with two sheets of paper.

Looking the list over quickly, I laughed. "This is dreaming. Hoping to find fillet mignon or pork roast may be a bit of wishful thinking, but I'll take this to Tico and see what he can do to fill this order," and I stepped off the boat and onto the rickety dock.

I started to walk away and seeing that the men had migrated farther away from the dock Anita called out to me, "Tell Carlos to have one of the boys come to watch the other two. I will want to go ashore soon."

When I walked up, the four men were conversing in rapid-fire Spanish. I interrupted them saying, "Lo siento." I paused until I had their full attention and went on in English, "I need to see about getting fuel and some provisions. We still have a fair distance to go and I would like to get moving as soon as possible." It was already mid-day and with any luck, I thought that we could make the Colombian border before nightfall.

"Capitan Brice," Carlos said. "We will stay here tonight. My brother. He practically owns this village and the police work for him. We are safe here. Tonight, we will celebrate being nearly to our destination."

Curious, I thought to myself. We were still in Brazil. But on the other hand, this remote area of the Amazon jungle really had no borders. The entire region was in the control of the drug lords, guerrillas and Indian tribes.

I just shrugged and said to Tico, "Here is a list of the provisions we will need. Can you help to find these for us?"

Tico took the list and opened it, frowning. "Some of these things may be difficult to get. But I will try," and then to Carlos he said, "I have some fuel arriving by small boat in a short while. It is coming from the dock of Capitan Olivier. I will need to pay for this in cash."

Carlos said, "I will be at the boat in a short while. Come to me then and I will get you this money."

With the conversation over for the moment, the four men split up. Diego and Carlos walked back down towards the boat. Santiago, no doubt intrigued by some of what his brother had told him of the previous night, sauntered over to the tavern and went in through the swinging doors. They squeaked in protest as he disappeared inside.

Tico and I walked up the street towards the house where the young Captain was staying, and I knocked on the door as Tico continued on to a small Chinese store, the only grocery store I had seen.

The older woman answered my knocking and opened the door a crack and then, seeing who it was, smiled and beckoned me inside.

Entering the room I saw Toby lying on the bed with what looked like a freshly bandaged leg propped up and the Indian girl sitting beside him, talking. When she saw it was me, she jumped up and ran to me, throwing herself in my arms.

Somewhat taken aback by this display, I held her for a moment and then gently eased her back away and looked into her eyes. She was crying. "What is it, Melowa? What's happened?"

"Oh, nothing, Capitan Brice. Forgive me. I just so afraid that you not come back! I am just happy!"

She grabbed my hands and pulled me over to Toby's bedside and by now, he had scrunched himself up into a semi-sitting position. "Mr. Toby tell me all about what has happen to the women on that boat, and he also tell me of his sister who is also prisoner of the evil men who made him stole the boat. Please tell me you here to help us!"

My mind reeled as I tried to decide how much to reveal. I finally decided to give into my gut feeling and responded.

"Listen, Melowa. I'm alone here. No-one else knows we are here and I really don't know how I'm going to help just yet. All I can promise you is that somehow I will do my best to get help."

Toby spoke up. "Actually, people do know about us. Or at least I think they do."

I looked over at him as he continued. "This morning, very early, I got a radio call out to that weather forecaster from Florida. Clint Barker? I gave him our coordinates and told him there are hostages. The police were coming so I couldn't tell him more. I don't know for sure if that will help or not, but I know he heard me."

I was stunned. What a brilliant and ballsy thing that had been to pull off and I said, "Good job, Toby. You may have helped more than you imagined."

Twelve

The RQ-4 Global Hawk unmanned aircraft entered the area of interest at fifty thousand feet. Crossing into Colombian airspace from the Pacific had already been arranged and as the pilot, secure in his work station onboard the navy carrier off the coast of Ecuador, made his turn towards the set of coordinates he had been supplied with, he began to ease the aircraft up to a more respectable sixty thousand feet.

At this altitude there could be no other air traffic and as the dark gray drone climbed further, people on the ground, even if they had been told where to look, would barely have been able to detect its presence.

Fifty-five minutes after entering Colombian airspace the aircraft crossed the Brazilian border and the sensor officer on the pilot's right began to collect data. The overflight was in broad daylight and it was a rare relatively cloudless day, so even to the low res cameras the target showed up. The target identification computer recognized the profile about fifty miles from where it had been set to look. After a slight adjustment in course, simultaneous infrared, hi-res photos and radar MTI and SAR data flowed in. A few minutes later, its mission competed, the aircraft banked to return to its base. *I wonder why anyone wanted photos of a sailboat?* the sensor operator thought and then shrugged, settling back in his chair as the pilot continued the aircraft's homeward flight.

◆◆◆

Roger Tatterson had set up what almost looked like a camp in his statehouse office. Since the call from the charter company, he and his wife June had been on virtually an around the clock vigil. Roger rarely got off the phone as he called supporters and colleagues for advice on how best to lobby the Defense Department to intervene. He didn't want to just sit idly by and hope for the best. He knew how slowly the wheels of government could move and he sensed that time was of the essence.

I suppose it's good, he thought, *that the media has not yet gotten wind of this,* and he wondered idly if some publicity regarding his daughter's kidnapping would help or hurt her chances of rescue. But he knew that as more people were brought into the loop in his effort to drum up support for a military intervention, it would not be too long before the media found out.

One promising thing he had heard was on a call from his friend Andy Winters. Andy had been able to allocate a single fly-over with an unmanned drone based on the information from the weather forecaster, and had promised Tatterson to follow up as soon as he heard anything, so when his secretary Marion interrupted him from a call he was on with a senator from Missouri, he quickly broke free and took the call.

"Roger? Good news. We've confirmed that a boat matching the description of the one your daughter was on is indeed in the area and that it is very likely the one we are looking for. Our people have been in contact with the charter company and supplied them with several photos. They've confirmed that its appearance matches the missing vessel. And the location is only fifty-eight clicks from the last reported position. It's got to be our boat."

◆◆◆

Rudy Bellows was at lunch at the Village Cay Marina in Road Town when his cell phone rang.

"Bellows? It's Cliff. Hope I'm not interrupting? Your secretary suggested I call this number."

"Of course, Clifford. I'm happy to hear from you. Please, tell me. What's the latest?"

Gaines started in, "We have been tracking what the Americans have been doing. As you know, our government has been rather deeply involved with an undercover operation in Colombia."

Bellows murmured an assent and the Interpol man went on. "Well, about two hours ago the Americans did an over-flight of the area where you had reported to me the stolen boat was located and, Rudy old boy? It's there all right. Your charter company there has confirmed it. It has to be the boat and so maybe your people are aboard too? Not quite sure what we're going to do with this intel just yet, but remember we have an asset on the ground there, so we may be able to assist. I'll keep you informed."

Rudy thanked his friend and started to hang up but Gaines said, "Oh, and one last thing. I've been authorized to tell you that our agent on the ground there has made contact with at least one of your people. Just thought you'd like to know."

Rudy thanked him again and finally disconnected from the call.

Stuffing the phone in his pocket he got up, paid his bill and went out to the parking lot. He often ate at the restaurant at the Village Key Marina, and the charter office for Sunshine Yacht Charters was just a ten minute drive away at Nanny Cay Marina.

Bellows opened his car up and climbed in. Ten minutes later he pulled up in front of the Sunshine Charters office and went inside.

The secretary greeted him warmly and buzzed the manager in his office. A minute later, John Johnson come out and enthusiastically shook Rudy's hand.

"I can't tell you how much we appreciate all of the personal attention you've been giving this, Mr. Bellows. Can you come into my office? Would you like a glass of water or some coffee or tea?"

Rudy followed him into his comfortable office and sat down, politely refusing the offer of the beverage.

Johnson's office overlooked the docks and you could see a number of catamarans and sailboats with crews either preparing to leave or offloading luggage, their vacations over.

"To what do I owe this pleasure?" Johnson asked.

Rudy began by asking him more about what he knew about the boat and where it had been located.

Johnson said, "Well Mr. Bellows, you certainly do seem well connected. I only just heard about this latest development a couple of hours ago and the American I spoke with refused to identify which agency he worked for, but did send me an email with some photos of the boat which I told him was indeed the boat we lost. The email address was a '.gov', so I think it's all legit."

The charter boss then went on about a few of the other minor and delicate details the man on the phone had related, surrounding the situation that was preventing them from immediately acting on the intel they had so recently acquired.

Rudy then filled Johnson in a bit more with what he knew, but did not refer specifically to any agencies or even mention his own people he had involved, but did inform Johnson that, "We have the situation well in hand and with luck, we may be able to retrieve the yacht sooner as opposed to later."

◆◆◆

"What do you mean, your hands are tied?" Senator Tatterson was incredulous and felt like he had just been punched in the gut.

When Marion had informed him that the vice president was on the line, he had perked up and felt excited. All of his lobbying had apparently paid off and now the acting administrative head of covert operations was going to get involved.

When he had been scolded, and then told that his actions were 'self-serving' and 'not in the interest of good government' he had nearly exploded at the man. "How can you say that retrieving one of our own citizens from a hostage situation is self-serving? Just because this person happens to be my daughter? What if it were your daughter out there? Would you respond the same way?" Roger was furious.

"Listen," the man on the phone said. "I'll be candid with you. If you had not voted against almost every piece of legislation this administration has tried to put through, we might have been more inclined to help. But you've been obstructive and small-minded, Tatterson. You're going to have to go this one alone. This administration cannot justify spending money on your personal problems." And with that, the vice president hung up.

What a total shit, Roger thought to himself as his mind reeled. *What next?* And then he had an idea...

Alex Peterson was sitting in a fashionable Lower East Side restaurant and was on a call with his editor when a call came in from a Maryland number. "Hang on a moment will you? Let me get rid of this other call," and he switched to the incoming call.

"Peterson," he said in his professional voice.

"Hello, Mr. Peterson. This is Marion Sanders calling from Senator Tatterson's office in Annapolis. The senator would like to speak with you if you have a moment."

What on earth the Maryland Senator could be wanting to talk to him about he had no idea, but he told the secretary to hold on for a moment while he went back to his editor and said "Sorry, Mitch, I've got to take this other call. I'll ring you back later, OK?"

"I'm here," he said and was asked to hold for a moment. Seconds later, the senator came on the line.

"Hello, Mr. Peterson. I know we've never spoken, and that you and I stand on opposite sides of the political fence on many issues, but I trust you are familiar with me?"

"Yes, of course," he said and Tatterson went on.

"I have a very important and extremely personal matter that may lead to some revelations that could be of great interest to the general public. I was wondering if you might have time to come to my office and meet with me, say, tomorrow morning?"

Alex Peterson had held his desk as investigative reporter for the New Times for almost five years and within that time had acquired a reputation for being thorough, unquestionably honest and not given to exaggerating facts or jumping to politically motivated opinions.

He got up early the next morning and made the three-hour drive to Annapolis and still had time to stop in at his old Main Street haunt for breakfast. By a quarter to nine he had already caught up with four old friends and had agreed to meet a larger group of people back there for lunch at twelve-thirty.

Alex was tall, standing about six foot four, and was fairly lanky. Although he had graduated from the Naval Academy some years back, after a few years in the service he had switched to journalism and yet he still kept himself in good physical shape. He had been a member of the Naval Academy sailing team and had been an accomplished collegiate sailor. Good-looking by almost any woman's standards, his wavy blonde hair, pronounced brow and shy seductive smile had won him many conquests and yet, to his close friends, he had many times declared himself a confirmed bachelor.

Shuffling up the street in the melting early morning frost, he entered the statehouse and found Senator Tatterson's office with five minutes to spare.

"Ahh you must be, Mr. Peterson." He was warmly greeted by a somewhat portly middle-aged woman who came out from behind her desk to shake his hand.

He had only just seated himself when the door to the senator's office opened and Roger Tatterson came out to greet the reporter.

"Mr. Peterson, thank you so much for coming on such short notice." Although Alex had never met the senator before, he was immediately surprised by just how much older and tired he looked than in his photos.

"Please, come inside." He held the door open for him and said to Marion, "Please hold all my calls."

Inside the office, Senator Tatterson said, "This is my wife June. June, this is Mr. Peterson, the reporter was I telling you about." They all sat down and after a few niceties, Tatterson started in.

"I suppose you are wondering why I called you here when we have never had any history of working together in the past. And after what I am about to tell you, I don't expect you to answer right away. But I do ask you to keep what we say here in the strictest of confidence. If word got out prematurely as to what is actually going on, innocent people could die."

Alex swallowed and answered, "Of course, Senator," looking calmly up at the senator who gathered himself before launching into his problem.

"Mr. Peterson, what do you know about the sailboat charter industry?"

Tatterson spent the next half hour explaining in as succinct a manner as possible the situation and dilemma he was facing. He started by telling Peterson about his daughter and her upbringing and sailing background and about how she had joined the charter industry. He quickly went on to tell about how the boat she had been working on had disappeared and that now there was evidence that this boat had appeared in of all places, a backwater of the Amazon River! He also told the reporter that in the strictest of confidence, he had told a member of the CIA of his daughter's disappearance and the strange events surrounding it, and that it was in fact through their involvement that the boat had been located. But that due to partisan bitterness, the vice president had refused assistance and had pulled the plug on any sort of rescue operation. He went on to say that he wished that Peterson could follow up on this story, verify what he needed, and expose the partisan roadblocks that were keeping his daughter from being rescued; or at least to make such a big stink of it over the media that the administration would have to back down and let the CIA do their job.

"Wow, Senator," Peterson said after Tatterson had finished. "That's a real story for sure. So how do you think I can help, beyond bringing this to the publics attention? I mean, you could have just called a press conference and blew the whistle yourself. Why involve me?"

Roger Tatterson had gotten up about halfway through his story and had been pacing. He now leaned back against his desk and, putting his hands across his chest, standing just a few feet from the reporter he added, "This is a bigger story than just what is going on with my daughter. Apparently there are other hostages, and there may be some involvement with Interpol regarding some big undercover operation they have going on there in Colombia. I don't know very much, but all I can tell you is that there are a lot of wheels in motion and I'm only being told a small bit of the whole story."

"I see," Peterson said and Tatterson went on.

"I think an investigative reporter like you could do a little snooping around and perhaps find out enough details that, number one, you could get a good story from this and number two, you could give me enough to work with so that I could force some action on the administrative side to help rescue my daughter and whoever else is being held there against their will."

At this point Tatterson's wife June jumped into the conversation saying, "Please, Mr. Peterson. She is our only child and I know she is in grave danger. We are out of other options and we're both very angry about the vice president's stand on this. We need your help."

Peterson looked into her tearful, imploring eyes and then looked down, gathering his thoughts before responding. "If you can supply me with a few contact numbers and emails, and give me a day or so, I'll snoop around a little and see what I can learn. I can't promise right now how far I can carry this, but if there's a real story here, and if there's a way I can help with retrieving your daughter, then you can count me in."

As Alex Peterson drove back up to New York, he was already on the phone with a few of his sources for more information on Tatterson's background and history and for some background details on Tatterson's daughter as well. He had already called the charter company and had a preliminary conversation with a Mr. Bellows in Tortola who apparently represented the insurers of the missing boat. Both of the Tortola contacts had been very guarded and had told him no more than that, yes, a charter boat was missing and that Jenny Tatterson had been on the crew. By the time he rolled up to his office, it was late afternoon and he hurriedly cleared his desk of several other projects he had going and began in earnest to try to find out the dynamics of what all was behind this apparent abduction and grand theft, which sounded more and more like the tip of an iceberg that was hiding a complex story.

◆◆◆

Juliet had spent the bulk of her afternoon at the poolside in the hotel where she had been moved at Javier and Ramon's insistence. Ramon had said "We can keep a much better eye on your safety here, and your boat is safe tied up next to my yacht. No-one will bother it there. I always have at least two of my men staying onboard. It is the best thing for you." With her 'bodyguard' Javier lounging somewhat uncomfortably in the chair opposite hers, baking in the hot tropical sun, she felt powerless and more than a little afraid.

Ever since the thwarted attempt on their lives at the restaurant, Juliet had noticed a change in attitude with both Javier and Frederica. They were much more guarded and succinct in their communications and Juliet was beginning to worry as she felt much more like she was being watched as a prisoner under house arrest than as a friend or guest who needed protection. It had been three days now since Brice had left for the Amazon and she was beginning to have serious misgivings about their situation. Wishing now that she had not been such an optimist, and that they had quit while they still could. Though realizing that those thoughts were anti-productive, she began to think of ways to get away from Cartagena and Ramon's cartel. Nothing she could think of, though, would ensure both her and Brice's safety. As long as he remained far away in the jungle, there was nothing she could do to help him and if she made a break for it, even if she was successful, it would almost surely affect him in a bad way. She was trapped.

She realized that she must have looked very worried and distraught when Javier sat up and looking at her with concern asked, "Señora Juliet, is there something that is troubling you?"

"Oh, yes, Javier, I'm sorry, it's just that it's now been three days since Brice left and we've heard nothing about how he is doing. Isn't there some way I can talk to him?"

Javier was clearly thinking about it when he said, "Let me talk to Ramon and see if he has heard anything."

Juliet watched him as he dialed a number on his mobile and waited patiently for an answer. Finally she heard him talking to someone on the line and then, waiting a bit longer before he sat up, he got out of the lounge chair and walked a few paces away.

Within a minute he was back and holding the phone to his chest he said, "I have just spoken to Ramon and he is trying to reach the boat now where your husband is. Please wait for a moment." He put the phone back up to his ear and waited.

A minute later he was talking again and Juliet was now sitting up in her chair. Ramon walked over to her and said, "Here is your husband. He is fine but make the call short. These calls are very expensive, yes?" He smiled at her genially as he handed the phone over, but stood by closely, listening to what she would say.

We had finally finished fueling and putting the last of the fresh food onboard when the satellite phone rang. I was a bit agitated that it was already 10:30 a.m. and we hadn't gotten moving yet, but had been bogged down in preparing the boat for its final run up the river to her eventual new home, so I was startled when I heard the phone and looked up at Carlos standing above me. He had been standing over me while I worked on changing out the starboard fuel filter and engine oil filters. I'd been at it since very early, going over both engines and making sure they were serviced properly. As I had told Carlos, "No-one has been taking care of these engines and it's a miracle that they haven't given you more trouble already. I just want to make sure they remain reliable and I'm sure Ramon would want that too."

Grudgingly Carlos had agreed and allowed me to do my work, looking at his watch periodically and occasionally saying, "How much longer, Capitan?"

So when, after I heard him speak briefly in Spanish on the phone, he looked down and me and said, "Capitan, it is your wife," I almost dropped the open container of oil I had in my hand.

Realizing that if it really was Juliet that she was undoubtedly being eavesdropped on, I tried my best to fall into our act. "Hi, honey! What a surprise! How are things back on the boat? What all have you been doing?"

She answered in a voice that I recognized as her most anxious tone. "Brice, I've been worried sick about you, Javier dialed you up and has handed me his phone. Tell me, are you alright?"

"Yes, of course, couldn't be better. Just going over to the boat right now, getting the engines sorted out. These Lagoon 62s have really nice engine rooms, nothing like our little one on Mahalo. I should have the thing up and running soon and it's only four hundred and eighty-five miles to where we are going, so it shouldn't be more than a week at most. This part of the river is too dangerous to run at night – too many shoals and sharp bends, and from what I understand, there have been problems with some of the natives so we're only traveling during the day, so it'll probably take us a little while. It's really beautiful down here in Brazil, You'd have loved it. But I think it's less than fifty miles to the border and so we'll be in Colombia later today and then from then on we have to stay on the right side of the river until we clear Peruvian waters."

Carlos was tapping me on my shoulder so I stopped and he looked at me, exasperated. "Do not say so much about where we are and what we are doing, just let her know you are OK and get off the phone. It is an expensive call."

Clearly he didn't want me telling so much, but I had now given her enough information so that she knew I had indeed found the missing catamaran, and she could get an idea of where I was once she got ahold of a chart of the Amazon basin. She'd be able to pinpoint my position to within a few miles. *Not that it would help anyway*, I thought to myself...

"I'm so glad you called," I said and continued, "How are Ramon and Frederica doing?"

"Oh, they're fine, but, Brice? There was a drive-by shooting when I was at lunch with Frederica, and I think Frederica was the target. I'm scared. Please finish up and come back. I don't like it here."

Javier grabbed the phone away, giving her an angry look and said into the phone, "Señor Brice, this is Javier. Your wife is perfectly safe. I am sorry she got afraid at the restaurant but we are now keeping her very safe and under constant supervision. So do not worry."

I was pretty pissed off that he had grabbed the phone from her, but in as nice a voice as possible said, "No worries, Javier. I know you'll keep her safe. I'd hate to think of what would happen to you if something bad happened to her."

My not-so-veiled threat was taken poorly when he seethed back, "Capitan Brice, you will have no cause for concern. She will be quite safe. You, however, will have to learn respect if you too want to remain unhurt." And he hung up.

As I handed the phone back up to Carlos he said, "You are not wise, my Capitan, to speak to Javier like that. He has killed many men for less insulting words," and he turned and walked back inside the yacht.

I quickly finished up and closed the engine room hatch and went inside to clean up at the galley. The American girl was there, preparing an early lunch and as I bent over the sink to wash my hands she whispered quietly, but in an alarmed voice, "They have brought Toby back onboard and they've got him tied up in the forward cabin with Bridget. He looks like he's been beaten!"

I looked her in the eyes and was about to say something more when Carlos came up the steps from his cabin and, seeing me at the galley said, "So will we now get underway?"

I nodded and went out the sliding doors to the cockpit where Santiago and Diego were just coming aboard from the town with the last of the provisions. I could see that at least we weren't going to run out of beer.

"Now that we are almost home, it is time to relax and enjoy ourselves a little, my friend," Diego said, and he and Santiago brushed past with three cases of beer each.

I climbed up onto the bridge deck and started the engines, and Carlos and the boys scrambled out to the side deck. Diego got off onto the pier and began untying the lines.

"Diego," I shouted, "Untie the stern line first, then the forward spring line and then the bow line. I'll keep the boat alongside by using the engines in forward, and then last thing, I'll slack the throttle and you can take the aft spring line off. Be sure to jump aboard right away after that!" He looked up at me and shook his head indicating that he had understood.

A few minutes later we were pulling out into the main current and had passed Captain Olivier's tug which was still tied up to the wharf in front of us. Carlos had vetoed my plan to hire him as our pilot for the next stretch of the river saying, "You will have no problems, Capitan. This river is not hard to navigate in the daytime and we will be in my own country tonight, so we can relax and enjoy our cruise. It is so refreshing!"

That's when I noticed someone standing on the steps behind Carlos. Melowa was onboard! I hadn't seen them bring her. It must have been when I was busy in one of the engine rooms and guiltily I realized I had forgotten all about her until now.

"When did she come aboard, Carlos?" I said, motioning with my head towards the diminutive Indian girl.

"Oh, she is a special gift for an important man up the river. She is beautiful, no? he said in English, not realizing that the girl understood and spoke the language. He then went on in Spanish for her to hear. "She will be a private teacher for her people up the river. I am sure she will be well loved." He chuckled to himself at his joke as he turned and left. "There will be a small town up the river a few miles inside my country's border. We will tie up there tonight. It is controlled by my brother's people and we will be very safe. But you might want to stay aboard and we must keep the women out of sight. We do not want to tempt the men with these;" he motioned his head toward the Indian girl 'special things'."

I spent the next several hours carefully navigating the winding river. The seasonal rains had not yet started in earnest and so the river was still fairly low. Sometimes the bends in the river seemed to go on forever in one direction until I was heading back the way I had just come and suddenly I would find us in another huge bend going in the opposite direction. I could see that this was going to be a long day and by late afternoon, when I saw from my chart plotter that we had finally crossed into Colombian waters, I shouted down to Diego who I had seen sitting in the lower cockpit. He came up and when I told him where we were, a few minutes later he brought his father up with him and they both sat nearby, anxiously looking ahead.

In this part of the river we were now wholly in Colombia. Apparently, a small section of the country juts far to the south, almost to the Amazon, something I had never realized. And so until we re-emerged on the opposite side of the political peninsula, we would be as deep in the Colombian Amazon forest as one could get.

A half hour later we rounded a sharp bend in the river and a dilapidated looking village appeared on the left hand bank. It had a very small and rickety wharf which Carlos directed me to come alongside. This landing looked even worse than the previous one, but the weather looked settled and so I was not too concerned. Within a few minutes we were tied alongside and I had shut the engines off.

Several scruffy looking men were on the pier eying us suspiciously. They were dressed in dirty tan and green camo T-shirts and pants, and all had small caliber automatic weapons slung over their shoulders and looked as if they had not bathed in a month. A mangy looking brown short-haired dog stood close by, glaring at me.

Within minutes Carlos had spoken with the men in an animated conversation and shortly after, the gunmen sauntered off. A few minutes after they were gone, a handful of the timid villagers came out of where they had been hiding behind doors and in the nearby forest and gathered around us on the shore, staring at what must have looked like a spaceship to people who were only used to seeing crude wooden or steel work boats and dugout canoes.

Carlos motioned me inside and asked me to sit at the dining table.

"Señor Capitan Brice, I have to apologize to you. My brother was wrong to have thought of you as unfaithful and it was my mistake to believe such a thing. We have found the person who is a traitor and he will be dealt with."

"Who is it, Carlos? Is it someone I've met?" I asked.

"You have met him. It was that young Capitan we had with us since the British Islands. Capitan Toby. It has been reported that he contacted a shortwave radio net in the USA and has put out a distress call. Some of our fishermen friends in Venezuela have heard this and it is apparently still being talked about a lot on a radio channel used by some of the people that sail yachts in the Caribbean. It is a radio program called the Caribbean Safety and Security Net. Well, these people talking on the radio have pointed out our man for us by clever deduction. So much of the work of identifying him was already done by the idle speculation from these people who chatter away on this radio channel. In any case, I have made him a prisoner and he is up in the forward cabin with the two women."

"Carlos!" I said. "Isn't it dangerous to keep him onboard if he really is the person who has infiltrated your operation? What will you do with him? Why not just get rid of him now?"

I had to inspire a greater trust from Carlos, so I was taking a calculated risk by suggesting that the young captain should be eliminated. It worked though, just as I hoped, when Carlos explained his reasoning.

"Capitan, we have his sister, a very beautiful Colombian woman, as our prisoner at my family's compound where we are taking this boat. We had her as insurance that Capitan Toby would cooperate with us, but now that we know he is a traitor, we will keep him alive in a jail and will turn that advantage around so that we can make her do as we bid. She will be sold along with the other girls and she will always know that if she does not cooperate with her new masters, her brother will be tortured and executed. This is the best way to ensure that the new owners of the girl have her complete compliance."

"Clever," I said and went on, "But how will you keep the French girl and the American woman from running away?"

Carlos chuckled and said, "We already have some close-up photos of the American girl's family, her mother and father, taken with telephoto lenses of them in their car, going into their house, and from outside the window looking into their bedroom. We will simply tell her that if she does not cooperate, that the camera lens will become the scope of a rifle and they will be killed immediately. The same will go with the French girl. We do not know enough about her yet, but we have her passport, and my brother's people will track down her family and do a similar thing with her. They always cooperate to keep their parents or brothers and sisters safe."

"And the Indian girl?" I asked.

"She is much easier. She knows we have many of her people under our control already. If any one of them is dearest to her, we will bring them to her and cut off pieces of their bodies to show her that we will not be trifled with."

I tried my best to not look too shocked and said, "What can I do to help, Carlos? Other than to keep them under wraps until we get to home base?"

He smiled and said, "Capitan, relax and enjoy the voyage. They will not try to escape from here just as they will not try to escape later on after they are with their new masters. We have done this many times. But if you wanted to help, Capitan, perhaps you could try to get to know the French girl. She doesn't know you, so she may trust you if you are nice to her." He chuckled to himself and went on, "Try to learn who are her favorites in her family and if she has a boyfriend, or anyone dear to her, and where they live. This would be a big help. And perhaps make her take a shower and give her some clean clothes. I will have Anita put some things together for her. We are getting closer to my brother's compound and we need to have her looking presentable when we arrive. So yes, Capitan, learn what you can so that my brother's people can find her vulnerable spot. This will make her much more valuable. This is how you can help me."

I said, "It would really help if I brought the America girl back with me when I question the French girl to help translate. I've heard them speaking together in French, and my French is terrible!"

Carlos nodded his head and said, "Good idea. But do not take your eyes off the French one, the American girl already knows that we have surveillance on her family, so she will not try to escape, but the French one, we still need to get her under control. So watch her, yes?"

I said, "My suggestion is to just enjoy the evening here and I'll learn what I can, and then I'll get us underway again tomorrow morning before eight, si?"

I got up from the table and on a whim said, "May I see the girls now?" Carlos stood up and, looking me closely in the eyes smiled and said, "Capitan, you are a married man!" He laughed. "Yes, have a little fun with them if you wish, but do not get them pregnant and don't let my sons see you getting too friendly. I have had a hard time keeping Santiago off the American girl, and I really do not want him messing around with her. Sometimes young men fall in love and want to become heroes. It is just not a good idea, I have found, to tempt young men with love. But I am not worried about a married man like you. Go at it!" And with that he chuckled a bit more and turned and got up to leave.

I called after him, "Carlos, I'm happily married and only want to see them so that I can learn these things for you. I will give you a report in the morning, si?"

He nodded his head and headed down the stairs to his cabin.

It was already after dark when I went up forward, opened the bow compartment hatch and looked inside. Toby was still tied up but one of the girls had removed his gag. He looked weary and afraid. I said to Jenny in hushed tones, "I have convinced Carlos that I am going to have both of you ladies in my room for showers and to learn more about Bridget, and so I need to see both of you now. So go along with the act if you can, OK?"

Jenny quickly translated what I had said to the French girl and I said quietly to Toby, "I'll do what I can to save you."

Bridget looked confused and Jenny again translated what I had just said. She nodded and stood up, climbing out of the cramped crew quarters for the first time since she had been taken, weeks before.

Stepping out onto the deck, she looked around, clearly afraid. I heard someone coming up behind me and turned in time to see Diego, followed by Santiago coming along the side deck.

"What are you doing with the women?" Diego asked.

I reached down and helped Jenny up and closed the hatch again, latching it tightly. "You father has told me to get these two cleaned up and to learn a bit more about each one," I said in English, motioning at her with my head. "Where are you two off to?"

"We are going into the village. There is a nice cantina there. Come up and see us later when you are finished."

Obviously, Carlos must have had a word with these two and so I nodded and said, "Maybe I'll see you two up there later."

Santiago said, "It is the place around the corner past the church, it is easy to find."

"I'll see you later then," I answered and both men then went aft, stepped off the boat and walked down the street. I motioned the girls to go ahead of me and I saw the boys look back at me as I slid the door open and led the ladies inside the yacht's main cabin.

Taking them down into my cabin I said very quietly in Jenny's ear, "It's entirely possible that they've placed listening devices here, so we'll need to act a bit, OK?" She nodded and I added in a whisper, "Go take a shower and then get dressed and call me in, but leave the water running," and then I said loudly, "Jesus, you stink! Get in the bathroom and take a shower. Both of you! In a few minutes, I'll be in. I want to see you both scrubbed and as clean as a whistle."

Bridget looked very confused but Jenny took her hand and led her inside the bathroom and closed the door. I saw her starting to whisper in her ear as the door shut.

I sat on the bed, giving it a few minutes until I heard the door open and stood up, walking over.

Jenny stuck her head out the door and motioned me over.

Speaking loudly again I said, "Alright ladies, you'd better be ready. I'm coming in," and I noisily banged the door open and went inside.

With the water still running and both girls now showered and wrapped in towels, I spoke to Jenny quietly, filling her in on the recent developments and of my vague plan for getting them away. She repeated this all to Bridget in French who nodded that she understood. Then I told them both to act like they were enjoying themselves and I carefully stepped out of the room, quietly closing the head door. The next few minutes were filled with the sound of the two girls noisily going about the motions of getting cleaned up. I knocked on the door gently and handed the new clothes I had been given by Anita earlier for Bridget to put on, and shouted for the benefit of our eavesdropping crew, "For crying out loud, shut the damn water off!" The water went off and they kept the sound going for a few more minutes, eventually coming out, and they stood in front of me where I sat on the bed, unsure about what to do next.

I whispered in Jenny's ear again, "Here is what you have to do."

Half an hour later, after I had also taken a shower and joined the young women once again in my cabin, we all went out to the salon where Anita and Carlos had been sitting. I realized that they probably didn't actually have a bug in my cabin and were only listening to what they could hear through the walls and doors. *This will make things easier,* I thought to myself.

I then led the women back up forward and locked them below. When I returned to the main cabin, Carlos and Anita had returned to their cabin.

I went back out to the cockpit and jumped off the boat, making my way down the poorly lit dirt street toward the sounds of the cantina.

A block and a half down and around the corner I saw a filthy, dilapidated looking low building with a rusty tin roof and remnants of some white paint that looked as if it had been applied twenty years previously. About twenty men and a few women were standing outside, smoking, drinking and laughing. As I walked up, silence fell over the small crowd and I began to wonder if this had been a good idea. A big brute of a guy with a ten days' growth of beard and a torn and filthy green camo T-shirt and muddy, greasy khaki pants blocked my way as I reached for the door to the cantina saying, "Where do you think you are going, amigo?"

His breath stank of cheap rum and tobacco and I was just trying to remember enough of my Spanish to come up with a good story when Santiago came outside and got between the two of us.

"This is our Capitan and he is Americano and very trustworthy. He is under my Uncle Ramon's protection, so please be nice to him! He is our friend."

This seemed to have a good effect on the crowd and they went back to talking and ignored me. The brute looked at me in a menacing way once more but turned and went back to his comrades. I followed Santiago inside.

The place was packed. At least fifty people were crammed into the noisy cantina with music blaring out of two partially blown speakers. Familiar Latin themes were intermixed with more popular songs and I was waved over to a circle of men and several women who were centered around Diego. Diego was telling a story and I did my best to follow along, but the gist of it was about the daring exploits of stealing the boat in the Caribbean and about their pirate attack on the sailboat before entering the Amazon. I tried to smile approvingly as he told the story and several of the men looked me over carefully. One of the women also gave me a seductive appraisal.

Santiago rejoined us and handed me a cold beer which I accepted gratefully and over the next hour as we all talked, I did my best to make it look like I was thoroughly enjoying myself. I was only questioned a little but the story Diego told about me saving his uncle's last drug shipment with scuba gear in a hundred and fifty feet of shark-infested waters, a slight exaggeration, seemed to get the most reaction and after that, I was considered a macho fellow who should be respected.

After an hour and a half things had begun to wind down a little, and people began trickling out of the bar to go their various ways and so I excused myself and walked back down the street, distancing myself from the din of the noisy bar.

Just as I turned the corner and onto the street where the boat was docked, a man came out of the shadows and tackled me. I tried to scramble free and was ready to hit him when I saw that he had a knife, and he quickly grabbed me in a half nelson and held the knife to my throat. He dragged me back to the shadows next to a dilapidated shack and shoved me up against the wall, my face crammed into the bare wooden siding of the abandoned structure and he put his face up next to mine, shoving the knife into my neck almost to the point of drawing blood and said in fairly good heavily accented English, "I have been following you on the river. You have my sister as a prisoner on that boat and I have come to get her away. You will have to free her!"

"You're Melowa's brother? Melowa is my friend! I am not your enemy!"

With this revelation, he loosened his grip slightly and I was able to turn my head slightly and look at the man who had me pinned. He was an Indian and at least five inches shorter than me, but was incredibly strong. A wiry, sinewy type of strength, like a powerful leopard or jaguar.

He said, "You are lying. I saw you locking those women away on the boat. You are one of the evil ones and I will kill you unless you do as I tell you."

I tried to reassure him. "Listen to me. I met Melowa a few days ago and I have promised to rescue her. But I also need to rescue the other people, so if you hurt me, then their best chance to survive and escape is gone!" The man loosened his grip a little more and I went on, "How were you following us and why didn't you rescue Melowa from the village?"

He hesitated and must have made a decision because he withdrew his knife and stepped back from me. I turned and rubbed my arm and face as I leaned back against the wall and said, "Tell me how you were able to stay up with us coming up river? And if we did get Melowa and the others away, where would we go?"

He shook his head. "No. It is only Melowa, and any of my people that I will save. The others are of the evil ones too. And so are you!" He started to grow agitated again and I tried to reason with him.

"Please listen to me, I am not your enemy, and where did you learn to speak English so well? Were you and Melowa in the same school?"

He nodded his head in the affirmative as he relaxed a little, realizing that if I knew this about him that his sister must have trusted me and said quietly, "We had a good teacher. He was a good man and maybe not all the white ones are bad. But they killed him when they killed my father and brothers that night, the night they burned the village and stole all of our women and killed the young children. The tribe that attacked us are terrible cannibals and they sold our women to the soldiers for guns and liquor. I have been searching for my sister ever since and now that I have found her, I am trying to find the right moment to take my sister away from these evil people!"

Just then we heard some noise from the street. Several men were talking loudly and coming in our direction. The young Indian man put his hand back on the hilt of his knife and looked uncertain about what to do and so I motioned him to draw back deeper into the shadows, away from the street.

We both stayed motionless as the men walked by and finally, after a few minutes, I went on quietly and slowly.

"I am trying to make a plan to get the prisoners away, but I have to be very careful. The men who control all these other men have my wife held as a hostage too, and if I try to break these prisoners out, they will surely kill my wife!"

The young Indian looked at me and softened his gaze as this became clear.

I told him, "I need to make their escape look like it was not my doing. You may be able to help with that! But first. Tell me how you were able to keep up with us coming up river?"

The Indian man told me, "I have a dugout canoe with an outboard motor. I have a lot of gasoline. I am a fisherman. I know this river and its tributaries very well and many of the other people who live by the river know me just as they also knew my father and brothers. Many of them have also lost their loved ones to these evil men."

He paused for a moment and drew up straighter, thrusting his chest out and speaking with anger and a new determination in his voice. "The men who have my sister. They own the towns and during the day they own the river, but at night the river is ours, and the jungle has always been our home. If we can draw them out into the river at night and into the jungle, we will kill them and free the prisoners."

I looked at him, my focus shifting between his two terrified but fierce-looking eyes and said, "Let me work on my plan. I have to get them as far as the compound where I am supposed to deliver the boat. I believe there may be other prisoners there. Maybe I can signal you when the time is right and I could create a diversion. Do you have enough people to attack the compound? I have no idea how many men are there."

The Indian said, "I have counted the men there. There are maybe one hundred including the soldiers. There are workers too, but they are slaves! I think that some of these slaves will help us once they see us attacking." And then he went on, "The river goes past more small villages and up the small rivers that feed this big river, there are more villages. I will go on ahead and gather the survivors of the attacks and meet you at the compound where the other shining boats are kept."

I asked, "What is this place like? When have you been there and how do you know about it?"

He shifted his stance and crouched down, drawing me down as well with his hands he said quietly, "After my sister was taken prisoner, I went to my cousins' tribe by the river and they told me that my sister would be taken to this place where you are going. So I traveled up the river and found the place. I spent weeks there, searching from the jungle, looking into the evil ones' compound to see if my sister was there, and looking for ways to attack the evil ones and kill them all. There are many of them though! But when I finally realized my sister was not there, I came back down the river, asking at each village about my sister. This is how I learned that so many other tribes have lost their loved ones too. The ones that lived were the ones that ran and hid, or that were like me, out fishing or hunting when the attacks came. Mostly now it is just older men and a few of the younger boys who are still alive, but there are also still some strong fighters like me! I think I can draw as many as a hundred men together if I spend the next days gathering them, and with these men I could take the compound and kill all the evil ones!"

"So, you think you could get enough of your own people together to assist us by making an attack? How could I be sure that your people would not also kill my friends?"

The Indian man said, "I will watch for you and you can signal me like this; drop me a white bag into the current with a note inside in English of when you want us to attack. Only write the day and the time. I will go to the place where the prisoners are kept and find you there. We will together free them and I will keep you and the white prisoners safe from my people."

I thought for a moment and said, "The best way for us to escape with them would be to get them all aboard the boat we have here now, and then drive it away. Maybe we could sabotage any other boats so that we cannot be followed."

The Indian man thought for a moment and said, "It will work."

He continued on, "There is a village two hours from here, I will go there tonight and I will begin gathering men to free the prisoners, I will see you next when you are up the river at the compound where the evil ones are based. We will wait for you there and wait for your signal, then we will attack."

The Indian stood up and started to leave. I touched his shoulder and he turned back to face me. I said, "What is your name? I must tell Melowa of you. It will give her hope."

He put his hand on my shoulder and, looking me in the eyes, said, "My name is Pulu. Tell my sister that I will free her!" and he quickly drew away and I lost him in the darkness a few seconds later.

I walked back out onto the quiet street. Music still wafted from around the corner at the cantina, but all was silent around me and as I walked back down the deserted street, my mind reeled with the revelations of the last half hour.

Climbing aboard the boat, I went up to the forward starboard cabin and knocked gently on the door before unlocking and opening it. Melowa lay there in the semi darkness with no clothes on and looked at me with big eyes, her expression hard to read. I crossed to her bed and she turned to her side. Crouching down, with my face close to her

I could smell her breath. She smelled good. I quietly told her that I had just met with her brother; she gasped, and reaching out she placed her hand on my cheek.

"I thought he was dead! Oh, Capitan Brites, thank you much for tell me! I have hope now that maybe my brother free me!"

She rolled to her side and propped her head up on her forearm while I continued. "Your brother and I have made a plan. He is gathering a force of men that will attack the place where we are going. This is to happen just after we have arrived. I will need you to tell the other people being held as prisoners of our plan once the attack is happening. But do not say anything about it until it starts. We will not know if perhaps one of the prisoners is a spy. So do not say anything about this before it is happening! You must tell the people they're not to be afraid, and to come with us when I come to get you. I am hoping to be able to free everyone and we will bring them back to this boat and try to escape down the river."

We talked for a while more in very quiet whispers and then I said goodnight and slipped quietly out and back to my cabin. Crawling into my bed, I concentrated on the plan as it was beginning to become clear to me. I lay there going over and over in my mind the details I was formulating, trying to find flaws or ways to improve upon it. Eventually I fell asleep.

Thirteen

Ramon opened the door to the study as Juliet and Frederica sat in the large, palatial living room. Frederica had picked Juliet and Javier up an hour earlier at the marina and had told her that Ramon needed to see her. Beyond that they had only spoken of inane things like shopping, clothes and about a hair appointment that Frederica had scheduled. She had asked Juliet if she would be interested in joining her and at first Juliet had said no. But then something in the glance that Frederica had given her had made her change her mind saying, "Oh, why not. I know Brice would like me to be saving our money, but I really could do with a new look!"

Javier had sat sullenly in the cramped back seat of the sports car listening to all of this with disinterest. He had been in Juliet's constant company for the last several days since the attack at the restaurant, and a second small car with three large men stuffed inside was following Frederica's Jaguar. Apparently, Ramon wasn't taking any more chances by risking a successful second attack on his beloved girlfriend.

"Come inside, Señora Juliet, please," Ramon said as he held the door open and added, "Frederica, my love, please also join us. I have an announcement to make."

Closing the door to the study the two women took seats in the armchairs and Ramon leaned against the front of his desk, looking down at them both. "We are going to go on a boat trip starting tomorrow. And I would like you to join us," he said, looking at Juliet.

"Well thank you, Ramon, is this a day trip or an overnight? I'd love to go, but I'll need to pack if it's overnight."

He chuckled and said, "Señora, this is for a week or two, maybe longer. So, you will want to gather most of your things, and maybe bring your valuables with you too. We will be going back to Panama. I think this is the safest thing for you both at the moment."

Juliet started to object but Ramon put his hand up, stopping her and went on, "I will of course inform your husband and in any case, we will come back to Cartagena when he is returned. Or he will meet us on the yacht in San Blas when he is finished with his job in the south. I have thought this over and it is best. I am still not certain who attacked you two the other day, and every day we stay here in Cartagena the risk of a second and successful attack grows greater. This is my decision and so we will leave tomorrow evening. Pack your bags, Señora Juliet and lock the boat up in the morning and move aboard my yacht. I will have Javier help you put your things aboard and my people will watch your boat while we are gone. It is the best idea."

Juliet could see that any argument would be fruitless so instead she decided to make an enthusiastic response. "Oh Ramon! This is so exciting! I've never cruised on a big boat like yours. I'd be thrilled of course! Thank you so much for thinking of me!"

Ramon was at first a bit surprised but then smiled and accepted the ruse. "No thanks necessary. We will be pleased to have your very gracious company aboard."

After a leisurely breakfast Juliet and Frederica, accompanied by their entourage, went to the salon appointment. It was in a nice part of the newer section of the city and was obviously a place used only by the very wealthy.

Going inside the waiting room, Javier and one of the guards from the other car sat on each side of the door and immediately lost themselves in their iPhones while Frederica spoke to the receptionist. A few minutes later, both the ladies were called and they walked into the main salon area beyond a swinging half door. Both women spoke briefly with a stylist who then had two assistants wash both women's hair and they were then led into a side room and were seated in chairs.

Frederica relaxed noticeably and said, "This is a safe place to talk. These people are working with me and this is where I always go to debrief."

Juliet was speechless as one of the stylists began cutting her hair.

Frederica began to recite the latest developments to her stocky balding male 'stylist' while Juliet's stylist, a tall blonde woman with green eyes and a serene, unlined face, listened while clipping away.

The male stylist then said, "We have discovered that the Americans did an overflight of the region with one of their unmanned surveillance aircraft and have located, as of several days ago, the ship that your friend's husband is on. Also, there is evidence that your cover may have been blown. One of our embassy officials was kidnapped and tortured.

His body was found mutilated and his throat had been cut. We believe that he may have leaked valuable information and that your position may have been compromised."

Frederica thought for a moment before responding. "This must have been what precipitated the attack the other day."

The stylist nodded and went on, "I'm awaiting instructions, but I believe that you're going to be pulled out."

Frederica reached up and stopped his hands just as he was about to cut another small section of hair, speaking insistently. "You cannot pull me out now! I am so close to completing my mission! We are being taken to the San Blas on Ramon's yacht starting tomorrow morning. He said it is to keep me safe, but I think there is a more important reason. Please, don't pull me out now! I have risked so much, and have compromised my own body for our government's goals. It is too late to pull me out now. Please!"

The balding stylist began cutting her hair again and said, "It is not my decision as you know, but I will pass on what you've told me. Just be very careful, Cynthia. You are too valuable to us to risk losing you!"

"Cynthia?" Juliet said.

"Yes, that's my real name. Cynthia Renaldo. But I've been under cover so long on this assignment that sometimes I almost forget my real name."

"That's one of the things our people are afraid of, Cyn," the stylist said and he went on, "You've been on this mission longer than is typically allowed. We really need to wrap this up and extract you soon!"

Frederica said, "Let's see what happens in the next week or so. Maybe you can pull us out of Panama. I'll contact you the usual way if I think we are in imminent danger."

The rest of the appointment went on with just a few words spoken by Juliet, the balance of the conversation being between Frederica and her stylist, and finally the women both stood up and admired themselves in the mirrors.

"Fantastic as usual, Quito," and she gave him two brief kisses and a hug and Juliet and Frederica emerged into the waiting room.

The two guards stood up from where they had been slouching and the four of them exited the building and climbed into their vehicles.

◆◆◆

It had taken only a half hour for the investigative reporter to pry the information he wanted out of Rudolf Bellows. At first the man had been obstructive and uncooperative, but after the reporter had mentioned the things he knew from what the senator had told him, the insurance man had finally agreed to cooperate on the promise from the reporter that none of this would be publicized until a rescue had been made, and that the identities of the key participants in the undercover aspects of the operation would be held strictly confidential.

The key to breaking down the stone wall the insurance man had put up had been the statement that, "I know all about your investigation and about the British undercover operation too. What I don't know is what is being done about it behind the scenes, and I need to find out who the bad guys are. If you'll cooperate with me, I promise I'll report what I find back to you and keep you in the loop. Look, Mr. Bellows. I'm very good at what I do and one way or another, I'm going to get to the bottom of this. So, you can either help me, or go this alone. But I'll blow this thing wide opened and I'd advise you to be on my team."

Six hours later Alex Peterson had arrived at Cartagena's Rafael Núñez airport.

Dressed in faded and artistically torn blue jeans and a worn 'Argentina Rocks' T-shirt emblemized with a profile of Andean mountain peaks, the blonde man picked up his dirty, well-worn backpack and went to the taxi stand outside. Two other backpackers were standing there and he quickly struck up a conversation with the young men.

"Where are you guys headed?"

"We're trying to decide," the shorter of the two said. "We thought we could fly out to Panama on standby, but the cheap seats are all gone. So flying there is sounding pretty pricey. We're thinking of heading to the waterfront. From what we've read, lots of boats go that way almost every day."

"I didn't want to take a boat ride," the taller of the two guys said and then added, "I get seasick."

"C'mon, Mitch, you'll be fine. Don't be such a wuss," his friend said.

Alex added, "I've heard it's a fun way to go and so that's where I'm headed. Let's share a cab."

A few minutes later the three young men were crammed into the back of a small taxi and on their way to the Cartagena waterfront.

A short while later they were walking the docks and Alex quickly asserted himself as the leader by finding out which boats were leaving soonest, and negotiating the prices to see which one was the best deal.

The men noticed a large and beautiful wooden motor yacht with a lot of activity onboard and Mitch said, "Too bad we can't go on that one!"

"Yeah, right. In your dreams," his friend said.

Within a short time Alex had located what looked like a promising boat. It was a fairly new looking Beneteau 473 sloop that matched the description he had been given by the insurance man in Tortola of one of the stolen boats, and after a brief conversation with the captain, a forty-ish looking Latino fellow, it was agreed that the men could join the crew later that day. The boat was set to leave that night for San Blas and on to Portobelo, so the two younger men enthusiastically heaved their gear onboard and started up to the restaurant to grab a few beers.

Alex told them he'd meet them there later but was going to look at a few other boats first and continued walking the docks some more. He wanted to try to get a feel for what kind of things might be going on in the background.

There were a lot of people coming and going and he noticed two large guys bringing some bags down to the sailboat his new friends had agreed to join. *I wonder what's in those bags?* he thought to himself as the bundles were quickly spirited below decks and out of sight. He took out his camera and began taking pictures, trying to look like a tourist but when he noticed one of the men whom he had spoken to on the Beneteau staring at him, he waved and put the camera down, turned and walked slowly down the dock in the opposite direction.

Looking out into the harbor he watched with great interest as a cool looking brigantine rigged schooner about sixty feet long came in closer and maneuvered stern to into the dock with what looked like about fifteen people on deck, and a pretty young blonde female captain shouting out orders to the line handlers. He noticed that the boat was being expertly handled and that its name was 'My World'. Another pretty young woman who appeared to be the first mate swung out onto the dock and began helping the people secure the lines.

He sauntered down the dock and watched as the passengers were debarking and finally, after about a half hour of pulling out bags, throwing stuff onto the dock amidst hugs and farewells, the two girls and a giant of a young man were left standing alone on the dock. Alex went up to them and tried to strike up a conversation.

"Hey! Great looking boat! She's a brigantine, right?"

The captain looked at him appraisingly and said, "You a sailor?"

"Did some sailing a few years back. Mostly dinghies but crewed on some race boats too," he answered.

"You from the East Coast?" the bright young captain said, scrutinizing him and looking him in the eyes.

He answered, "Yup, good guess! Annapolis, born and raised. But been living in New York lately. Name's Alex Peterson," he said, sticking his hand out.

The pretty first mate moved in closer and said, "THE Alex Peterson? As in the Alex Peterson who works for the New Times?" she said with great interest in her voice.

"Sorry to say, yes, that's me," he said and went on, "Just checking things out down here Colombia way. Seems like a pretty cool place."

The captain took the conversation back over. "So you writing a story about the backpacker trade or are you here on some other story?"

Wow, he thought, *this girl is quick*, and so he said, "Nah, just here checking out the city and found myself gravitating to the waterfront. I've always liked boats and yours is really cool."

Just then Mitch, one of the guys he had met at the airport, walked up and said, "Hey, Alex, you gonna come on our boat or have you found a different one?"

The captain narrowed her eyes, staring straight into Peterson's and said, "Uh huh. Well, if you want to sail with the best boat in the fleet, come talk to us later. But if you're just looking for a story, then come see me tonight, I'll be aboard any time after six." And with that she turned and left, going about checking lines and securing rigging lines on deck.

Her mate followed but the deck hand, a big burly dark haired fellow who looked more like a bear than a man, lingered, smiling in a disarming way and put out his huge hand and said in a strong South African accent. "Name's Ben. Nice ta meet ya, Alex," and Peterson shook his firm hand. "Hope you sail with us. We have a great time." At which the deck hand turned and walked back down the dock and climbed aboard the schooner.

Peterson spent the next hour taking photos and chatting with a few of the other backpackers who were coming and going. He found out about a cheap but relatively clean youth hostel nearby and was invited to accompany two girls he met on the dock who had just arrived from Panama for a couple of drinks.

After a few beers with the girls where he learned more background information about the backpacker sailing trips between the two countries, it was just after 6 p.m. when he shuffled back down the dock again.

As he made his way past the Beneteau that Mitch and his friend were just boarding the taller man said, "Hey, Alex! You gonna come sailing with us or you gonna go on some other boat?"

You guys have fun, I'll probably be seeing ya down there. I'm thinking about sailing on 'My World'."

He arrived alongside the steel schooner and knocked on the hull. Ben the giant stuck his head out the middle hatch and said, "C'mon aboard, man, capn's waiting for you in the main cabin, so c'mon up here and I'll show you around."

Clambering aboard, Alex made his way up the side deck and climbed down the hatch into the big comfortable main cabin. The captain was seated at the heavily varnished dining table with another young woman he had seen earlier on the docks, and he joined them and Ben at the table just as the first mate brought a bowl of chips and some salsa out and set them down in the middle.

"This is my girlfriend, Bianca," the giant said, motioning to the girl seated at the table next to the captain and he then went on, "And I don't think you've been formally introduced to the captain and mate. These two are sisters. Meet Captain Sarah and her sister, First Mate Valerie."

"Wow, two sisters running such a big boat. Who owns her?" Peterson said as he appraised the rustic woodwork and eclectic décor.

Sarah said, "My sister and I own the boat. Bought it a few years ago from a famous writer. Had to borrow some money to pull it off and we've been running trips on her ever since. She's a great boat. Want a tour around?"

She stood up and led Alex aft, showing him the engine room, workshop and the after sections of the small ship. They then went up on deck from the aft hatch scuttle and in the twinkling lights from the marina and glow of the city, she walked him around the deck, explaining about the several thousand feet of running rigging and showing him how the yardarms worked for controlling the square sails, telling him a bit of the history of the design and about the boat's individual history as well.

Finishing up her deck tour back at the aft hatch, she then leaned up against the hatch scuttle with her arms folded under her breasts and looking at him coyly, her blonde hair falling partly across one eye she said, "So tell me, why are you really down here?"

Alex thought for a moment as he made a decision about how much he could reveal and then said, "I'm here investigating a very complex international incident that is still ongoing as we speak."

She blinked at him impassively, saying nothing, and so he continued. "I'm trying to find out what, if any, connection the backpacker trade may have with some boats that have been stolen from the Caribbean, and in particular about a specific boat, a large catamaran, which has at least one, probably more hostages onboard."

Sarah looked a bit surprised and said quietly, "Let's go down to my cabin. I'll tell you what I know." And she opened the aft scuttle door and took him down below through the navigation cabin and into her private cabin.

Sitting down at the small desk there, she asked him to shut the door and motioned him to take a seat at the foot of the bed.

Sarah leaned over from the small desk and opened the door, shouting towards the main cabin down the hallway saying, "Hey, Bianca, can you ask Valerie to bring us a couple of drinks and some of those chips and salsa?"

They spent the next two hours behind closed doors with Sarah chatting about the backpacker business and about the various boats and crews she had met.

Yes, she remembered the dubious captain of the boat that was lost in San Blas several months before and knew that he was working with a group of people who she did her best to stay well away from. She also said that the Beneteau that the young men from the airport had joined was definitely with the same people who had the boat that had been lost, and that she had little doubt that drug smuggling was going on. But she elicited a promise from the reporter that he would not mention her or her sister or in any way make it obvious where this information had come from.

"I've been in this business now for four years and I can't afford to cross any of the criminal elements that operate down here. So far they've basically left us alone. But I have no doubt that they'd kill us all if they thought we were a threat."

There was a knock on the door and Valerie came into the aft cabin bringing in two more drinks. She said, "The boat your friends are on is leaving, if you want to know."

Alex and Sarah scrambled out of the aft cabin and up on deck in time to watch the Beneteau sailboat pulling out away from the dock and make its way off in the darkness towards the harbor entrance.

"Never thought about it before, but those boats always seem to leave at night," Sarah said.

◆◆◆

It was 10 a.m. when Alex Peterson boarded his flight at the Rafael Núñez airport bound for Bogotá where he caught a connection to a small river town on the Putumayo. The flight was the best thing he could find to get him within range of where the boat he was looking for had last been reported.

Through careful deduction he had reasoned that the boat was probably heading into Colombia, and so he decided to land at the El Encanto airport and to try to pick up the trail there to wherever it led.

He had spoken with his editor and had made a brief phone call to the senator, filling him in on what he had learned, and went over in his mind again the cover story he was going to use for the snooping around that he was going to have to be doing on the guerrilla-controlled region he would be traveling in.

The aged twin engine DC-3 had dodged some large thunderstorms on the exceptionally bumpy flight from Bogotá into the interior and the arrival at El Encanto airport's pothole-infested strip had seemed more like a controlled crash than a landing. He had learned that only weekly fights arrived at this small military strip, and he had been lucky to have learned this in time to make a connection in Bogotá from Cartagena earlier that day.

Dragging his backpack off the plane he had hoped to find a taxi driver, but soon learned that no such infrastructure existed. The small river town was mostly known as a military base and was one of the few government strongholds in an otherwise widely disputed area full of FARC rebels, drug lords, and hostile Indian holdouts who were resisting the intrusion of these outsiders into their native homelands.

Over a century of persecution had begun with the rubber barons of the early 1900s when thousands of Indians were forced to work in labor camps, their own villages destroyed by military groups funded by Peruvian and Colombian merchants interested only in the huge profits of the viscous material on which the industrial revolution was so dependent.

Entire civilizations of indigenous tribes had disappeared or had been driven deeper into the Amazon jungle by this corrupt trade and when the rubber boom finally died down in the 1960s, it was replaced by the drug trade which was even more ruthless, and was being resisted fiercely by the holdouts who were lucky enough to live in remote areas that had not been economically viable for plantations, and so had been left alone.

Alex had learned that the largest number of citizens in the town were for the most part native Indians who had moved in after their own villages had been destroyed, or after so many of their young people had been enslaved in the rubber business, and then the drug trade made it so that continuing on with traditional life in the jungle had no longer been possible.

Finally, as he sat outside the small terminal, the only taxi driver in the town rolled into the grassy parking area and stepped out of his rusty old Chevy sedan. He was a Mestizo man who appeared to be in his early fifties and had graying hair, a short stubbly beard and a gleam in his eyes that promised some semblance of intelligence, the reporter thought to himself.

The man walked up to him as he got up from where he had been sitting on his backpack and introduced himself in Spanish. Alex struck up a bargain on the price of transport into the town and loaded his bag into the trunk.

Settling into the back seat he said, "Necesito un hotel bueno grande," in his terribly improper Spanish to which the taxi driver replied,

"You Americano? I speak."

Peterson then said, "Please take me to the best hotel, and where is the best restaurant in the town?"

The taxi driver said, "I will take you to the Grand Hotel. It is the best we have, and also the only one!" He chuckled and went on, "And you will like it. Please, tell me why you are here and maybe I can help you."

As the car pulled out onto the broken pavement of the street, the reporter thought for a moment and said, "I am doing a story on river traffic for a newspaper in the United States. I did not know until recently that the Putumayo River is an important trading river and I am here to do a story on it and about the villages that line its shores."

The car driver said, "This is a good story to tell for sure. But this can be a dangerous river too. And not just after the big rains when the floods come, but if you are going to be traveling on the river, you will need to find a trustworthy boat driver and follow his instructions. There are many types of trading going on along this river and not all of it is what you will want to write about."

The driver let this sink in for a moment and went on, "I have a brother who runs a small ferry and cargo boat and I will speak to him, how far along the river do you want to travel?"

Peterson said, "I'm not really sure. I think I'll want to start out by going down river and then maybe go up river after that. Would your brother be able to take me as far as the border to Brazil?"

The taxi man said, "I will speak to him tonight. Tell me, how long will you need his services? He will surely ask this of me."

"A few days to as much as a week, is my best guess."

Just then they pulled up in front of a somewhat worn looking two-story hotel with dingy shutters and mold growing in the shady areas of the siding. He guessed that at one point the building had been white and pink but it was now just a faded and filthy shade of those two colors. A large, mean looking dog of indiscriminate breeding was tied up on the side lawn, and the steps leading up to the front door and reception area had some broken planks and were missing paint in the traffic area, but all in all the structure appeared more inviting than the rest of the buildings around the area had looked, and he got out, paid the taxi driver and then climbed up the steps and opened the door to go inside.

Just as the taxi was pulling away the driver stuck his head out the window and shouted, "When do you wish to start your trip, Señor?"

"As soon as possible," the reporter responded and the taxi driver waved his hand as he drove off. Peterson went inside and closed the door.

Peterson checked into the hotel where his Spanish was apparently good enough that he got his point across that he didn't expect to be there for more than a few days, but would like to keep the room for as much as a week, and so wanted to pay for it in advance for that period. This would allow him to leave most of the contents of his backpack behind. Somehow, he expected that it might be best to travel very light.

He was disappointed that he seemed to be the only guest and found out from the young receptionist that this was the end of the dry season. By next month, when the rains were coming down in earnest, the hotel would be full of military personnel. When he asked why, he was told that it was in the wet season that most of the cargo traveled on the rivers and this was when the patrols would be constant. Trying to keep the rivers free of danger was the primary reason for the patrols, he was told.

As it was nearing dinner time, after he had settled into his room, he went back downstairs and asked where a restaurant might be found. Just then, the taxi came back into the yard and Peterson walked down the stairs to speak with the driver who had just gotten out of the car.

"Ah, *buenas tardes*, Señor Peterson. I have spoken to my brother and he would like to meet with you."

"I was just thinking about trying to get some food. Maybe I could speak to him after eating?" the reporter said.

The taxi driver said, "Actually, you are in luck because my brother, he keeps his boat at a dock where there is a restaurant just across the street. It is always open because the military men who can afford it eat there. The food is much better than at the navy base!"

The old car trundled down the bumpy dirt road towards the waterfront and pulled up a few minutes later in front of a tin building with a sign out front which said 'Cantina' in flowing orange letters. The place looked amazingly clean and well cared for, and both men got out and went inside.

The driver said something in Spanish to the man at the front desk and Peterson was led to a nearby table to be seated. The tables were plastic with white plastic chairs and there was a red and white checkered table cloth made of plastic also. The silverware and plates though were more substantial, and a few minutes later, a portly native Indian waitress appeared.

The taxi driver departed after saying, "I will bring you to my brother after you have eaten." And then he leaned closer and lowered his voice. "I would suggest that if the military questions you, tell them you are here to look at the wildlife and the trees. Do not tell them you are interested in the trading that takes place on this river. It may be taken the wrong way."

The reporter nodded and said thanks and the older man walked off.

During his dinner, several men came in and sat at some of the other tables. All were dressed in military uniforms and two in particular stared at him and then conversed quietly amongst themselves, looking back at him occasionally while he hurriedly finished his meal. He got up and paid his bill and walked outside. The taxi driver was waiting for him.

"Ah, Señor Peterson. I am here to take you to my brother. I trust that the food was good?"

They walked a short distance across the street and down to a small house with a rusty tin roof. The reporter was led inside and in the dim light he saw three Mestizo men at a table with a bottle in front of them. As they entered, two of the men got up and left the room. The man remaining motioned to Peterson to sit down and said in fairly good English, "My brother tells me that you wish to hire a boat to go down the river." He was a bit younger than the taxi driver but bore a strong resemblance. Stocky of build and about five foot six tall, he looked much rougher and his face and arms showed some scars. Perhaps he had been in the military or had worked on some manual labor job when he was younger?

Peterson said, "Yes, I am a writer and am doing a story on the river, its wildlife, the villages and of the people that use the river for commerce." This was an adaptation of the story he had originally been telling.

Over the next half hour, a price was negotiated and a time agreed upon for a morning departure. He had been told that they would stay in villages ashore and that he should not bring valuables with him unless he could keep them on his person at all times. He was also told that if they ran into patrols; either rebel or military, that he was to act as if he understood no Spanish and to let the captain speak for him. That this was the only safe way to travel on the river and that he must tell the men he saw that he was a nature photographer only. He must not talk of trade on the river or be seen taking photos of gunboats, villagers or any other goings on that they might witness.

Seven a.m. arrived and his friend the taxi driver drove him the short distance down the street and dropped him off at the wharf where he climbed down into the brother's boat.

The boat was about thirty feet long and had a small cabin in the front with a large open cockpit with a canvas awning to protect it from rain but allowing good visibility. There was an eighty HP Yamaha Enduro outboard motor on the stern which looked a bit worn and there were two large portable gas tanks in the somewhat dirty bilge. The boat appeared to be about ten years old and was built of heavy timbers, and looked quite sturdy.

Firing up the outboard motor, the captain cast off and pulled away from the dock. Taking a cigarette out of his pocket the captain lit up, offering one to the reporter who politely refused.

A few minutes out away from the dock they lost the town from view and the captain visibly relaxed. Putting his feet up and steering with one hand, he said, "So tell me Señor, what is it you are really looking for on this river?"

Peterson had decided to tell a story very close to the truth as time was short and there was little time to waste if he was to hope to intercept the stolen boat. "I am looking for a big shiny new looking sailboat. One that may have been stolen and where there are prisoners onboard. Do you have any idea where a boat like that may be kept? It was spotted two hundred miles down river three days ago. This is what I am really looking for."

The boat captain looked sullen and finally said, "I do know where this boat may be going. There is a tributary not so far from here, this is where there are other boats maybe like what you are seeking. But I cannot take you there. It is very dangerous! This is an area owned by drug lords and patrolled by the FARC rebels. The military will not even go there."

With this the boatman slowed to a crawl and folded his arms across this chest. "I cannot take you there. It is too dangerous."

The reporter thought for a moment before responding. "I will pay you two thousand U.S. dollars if you will take me close, and wait for me. I need to get photos and to see with my own eyes."

The boatman looked unhappy but was clearly motivated by the money and responded, "If you make it five thousand, I will bring you to this place but by a small river that is close by. You can walk in from there. It is only about forty miles from here. And then I will come back a day later to fetch you. I will not wait for you, it is not safe for me and it is really not safe for you either. But this is the only way to approach that place without being caught immediately. And maybe you can say you are a nature photographer searching for a rare species of bird. It may not help you, but that is your best chance to survive if you are caught."

The reporter negotiated further, "I only have a few thousand with me, but I can give you the two now and three when you pick me up. But I will need at least two days to get what I need. You must wait for me or return for me and bring me back and then I will pay you the rest of the money when we are back at the town. And I will need a guide to help with finding my way in the jungle. I am not familiar with traveling in the jungle and will surely become lost without help. Can you find me a local Indian guide? I need your help!"

The boatman reluctantly agreed and they resumed their trip down river. He was silent for a while and appeared to have been deep in thought when he said at last, "There is a village a few miles farther down the river from where this small river is and we will go there and try to find a guide for you. I am not sure how much this will cost but probably only a few hundred dollars. That is your best chance, Señor."

The small boat cut a wide V in the smooth surface of the river as they sped downstream and soon a light rain began to fall. The boatman told the reporter that this was the beginning of the rainy season and that in a few weeks the river would have risen so much that it would be possible to take a boat right into the forest. Huge areas of the surrounding bush would be submerged and the entire face of the land would change dramatically.

Several hours later the boatman pointed to a small river off to the left which disappeared into the dense jungle. "This is the river I was telling you about where I could take you to the back way of where that place is," and a short while later they passed a much bigger river which the boatman said led to the place.

Fifteen minutes later they made a turn onto a small tributary and soon pulled up to a small Indian village and ran the bow of the boat up onto the steep, muddy bank. The boatman tied the bow of the boat to an overhanging tree and the two of them prepared to get off the boat. The boatman locked the cabin securely with a large padlock explaining, "These savages will steal anything they can see."

They scrambled out onto the embankment and saw that about thirty Indians had gathered, mostly older men and women and a few children. In the front of the group were two older men who stood proudly holding spears at their sides. The boatman walked up to them and spoke in a dialect that the reporter guessed was one the indigenous languages.

A moment later, the boatman turned to him and said, "We will go speak with these men in private. Come."

Walking up the muddy trail into the main part of the small village, they threaded their way through a labyrinth of passages amongst bamboo walls and entered a small hut to a room with about ten older men all sitting in a circle. The boatman removed his hat and, holding it in his hand, motioned the reporter to sit and join him on the dirt floor. Peterson took his hat off as well and waited to see what would unfold.

A man who appeared to be the leader of these older men spoke earnestly to the boatman and at the end of the exchange, the captain turned to Peterson and said, "He tells me that there is a plan to attack the compound of the place you are seeking. The young men have all been preparing for this and are out in the jungle gathering supplies and poison for their weapons. He tells me that this attack will come soon."

Peterson said, "Ask them if I can accompany them on this attack."

The boatman looked shocked, but relayed this to the elder, who looked appraisingly at the reporter and said something to the boatman who then relayed what was said.

"This cannot be allowed. They do not know all the details, and only know that soon another man will come with a group and that the attack will happen very soon after this. He suggests that you do not try to go close to the compound. He says you may be killed because of a mistaken identity. He recommends that you return to where you came from and let them take care of this problem themselves."

Peterson responded, "Please tell them that there are some prisoners that are being held by these people that they plan to attack and that it is very important that they are freed. Tell them that I have made a promise to the parents of one of the prisoners who is a young woman that I would try to free her, and so with or without their help, I am going to go there to help them. Tell them that I cannot walk away. I have flown and traveled from very far away and that I must help these people."

The boatman explained this as best he could and the older men then all began speaking to each other in a very animated fashion. Several of the older men became agitated and finally the conversation calmed down and the elder spokesman relayed what had been said to the captain, who then told the reporter, "They will allow you to join them, but you must stay back and not get close to the fighting when it happens. He says he cannot guarantee your safety but that he understands your need to help the prisoners and your oath to the parents of the missing girl."

The man went on to say, "For my part, I will go back up the river and will return in a few days to see if you are still alive and need to be picked up. You will stay here in the village for a few days and either this attack will happen, or it won't. But you may learn more here than on your own. If things go wrong and you are captured, I will also inform the military of the situation and see if they can be brought out to try to assist. But do not count on that! The military has only a few gunboats, and they are well overpowered by rebel forces here in the jungle and are afraid to be drawn off the main river. The military men will not go into the jungle willingly because the few that have are almost always killed."

Peterson thanked the man for his help and the two of them went back down to the river boat. The reporter gathered the few things he had brought and gave the boatman his two thousand dollars with the promise of more on the successful completion of the investigation.

It was late afternoon by the time the reporter watched the wooden skiff head back up the river. He turned and walked back up the embankment and was led by one of the older women to a small empty hut where he understood he was to sleep.

As night fell on the jungle, he was summoned to a fire and given some food. The sounds of the jungle and the fire-lit panorama of thatched huts amongst dense jungle surrounding the gathering of Indians was like something straight out of *National Geographic*. It could have been 1400 A.D. He tried, as inconspicuously as possible using a small digital camera, to snap a few photos and to observe as best he could while he waited for what was to unfold.

◆◆◆

Night was falling as the palatial and elegant classic wooden motor yacht 'Inca Gold' cleared the Cartagena breakwater and made her way to the west towards the distant San Blas Islands.

Ramon's captain brought the yacht up to an easy twelve knots and they all settled in for the comfortable ride in the light easterlies with small following seas.

Frederica and Juliet sat with Ramon, and Javier and the other woman whom Juliet had been introduced to as Javier's friend were all relaxing around the teak cockpit table as the twinkling lights of the city faded into the distance.

◆◆◆

Carlos felt that things were now back under control and that the damaging problem of the infiltrator had been addressed. The young captain, Toby, had been taken prisoner and he would be interrogated once the new catamaran was safely docked at the compound deep in the jungle. The young man would surely divulge all they needed to know. He knew his brother's sons would enjoy the questioning process as they cut pieces off the man's body until he spilled all he knew.

◆◆◆

The following afternoon the elegant motor yacht slipped through one of the poorly charted southern entrances through the San Blas barrier reef, and by 4 p.m. she entered a remote mainland anchorages. Surrounded by high hills and well up into the bay, the yacht came to rest and was soon riding quietly at anchor with only a hint of the ocean swells to sway her lightly.

The captain, who had traveled all of these waters since his early days doing smuggling and regular commercial runs, was surely one of the most knowledgeable local pilots in this far southern frontier of the Kuna Yala nation. Few, if any, patrol boats ever came this far south and the close proximity to the Colombian border made it a safe and secure port from which to wait out further developments. Situated just an hour's ride from the Colombian border town of Sapzurro by the yacht's fast dinghy, and with his sat phone and data links, business could be done just as easily from here as back in his own office in Cartagena.

◆ ◆ ◆

Alex Peterson had made good use of his first full day in the village and had even found a homely little twelve-year-old girl who spoke English fairly well and whose foster parents had agreed to make her available as an interpreter.

The reporter learned from the girl that she had lived in a village far down river up until several months earlier when their village had been attacked by another tribe who had modern weapons. Most of the young men had been killed and the few survivors had run into the forest. She too had run and hidden for two days but was finally captured by one of the attacker's scouting parties. She was then repeatedly raped and beaten and had then been sold to some white men from one of the river boats, who also beat her and raped her and eventually grew tired of her and threw her into the river off their boat at night. She had been barely alive when she was found by one of the fishermen from this village and had been brought up river to the tiny settlement. She had lost everyone in her family and was alone, so an older man and woman who had lost their own children many years back had adopted her and they kept her hidden whenever strangers came by the village. There were other young men and women who also were hidden away in a cave near the village whenever the soldiers or the drug runners came by.

Peterson was appalled by her story and he vowed that he would make this whole episode front page news. But first he had to get the rest of the story and to try to save as many of the prisoners as he could. Although he could almost smell a Pulitzer Prize, he had quickly put that out of his mind. It was his moral duty to do what he could to save them and bring these atrocities to the world's attention.

That night he made a sat phone call to his editor and then another shorter call to the senator in Maryland. He reported what he had learned so far and quickly signed off. He wished he had brought a spare battery. He had no way to charge one again until he returned to the main town and he was unsure about how long that might be.

In one of his conversations with the young girl, he asked her to ask all the other men and women who went out fishing and hunting near the main river to tell him if they heard or saw a big shining yacht go by. She assured him that even though they were a few miles off the main river, there was no way it could pass unnoticed. The tribe kept a twenty-four-hour guard at the entrance to their creek and through a series of animal calls they could relay information quickly up river to the village of any traffic coming their way. So, relaying this information of a boat passing would be easy, and she came by his hut later that night to tell him that this had been done.

◆◆◆

"We are getting close to the side river, Capitan Brice," Carlos said. It was evening and we had anchored off to the side of the river, having been unwilling to tie up to the poorly maintained dock at the last village we had passed.

"Tomorrow we will be home at our safe compound and you will get to see some of the wonderful things my brother and I have been doing here in the jungle."

Carlos had been celebrating and had enjoyed several drinks, so was in a particularly boastful mood. His demeanor around me had been much more relaxed in the last few days as we made our final approaches to the base, and now that he was convinced that Toby had been the informant, he spoke freely in my presence when discussing details of the business with his sons and wife.

I had been allowed to speak with Toby myself on two brief occasions while Carlos or one of the boys were there, in the belief that perhaps I could glean some information from him and I had been able to relay to him via the girls that he was in very grave danger and that I would try to help, but that until I said so, he was to comply as much as possible. Whatever he did, I had told them to tell him, he must not fight back yet. I had also told them to tell him to act as if he was very ill and weak. I had told Jenny that when the attack finally came, it was going to be up to her and Melowa to gather all the prisoners together and assuming that by then they were being kept in some sort of common area, to wait for me or one of the other rescuers to lead them to safety.

I was very unsure about the plausibility of this plan as I had not even seen the lay of the land of the place we were headed, but I saw no way to stop the wheels that were already in motion. It was one of the most frustrating and stressful few days of my life as I felt truly helpless to stop what was happening, and knew that the only way to help was to do as I was being told and to make it appear that I was a hundred percent behind my employers' actions.

I wondered if I was laying it on a bit thick when Carlos, noticing my apparent unease in what I thought was a private moment, said, "Capitan Brice, why do you look so concerned?"

I had quickly responded, "I'm just worried about money, Carlos. I really appreciate the work you and Ramon have given me and now that we are nearing the completion of this delivery, I'm just worried about what I'm going to do to come up with the rest of the money I need."

Carlos had laughed and said, "My friend, you have proven yourself to be a trusted and competent employee. We will make sure you are kept working, so do not worry, OK?"

I had smiled and thanked him as I thought to myself with a bit of irony; *Great. Job security at last with one of the most dangerous drug cartels in the world. I can just imagine how their retirement benefits are meted out...*

In the morning we got underway at seven o'clock and by ten-thirty we were nearing the area where Carlos told me we should be watching for a side river coming in from the right hand side.

A few miles later I saw that the river appeared to fork and Carlos told me this was the branch we must take. I throttled back and we carefully edged our way up the smaller river. The tall mast was almost brushing the trees at times as we threaded our way up the winding course, and the depth sounder made alarm sounds twice as we nearly touched the bottom on the bends while I tried to keep the mast out of the trees. After nearly an hour of this I was fairly exhausted when, coming around a bend, I saw a sight which made me nearly drop my jaw.

Amongst the jungle was one of the most beautiful settings I had ever seen. The tall jungle canopy had been left intact, which shaded the entire area and a huge fenced-in compound hove into view. We passed by sentries who were poised with mounted machine guns on either side of the river and as we passed a twelve-foot-high fence which appeared to be electrified and had coiled barbed wire at its top, we entered a dredged basin with several docks. Several small boats which had the look of patrol boats shared dock space with two modern catamarans; a 48' Robertson and Caine and a 45' Lagoon were tied up alongside one of the docks near what looked like a guardhouse and I was directed by Carlos to dock the big cat at the other end of the second pier, far away from the other yachts, in an area with another set of lower fences and a guard hut off to the right. We were now several hundred yards into what looked like a cross between a botanical garden and a maximum-security prison.

As I maneuvered the boat into the slip, several men in green coveralls appeared on the dock to help with lines. Carlos and the boys and Jenny all helped to position fenders and adjust lines, and in a short while we were secured and so I had shut down the engines. A shore power cord was pulled out of the cockpit locker and hooked into the receptacles on the docks. It was amazing. It was like one of the finest marinas in the world had transplanted two of its finger piers into a fairyland setting deep in the Amazon jungle.

Above and in front of the cat, off to our left there was a beautifully constructed pool house with an outdoor pool completely covered over with trees. A series of what looked like hotel rooms opened onto the terrace of the pool, and workers cleaned and trimmed shrubbery. The complex around us was built of natural stone and was all single story and blended into the surroundings like Hobbit houses in the Tolkien Trilogy. Turf roofs with vegetation growing over them were interspersed with huge trees from the first growth forest which reached up nearly two hundred feet. I realized that the entire place would be virtually invisible from the air and yet, the sheer magnitude of the surrounding structures was awe-inspiring. Dozens of people seemed to be working and running about and it took me a while to take it all in.

"An amazing place is what I had promised you, yes?" Carlos said as he stood behind me at the helm. "Did I not tell you?"

He was smiling as I turned to him and said, "You were right. This is more spectacular than I had ever imagined. How long has this been under construction?"

Carlos laughed. "Do you see how the hills began a short while back and that they end here?" he said as he motioned with his arm to the craggy low cliffs along the riverbanks with low hills behind them. Vines and dense foliage engulfed the cliffs and everything that wasn't bare rock, and it was hard to see the sky through the dense forest canopy. "And do you see the embankments? This place is unique and is full of natural caverns. It has been inhabited, from our estimates, for possibly ten thousand years – since the earliest ancestors of my people came here from Asia. This place has been a sacred place for many civilizations. The most recent were the Incas who used this as their secret treasure trove. It was my fathers' fathers' ancestors and their ancestors who were entrusted with protecting the treasures that were stored here to keep them from the marauding Spaniards and ever since my great grandfather rediscovered this place, it has been my family's legacy to protect these treasures from the outside world."

I thought to myself of the treasures that had already been smuggled out of the country with backpacker boats and said, "Why sell these treasures now, Carlos? It seems as if these are irreplaceable and worth preserving for history."

He snapped at me, "The things we have been selling are but trifles! If there is time maybe I will show you what the real treasure is like. But our country is under siege from the untrustworthy enemies of my family and since the United States helped the military in the big drug crackdowns a few years back, when so much of what my father had built was captured or destroyed by our enemies, we have had to sell some of the treasure to keep an army going that is protecting the majority of what we have pledged to our fathers, and our fathers' fathers to hide from the greedy world. It is these treasures that matter. And we have been very successful in other business ventures in the past as well. Up until recently we were the undisputed leaders in exports of the coca and only now, with the interventions of the corrupt politicians and their friends in the government of the United States, are we finding it necessary to sell some of our heirlooms in order to protect ourselves."

A tall, heavyset uniformed fellow with an angry scowl on his face and a large scar across his cheek came walking down the docks, and Carlos turned and went down the steps to meet this man as he stepped aboard the boat.

"Sergio! How are you, my friend?" Carlos said and the man said,

"You are late! I have been expecting you for hours!" The man couldn't hold his false scowl any longer and his face broke into a huge smile which showed a missing front tooth, and he stepped forward and embraced Carlos. "I am happy to see you, my cousin! It has been a long time!"

Carlos said, "I missed you too, my uncle's favorite son! It has been a long and dangerous voyage. But now we not only have this beautiful yacht to enjoy, but also some very nice young ladies to help keep us company in our solitude."

Carlos went on with a lowered voice, "I also have a prisoner. A traitor who nearly ruined our voyage. He is a young man, the brother of one of the women you have here, the one we call Camila."

"Yes, the troublemaker. She has been a hard one to get to know," he laughed and added, "But maybe now, with her brother here, she will be more... cooperative."

Carlos slapped him on the back and said, "Yes, yes, and come see this beautiful new plaything we have here! You and our best men can have a very good time on this yacht. It is truly wonderful." And with that he led the big soldier below to show him the yacht.

Just as they were disappearing from view I heard Carlos say, "Please arrange to have the women and the prisoner taken to the cells as soon as possible, but we will keep the blonde one here for a few hours. She has proven to be very useful and knows the operation of the yacht and systems well."

◆◆◆

It was mid-morning when the young Indian girl came to the hut that the reporter had been staying in, and Peterson went outside to speak with her as she said in a nearly breathless voice, "The boat you have been asking about? It has passed us within the last hour. And it is also reported that there are several canoes full of men coming our way. My new parents say I must go hide in the cave in the forest." And she quickly left, running up the small hill behind the village, and disappeared from view into the jungle.

Peterson then went to seek out the tribal elders and saw that they were already assembling along the shoreline. A few minutes later three large dugout canoes full of young and middle aged men came around the bend and nudged up on the shoreline, the occupants pouring out and scrambling up onto the muddy embankment.

With his interpreter missing, Peterson could only guess at what was being said, but it was clear that the older men were of mixed emotions. Some appeared happy to see the younger men, but others were clearly distressed. A short while later several of the newly arrived men went off with a group of the elders and the rest began pulling supplies and weapons from the canoes, depositing them on shore. Several of the men looked at the reporter with distrust, and he was glad when a few minutes later, his young interpreter friend reappeared, it apparently having been decided that there was no threat from these people.

The young girl stared at the men from the canoes and then shrieked with joy. She ran down the embankment and threw herself at one of the younger warriors, wrapping her arms around him and crying out in delight. She looked back at Peterson and said, "This is my oldest brother Miamu. I thought he was dead!" and she hugged him again tightly. He too was overwhelmed and tears flowed down his face.

All that afternoon and evening there was great commotion in the village and everywhere the reporter went, people were talking in groups or carrying bundles, hurrying in one direction or another. Several times he saw people point at him or motion towards him while talking animatedly with some of the newcomers. By nightfall he decided it was time to make a call to his editor and fill him in. Peterson had no idea what the next day would bring and so just in case this was to be his last transmission, he decided to tell the man as much of what was going on as possible.

After a thirty-minute conversation where he dictated his initial installment of the story and said as much of what he wanted to say to his editor, he made another quick call to the senator from Maryland, hoping that it wasn't too late to be calling.

"Of course I was awake and thank you for calling, Mr. Peterson. I know you probably don't have a lot of battery, so please, tell me what you know."

Peterson quickly filled him in with what was happening and with the approximate coordinates of the area they were in. "I don't know exactly what's being planned, but my best guess is that either tonight or tomorrow night, probably not tonight actually, and maybe even the day after, these people are going to attack the compound where your daughter is being held. I'd say that if there was ever a time to be thinking about calling in the Marines, it would be soon!" Then Peterson went on with, "Just so you know, I've dictated my first installment on this story which will come out in tomorrow's paper. After that hits the news stands at 7 a.m., you'll no doubt get complete cooperation from the White House. Oh, and, Senator? I'd tell them that they should hold off on any intervention until I call them again with an update. Coming in early with guns blazing may only result in getting all the hostages killed. So please, be patient." And with that the reporter signed off. He grimaced when he saw that his battery was now down to nineteen percent.

◆◆◆

I was dismayed to see that only a short time after we had arrived, several guards came and took Toby away. As they dragged him down the side deck, one of them punched him in his gut and I saw the young man double over in pain. I couldn't help saying, "That man is sick. Unless you want to be vomited on, I'd suggest treating him a bit more gently." One of the guards got my meaning and they shuffled him off the boat and down the dock. I watched as they took him through the set of inner gates and down a long row of overgrown buildings with tiny slits for windows that I had noticed when we were docking. At the final door they went in and a few minutes later the guards returned and took Bridget and Melowa down to a door closer to the boat, but in that same building.

That must be the prison block, I decided and a few moments later Jenny came up behind me and said quietly, "I guess I'm going to be next."

I told her, "I heard Carlos and his cousin, the chief guard, talking. I think they're going to keep you here for a little while longer today. I think I'll come up with a bunch of distasteful jobs that need doing and that way they might leave you for even longer."

But she said, "I have a better idea. Why not let them take me, and then call for me later on? That way I'll have a chance to see what it's like in there and maybe we can figure out a way to break everybody out."

I looked at her with amazement. "That's a good idea, but don't get ahead of yourself here. Just concentrate on observing." And I noticed Carlos walking down the dock with his cousin.

I went out of the side deck and said, "Hey, Carlos, do you mind if I take a few hours off and relax? That last bit, coming up the creek, was really taxing and I'm bushed. I have a lot of stuff that needs doing. I've gotta clean the holding tanks, set up the Y valves for the toilets and clean up a lot of the oil and sewage that leaked out. So, I'd like to get some rest before I start that and if I could get some help with that, it'd be great. Maybe one of your sons could help? I really need someone who speaks English and knows this boat's systems like how to operate pumps and breakers and so forth."

Carlos took the bait and said in Spanish, "My sons are in no condition to help right now. They're going to be blowing off steam. I'll put the American girl in her cell and then just tell the guard at the end of the dock when you are ready for her. I'll have them bring her and she can help you. That may be best, yes?"

I nodded and thanked him and turned and went inside. The air conditioning was already running off the shore power so I went into my cabin, closed the door and took a nap.

Awakening at 6 p.m., I went up into the deserted main salon and looked out across the twilit basin. I hadn't seen either Diego or Santiago since shortly after our arrival and I realized why when I saw both of them across the water on the larger of the two catamarans. They were sitting in the front cockpit and each had two topless Indian girls on their laps. They were groping the girls, drinking and speaking very loudly to some of the other men, undoubtedly bragging about their exploit of stealing the big catamaran and of killing the yachtsman off the mouth of the Amazon. They seemed to really enjoy telling that story.

I sauntered down the dock to the guard station and said in my best Spanish "Tráeme la chica rubia ahora." "Bring me the blonde girl now."

The guard got on a phone in the guardhouse and punched a couple of numbers on his keypad and quickly relayed what I had said. I then started walking down towards the prison block and ignored the guard when he shouted after me, "Deténgase. No puedes ir allí!"

Walking briskly, I was soon alongside the first set of doors and they suddenly burst open. Two guards had Jenny by her arms and one said in Spanish, "You are not to be down here. This building is off limits to everyone."

I smiled my biggest toothy grin and responded, "So sorry, amigo, I just needed to stretch my legs. I'm sorry but my Spanish is not so good."

I turned and walked back up the walkway to the gate where the irate guard glared at me as we went through and down the dock to the catamaran. The guards then left us and Jenny and I climbed aboard. I gathered a few tools and we opened up the engine room door farthest from the dock and climbed down inside.

"Holy shit," she said. "You really pissed those guys off! I'd advise against doing that again!''

I ignored her concern and asked, "So what's it like inside the building? Is it individual cells or are the prisoners held in a common area?"

"It's a big common cell for the girls," she said. "Not sure about the men's cells, but I imagine it's the same. I have no idea what's inside the last door though, but I bet it's not nice."

I asked about how many women were in the cell she had been held in and about what had happened to her since I'd seen her a few hours earlier.

"There are six girls inside counting us. Toby's sister is one of them and they took her away a short while after they put me in there. When they brought her back they had beaten her and she was crying."

I asked about the others.

"The other two are both really pretty and about my age, maybe a little younger. They don't speak any of the languages I know. My best guess is they're Russian or Ukrainian. Not sure. They seemed very resigned to their fate and were largely uninterested in us. I have no idea what's happened to them or how long they've been there."

"What did they do to you?"

"Nothing really," she said and went on, "They took Melowa away for a while but brought her back. She had showered and was dressed in nice clothes. Just before I came here they took Bridget and my guess is they're doing the same with her. I suppose they're getting readied for photos or something?"

"What's the security like inside? I wanted to get a look at the doors and the locks, but you came out just as I was starting to examine them."

She responded, "We had a single guard inside. A big burly woman who looks like she could break a man in half over her knee, and then there were the two guards you saw but they didn't stay inside. I'd say it's just the one guard in there. But they might have more nearby. I just don't know."

Just then I felt someone step aboard and I quickly took some greasy oil from under the engine and put it on Jenny's cheek and hands. She pulled back at first but then got what I was doing and smeared it around even more.

Carlos's cousin stuck his head into the hatch opening and said, "Ah, there you are, Capitan. I see you are working hard so I will not keep you long, but one of my guards said that you were walking around unaccompanied outside of the marina, inside the inner fence. I just need to tell you that you are only allowed inside this inner fence unless you are with one of our guards. The area is off limits, so please do not do that again. Our guards have been instructed to shoot anyone who is not known to them and is not in uniform and so you are a lucky man that this did not happen. So please, for your own safety, stay on the boat or in the pool area and you will be fine. Oh, and I came to tell you that dinner is served at eight in the main dining area. It's just behind the pool house here in the inner compound. We'll see you there then?"

Jenny and I worked for a while longer in the engine room and cleaned things up quite a bit, and then by the time we emerged we saw Carlos coming down the dock with Anita. Both of them looked well cleaned up. There was still no sign of Santiago or Diego.

"Capitan Brice! How is it going with the jobs?"

I said, "Well, I've got one engine room done but there wasn't enough time to tackle the sewage problem. If it's OK with you, I'll work on that tomorrow."

He smiled and said, "Of course, of course. Please, get cleaned up. I have someone I want to introduce you to and we can have the girl brought to you any time you need her. We're going up to the pool house to have a drink and so once you've gotten cleaned up, please join us there, or if you get delayed, just come up to the dining room. It's up the steps and over behind the pool house. You can't miss it!"

The two of them then reeled about and strolled back down the dock. I saw him say something to the guard at the gate and they then turned and strode down the walkway along the water inside the inner fence and made their way up to the pool house, disappearing inside.

A short while later I saw the two guards I had seen earlier emerge from the last door and come our way.

"I guess you'll be heading back to your fine quarters?" I said to Jenny.

"Yeah. Great. I'll try to learn more and hope you can get me out of there again in the morning. About what time, do you think?"

I said, "I'll send for you at about 8 a.m. if that's OK."

The guards arrived and walked the pretty blonde down the dock, out past the gate and down to her quarters in the prison block.

I turned and went inside, showered and dressed and went up to the pool house just as Carlos, Anita and one other powerful looking man I had not met were all getting up to leave.

"Capitan Brice! So good of you to join us! Please, I want to introduce you to my friend."

"General Alverado, this is the Capitan I have been speaking of who has done us such a great service. Capitan Brice, meet the most powerful man in southern Colombia, General Alverado."

I shook hands with the man and grimaced slightly as Alverado tried to crush my hand. We all then walked out and around to the dining room.

Inside there was an elegant mahogany table with eight chairs and settings for five. I wondered who the missing person was as we all sat down and a waiter appeared, offering us drinks. I ordered a scotch on the rocks and sat back, surveying my surroundings.

The room was old. Much of the décor was colonial and older. I saw a number of glass cases which displayed some gold figurines and other objects made of jade, gold and obsidian. The richly carved chairs we were sitting on were each unique and the armrests were intricately carved with the figures of naked humans being consumed by wild beasts, copulating couples and warriors with stone axes cutting off the heads of prisoners. Not exactly the kinds of scenes that made my appetite grow and so I concentrated instead on the artwork on the walls,

Beautiful oil paintings of pastoral scenes with stone temples in the jungle and mountainous vistas were for the most part represented, and a few of the paintings were of Indian peasants being led off in chains to mines, or pulling plows while overseers whipped their backs. Nice.

Just then my curiosity about who the fifth person to join us might be was satisfied when an inner door opened and in walked Melowa. She was dressed in an elegant full length lace dress which showed off her stunning figure and pushed her smallish breasts up and out making them appear larger than they really were. She was bedecked in diamonds and emeralds. Her hair was done up in an elaborate braid and was stacked up on her head so that the loose ends tumbled down onto her forehead and cheeks. She was absolutely stunning, and I was not alone in my assessment. The general was spellbound. She then looked at me briefly with eyes that were so sad that I almost said something, but thought better of it.

Then Carlos said, "general, this is the one that I told you of. Is she not the most delightful full-blooded woman? She is surely a direct descendant of the ones who built the greatest empire in the history of mankind. The empire that one day I hope we shall see rebuilt and reclaimed. And I give her to you as a token of my appreciation for all that you have done for us in the past and in appreciation of your continued support in the future."

The general continued to stare at the girl appraisingly and Carlos told the girl, "Turn around for us my dear. Show them your beautiful grace and form."

She did as she was told and was then told to take a seat. The general seemed entranced by the girl's beauty and I too had trouble taking my eyes off her. The transformation had been quite remarkable.

Carlos started in again, "As I was saying, general, this fine creature is surely a direct descendant of our old ones and she is as perfect in every way as any woman on earth, I can assure you."

The man murmured agreement and was finally distracted when a waiter came in, bringing the first course of the meal.

Throughout the rest of the meal the two men talked of how the struggle with the government was going, about how the traffic on the river was as safe as ever, and were exuberant when Carlos told them that his brother Ramon had arranged to get another large sum of money to them soon to help with the revolution.

"I am hoping that with this new money and this gift of the young maiden that you will help us to reacquire some of what we lost in the days since my father was murdered." The general nodded but I had trouble following much of what was said in the rapid-fire Spanish, so I was beginning to lose interest when the conversation was turned in my direction.

Carlos said, "Capitan Cannon, please answer the general." I hadn't heard the question so General Alverado repeated it as the waiter poured him another drink.

"I was asking if you would be interested in helping us with a problem we are having with a shortage of river gunboats for our own patrols on the Putumayo and other rivers. Surely if you can bring such a grand yacht as the one you just delivered, bringing us some fast gunboats would be an easy job for you, yes?"

Luckily Carlos jumped into the conversation. "General, it is not so easy. Bringing a large shiny yacht up the river through Brazil was no problem because the officials, they all assumed we were rich yachtsman and they left us alone. Only once were we boarded coming up the river, and our forged papers and a bribe were enough to send them on their way. These officials are never familiar with all the different styles of registry forms. But a gunboat? We would have been stopped a hundred times and would not be sitting here speaking to you now. It is just not a possible thing to do."

I jumped into the conversation saying, "General, there is a way to get your gunboats." Both men looked at me as I continued. "All you would need to do would be to attack a naval base on the river. We have passed several. Why not just attack one of those bases and take the boats from there?"

The general laughed as he finished his drink and said to Carlos, "Your Capitan has more balls than brains!"

I held up my hand and continued. "What I would do would be to pick a base with several boats tied up, then I'd bring in a lot of booze on a small boat and leave it at the dock. Maybe a few girls too, and have the boat appear to have 'broken down'. Surely the navy guys would steal the booze and the girls could entice them to drink a lot. Then in the middle of the night I'd attack the compound and kill all the soldiers and sailors and take the boats up a small side river where they could be repainted, camouflaged, and would move them where they were needed under cover of darkness."

"Ahh, good idea, Capitan, except for one thing." I noticed that the general was slurring his speech somewhat now as he continued, "The river is not always safe to travel on at night. In the day the navy patrols it, but at night the Indians take it back. We have lost many of our men in this way."

I said, "But we met one of your patrols on the river in Brazil? These are gunboats, general, they have armor and surely they could be moved safely?"

"Perhaps," the general said, but clearly he was losing interest in the conversation and he ignored me for the remainder of the dinner.

After dinner more drinks were poured and eventually the party broke up. I felt a tinge of guilt as I saw the general grab Melowa by her waist and pull her along with him as he stumbled out of the dining room and walked out into the night towards the rooms that surrounded the pool in the inner compound.

By 11p.m. I was back aboard the boat alone and wracking my brain to think of what to do next. I wondered about how much faith I could put in Melowa's brother coming through with the attack he had proposed. How would I ever know? But then I remembered the note I was supposed to float away from the boat and I quickly went back up into the galley and pulled out a garbage bag, filling it partially with air. I then wrote down the code we had agreed on and went up on the stern of the boat to release it into the river. It was only then that I realized that it was hopeless to think that the bag could make it all the way out to the open river and be found. The current this far up was negligible. The chances were much greater that it would be found by Carlos's people and that questions would be raised. I crumpled up the bag and stuffed it into the trash and was dismayed and upset by the time I finally went to bed.

Falling into a fitful sleep, I worried about what was happening to Melowa, and to Toby, and to my wife back in Cartagena. Clearly this situation had gotten completely out of control and I couldn't see a clear way out of it. My plan now seemed feeble and full of holes. So much could go wrong and any mistakes I made now could get us all killed.

Fourteen

It was after midnight when Alex Peterson awoke to the sound of voices and commotion outside his hut.

Dressing quickly, he emerged from the low doorway and made his way in the dark down towards the river where in the ambient light of a nearby small cooking fire he saw that a large group of men had assembled on the embankment. As he approached the water he saw that a dozen or more canoes had arrived during the night and approximately a hundred or maybe more men of all ages were milling about on the nearby shore, unloading the canoes and talking to each other in a variety of dialects.

Making his way closer to the center of activity, he was challenged by a young man with a spear. The warrior began shouting something at him and shaking the weapon near Peterson's chest. The reporter pulled back, but then a familiar face — one of the older men he had met in the first gathering — came forward and spoke to the young warrior and this seemed to calm him. While this had been going on, a group of warriors had gathered around them and soon an animated and urgent conversation ensued around him.

About this time, he noticed that his young interpreter had arrived and she sidled up to him, placing her hands on each side of his torso as if to protect him as she bravely joined in the banter. She quickly looked up at him and explained that she was telling them why he was here.

Soon the situation diffused and the men wandered away and back to what they had been doing. A few minutes passed and then a strong and insistent looking man in his early twenties came up to him and said in fairly good English, "So you are the reporter who will tell the world of our problems?"

"I'm a reporter, yes, but I'm also here to help as best I can. I want to accompany you on your attack of the place of the evil ones," Peterson said.

The native answered, "Yes, I have been told this. I will speak with my brothers and we will discuss this. We are planning to attack this place tomorrow night. I will not promise you, but I will see if I can convince them to let you come along. Can you fight?"

Peterson said, "I am a naval warrior and I know how to fight."

The young man looked up at him more closely in the firelight and nodded his head, turned and disappeared into the throng.

The young girl took the reporter's hand and led him up and away from the gathering saying, "Let them do their work and you should get some rest. I believe that tomorrow will be a long day."

Once he was back in his hut, he pulled out his sat phone and dialed his editor in New York, quickly telling the man, whom he had gotten out of bed, about the events that were about to unfold. He then signed off and called the senator. The low battery light was flashing by the time the senator came on the line and Alex tried to fill him in as quickly as possible about the recent developments and that he believed that the attack on the compound where his daughter was being held would happen within the next night or two.

♦♦♦

As soon as Senator Tatterson had hung up with the reporter, he dialed his friend Andy Winters at the CIA.

"Andy? Roger! Big developments!"

The agent responded, "What have you got, Rog? What's new?"

Tatterson quickly filled the agent in on the most recent intel from the reporter in the Amazon and also mentioned that the man had promised him that the morning edition of the New Times would likely erase any roadblocks that the White House had been putting up to prevent a military intervention.

"I'll see what I can do, buddy. Let's see what the next several hours bring," and the two disconnected.

SENATOR'S DAUGHTER KIDNAPPED. WHITE HOUSE ROADBLOCKING HELP, was the headline that erupted across the country that morning.

By 10 a.m., Tatterson's secretary had fielded dozens of calls from all over the world from reporters who were fishing for who the senator was that had lost a daughter, but so far they had been unsuccessful in tracking Tatterson down personally as the aggrieved man.

Marion had put through a few of the more important calls to the senator, who was entrenched in his office along with his wife June. These calls included a few of the senator's close friends and colleagues who had also been contacted, asking about when or if they could come forward with what they knew of this situation. Tatterson had elicited promises from them all that they would wait for a little longer, but knew deep down that it was only a matter of time until the best investigative minds in the media would fill in the blanks in the story and his secret would be out in the open. He prayed that the CIA would intervene soon enough to save his daughter before she was eliminated by the dangerous people who were holding her captive. He realized that it had been a calculated risk involving the reporter, but still felt that the hope that his daughter might be rescued by the military had outweighed the risks involved in getting the story public enough to elicit the proper response from the White House.

The one call that he had been waiting for came through at ten past ten. The president was on the line and said, "Roger? Nate. I've just read the newspaper and have been briefed by my advisers. I've been told that it was your own daughter that has been kidnapped. So sorry to hear about what happened. This is the first I've heard of this and I just want you to know that I've put my top people on this to see how we can intervene and rescue your daughter. What I'm hoping for is that you'll be able to tell us something we don't know. Can you come by my office in an hour? I'd like to have something settled by mid-afternoon and to issue a press release statement by 4 p.m."

Roger assented and the president quickly signed off. Tatterson was thinking, *Yeah, right. First I've heard.* And realized that by saying his top people would be responsible, the president meant that the vice president himself would be in charge of the operation. Great.

Tatterson re-read the article to try to reassure himself that his daughter's situation had not been endangered more by this recent development.

New Times reporter Alex Peterson has been traveling in secret, deep in the world of shadows that surrounds one of the most sinister offshoots of the burgeoning planet-wide drug trade.

Human trafficking in young women has been reported for some time and Peterson has recently discovered that one of our nation's own senators has recently lost his own daughter to this vile trade.

The New Times has learned that the senator has been refused help in recovering his daughter from the White House due to partisan obstruction and has been told by officials high in the administration that he must go about trying to solve his problem on his own.

Through personal observations, our reporter has unearthed evidence that many hundreds of young women are taken every year in our hemisphere alone and that due to the desire to not inflame international relations with the countries which are most often involved in this activity, the actual facts, nature and full scope of this trade have been hushed or ignored by people within our own government.

Further developments on this ongoing story will appear as they are reported.

Tatterson reflected that indeed, the story was vague enough that those who were not 'in the know' about the particulars of this situation would not likely be able to put the pieces of the puzzle together quickly enough to endanger his daughter's already precarious position.

At twenty past eleven Senator Tatterson was ushered into a small conference room deep under the White House.

Seated at the table were several high ranking military officers representing the Navy, Marines and Air Force. Tatterson also noticed Andy Winters and another man who he presumed was also CIA and the vice president all seated. He was shown to an empty chair by a guard and shortly after, the president entered the room through a small door at the far side of the room and sat down.

"OK," the president started in, "What have we got?"

He was looking directly at Winters from the CIA, who stood up and filled the men around the table in with what he knew of the situation. He went into great detail about the background of the cartel he believed was involved and about how there was another ongoing operation by Interpol that needed to be taken into account.

Just then there was a knock on the main door and when the guard opened it, two more men entered the room. They were quickly introduced as representatives of Interpol and the older of the two agents begged forgiveness for being tardy. "I had forgotten just how thorough and time-consuming your security precautions were when entering this level," he said in a dismissive way.

The vice president spoke up. "Please, tell us what you can about your own operations. As you have been briefed, one of our own senators' daughters has been abducted by elements of the same cartel you have been investigating, and it is this government's sworn duty to protect our citizens, so a military intervention is being considered at this juncture. Anything you can tell us that may assist us in the safe return of our citizen to her family is of the utmost importance to this government."

Tatterson thought to himself, *you creep, now you make it sound like all you wanted all along was to help.*

The Interpol agent immediately responded. "Mr. President, Vice President, esteemed colleges, for the last two years our agency has been involved in a deep cover operation with one of the most powerful drug cartels in Colombia. Through this operation we have learned not only of the actual levels of involvement of many of Colombia's most influential criminal elements in the running of the country's infrastructure, but also of how deeply intertwined the FARC rebellion is tied into the actual legitimate government's own elected officials. In many cases we have learned that both sides are being led by the same people! Through our agents' efforts, we have been able to compile a list of over twenty of these traitors to the legitimate government but believe there may be more of these people who we still have not identified. Through intel by our undercover agents, we have also by sheer luck learned of a possible cache of ancient artifacts that it has been speculated may be equal to, or possibly even greater than all of the wealth in gold and precious stones that were plundered by Pizarro and during the subsequent quelling of the Inca Empire."

The Interpol man let them ponder that for a moment, and then went on. "We are very close now to being in a position to not only provide a list of names of the traitors to the government of Colombia, but to also pinpoint the actual location of the alleged hidden treasure trove of ancient artifacts that may result in one of the greatest archaeological finds since the discovery of the treasures of ancient Egypt or the unearthing of the tombs of the Ming Dynasty."

As the Interpol agent finished, there was a murmuring of voices around the table.

The president was the first to speak. "Thank you for the information, sir, and you may have a seat."

Turning to his own CIA man, the president said, "Agent Winters. What is your assessment about the possible effects any intervention at this time might have on the ongoing operation that Interpol is conducting, and specifically, how could a rescue of Senator Tatterson's daughter, and any other hostages being held be best effected in such a way as to not undermine our allies' operations?"

Agent Winters stood up again and answered. "Mr. President, gentlemen, our agency has been informed of this situation for several weeks now and have in fact gathered valuable intel regarding the approximate location of the place where the hostages are being held. It is however not known whether there is any cache of artifacts hidden as this has not been brought to our attention until just recently. We have already performed one overflight of the area by one of our unmanned drones last week, and another flight is underway as we speak. It is possible that within an hour or two at the most that we will have the necessary intel to allow us to plan a military intervention. What we're missing, however, is an 'on the ground' asset. So, my suggestion will be that prior to any military intervention, we should endeavor to place an agent on the ground to provide us with the exact placement of defenses, where the prisoners are being held and ground level imagery of the best avenues of infiltration and of course, the most likely routes for extraction. These steps must all be taken before a successful intervention can be safely executed."

Senator Tatterson spoke up, raising his hand. "If I may, Mr. President?" The president nodded and Tatterson went on, still seated in his chair. "The source of the story we have all no doubt read, and which is undoubtedly the real reason why we are meeting here today," he said as he glared briefly at the vice president, "Is a reporter by the name of Alex Peterson who is at this very moment, near the epicenter of a rescue mission that is being undertaken by the native population of the immediate surrounding area."

"Please tell us all you can of this," the president said and as the CIA man sat down, Tatterson leaned forward in his chair and took the lead.

"As I am sure the vice president knows, because I was told several days ago that our government could not become involved in what I was told was 'my personal problems,' I contacted a reporter whom I'm sure most of you are well familiar with. Alex Peterson agreed to investigate this situation and has placed himself in the way of possible grave bodily harm in order to locate my daughter, and help to bring about her rescue. As of early this morning he contacted me by satellite telephone and informed me that the local Indian populace have mustered a force of over a hundred men with the intention of attacking the compound where the prisoners are being held in an effort to rescue them. From my understanding, as many as fifty or more of these natives' own family members or kin are also being held as slaves by the people who have taken my daughter captive. So any intervention that occurs must take into account that there may be another force on the ground which will be fighting for the same goals as us, but who may not be aware of our purpose or goals. This could result in, at the very best case, confusion in battle and in the worst case, unnecessary loss of life. Friendly fire deaths and even jeopardy of both rescue missions could be the result, and so I ask you to carefully assess the situation, as Agent Winters has suggested."

One of the military commanders spoke up. "Senator Tatterson, do you have the ability to communicate with this man at the site?"

"He has called me twice, but from what I understand, his sat phone battery is almost dead. I cannot be sure he'll try to contact me again, but if he does, what would you want me to tell him?"

Tatterson sat back as the men around the table began a heated debate about the best plan of action. Tatterson noticed the president listening carefully to the general drift of the debate and after several minutes he spoke up loudly saying "gentlemen please, may I have your attention?"

He went on, "I have made a decision. General Johanson, how quickly could a suitable force of Marines be assembled aboard our aircraft carrier off Colombia?"

Johanson said, "I can have a force there in twelve hours, if I give the order now."

The president then asked the air force general, "Would you be able to provide air power to support this operation in fourteen hours' time?" To which the general assented, and then the president asked the Admiral if his carrier force could steam in the direction closest to the area to provide a launch base for the Marine contingent and he was told that this would not be a problem.

The admiral added, "In anticipation of this eventuality, I have already placed my carrier force just off the coast, a little over an hour's flying time from the area of interest."

The president raised his eyebrows at this and with a slight nod of his head he then directed his attention to the CIA men. "I want you to have an agent on the ground within the next four hours, I will want hourly updates as the operation unfolds," and he addressed the Interpol agents who were looking a bit bewildered at the speed with which developments were unfolding.

"Gentlemen, please tell your superiors that this operation will be undertaken within the next eighteen hours and that under no circumstances do I believe that this will adversely affect the agents you have on the ground, unless of course they are in the immediate area of the intervention. If that's the case, I suggest that you warn them. I thank you for your input."

He looked up at the surrounding men and said, "Now. Let's get going on this. Dismissed."

The president quickly got up and left through the private door behind his chair.

♦♦♦

I woke up before dawn, having had a lousy night's sleep. I had been worrying about my wife, about the Indian girl and wondering what was being done to the young captain Toby.

I got up and went into the galley to make some coffee and noticed that it was raining fairly heavily outside. The air conditioners had drowned it out while I had been in the sleeping cabin. In a short while the rain began to come down so hard that visibility was reduced to almost zero. This gave me an idea.

If I could get over to the prison block in heavy rain, I might be able to gain access to the first cell and if indeed there was only one guard there, I might be able to overpower her and free the girls, and if the guard had keys and a gun, I might be able to free the other prisoners too.

As the dawn began to break, I ate a little breakfast and as soon as the rain subsided, I walked up to the guardhouse and spoke to the guard there. "Carlos told me to let you know when I was ready to have the blonde American girl come down to the boat to help me. I am ready for her now."

The disinterested guard stared at me sleepily, and I realized that I had just awakened him. Maybe he had slept through most of his shift.

"C'mon! I have a lot of work to do! I need her now!" I shouted. He jumped up and dialed a two digit number on the intercom I noticed that it was 24.

I turned and walked back down the dock and climbed aboard just as the rain started to fall more heavily again. About ten minutes later I saw two people coming up the dock and climbing aboard. I slid open the glass doors to the main salon, and the drenched American girl and a young guard I had not seen before came in.

"Whoa! You're both soaked!" I glared at the guard. "You, get out of here! I'll call for you when I am finished with her."

The guard quickly bowed out into the driving rain and I slammed the door shut. As soon as he had departed I took Jenny's arm and led her down to the aft cabin and told her to take a shower and warm herself back up. I gave her some dry clothes that I hoped might fit and went back up to the galley and made her some food. A few minutes later she reappeared, dressed in my clothes. She actually looked pretty good in my too big boxer shorts and button-up shirt.

I motioned her to sit down and as the rain continued to drum heavily on the cabin top, I placed some breakfast in front of her and took a seat opposite, cradling my coffee cup in my hands.

"So, tell me about your night," I said.

She finished her first mouthful of food and said, "Pretty damn awful actually. I hardly slept. The troll that was there earlier in the day left after dinner, which by the way totally sucked, and a male guard was there all night. He never stopped leering at us and made lewd comments off and on all night. Seemed like the two Slavic girls were pretty used to it and they ignored him, and Bridget is still so far in shock that she seems almost oblivious, but he could tell he was getting to me and seemed to love taunting me. I'm so fucking tired I feel like my bones ache."

"What about the sister? Captain Toby's?"

She said, "I never saw her all night. Guess there's another cell somewhere else?"

I told her to just relax and finish her food and asked her if she'd like some coffee or a nap instead. She said, "If I could just take an hour nap, I'd probably be a lot more useful."

"Jenny," I said, "I really don't need help on the boat, that was just an excuse to get you out of there. What we really need to be doing is to figure out how to break the others free and escape from here somehow. I've got a basic plan, but there's a lot of rough edges, so yeah, you get some sleep and as soon as you're back up and around, we'll start working out how this is going to go."

She nodded her head and got up to leave, picking up her dishes and I said, "forget the dishes, just go sleep." And she put them in the sink and padded down the stairs, went into my cabin and crashed.

The rain continued to thunder down.

◆◆◆

Alex Peterson woke up to the feeling of a wet bed. It was still dark and he realized that a pool of water had formed inside the doorway where he had failed to place the rain barrier. He quickly climbed out of the bed and stuffed the heavy cloth in place behind the door just as the rain began to come down even heavier. Crawling back into his bed, he listened to the solid roar of the rainfall and realized it was still probably another hour until the gradual lightening of dawn would come. Suddenly he realized there was someone in the hut with him, crouching in the shadows on the far side of his bed. The intruder spoke to him in fairly good English

"I have been told by the villagers that you are here to help bring the story of our people to the world. I am here to rescue my sister and the others that are being held as prisoners."

The man came out of the shadows and Peterson could see that he was the same young Indian man he had seen earlier that night down at the canoes. The one who had seemed like some sort of a leader.

The Indian said, "My name is Pulu. I came here to ask you to come with me now. I am going to go to the place where the prisoners are being held. I know a secret way there. If you wish to see this place, come with me now." The Indian stood.

Peterson quickly scrambled to his feet and, telling the Indian man he wanted to go, threw on some clothes and grabbed his camera.

"No, do not bring this or any other extra things. We will be swimming and we must go under the water to get into the caves. Just come with me now."

Peterson put his camera down but picked up his small waterproof flashlight and, stuffing it in his pocket, followed the man out into the predawn darkness.

They went down the embankment and together launched a small canoe that had an outboard motor. He hadn't noticed this boat earlier and realized it must have been hidden in amongst the other larger boats.

Only a few of the men were still moving around the landing; most of them had taken shelter in the huts and were asleep and so noiselessly the two slid the canoe out into the river and climbed in. Each grabbing a paddle, they worked their way out away from the bank. The Indian turned and lowered the outboard motor which started on the first pull. The rain began to ease a bit and the Indian said, "Pray the rain stays for a little while longer, *hombre*, we will need the noise to cover our approach."

The canoe headed further up the small tributary away from the main river, and in a short while they took a fork in the stream to the left which within ten minutes entered an area of small hillocks and deep ravines. The forest canopy in this area was very high, almost two hundred feet by what the reporter could see in the early morning twilight, and about a half hour into the trip the Indian edged the canoe into an embankment. They both jumped out into waist-deep water and pulled the canoe deeper into the bushes which overhung the bank, effectively hiding it from anyone passing by in the main channel. The Indian tapped Peterson on the shoulder and motioned him to follow.

Scrambling up the muddy embankment and over a slight rise they came upon a low swampy area, and within a few minutes Peterson saw that they were at the mouth of a low cave. The Indian crawled inside and Alex followed. It was immediately dark inside, but it was nice to be out of the rain, at least for a short while, he thought.

The Indian man turned on a small flashlight. *Glad he has that*, Peterson thought and he followed the man deeper into the cave.

"How did you find this place?" Peterson asked.

The Indian signaled with his finger to be quiet and said in a hushed voice, "I spent several weeks looking for a way into the compound where I thought my sister was being held. I found this place by accident. We are only a short distance from the place they hold the prisoners, but we must swim under a low place up ahead. It was not so hard last week, but now the river is already rising. In a few more days, if this rain continues, it will not be possible. Follow me now."

Peterson nodded and followed the Indian into a dark pool with a low ceiling. The Indian entered the water and whispered, "Keep closely behind me. Sometimes there are people on the other side. It is about thirty meters away under the water but it is straight and easy. Just keep my feet in sight. This is why I waited until it was light out, otherwise it is easy to get lost. There is a current about half the way across in there, so be careful! Follow me. Do not hesitate!" And with that the Indian ducked under and swam away. Peterson quickly followed. Taking a deep breath, he plunged into the inky darkness and swam down.

Looking around he saw a glimpse of bubbles and a faint light down and to his right. He swam down and followed the bubbles. In about thirty seconds he felt a strong current pulling at him and the darkness was encroaching all around, but he could still see a glimmer of light ahead and he fought harder to keep up with the small man.

Within another twenty seconds, just as his lungs were beginning to burn, he saw the light get much brighter and he realized he was nearing the end of the tunnel. Seconds later he burst to the surface, taking a deep breath.

"Shhhh!" The Indian grabbed his arm and tried to quiet him, whispering in his ear. "Be very quiet! We are close to their guardhouse!"

Peterson saw that they had surfaced under a low overhang with roots and vines nearly covering the recess. Just a few feet away, there was a walkway and as his eyes adjusted, he could see that there was a wire fence and a small building. The Indian signaled him to follow and they both gradually emerged from the shadows of the roots and entered a pool of water adjacent to the guardhouse. Peterson realized that he was on the far side of a small basin and across the water, about twenty yards away, were several boats. On his right there were two medium size catamarans and three smaller boats that looked like patrol craft, and across the lagoon to his left, inside a second fence was a much larger catamaran. The rain was thundering down heavily now and he felt a tug at his arm. The Indian was signaling him to retreat back into the shadows of the overhang.

Back in amongst the roots the young Indian man said, "I want you to stay here. I will swim across the lagoon under water and try to get inside the inner lagoon. If I can, I will go to where the people are being held and see if I can see or hear my sister."

Before Peterson could object, the Indian ducked under water and swam away. Peterson paused for a few seconds, gathering his thoughts and then took several deep breaths and followed, making for the big cat across the breadth of the lagoon.

With the floodlights from the compound to help him judge his direction and in the gradually lightening day, Peterson swam powerfully under water towards the inner harbor area and within a short while saw in the gloom the bottom of the heavy inner fence. Working his way along the bottom of it, he found the opening and continued on towards the bright lights he had seen that illuminated the dock area where the cat was tied up.

About thirty seconds later, he saw a dark shape up ahead and realized it was one of the hulls of the big cat. Carefully swimming along the bottom, he dodged under the boat and surfaced noiselessly between the hulls, directly under the low cockpit area.

He was alone. The young Indian had obviously gone a different way.

Peterson took stock of the situation and was just about ready to make for the nearby shore where he heard footsteps on the pier and the noise of people coming aboard the boat.

Pulu surfaced under the walkway on the far side of the inner lagoon. He had come this way several times and knew it well, but this was the first time he had ever dared intrude in daylight. Still, it was quite early and it was raining heavily, so he edged his way into the shore and slid up onto the stones that lined the lagoon and crawled up onto the edge of the terrace of the pool house, using the beach chairs and tables as cover. He sensed that no-one would be looking this way so early in the morning and he flitted from the cover of the furniture, scrambling from table to table until he was near the first of the glass windows that looked out onto the terrace. Just then, he saw movement to his left and he froze. One of the sliding doors had opened and he silently withdrew his knife. With his back against the wall he slid in alongside one of the small planters that lined the poolside walls of the sleeping rooms and waited as a person walked towards him. Just as he was about to lunge he saw two small brown feet and part of the leg of a small woman or perhaps a child. He held his breath as a woman came into view. She was facing away from him, unaware of his presence and was looking left and right, clearly unsure of what to do. She was dressed only in a white nightshirt and his heart skipped a beat as he realized that it was his sister Melowa!

Risking being heard, he made one of the animal calls he and his sister had used years ago when they were children playing in the forest.

Melowa nearly shrieked when she heard the bird call close behind her. She knew this was her brother's own special call and it was so close!

Looking over her shoulder to her right she saw him immediately, hidden behind a planter.

Melowa froze. The danger they were both in flooded her every pore, and she stared at him silently, not sure of what to do next.

Pulu signaled her to follow him and he led her quickly across the patio to the edge of the water. They both slid into the lagoon, Melowa shedding her cover-up which was white and would make it too easy to be seen in the rapidly lightening day. The rain was coming down so heavily now that the guardhouse was invisible and they both swam a short way along under the pier and then ducked down under the catamaran, surfacing in between the hulls.

Peterson nearly gulped water as the two Indians emerged next to him and Pulu, seeing him there, did a double take too. Neither said a word and Melowa looked at her brother inquisitively. Pulu said very quietly, "We will need to swim back the way we have come. It is much harder to find the opening swimming that way. It is all darkness. Both of you must follow me closely."

Peterson said, looking at the Indian girl, "I need to know where the American girl, the one they call Jenny, is being kept."

Melowa whispered quietly, her voice barely discernible above the roar of the rainfall. "I know this girl Jenny! They are keeping the people all down in the three rooms past the guardhouse. You will never be able to get there in the daylight!"

Pulu said, "You must come away now, you will be captured if the rain stops."

Peterson shook his head and answered, "I'll stay here. I need to find the American girl. You two escape. I'll find my own way back, but can you wait for me on the other side? Give me a half hour, then if I'm not there, go on back to the village and I'll find some place to hide 'till tonight. Now go!"

The two siblings looked at each other and then Pulu took a deep breath and slipped beneath the water and Melowa followed. Peterson continued to silently tread water while he planned his next move.

Swimming quickly under water, Melowa followed her brother closely. Taking special care not to get too close to the surface, she brushed the dark muddy bottom several times and only just managed to keep him in sight as they passed the edge of the fence and made their way across the outer lagoon.

A minute later they both surfaced inside the small overhang and, breathing heavily, regained their strength for the next swim.

"How do we get away from here, my brother?" Melowa asked urgently and her brother whispered,

"Follow me closely." Pulu produced a short length of rope and continued. "It is a long swim. Do not lose hold of this rope!" He began breathing rapidly and Melowa did the same. Then he slid underwater and Melowa followed.

A minute later they both emerged in the small pool on the far side of the hillock which separated the two tributaries.

◆◆◆

"What the hell are you telling me?" Carlos shouted. The guard had awoken him and Carlos saw that the general and two other guards were all standing outside his door in the driving rain. "Come inside, quickly!" he said.

The four men entered Carlos's room and Anita closed the door to the adjacent bedroom.

"Now, tell me again, what has happened?"

General Alverado said, "Your 'Indian Princess' has escaped! Why did you not tell me she was unfaithful?"

The general was obviously very upset and Carlos thought quickly before responding, "General Alverado, please understand, I had no idea she might try to leave! We have so many of her people here as prisoners, I never expected her to try to escape! Are you sure she has not just gone off to the bathroom or back out to the catamaran?"

The general turned and spoke to the guards saying, "Go search the pool house and the marina complex. Now!"

◆◆◆

A few minutes after the two Indians had left, the rain began to ease. Peterson edged closer to the stern and tried to overhear the voices above him. He recognized a man and a woman's voice and, pressing his ear against the underside of the cockpit, heard what they were saying.

It was the woman talking. "I'm sure I heard voices, Brice. Just listen."

"Jenny, please, try to relax. I don't hear anything. The rain can do that sometimes. Makes you think you're hearing voices."

Peterson couldn't believe it. What were the odds that the girl he was looking for would be standing right above him? He edged out past the stern, which luckily was facing away from the shore and was not visible from the main area of the compound. Looking up he saw that the man and woman were standing right above him, peering out across the lagoon.

She said, "I think I saw something over near the inner gate. Bubbles, I'm pretty sure of it!"

Peterson spoke quietly. "Hey! Are you Jenny Tatterson?"

We both jumped back and then looked intently into the water

"Who the hell are you?" I asked.

Seeing the big blonde man treading water directly below me gave me quite an adrenaline shot. I crouched down, looking to my left to make sure I wasn't being observed. The rain had lessened so much now that the guardhouse was easily visible.

I didn't see any movement there so I ventured a further exchange. "How'd you get in here?"

The blonde man looked up at me and said, "My name's Alex Peterson. I'm a reporter from New York. I found out about you from Senator Tatterson and your employer, a Mr, Bellows, and have tracked you down. I need to get Jenny out of here. Will you help me?"

My mind reeled as I thought about all the implications for the other prisoners and my wife if I tried to make a break for it now. I said, "It's too dangerous for us to try to escape now. My wife is being held prisoner in Cartagena by a man named Ramon. He's the head of the cartel that owns this compound. His brother is here, a guy named Carlos. If we try to escape now, I'll just get my wife killed and maybe the others too."

Jenny cut in, "I need to try to help the others escape. I can't just run away now!"

Peterson said, "There are about a hundred Indians getting ready to attack the compound tonight. I'm not sure what time, but maybe we can do something about the others then?"

He was clearly unsure of what to do and as he held on to the transom of the boat, I heard voices off to my left behind me on the shore. In a moment, we'd be seen.

I said, "There are people coming. We'll wait for tonight. If you can have them create a diversion, I may be able to get the prisoners down here to the boat. Maybe we can make a run for it then."

Peterson said, "I'll try to warn you," and he ducked under the water just as I heard footsteps on the finger pier next to the boat.

I grabbed Jenny by her hair and pulled her head back and shouted, "I told you to get back to work!" just as Carlos and General Alverado came into view alongside the boat.

"Capitan Brice!" Carlos shouted. "What are you doing with the girl?"

I released Jenny, who stumbled backwards but quickly regained her balance. She realized what I had done and why and rubbed her neck saying "I'm sorry, Carlos, I couldn't help it. I'm just so tired. I'll try harder to help out though. Please don't send me back to the cell yet!"

I took the cue and added, "I'm sorry too, Carlos, I didn't mean to hurt her. No harm meant!"

Carlos lowered his voice and said, "Never mind. We're looking for the Indian girl Melowa. Has she come out here?"

"I haven't seen her," I answered "But I was asleep for quite a while, so I can't be sure. Maybe we should search the boat?"

Carlos seemed mollified by my response and Alverado said, "Yes, search the boat!"

Two other men who had been following the general and Carlos scrambled aboard the cat and slid the door to the cabin open. I said, "At least take your shoes off down below! This ain't no damn work boat!"

I turned to Carlos and said, "When did she go missing?"

Carlos said, "The general isn't sure. Sometime during the night."

Alverado spoke up. "When I woke up, she was gone. But her side of the bed was still warm. I think she has not been gone long."

I thought for a second and said, "Maybe she's just gone for a walk. I'm sure she'll turn up."

I turned and went into the main cabin and the two older men followed. Jenny stayed out in the cockpit, watching us.

Over the next five minutes the two soldiers searched the boat thoroughly and announced, "She is not here."

Alverado said, "We will go search the rest of the grounds."

Carlos added, "I will get more men to help with the search."

The four men left but just as Carlos stepped off, he looked back and said, "The girl is not to be marked or damaged, Capitan. Just remember, she is mine and so do not blemish her."

He turned and walked away.

Jenny collapsed against my side with the suddenness of the passing of the danger we had just endured and said, "That was close!"

I put my arm over her shoulder and said, "Sorry if I hurt you. It was the only thing I could think of on such notice"

Jenny smiled and said, "It wasn't so bad. Now, what should we do next?"

I led her inside and slid the glass doors shut but then saw Carlos reappear in the cockpit. I went back outside and he said, "Capitan, we are going to go search the tunnels. I wondered if you would like to see more of this place? It is quite amazing."

He was smiling now and I said, "That'd be great, Carlos, I'll send the girl back to her quarters." And then I added, "Wow, the general sure looked upset!"

"Yes, he has bad luck with women," Carlos chuckled and said, "If I had to sleep with that man, I'd run away too!" and then he grew more serious and added, "But we are going to go search for her in the tunnels in a short while. First I must go speak with Santiago. He has been interrogating the young Capitan Toby since last night and says he has some information for me. Meet us over at the guardhouse in a half hour. We will go in from there."

◆◆◆

Peterson waited under the boat while things calmed down onshore. After a flurry of activity and loud conversation on the boat, the group of men had left. A short while later he heard Brice and Jenny go onto the finger pier and he heard Brice say, "If you can hear me, Peterson, I'd give it a few minutes before I tried to make a break from here. They'll all be on high alert looking for the girl." And the two walked down the pier and on to the shore.

About a half hour later, it started to rain again and in a short while the rain had begun to come down hard enough that he decided to make a break for the tunnel.

Swimming powerfully across the bottom of the lagoon, he got slightly lost and only just found the fence in time as his lungs were beginning to feel as if they would burst. He edged around the opening and risked surfacing for a moment next to the post. The rain was still thundering down and the guardhouse was barely visible, but only about forty feet away. He got his bearings and ducked down to continue his swim.

Surfacing inside the overhang, he heard shouting onshore. He had been spotted! Several rifle shots erupted and broken branches and parts of roots hit him in the face. Without a seconds hesitation, he took a deep breath and ducked under the water, swimming quickly away from the opening.

As the light faded behind him he tried his best to figure out which way to swim to make it through to the other side. In a moment he felt a strong current and realized he was at the fork he had swum through coming in. Trying his hardest he struggled to get out his Maglite, and correcting for the current, struck out for where he hoped the tunnel was but in a moment hit hard on a rock and nearly gulped water. The water was muddy and the light was of almost no use. He felt himself being dragged away by the current and fought to pull himself up against the stream of water. Nothing he could do could overcome the pull and in his struggle to hold on he nearly dropped his light. He realized that with all the rain that had been falling, the current had become a torrent. Surely this was what had formed all these tunnels in the past and he felt himself being pulled along. He banged into another rock and was nearly knocked out. As his lungs began to burn he realized that he was probably going to drown.

Just as he was feeling like he would have to gulp some water — the reflex was so strong it took all his thoughts to keep his lungs closed, suddenly he felt the current lessen and his head broke the surface. He gasped for breath and desperately reached out, clinging onto a rock to keep from being swept farther along the tunnel. Gradually he felt the strength returning to his limbs.

After a few more minutes his heart rate had slowed and he was able to take stock of his situation. It was pitch dark and there was no way he could swim up against the current. He shone his light in a sweep around the small air pocket he was in and saw that there was a low arch with darkness behind. He decided to see if there was a lip to the tunnel or a place where he could climb out of the water, and slowly he swam away from the current, deeper into what sounded, from the echoing of the water, like a fairly large cavern.

Suddenly lights came on! He quickly glanced all around to get his bearings and saw that he was in a very large pool. The pool was probably a hundred feet across and he saw that there was a landing of sorts off to one side with quite a few steps leading up to a level area. He swam slowly along the side and climbed out onto the landing.

The lights were crudely strung up along the sides of the dry side of the cavern, and illuminated a tunnel which led off at an angle from the dark pool. Regaining his resolve, he stood up and made his way off along the tunnel.

His every nerve and sense were heightened by the danger he was in, so when he heard voices in the distance, he froze.

♦♦♦

Melowa jumped as the rifle shots rang out a short distance away just over the small hill.

Her brother Pulu said, "We have waited too long already. They have probably shot him. We must go."

He dragged her along and she reluctantly got into the small boat which they paddled quietly out of the tributary and into the larger stream, heading back down river toward the village. After ten minutes he started the outboard and in a little over an hour they were ashore in the village.

Pulu gathered the other warriors around him as he gave them a briefing of what he had found in the compound, and told the men that they should all hide their canoes. With the escape of his sister, and the other American man still missing, he expected that a patrol craft might come this way and would surely report seeing such a large group of boats.

He told the men that they should be ready to start the attack just after darkness and the Indians all scattered and paddled off along the river, finding hiding places along the banks.

♦♦♦

I led Jenny back to the guardhouse and the guard motioned me to escort her on down to the detention block. Surprised that I was being allowed to go to the cell block unaccompanied now after my experience the previous day, we sauntered down the walkway and knocked on the first door which, after a few seconds, opened. The same brute of a woman I had seen earlier was there and appeared to be alone. I said in my poor Spanish, "I have the girl for you now. I also must see the other girl I brought. I have been told to check on her now."

The guard looked unsure but then swung the door open and let us both in. I saw that there was a single door to a large fenced in area. The cage was only light chicken wire and I saw that it would not be hard to break in if I had the right tools. The woman said, "You see, she is fine."

I looked into the pen and saw four women. Aside from the French girl Bridget, there were two other blonde women who appeared to be in their early twenties and who looked dirty and rather disheveled, and a strikingly beautiful Latina woman who I guessed was Toby's sister. She had a black eye, and had abraded wrists and a nasty bruise on her thigh. I imagined they had been using her to gain information from the young captain.

I said to Jenny, "You will stay here until I call for you again," and I turned to the guard as I motioned towards Jenny, saying, "I will come for this one later," and I turned and left.

Walking briskly back down the walkway I came around the corner and went up to the far guardhouse. This one was at the far end of the compound past the lagoon and up against a cliff face that was alongside the inner fence. I saw that Carlos and one of his men, the same huge man whom I had been introduced to when we first arrived, were already there.

"Where is the general?" I asked.

Carlos answered, "He is conducting his own search along the river. He has taken two of his patrol boats and believes he will find his woman that way. This is good actually." Carlos smiled and added, "There are some things I would like to show you that I do not wish the general to see."

We all entered the guardhouse and I saw that there was a heavy steel door in the face of the cave inside the room. The door was set in bricks and mortar which was closing off what appeared to be a natural opening in the rock about six feet square.

The large menacing looking guard I had met the previous day at the other guardhouse was there, and stood aside as he swung the heavy door open for us, staring at me as the three of us went inside. The door closed behind us and my eyes adjusted to the gloom. A long string of lights was suspended out along a tunnel which led off into the cliff face.

I followed Carlos and his man and we walked through the winding tunnel which at times came to branches leading off to God only knows where, but these side tunnels were only sporadically lit. After a short while, we came to a large room and a narrow shaft which led up to the right. We all stooped down and one by one climbed some crudely cut but well-worn steps which in a short while led to another smaller room. At the far end of the room was a heavy door made of wood with strong looking hinges made of what appeared to be solid gold. I was shocked to see that the doorknob was a golden human skull, and Carlos produced a large key of unusual design which he inserted into the mouth of the skull. He turned it with a judicious use of force and I heard a loud click. The door swung open.

Inside was a room about thirty feet by eighty feet which was absolutely filled with treasure! I had never seen so much gold and so many rare gems before, even in photos. I was speechless and Carlos said, "This is the treasure that has kept my family strong and powerful for many generations. It is from this treasure that we are now selling some pieces. It is unfortunate, but it must be done."

Carlos reached over to a small pile of items near the doorway and took two hand-sized figurines, holding them up for me to see. They were erotic representations of women in unusual poses, and appeared to be made of gold.

"You see, these are small, but very special. We will smuggle these to our buyers in Europe on the next backpacker run and each one will likely fetch over two hundred thousand dollars."

I said, "This is amazing, Carlos! I had no idea such things still existed. This reminds me of the story of the lost city of El Dorado!"

Carlos chuckled and said, "You are correct, Capitan Brice, this *is* in fact the treasure of the lost city. It was saved here by the Incas when the first of the Spanish invaders fell upon our people. It has been hidden here ever since."

I looked around again and said, "Why show this to me though, Carlos? Don't get me wrong, I am very impressed, but what can I do to help you with this?"

Carlos suddenly became very serious. "Capitan Brice, we will need a new way to get this treasure out of the Amazon. And we need to make a much larger shipment this time. Taking it by boat might be the safest way and our route through the San Blas is becoming too well watched. I am thinking that you could bring some of this treasure out on one of the smaller catamarans and deliver it to Europe for us. It seems to me that many boats travel that way every year and so one more boat coming into France would not be noticed, yes?"

I replied, "That could work, Carlos, but what if we were stopped along the way by one of the patrol boats?"

Carlos smiled and said, "You are an American yachtsman, and you will bring your lovely wife with you, and maybe also a crew of nice looking people. You will have the necessary papers and you could make this trip in a short while. How long do you think it would take to go back down the river and sail up into France?"

I said, "Well, I'd have to see the other boats, and to prepare. It might take a week or two to get a boat ready, and then three weeks to get down the river, and another three to four weeks across to France. When would you like this to begin?"

Carlos laughed, "This a crazy plan! No, Capitan, we will not do it this way. I was just playing with your mind."

I looked at him with confusion as he said, "No, if we need to move this much treasure, we will put it on a freighter. I just wanted to see your face, Capitan!"

The guard laughed also now and I stood uneasily, shifting my weight a little as I waited to see where this was leading.

"Why show this all to me now then?"

Carlos suddenly became serious. "Because this treasure chamber will become your tomb, Capitan!"

The guard that was standing next to Carlos pulled out a gun and clubbed me over the head. I tried to turn to defend myself, but stumbled and he hit me again. I fell to my knees and heard Carlos speak in a voice that was seething with anger. "Capitan Toby has told me all about your involvement and that it was you all along who has been betraying us!"

I was struck again on the head and darkness came over me as I collapsed on the ground.

◆◆◆

After Alex Peterson had regained his composure, he followed the sound of the voices along the passageway until he came to a better lit, broader tunnel. He heard the voices much closer now coming from the left and he stealthily edged his way along the damp craggy wall, ready to bolt back the way he had come if he was spotted or if the men turned to come back.

A minute later he saw in the gloom that there were three men standing in a small room. They were all looking up at something to their right and so Peterson stayed silent, jammed up against the slight bend in the tunnel.

A moment later the three men disappeared from view and after about thirty seconds, Peterson went on. He emerged from the main tunnel into the room and saw that there was a worn stone staircase going up from there. He gathered his resolve and quietly edged up the steps, listening for sounds. In a short while he emerged into another small room and saw that there was a large doorway which was open. He heard voices coming from inside and crept closer to see if he could overhear what was being said.

Listening intently, he heard two men. One sounded like the American captain and the other sounded Colombian. They were talking animatedly and then suddenly, there was laughter and a loud thud, followed by another thud and the sound of something hitting the floor. Peterson heard more conversation and then another thud followed by a another quick exchange in Spanish with a third man, and then he heard the voices coming his way. He stole back down the staircase and went down a small side tunnel he had seen coming in and hid just around a bend.

No sooner had he taken his hiding place than he heard the men emerge into the small room, and after a short exchange they went down the passageway the way they had come. Peterson stayed put for another minute and then quickly went back into the room and climbed the steps into the upper chamber with the door. The door was now closed and he tried the knob, but it was clearly locked. Searching around from left to right he looked for something with which to pry the door, just as the room was plunged into total darkness.

The reporter carefully felt his way along the floor and edged up to the doorway. He could feel the planks of the door and listened carefully for any sound from the other side. Nothing.

The dark was oppressive and almost suffocating, and with absolutely no light, his eyes began to play tricks and he could imagine seeing things. But his experience had taught him that this was an illusion that must be ignored. He didn't want to waste his light because he had no idea how long he might be trapped in this labyrinth. Leaning up against the heavy door he rested, thinking about a plan of action.

◆◆◆

I woke up with a bad headache. As I gradually became aware of my surroundings, the events of the recent past came flooding back to me. I realized that I had been duped into thinking that Carlos still trusted me and imagined that Toby must have spilled what he knew in an effort to save his sister. I could hardly blame him. That would explain the bruises I had seen on the girl.

I sat up and felt around in the dark for my small flashlight which I always carried out of habit. Thankfully I had remembered to charge it not long ago.

I fumbled around until I found the switch and turned it on.

My thin bean of light cut across the treasure chamber and I scrambled to my feet. Standing somewhat unsteadily, I panned the light around the room to see more of where I was. I then focused on the heavy door handle and realized that it was a blind lock – no way to open it from the inside. Just then I thought I heard something from outside the door. It was a faint voice and I listened carefully.

"Cannon, is that you? Can you hear me?"

I shouted, "Yes, I can hear you! Who is it?"

"It's Alex. I'm just outside the door, I can see light coming from in there. Do you have a flashlight?"

I said, "Yes, it's only a small one and doesn't last very long. Do you want me to pass it that way? I can't see anything in here that might be used as a pry bar. If you can't see anything out there, please pass it back!"

He said, "I have my own light but I'm saving it for when I really need it. I suggest you do the same."

I turned my light off and once again was plunged into complete darkness. I saw his light come on from the other side of the door, a faint glow coming in through the crack at the base of the heavy door, and heard him speaking again.

"I don't see anything out here. Let me go back down the passageway and see if I can find something. I'll be back soon!"

I realized that relying on the reporter was my best chance and so I said, "Good luck."

I sat down with my back against the door. The minutes turned into an hour, then two. I was beginning to lose hope.

Fifteen

Juliet awoke to a hand over her mouth. She struggled for a moment until she realized that it was Frederica who was trying to awaken her without sound, and so she stopped struggling and lay quietly as the woman withdrew her hand, making a shush motion with her finger over her mouth. She then leaned towards Juliet and whispered, "I have just overheard a telephone conversation from Ramon's brother Carlos's son, Santiago. Apparently they have found out about you and Brice and they are about to take him prisoner."

"What happened?" Juliet asked and Frederica said,

"From what I could understand, they were torturing one of the prisoners and he or she told them that your husband was there to rescue them. That's all I know. I think that Ramon will lock you up soon, or maybe even kill you. I think you should try to slip over the side and swim to the shore."

Juliet quickly got up and threw on some clothes, trying to be as quiet as possible. Frederica continued, "I'll leave the door unlocked. Just go quickly. It should be light in less than an hour but if you can get into the woods, then make your way north over the mountain. I think there is a Kuna Indian settlement over on the other bay and you should be able to get away north from there. I'm sorry, Juliet. I really am."

Juliet thanked her and Frederica quickly withdrew.

One minute later Juliet crept stealthily out along the passageway and onto the side deck; she slid over the side and slipped into the water, hoping the splash wasn't heard and as she surfaced alongside, she listed carefully for any sound of alarm. Nothing.

Calming her nerves, she tried not to think about sharks or salt water crocodiles, and made her way as quietly as possible in gentle side strokes towards the gloom of the distant northern shore. It was at least a mile and after forty minutes, she felt the bottom under her feet and scrambled ashore amongst mangroves and low trees.

She managed to make her way onto firm ground but was badly scratched up in the process. She was still breathing heavily as the sky was gradually beginning to brighten and as soon as she could see well enough to make her way through the underbrush, she started to climb the hill, making her way as best she could to the north.

As she climbed, the trees became thinner and soon she could occasionally get a glimpse of the bay where Aztec Gold lay at anchor.

After about an hour she was nearly at the crest of the ridge and she came to a clearing where she could get a good look at the bay. Below her she could see that there were people running around on the deck of the boat and that they had launched the dinghy. She watched in terror as she saw three men jump into the dinghy and speed towards the shore where she had been only a short time earlier. She immediately got to her feet and ran for the top of the mountain.

Ten minutes later she had crested the top of the ridge and saw below her another bay, smaller than the one she had been in. She saw that there was a small village against the opposite shore and she moved as quickly as she could down the slope towards the smaller bay. All she could think of was to get as far away from the men as she could and so thirty minutes later she was at the water's edge, unsure of what to do next.

She stopped in her tracks when she heard behind her, from high up on the ridge in Spanish, "She came this way. I see how she has traveled."

Juliet plunged into the forest again and tried to make her way parallel to the shoreline in the general direction of the head of the bay, but the going was difficult. Lots of close brush blocked her way and she was forced to move part way back up the slope, which she realized put her closer to the men who were in pursuit.

Moments later she burst through some brush onto a clearing. It was a farmed plot of land and several Kuna Indian men, alarmed by her sudden appearance, dropped their tools and stared at her in disbelief. She realized she must have been quite a sight – torn clothing, drenched and covered in dirt, her hair wild and full of branches and twigs. She tried to speak calmly in her rudimentary Spanish, hoping that one of the Indians would understand. "(So sorry! I am afraid! I am being chased by bad men with guns who are trying to kill me. Please help me!)"

The Kuna men stared at her for a moment and then conversed rapidly in what she assumed was their own language and then the older of the three said in Spanish, "Who are these men? Where are they now?"

Just then they all heard a shout from not far behind her, part way up the hill. "She's doubled back, I think she is heading for the Indian village!"

The older man said quietly, "Come. Follow me," and to the other two young men he said, "Tell them we have not seen any white women. Try to stall them, but be careful!"

The man signaled Juliet to follow and they both ran off down a well-trodden path towards the village she had seen.

Halfway past the head of the bay they came to a fork in the trail and the man signaled her to follow him up a hill. Juliet was beginning to become winded but did her best to follow the older man who seemed to run with almost no effort. Ten minutes later they crested another ridge and they went down a steep incline towards the sound of a rushing river.

The pathway ended at a landing where there was a dugout canoe tied to a tree. The man signaled for Juliet to get inside and he quickly untied the boat and pushed it away from the shore.

The canoe was soon gripped in the gentle current and making good time downstream. She crouched down and then heard the men who had been pursuing her. "She must have gone up this trail, not into the Indian village. Follow me!"

The older man understood this and pushed her down into the bottom of the boat saying, "Stay still. I will cover you with my fishing nets."

A few minutes later she could feel that they had entered calmer waters and the man paddled rapidly away from the shoreline. She lay still in the bottom of the boat but never heard any more sounds from the pursuing men. An hour later, the man tapped her shoulder and told her that it was safe to sit up.

She looked around and saw that they had entered a huge section of water with dozens of distant islands dotting the horizon, and the dense jungle coming right down to the water's edge was close alongside on their left. They were traveling north and soon the man rigged the small sail and they leaned over in the medium strength trade winds, making good speed to the north, away from danger.

She said, "Thank you so much for rescuing me! I don't even know your name!"

The old man said, "My name is Arturo and I am happy to save you from the bad men. Life has been too calm for me lately." He said this with a slight smile in his eyes and went on, "This will make a good story for my grandchildren to hear! Who are the men, and why were they chasing you?"

Juliet did her best to explain all that had been happening, and that she needed to get to a settlement that had a telephone so that she could contact her people.

The old man said, "I will take you to a place where you will find a phone. It is a place where some of the gringo boats go. They always have phones! It will take us half the day to reach there, so relax and here, have some water."

The old man settled back against his steering oar and they slid along nicely, doing close to six knots.

♦♦♦

"What are you telling me? She has escaped too?" Carlos couldn't believe what his older brother was saying. "Why can't you find her? We must eliminate both of these people. They know too much about our operation!"

Ramon laughed and said, "Relax, my brother. The woman knows nothing. And she will not last more than a few days in the jungle. The Indians here will kill her, or maybe eat her. They are savages. Just relax. It is all fine."

Carlos said, "I have locked her husband in the treasure vault to die. But perhaps I should have questioned him?"

Ramon thought for a moment and said, 'Yes, this would be a good idea. Torture him and find out how much he knows. Tell him that we will torture his wife if he does not tell us everything. And kill the young captain. He is of no further use to us."

"What about keeping him alive so that his sister will cooperate for sex?" Carlos asked.

"Kill her too. I am tired of all this. It is time to clean up the messiness. Just do it."

Ramon punched the end button on his sat phone and looked over at Frederica, who was tied up in a chair and bleeding. He had been beating her for almost an hour, questioning her about the disappearance of the American woman, but so far she had only said that she loved him and was still begging him to stop. She sobbed quietly and Ramon wondered if perhaps she really was innocent.

He said, "Tell me again. Why did you help the American woman to escape?" He struck her across her broken jaw and she howled in pain.

"I did not help her! I went to make sure she was still in her cabin. I did not help her! Please, Ramon. Why would I help that woman? She is nothing to me! You are my man and I only want to help you! I only want to have you forgive me. I did nothing wrong!"

Ramon looked over at Javier and said, "Cut her free and have her get cleaned up. We will continue this questioning later."

♦♦♦

Melowa and Pulu were in the largest hut as food was brought and the elders, as well as some of the warriors from the other tribes, crowded around them listening to what they had to say.

Pulu was telling them, "The water has risen in my secret way into the compound, but if the rain does not continue, I think I can still get inside again tonight. I will take two or three good warriors with me and we will kill the guards that stand at the gates to the compound, then the rest can come over the hill and enter the water outside the gate. It is only a short swim across to the buildings and we will surprise the soldiers and workers."

One of the elders said, "How will we be sure our men can make it into this compound without being observed?"

Pulu said, "With my men, we will use poison darts to kill the guards, and then we will give the call of the toucan to signal that it is safe to come."

One of the younger warriors from outside the circle said, "I will come with you, Pulu!" The young man was the older brother of the American reporter's interpreter.

Two others spoke up and asked to join and it was quickly decided who would accompany the initial probe into the compound.

Then Melowa stood up and spoke defiantly in her native tongue. "I will come with you also. It is my friends and my people too that are held prisoner there. Many of them know I have been brought there and so they will know that I have escaped too. This will give them hope and if I am there to speak to them, I will rally them to revolt against the masters and help us take over the place."

Pulu started to object but one of the elder tribesmen put his hand on Pulu to stop him. There was silence and the leader removed his hand from Pulu's shoulder and said, "This is a wise plan. This is how it will be done."

The elder then looked Pulu in the eyes and said, "Many of our own people are prisoners and slaves of these men, and many of us have lost loved ones from the evil these men have brought on us. It is your sister's right to be allowed to help. We will all be helping in every way that is possible." The old man looked at the men around him and stood, raising his voice to be heard outside the hut as well, saying "Hear me now! This night marks the beginning of the time when we will avenge the wrongs that have been brought against our people. This night we will kill the evil ones and set our people free! Go now and prepare for battle!"

A cry rang out from the men in the hut and was echoed throughout the village. A cry for war. A cry for vengeance.

◆◆◆

Senator Tatterson hung up the phone and slumped in his chair. His wife June spoke to him. "What is it, dear? What did they say?"

Tatterson answered, "That was Andy at the CIA. He says that the weather's too thick to get a good idea of what's happening on the ground, and that until things clear up they can't move forward with this. Jesus, June, I have no idea what to do!"

His wife said, "Maybe the reporter has made some progress. Didn't he say the Indians were going to try to free the prisoners?"

Tatterson said, "We have no idea what's going on down there. Andy said he doesn't even think they can get a man on the ground there until tomorrow morning at the earliest. The weather is looking like it is going to be really bad later today and through the night. He did say that maybe by tomorrow the clouds will break up and we could get some people in there then. God, I feel so powerless!"

June said, "Just pray that the Indians can pull off their rescue. And if they don't, that the Marines or whoever can get there in time. That's all we can do, Roger. Just pray."

Tatterson then added, "One thing that just happened is that apparently the CIA has picked up two guys who have been keeping us under surveillance. They have them in for questioning now. Seems like they were mostly interested in talking pictures of us. I have no idea why."

June looked worried.

◆◆◆

I looked at my watch and saw that it had been four hours since I had been locked in the treasure chamber and after I had napped, my headache had become more of an acute pain in the back of my head where I had been struck. But at least I felt stronger and so I turned on my light and stood up, having decided to make a more thorough investigation of the room I was trapped in.

It was an overwhelming sight really. Huge gold statues of regal looking men in strange costumes were lining the walls and carefully placed stacks of gold and silver urns, cases and tables full of figures and sculptures of buildings filled the place. There were wooden trunks with heavy hinges and intricately carved panels stacked in rows. Along the back wall were recesses in the cavern walls which each had a human form inside. All except one. I went to this empty recess and shone my light at the back wall. I realized that it was in fact a doorway to another chamber and I carefully squeezed through to a much larger room filled with even more treasure. I was absolutely stunned by the enormity of what I was witnessing. Hundreds of millions of dollars worth of some of the most exquisitely preserved pre-Colombian artifacts were packed so tightly into this larger room that it was hard to walk in the narrow passageways between the rows of trunks and artifacts piled higher than my head.

Just as I got to the far end of the chamber I heard a voice coming from the other room. I went back quickly and heard Peterson calling my name from on the other side of the door.

"Cannon, you there? Cannon!"

I crossed quickly to the door, switching off my light and said, "Yes, yes, I'm here. What have you found? I was afraid you'd forgotten about me!"

The reporter said, "Not great news, I'm afraid, but some interesting finds. Here's what I know."

He told me that over the last several hours he had explored most of the tunnels and found that virtually all of them were dead ends but that some led to other rooms. He had found one room with some tools and had brought back a shovel and a pickax.

I was ecstatic but then the reporter said, "Hang on. I think I hear something!" A few seconds went by and he added, "I've gotta go hide. Hang in there!"

I heard nothing for almost ten minutes and then was surprised when the lights came on in the chamber. Another five minutes went by and I heard the door to the room open and saw the big blond reporter stick his head inside.

He said, "Well, you coming or have you decided to hang here a while longer?"

I said, "Tell me later how you did that, but take a few seconds to look around here."

The reporter then noticed that the room was filled with treasure and he appeared stunned as he took it all in. I said, "And there's another bigger room beyond this one. This place is beyond amazing."

The reporter said, "We'll have to come back and see this, but right now? We've gotta get moving. I have no idea how long it'll be until they come looking for their friends."

I followed him out and down the stairs to the lower level and we struck out in single file back the way I had come in. But just before we came to the main door, there was a tunnel off to the right and Peterson said, "Follow me. This leads to another way out."

We ended up at the large pool of water and I saw that there were two men who appeared to be dead, lying alongside the water's edge.

"Who are they?" I said and Peterson said,

"They were coming for you, pretty sure. I made them change their minds."

I said, "Do all reporters specialize in murder or is this a special trademark of yours alone?

He said, "I was a Navy Seal before I got into journalism. That training is hard to forget." And then he added, "The water level has gone down a lot since I came in this way about five hours ago, and if we can swim upstream for about maybe thirty or forty feet, there's a way out that's across the hill from the compound."

I said, "You mean we have to swim underwater in a pitch-dark cave against a current trying to drag us to our deaths just to get out of here?"

Peterson smiled at me. "Like I said, I think it's the only other way out of here, unless you want to go strolling out the front door."

Just then, we heard a loud noise which sounded like the main door being opened and several voices not far away, up in the main tunnel. We both instinctively crouched down and the voices receded as the men made their way up towards the treasure chamber.

"They've come looking for these two, no doubt," Peterson said.

"I guess our time is up then?" I replied.

"Follow me into the water and keep me in sight and here," he said, handing me a handgun, "I borrowed these from our friends here. Didn't think they'd mind."

I tucked the handgun into my shorts as the reporter slid off the low ledge into the water and I followed. We edged our way out towards the far wall and he said quietly, "Take a bunch of deep breaths and on the count of three, follow me. I'll keep my Maglite on so just follow that. It's not far, and then we'll be turning to the left."

He ducked under the water and I did the same. The water was murky but I could see well enough so that his light was easy to follow. The current became stronger as we worked our way into a second chamber and surfaced. Peterson said, "This is where it gets more difficult. Just stay close," and he ducked under again. I swam down and nearly lost him as he made a turn into a much stronger current. Swimming as hard as I could I was only making slow progress and started to panic when I realized I had lost sight of the stronger swimmer. Suddenly I saw he had turned to the left and I followed. I was instantly out of the strong current. I continued to swim hard, catching up to him in short order and in about twenty seconds we both surfaced in a small pool in a cave covered under a bunch of vines and roots on the edge of a cliff. We crawled out to the mouth of the cave and both collapsed at the edge of some shrubbery and grass, well-hidden and still under the edge of the low overhang by just a bit.

"Holy shit," I said as my breathing returned to near normal. "That's something I wouldn't have tried it if I'd known what it was like going in!"

He smiled again and said softly, "You did fine, we're out. Now we just have to wait for the Indians to come and we'll go back in the way we came and help them attack the compound."

I didn't say anything as I continued to catch my breath but finally said, "Explain."

Over the next half hour, Peterson brought me up to speed with what he had been doing since he arrived in the country and what he believed was going to happen. Then we both settled back in the weeds to try to get comfortable as we waited for the day to pass. With several hours to kill, my mind raced through all the possible scenarios we might run into when we re-entered the compound at night. Not many of them seemed survivable, but I tried not to dwell on that.

◆◆◆

It was mid-day when the Kuna man said to Juliet, "There, do you see them? It is a place the gringo boats come and there are several. See?"

Juliet had dozed off and so scrambled up to more of a sitting position and looked out where the man was pointing. Off about two miles away was a small palm-fringed island and alongside it and just behind it were what looked like three cruising yachts. One was a schooner, she noticed, the other two were sloops.

Thirty minutes later the Kuna man expertly brought his dugout alongside one of the sloops and about eight eager backpackers helped hold the boat off while the Kuna dropped his sail and stowed his steering oar. A middle-aged British sounding man said he was the captain and asked what was needed.

Juliet said, "I need a satellite telephone. Have you got one?"

The captain laughed and said, "Not on this boat, lady, but maybe try the schooner over there. They make a lot more money than me and probably have one."

Juliet thanked him and the Kuna picked up his paddle and they made their way over to the larger boat.

Coming alongside the schooner, there were already a bunch of young backpackers gathered. While it was a common sight to see Kunas paddling and sailing around the islands in dugout canoes, seeing one with a disheveled but beautiful red haired white woman onboard, wrapped in fishing nets, was not so common.

Juliet looked up and saw that it appeared as if there was a young woman in charge. Standing next to her was a huge man and another woman who looked like she could be a sister of the apparent captain.

"My name's Juliet," she said, hoping that the crew spoke English and added, "I need to find a telephone. It's a matter of life and death!"

The captain spoke up. "My name's Sarah and this is my boat. Yes. We've got a phone. Come aboard."

Juliet looked over at the Kuna man who had risked his life to bring her so far and said, "Thank you, my friend. Someday I hope I may find a way to repay you for your kindness."

The old man smiled, his kind eyes squinting and said, "I have only done what you would have done for me," and he quickly paddled away, setting his sail as soon as he was clear. Juliet looked back one last time as she was being helped below and saw the lone Kuna sailing back towards the south.

"You look like you could use some water, or a drink!" the younger of the two sisters said and introduced herself. "My name's Valerie. Val for short. Pleased ta meet ya," and the younger woman thrust out her small but strong hand.

Juliet said, "Thanks. Water would be great. My name's Juliet, Jules for short. Is there a place I can clean up a bit please?"

She was led below and the dozen or so young passengers murmured, wondering what all this could be about.

As soon as Juliet got out of the bathroom, she was handed a glass of water by the giant crewman and the captain, Sarah, showed her to a door to a side cabin saying "Please, come inside. Let's see how we can help."

Juliet entered the small cabin and the captain closed the door and sat at a small desk, motioning for Juliet to sit on the foot of the bed. The captain said, "So tell me what's happened and how I can help."

Juliet was unsure at first of how much to share of what was really going on, but made a snap decision to level with the younger woman.

"I'm an insurance investigator and I've been held prisoner on a large yacht called Inca Gold. My husband is being blackmailed by a drug cartel to help move a stolen boat that disappeared from the BVI a little over month ago. We'd been tracking the boat but found out that a senator's daughter was onboard and that other people have been kidnapped too. So he's trying to help, but now we're both in real trouble. The cartel knows who we really are and I only just barely escaped. I need to make a call to my employers to let them know where I am. Please, help me!"

Sarah was speechless for a moment and then regained her composure. The last thing she wanted was to have a run-in with the dangerous people this woman had claimed to have escaped from, but by the same token, the story she told was so alarmingly similar to the story she had heard from the reporter back in Cartagena that she felt like she had to assist.

"Look, I'll get you the phone but you have to understand something." The young woman paused for a moment and looked down, then her eyes met Juliet's and she went on. "I've been making a good living here for the last few years and we've kept out of trouble by staying away from the people you're talking about. I can't afford to get involved in this, but I can't refuse you help either! I'm going to give you the phone and walk out of the room. I don't want to know any more than what I already know now. I can get you to port where you can get to an airport, and you can fly out, but I really have to be careful! We could all be killed very easily. Those people are the worst!"

Sarah then reached into the desk and pulled out an iridium satellite telephone saying, "This is routed into a masthead antenna. It works just like a regular phone. Just dial plus one and the country code and number and wait for the beeps. It should connect straight away. I'll hang out long enough to make sure you get through."

Juliet quickly dialed the number for Rudy Bellows, the insurance man in the BVI, and after a few rings his familiar voice came on the line.

"Bellows here, how may I be of assistance?"

"Rudy? It's Juliet! We're in trouble!"

Rudy Bellows had been worried sick about his favorite insurance investigators and good friends for days now. Since he had spoken with the reporter from New York, he had heard nothing and so he bolted out of his large leather chair and said, "Juliet! Where are you? Tell me everything!"

Juliet started in and told Bellows, in as abbreviated a manner as possible, about the events of the last two weeks but after five full minutes of talking he finally interrupted.

"Julie, listen. You sound very distressed! I'll send a private jet for you to the closest airport. Can you put the captain on the phone? You said her name was Sarah?"

Juliet realized that she had probably sounded hysterical as her recounting the incidents of the last several weeks came flooding out in only a partially coherent jumble, and she sighed heavily. She then stood up and opened the door.

Captain Sarah was standing just outside the doorway and had obviously been listening in. Juliet smiled to herself and said, "This is my boss at Ainsley and Dunbar Insurers. He wants to talk to you."

Sarah said, "Ainsley and Dunbar? That's who we have our insurance with!" and she took the phone Juliet was offering, placing it to her ear.

"This is Sarah Andrews. Who am I speaking with?"

"This is Rudy Bellows. I represent Ainsley and Dunbar Insurance and am employing Juliet Sparks. She is one of our most valued employees and we have been very worried about her since we lost track of her over a week ago. Can you get her to the closest international airport? I'll pay you ten thousand dollars if you can get her on a flight to Miami within the next few hours."

Sarah looked stunned as she held her hand over the mouthpiece and said to her sister Val who had come back to the navigation cabin when she heard her sister on the phone, "He wants to give us ten grand to get this woman on a flight out of here today!"

Sarah went back to the call saying, "Mr. Bellows. We're in a very remote part of the San Blas Islands and are probably ten hours' motoring time from the end of the road where we might be able to hire a taxi, and then it's another three hours to the airport and this is Panama. They only have a couple flights a day to Miami."

Bellows then said, "How about the closest small airport? I think I can get her a charter flight out to one of the small strips down that way. I can probably find someone to fly in to get her within the next few hours."

Sarah thought for a moment and said, "I could get her to Sanadup-dup in a few hours. It's a little island and just off the mainland. They have a small airstrip, but it'll be close to dark by then. That's the closest airport."

The insurance man said, "OK, head for that. The ten thousand dollars still stands. Just get her out of there safely. I'll work on getting a pilot lined up. Call me when you are getting close, like an hour away."

He then asked to speak to Juliet again and after a few minutes, they both signed off.

◆◆◆

Andy Winters looked at the two Colombians handcuffed in the observation room. From behind the two-way mirror, he noticed that the older one looked calm and collected but the younger one was obviously very distraught. He decided to bait them.

"Walters." Winters looked at the other agent in the room. "Get the smug looking one out of there and let's see if we can crack the smaller nut."

A few minutes later three CIA men came in and roughly removed the older criminal from the room. Ten minutes after that, Winters walked in and sat down opposite the younger man.

"My name is Winters." The agent was ad-libbing. "That's a nickname actually. It's because after people see what I do to creeps like you, they get chills."

He let this sink in for a moment. The young man looked concerned, but not overly worried until Winters added, "So I need to ask you. Would you rather die by drowning, burning or disembowelment?"

The young Colombian looked stricken and said, "You will not do this to me! This is America! You do not do these things to people here!"

Winters laughed and said "This is not America. This is No Man's Land. You've been spying on one of our most important people and we want to know why. And if the answers you give don't sound true to me? I'll show you how people disappear here in No Man's Land." He let the man stew on this for a moment and then added, "If you think for one minute that you're going to walk out of here unharmed by lying to me, think again. And if you want to live through this experience, and still be able to walk and still have a dick, then you'd better answer me NOW!" Winters slammed his fist on the desk and the man jumped.

Winters turned his head and spoke to the large mirror. "Bring them in."

The young man looked quickly left and right and just then a door opened directly behind him and two huge men walked in, dressed in black with hoods over their heads. One was holding nunchucks and the other a large fillet knife.

Winters said, "I'd like you to meet my two assistants, Death and Dismemberment."

The man with the nunchucks slammed them down on the table right next to the Colombian and the man with the knife grabbed the young man's ponytail and pulled down hard, exposing his neck which he thrust the large blade against, pushing just hard enough to draw a little blood.

"Now that I have your attention. Suppose you tell me what you know about why you were watching Senator Tatterson and his wife."

Over the next half hour, the Colombian told everything he knew and as they got up to leave him, Winters said, "Oh, and just so you know, those things I told you would happen to you probably will, but not by us. We're going to play your confession for your friend and see what he agrees with and what he thinks about your version. Then we'll release you both to Colombian officials here. What they do with you is not of our concern."

As Winters left the room, he got on the phone with the commander of the Marine contingent that was standing by, ready to go into action.

"Commander? Andy Winters, CIA. I've just gotten out of an interrogation with a man who may have the intel you've been hoping for."

The CIA man spent the next fifteen minutes filling the Marine commander in with the details of the compound, the personnel and the possible weaknesses in the defenses that the young Colombian had so kindly offered.

◆◆◆

Toby Meyers was very weak and felt like he was about to lose consciousness again. After a full night of beatings and then seeing his own sister brutally raped and beaten repeatedly, he had finally told the men there all they wanted to know. They had then beaten him again and had left him tied up in a chair. The bindings had long since worn through his skin and he had lost feeling in his legs. His head bobbed against his chest once more as he nearly fell asleep but the chokehold they had him secured with wouldn't allow him to rest his head. He had been given no water since the previous night and now the sun was beginning to set again. He felt like he might not make it through the night.

He was barely aware that there was a person in the room with him and he looked up through his swollen eyes at his tormentor, there in front of him again.

"Ah, Captain Toby! I can see you are still with us! This is good! I have some more fun times for you to endure."

Santiago was standing in front of him with a sadistic leer and the man shouted to someone outside the room,

"Come in and take this thing and get him cleaned up. Then we will take him up to the caves!"

Two large guards came in and untied him from the chair, but left his hands tied behind his back and they pulled him roughly to his feet. Toby staggered under his own weight and the smaller of the two guards punched him hard in the gut. Toby doubled over and fell crumpled onto the floor.

Santiago said, "Unless you want to carry him, I suggest you let him gather his strength. Give him some water. I would not want him to die before he sees what we will do to his sister."

The men pulled Toby to his feet and half dragged, half walked him out into the darkening evening and down the lit walkway towards the first door on the prison block. They waited there while Santiago banged loudly.

"Open up, you stupid slut!" he screamed. The giant woman swung the door open and glared at Santiago hatefully as he said, "Bring me the little Colombian witch. We have use for her again."

The guard sullenly turned and walked over the main door, unlocking it and went over to where Toby's sister was crouched, leaning up against the chicken wire. The girl shied away as the guard grabbed her and pulled her to her feet. The guard then said, "Come now if want to see your brother one last time."

The young woman reluctantly did as she was told and followed the guard out of the main cell block doors.

She saw her brother and ran to him, but the big guard threw her to the ground and Santiago said, "Ah yes, my little princess! Come with us now, we have some nice plans for you and your brother tonight."

The Colombian girl started to cry and Santiago bent over and struck her across the face. "Save your tears for later, bitch," he said as he grabbed her and dragged her roughly to her feet, pushing her along towards the showers. "Get them both cleaned up and I will be back shortly and then we will take them to the caves at the far end of the compound."

◆◆◆

Peterson was the first of the two to hear it.

"Listen!"

I had dozed briefly and came fully aware as I too heard quiet voices and the sound of paddles hitting the water. We both crawled out of our hiding places in time to see two small canoes come in close to our hiding place and land along the bank on the far side of the small swampy area. Four men and what looked like a child leapt out and scrambled up the bank.

'Melowa!" I said

"Capitan Brites!" She threw herself into my arms and said, "I think they kill you! I so worried!" Turning to the reporter she said, "I so happy to see you too, Mr. Alex. My brother sad to think you been killed."

Pulu stepped up and entered the conversation. "We heard gunshots and feared the worst."

Peterson said, "I managed to get away and found the captain in the process. He was headed for oblivion but we managed to get away."

The other Indians were standing around us now and Pulu said, "Let me tell them what is happening. They do not speak English."

He spent a couple of minutes explaining our presence and then looked back at us and said, "After it is fully dark, we will swim into the compound and kill the guards. The other warriors are coming soon and they will all come over the hill. And some will come up the river too. We will swim across the compound and free the prisoners while the main body of men kill the evil ones' soldiers and guards."

I said, "We will go with you on the first thrust. We know the way and will be able to help!"

Pulu nodded and explained this to the other Indians.

It was now nearly fully dark and several other canoes arrived. More came and men began to flood ashore. Soon there was a sizable contingent and a few of the more agile warriors were scouting possible routes to the top of the low hill that separated us from the compound. Almost no one spoke now as the rain had stopped and so the jungle was very quiet.

Pulu spoke to me quietly saying, "We will go when the shadows are deepest. This will happen soon."

He was right; as the darkness took over the jungle, the shadows, to our eyes that were still accustomed to the daylight, became so dark that nothing could be seen in them. This time, until the guards' eyes became adjusted to the night, was the best time for our attack.

We crawled back into the low cave. Pulu eased himself into the dark pool of water and said quietly to me, "Follow me closely. We will have a light for the first part, but I will have to turn it off when we get close to the other side or we will be seen."

I nodded and he quickly related what he had said to the Indians, and his sister came up close to me and whispered, "I will stay right next to you. I want to help rescue my people, but we will get to your people first."

Peterson slid into the water and we all followed. We were bobbing in the pool, waiting for the right moment.

Soon Pulu said, "Now we go."

Pulu slipped under the water and I followed immediately. We all began to form a single line in the weak beam of Pulu's flashlight and started our swim through the treacherous tunnel, towards the inky blackness.

Forty seconds into the swim we had passed the area of current and Pulu turned his light off. I put my hand out in front of my face to feel the roof of the tunnel and blundered along cautiously. Just as my lungs were beginning to burn, I felt the top of the tunnel disappear and saw a faint glimmering of light ahead. Seconds later I silently broke the surface, coming alongside Pulu with Melowa surfacing seconds later. Within fifteen seconds Peterson and the other three men had arrived and we were all silently treading water or holding on to the roots above our heads and Pulu whispered quietly, "Capitan Brites and Alex, Melowa; we will swim across to the inner guard station." He then turned his head and said to the other three Indians in their dialect, "You three take the outer guardhouse. Leave none alive, and be silent!"

Like a gift from God, as suddenly as if a switch had been thrown, a torrential rain began to fall.

◆◆◆

The Marine commander aboard the carrier spoke belligerently into the phone.

"General, my men can land in rain and we can find our way to the target area without moonlight, we've been trained for this and we're ready to fly."

The general said, "Commander Bruske, I appreciate your eagerness, but there's a huge thunderstorm system moving into the area beginning just about now, and it may be several hours, or even until the morning before it has moved through. So, until these rains stop, the president will not authorize deployment. I have no doubts about your abilities, but I am only following orders from above. Just stand by and our meteorologists will get you into the drop zone just as soon as an opportunity comes. That's the best I can do."

The general signed off and the commander snapped his headpiece into his vest, muttering under his breath and then spoke up to his men.

Twenty-five of the finest men he had ever had the opportunity to lead were all staring at him when he said, "We have been ordered to stand by. They're looking for a weather window to bring us in. I suggest you men relax and try to get some sleep, but be ready to deploy on five minutes' notice."

He turned and walked back down the corridor of the carrier to the cabin he had been sharing with a junior naval officer and sat down on his berth to wait.

◆◆◆

The schooner My World was making great time with the winds which had cranked up to a solid twenty knots. She was carrying full sail with her topsails set as well and so by 4:30 p.m. the boat rounded the corner of the small island and made its way into the harbor. No other boats were there but the small Kuna village was close by and they could make out the small runway behind the village on the mainland, about a quarter of a mile away.

Juliet had called Rudy Bellows back as she had promised and so it was only a short time after the schooner had dropped anchor that they heard a small airplane come in over the harbor, circle once and then land on the short airstrip.

Within minutes the giant deckhand and pretty blonde captain were ferrying Juliet ashore and by five-thirty, as darkness began to fall, she was looking down at the San Blas islands spreading out below her along the edge of the barrier reef as the single-engine Cessna airplane made its way to the northwest.

Sixteen

The pilot had obtained a clearance to fly all the way to Panama City and it was fully dark by the time the Cessna landed at the smaller regional Albrook "Marcos A. Gelabert" airport. A twenty-minute taxi ride, and a few hundred dollars changing hands over the fact that Juliet had no passport with her, resulted in her being taken to the U.S. Embassy where she was met at the gate by a Mister Jeffers.

Jeffers introduced himself as a special attaché and ushered Juliet into a comfortable sitting room and within a few minutes two men and a woman, all middle-aged and dressed in business suits, came in and introduced themselves. They asked Juliet to tell them everything she knew about Ramon's operation and assured her that they had been briefed by the highest authorities and that she was to provide them with her best descriptions of the physical layout of the various places she had visited during her time with Ramon and his entourage. They went on to ask her if she would mind if the chief investigator for this situation could be allowed to join in the interview via satellite link, and Juliet agreed.

Andy Winters' image came over the screen on the far side of the table and he introduced himself. He then filled Juliet in with what he thought she should know about the investigation thus far, and told her that he knew about the infiltrator known as Frederica and that they had Ramon's yacht now under close observation via satellite. It was still being decided whether an intervention there would need to be done and so Juliet broke into the monologue saying, "Mr. Winters. It is my belief that Frederica, I mean Cynthia, because that's her real name, is in grave danger. She helped me escape and Ramon is no dummy. He'll probably figure out that she helped me. If it hadn't been for her, I'd still be on that boat and probably already be dead, we've got to help her!"

There was a pause while Winters spoke to someone out of view to his right and then he came back on and said, "How reliable do you think this observation is? Would you say, ten, twenty-five, fifty percent? We need a risk assessment here and although we know you're not a professional in this field, we do know that you're an insurance claim investigator, so we're asking you honestly, how strongly do you believe that this Interpol agent is in danger right this moment?"

Juliet answered without hesitation, "One hundred percent, sir."

There was more consultation off the screen and Winters finally came back to the conversation saying, "Thank you, Ms. Sparks, you have been very helpful. I've been informed that you will be issued a new temporary passport and will be flown out of Panama tonight. I believe it has been requested that you report to headquarters here in Washington, DC. I will meet with you personally tomorrow. Thank you and good night."

Juliet jumped in before he signed off. "Mr. Winters! Excuse me." The agent looked back at her across the screen. "Mr. Winters, I can't come up there as long as my husband is in danger and I need to try to help Cynthia. I need to try to rescue her!"

Winters looked at the woman blankly and then turned once more to the person or people with whom he had been speaking off camera. He then looked back at her and said, "Ms. Sparks, what would you do if you could help the Interpol agent?"

Juliet was ready for him and said, "I'd try to come nearby in a boat that they wouldn't suspect... like one of the backpacker boats. We could pretend we needed help, Like engine problems or something. And then come alongside and board them. I know how many guards they have and where they hang out, I know that with just a handful of people we could take that yacht, save Cynthia and probably capture Ramon too."

Juliet heard the two men in the room with her speaking to each other quietly and saw that the sound was off and Winters was once again speaking off camera.

A few minutes went by and Winters turned his head back to her and when the sound came back on he said, "OK, we're going to send some help down there. These are highly trained professionals. Can you think of a backpacker boat you could rent or borrow? We'll need to move quickly if this is going to happen."

Juliet said, "I'd say we should see about renting the schooner My World. That's the boat that helped rescue me and brought me to the airport in Panama. I have the captain's number and could get ahold of her to see if she'll help. But I know she'll be afraid of stirring up a hornets' nest. What kind of assurances can I give her?"

The CIA man put his hand to his left ear and then said, "Tell her we'll pay her a hundred thousand dollars and will guarantee her safety. We've just been given full authorization for this operation to begin immediately."

Juliet asked the man to hold on and asked for a telephone. A few minutes later she had Sarah from My World on the line.

"Sarah? This is Juliet. I wanted to thank you again for helping me earlier today and I'm sorry for calling so late."

Juliet went on to tell the woman about what was going on and about the plan to begin a rescue operation in the morning, and that the pay would be substantial. The shrewd young captain then said, "I'd love to help, but if my boat is lost, my insurance won't pay for a loss initiated by direct armed intervention. I'm sure of it. If I lost the boat, I'd be out four hundred thousand dollars and out of business. So I'll need an assurance that I'll be compensated for the full insured amount if my boat is lost."

Juliet asked her to hold on and relayed this request to Agent Winters who, after a brief exchange off screen came back on the camera.

"Tell the captain it's agreed."

Juliet then came back on and asked if it would be OK for her to pass the boat sat phone number on to the CIA so that they could coordinate with her directly from there on out, and Captain Sarah agreed.

Juliet then asked if she could be driven to Portobelo that night stating, "Brice and I have a very good friend there and I need to tell him what's going on. You can ask My World to meet us in Portobelo. That would be a good place to take on the people and supplies needed to go back down to where Inca Gold is anchored."

Agent Winters agreed and then signed off. The three other officers in the room got up too, each one each shaking Juliet's hand and offering wishes for a safe operation and for the safe return of her husband.

Juliet was then shown to a room and given some fresh clothes and told that she would be summoned in a short while when it was time to leave for her transport to Portobelo.

Twenty minutes later Juliet answered a knock on her door to tell her that her helicopter was ready.

"My helicopter? I thought I'd be taking a taxi!"

The man at the door smiled and said, "Time is of the essence, and it's just easier this way."

Juliet thought to herself. *Easier?*

Thirty minutes later she was landing in the central square in Portobelo. By now it had been dark for hours and so the helicopter only attracted a small crowd. Juliet was helped off and two large men escorted her up to Captain Mack's Bar. The place was still open with tecno music blaring from the bar as Juliet and the men climbed the steps to the restaurant.

Mack was behind the bar and noticed Juliet and the two menacing looking men right way.

The place was fairly crowded with young people. Several backpacker boats had just come in and so the usual crowd was augmented by the newcomers and in addition, there were forty or so people waiting to catch the next backpacker boats going south.

He came out from behind the bar and met them halfway across the crowded floor. "Julie!" He put his arms out and she came to him, giving him a crushing hug.

"God Almighty, Mack, I'm sure glad to see you!" and then she looked at the two men and said, "I'll be fine now. Just call me on that phone you gave me when I need to be ready to move out."

The taller of the two men nodded and said, "Best of luck to you. We'll hope to see you on the other side." And they both turned and made their way out past the throng of young bodies, walked down the stairs and disappeared into the night. A few minutes later, for anyone who was listening, the helicopter could be heard disappearing into the night.

"C'mon back to my office, Julie. You've gotta tell me what's happened and... where's Brice?"

Over the next hour Juliet filled Mack in with everything she knew, including the fact that in a short while there was going to be an assault team meeting the schooner My World which was expected in sometime after dawn.

"My God, Julie, I had no idea you two were so well connected," Mack said, referring to the CIA involvement and the suggestion that Interpol was involved as well.

"I never knew it either, Mack. It all just sort of came up at the last minute." She smiled weakly and added, "But at least now there'll be a chance for us to rescue the woman who helped me... if she isn't already dead that is."

Juliet looked out the window of the office into the dark jungle night and added, "I'm so sorry we had to lie to you earlier, Mack. We were told to stay undercover and we didn't want to involve you unnecessarily. But now things have gotten so far out of control! I just had to come and see you and to explain. You're one of our best friends and we just wanted to keep you safe."

Mack smiled at her and said, "Look, I'd have done the same thing. Thing is, I've got to help you now. There's no way we can just leave this all as it is. We've got to rescue your friend and then we'll go find Brice and get him out of whatever predicament he's gotten himself into. I'm coming with you, and there's no stopping me!"

Juliet felt tears welling in her eyes and she went to Mack, holding him close and kissed him on his cheek. "You're the best, Mack. You really are!"

◆◆◆

Captain Sarah had gotten the call a half hour after she had hung up with Juliet.

"Sarah? My name's Agent Winters. I'm in charge of this operation and I've been authorized on behalf of the president of the United States to guarantee your financial safety in this intervention. However, I want to warn you that we will be trying to approach very dangerous criminals and there is the distinct possibility of harm to your vessel, and possibly even to yourselves. So if you want to back out, now is the time to say so."

Sarah didn't need to think about it as she had already spent the last twenty minutes discussing it in hushed tones with her crew in her cabin.

"We're in. Just tell us what we need to do."

"Where are you now, and what's your ETA to Portobelo?"

"We got underway the minute we dropped Juliet at the airport, so I expect us to be arriving in Portobelo around 6 a.m."

"Good. I have a team arriving there by transport by around dawn. They're Marines coming from an aircraft carrier off Colombia, otherwise they'd have been there sooner. What I'd like you to do is collect Juliet and be ready to leave as soon after that as possible. Is there anything I can do to help?"

Sarah thought for a few seconds before responding. "We'll need some provisions and diesel. Other than that, we need to get our passengers off. But I can be ready in time, or at least close to ready."

Winters said, "Good. I'll call in the morning with an updated ETA and rendezvous instructions. Where's the best place for them to meet you?"

Sarah said, "There's a small music school on the waterfront. Have your men meet us there on the dock. Oh, and Agent Winters? Have them dress like hippies. The only way we'll be able to get close to the boat you want us to board will be to have a crew that looks harmless!"

Winters thanked her for the suggestion and signed off.

The crew of My World took alternate watches all night and arrived uneventfully off the Portobelo waterfront at five-thirty, just as the sky was beginning to lighten. They anchored close to the music school wharf, and Sarah and Valerie got all the passengers rounded up and on their way so that by six-thirty they were ready to take on fuel and water, and get provisions.

Ben, the giant, and Valerie went down the street to awaken the Chinese storekeeper so that they could get a jump start on getting the food while Sarah went down the harbor in the dinghy to the fisherman's fuel dock to arrange for a barrel of fuel to be delivered to the boat.

◆◆◆

Juliet had finally fallen into a deep sleep in the guest room in Mack's apartment in the hotel, but was up at six after Mack's young wife knocked on her door.

"I've been told that the passengers from My World are coming up the street. So you'll be leaving soon. Come and get some food. Mack has been cooking since five-thirty."

They ate in virtual silence and Mack finally said, "Let's get down to the waterfront."

Just then Juliet's embassy cell phone rang and a familiar voice came on the line. It was the same Mr. Winters who said, "The Marines will be there within forty minutes. They'll be coming into the town by small truck. Meet them at the waterfront and direct them to the wharf if you can."

Juliet said, "We're on our way." She hung up.

Mack looked at her inquisitively and said, "Time to rock and roll?"

Juliet nodded her head and said, "Let's do this."

Mack kissed his wife goodbye, promising her, "I'll be back in a few days. Hold the fort down, OK?" and he turned away to hide the tears in his eyes.

They both grabbed the two small bags Mack had assembled and walked down the stairs and down the quiet sloping street to the waterfront.

The morning mist was finally beginning to burn off when they met the inflatable dinghy which came in from My World as soon as they were seen on the dock.

No sooner had they gotten their gear aboard when Juliet heard a shout from shore. A large muscular man in dumpy looking bib overalls and a checkered shirt was standing on the dock waving at them.

Juliet said, "I think this could be our new crew," and she and Ben jumped into the dinghy and zoomed into shore to meet the stranger.

Sure enough, the man in the hayseed outfit proved to be a Marine lieutenant named Jamison and within a few minutes, and two more quick dinghy runs to shore, he and his four equally disheveled looking companions and all their gear were safely transferred to the schooner My World and in a short time their gear was stowed away below decks. By the time the harbor was finally coming to life, My World was already a mile and a half away, heading for the southern San Blas Islands, a hundred and twenty miles distant.

Seventeen

Now with a heavy rain falling, I silently followed Pulu out across the water and saw that Melowa was following. Peterson brought up the rear of our small party. The rain was so heavy that we were following Pulu closely and he was likely finding his way across the river by instinct. The nearby guardhouse was invisible, so luckily, swimming underwater was not necessary. It would have been exceptionally difficult to find the opening in the fence in the dark while underwater! Soon, a faint light loomed ahead and shortly after, we came to the inner fence. A few minutes passed as we swam the length of the inner basin and we made for the underside of the catamaran, which was dark and appeared empty.

Pulu looked at Peterson and said, "Follow me and after I have killed the guards, we will go down to the prison block and free the people. Then we will await the main attack and in the confusion we will come to the boat here and make our escape."

He then said to me, "Capitan, you get the boat ready to go and I will bring the people to you."

I said, "Even with the attack going on, there will be a huge risk to the people! One man with a machine gun could kill us all in a few seconds. We will need a diversion!"

Pulu thought for a few seconds before saying, "I am not sure how long this hard rain will last, but you are right, if it does not continue, we would be too exposed. What do you suggest?"

I said, "Just across the compound, behind the cell block, I noticed a large garage. I think that is where they store the fuel for the boats and I think there is a road coming in here from the interior. So there are probably trucks there too. If I can get in there, I could maybe start a fire, and maybe that would divide the guards up trying to deal with that."

Pulu said, "After I have made the call of the toucan, it will take maybe ten minutes for the main body of our warriors to come into the compound, so you will have that long to work. Do not destroy the building until you have heard the first shouts of alarm though! If you start a fire too soon, the guards will come and see our people swimming across the river!"

Alex Peterson, who was silently treading water next to us, interrupted.

"Excuse me, but I was in the navy and was a Seal. I'm sort of a demolition expert. I should be the one to go and if those trucks run on gasoline, I can probably blow the whole damn place up. Brice, why don't you go rescue the people and as soon as I hear the first gunshots, I'll blow the place and go back down to the boat. If you're gone by then... and don't wait for me, if you're gone, then I'll swim out the way we came in."

Pulu looked from Peterson to me and then his sister and said, "This is a good plan. Capitan, go up on the boat now while it is still raining hard and make it ready to go, then as soon as you hear the toucan call, come down to the guardhouse and we will go free the prisoners."

With that Alex pulled himself out of the water on the far side of the dock and disappeared into the driving rain in the direction of the storehouse and I swam to the stern of the cat and pulled myself aboard. I caught a slight glimpse of Pulu and Melowa swimming towards the guardhouse but lost them quickly in the rain.

I climbed up on the port hull which was farthest from the buildings and crawled to the main door which thankfully was unlocked. Sliding it carefully open, I went inside and stood up.

The main electrical panel was lit and showed that we were still plugged into shore power, and I quickly went about throwing the switches for the ignitions and I went down into each hull to check to make sure the engine battery switches were in the on position. The voltages on the panel looked good and I went back outside and climbed up into the cockpit to check to make sure there were keys in the ignition. There were.

Just then I heard voices and saw that there was a small group of guards walking right past the boat on the shore in front of me. I crouched lower and crawled to the edge of the bridge deck to peer over as they passed by. They had two people who appeared to be prisoners and I suddenly realized it was Toby and what I guessed was his sister. Both appeared to be badly injured and were stumbling along, occasionally being shoved or hit. I also recognized Santiago in the group and they disappeared in the driving rain in the general direction of the entrance to the caves. There was nothing I could do about that just then, I decided.

Several minutes later I heard a faint toucan call. It was answered by another call from across the basin and a much louder call then was made. We had about ten minutes before all hell would break loose!

I quickly made my way back to the lower cockpit and onto the dock, running in the direction of the guardhouse. By the time I arrived at the gatehouse Pulu and Melowa were outside and, after I reached inside and punched in #24 on the gate lock, we all ran down the walkway towards the cell block.

The rain was now beginning to let up and as we came to the first door I said, "Let me try something. Pulu, you stay hidden, Melowa, pretend you're my prisoner."

I knocked on the cell block door loudly several times and stepped back. As the door opened I saw the large and very ugly Latino woman standing in the doorway. I roughly pulled Melowa in front of me and said in Spanish, "Carlos sent me with this prisoner. She is the one that escaped."

The ogre changed the doubtful expression she had been looking at me with when she recognized the Indian girl as the one she knew had escaped and stepped aside to let us in. The moment her back was turned to the door, Pulu slipped in behind her and hit her hard on the head with a short club he was carrying. The giant woman staggered but did not fall! She turned and stared to shout, but Pulu hit her again hard in the face and she went down with a solid thump. Pulu quickly shut the door and we looked over at the fenced area. There were about a dozen girls in there including Jenny and Bridget, two other Caucasian girls, and a bunch of Indian girls whom I realized must be the prostitutes I had seen across the harbor on the other catamarans.

Pulu spoke urgently to the prisoners in a dialect I did not understand, but I guessed it was something like, "We are here to free you. Come with us now!"

I saw that the key to the lock on the wire fence was hanging on a nail on the far wall and I grabbed it as Pulu and Melowa dragged the big guard off to the side, and he grabbed a section of rope he saw lying on the ground and began to tie her up.

I worked the lock open and then ushered all the girls out. Jenny threw her arms around me and said, "Thank you! Where's Toby?"

Before I could answer, we heard gunshots outside.

I grabbed the gun out of my belt and said, "Jenny! We're going to try to free the other prisoners. I have the catamaran all ready to go and we need to get everybody aboard. In a short while there's going to be a big explosion and when that happens, I want you to take the girls all down to the boat as quickly as possible! Melowa, you go with them and Pulu and I'll be there was quick as we can."

Just then a huge explosion shook the walls of the prison block and dust and debris came in through the windows and down from the ceiling.

"Now! Go now!" I shouted.

We all piled out and I made a quick sweep of the area. I shot two guards who were running towards us and then signaled the girls to run for the boat. Pulu went along with them as far as the dock and then turned around and ran back towards me.

I reeled around as I heard shouting behind me just in time to see three more guards emerge from the second cell door. I took out two and Pulu got the third with an arrow in his chest before they could return fire. Then we ran the short distance down to the cell block doors and entered. Inside a chain link fenced-in area there were about thirty men. I realized that these must be some of the workers and said in Spanish, "We are here to rescue you. Go down to the water and there is a large white boat that you saw come in, it is our way out of here. Go to the boat and get aboard and hide. We will be there soon!"

I shot the lock off and the men all piled out. Pulu said to me, "I guess your friend's not here."

I told him that I had seen Toby and his sister being taken to the caves and we followed the last of the men out. By now there was a lot of shooting going on down by the outer basin but we didn't see any guards as the large group of men ran down towards the water. Alex, Pulu and I went to the third door and tried to open it. It was locked. I then shot the lock twice and the door gave way. Inside Diego and the large menacing guard with the scar on his face I had met the first day were standing with small machine guns aimed at our chests, and we both dropped our weapons. The guard was closest to me and hit me in the head with the stock of his gun. For the second time that day, everything went black.

The main body of the attack had routed the guards at the outer compound and many of the surviving guards from the outside post were now streaming into the inner compound. As they ran for the inner fence, three more dropped with arrows in their backs.

A small group of the guards saw that the cell block doors were all open and stopped by to investigate while the main contingent of the surviving guards retreated to the pool area and took up defensive positions there.

The leader of the group of soldiers at the cell block sent three men into the first door and the men quickly came out to tell him that the room was empty and that there was a guard unconscious and tied up inside.

They then went to the third door and came upon Diego and their leader who had two Indians and an unconscious white man held at gunpoint. Diego snapped at the guard "Take over here. Lock these three inside and keep them guarded. We need to start a counter attack immediately!"

Diego and the giant guard left and took the majority of the other guards with them and ran up towards the outer fence, disappearing into the rain after only a dozen yards. The remaining three guards brutally threw Melowa and Pulu into the fenced-in area. By now I had started to come around and felt them pick me up by my shoulders and legs and toss me inside the fenced area where I landed hard against a bench along the far wall. The new pain of feeling a rib break brought me out of semiconsciousness immediately and I groaned and clutched my side as they slammed the door shut and I heard the lock click closed.

Just then I heard gunshots and all three guards collapsed. Alex Peterson poked his head in the door and quickly entered the cell area saying, "Sorry to break up your party, but you've got a boat to drive!"

I said, "Isn't there another whole group of workers we're missing? I thought there were a lot more workers being kept here!"

Melowa spoke up as Peterson worked the old rusty key he had taken off one of the guards to open the inner fence. "The main workers all kept in outside area. I sure they all run off to forest by now, so we not worry about them. It is the people we have rescued that we must get away from here."

The rusty lock finally came open and we all tumbled out of the holding cell. I quickly picked up the gun I had dropped and checked it to make sure I had chambered a round, then picked up two of the guards' weapons and handed them to Pulu and Melowa. Melowa looked at the machine gun she was holding apprehensively and said, "I not sure how to work this thing!"

Peterson quickly explained how to fire it as Pulu looked on, mimicking Alex's actions of cocking, taking the safety off and on and aiming, and he explained that she must hold it firmly and point it at the middle of a target because the gun would jump when it was fired.

By now I had already gone outside and was crouching down next to a small tree across the sidewalk. I motioned the others to come out and we all fled single file back down the walkway towards the water. As we approached the end of the building, an arrow bounced off the stone just above my head.

Pulu shouted something and he was answered from across the compound. The rain had now eased to the point where we could see the empty guardhouse and make out the docks just past it. The catamaran was around the bend to the right and was right in front of the edge of the pool compound. I silently prayed that the escaped prisoners we had freed had not been discovered and hoped that Jenny had managed to keep them all quiet and down in the hulls, out of sight. I suspected that the guards may have been retreating to the pool area as it was higher than the surrounding compound and had good cover with all the plantings, the low wall and the rooms in behind. Alex confirmed this when he turned back to me and said, "I saw about twenty guards head this way about three minutes ago. Otherwise I would have gotten to you sooner."

Suddenly about fifteen Indians came running low across the grass and took shelter with us along the wall. Pulu spoke to them and four of them turned and went back up the sidewalk and disappeared around the back of the cell block.

Alex said, "They're going to get behind the pool compound and create a diversion. The guards were expecting a frontal attack and this will cause them confusion."

I said, "We'll need to clear those guys out of there before I can take the cat away. What can we do?"

Peterson looked down at the dirt for a moment and then looked back up at me and Pulu and said, "I'll go around the back too. I'll go back to where they are keeping their trucks. I kind of made a mess of things when I blew that fuel, but maybe one of the trucks is still drivable and maybe I can drive one in through the back of their building. That ought to bring the guys from the front over my way. Then, Pulu, maybe you can get your men to attack any stragglers while el Capitan here steals the boat and gets the innocents away. Whaddaya say?"

I was about to object when Pulu said, "We will do this. Go now!"

Without a seconds hesitation, Alex and three of the other Indians all fled up the back way just as another group of Indians who had cleared out the outer compound came to reinforce our position.

Suddenly there was an eruption of gunfire from outside the compound and with the rain now down to a light drizzle, we saw a large gunboat enter the outer harbor. They slammed into the outer pier and we watched in the bright compound lighting as about fifty heavily armed soldiers piled off the boat and began to attack our flank, just out of range from us. It would not be long before we were in serious trouble and the Indians and Pulu all looked at me as if I could somehow offer a suggestion of what to do next.

"Pulu," I said, "Take your men back to where Peterson is starting his diversion and warn him. He needs to hold off on that. Take your men and hide them and we need to see what happens next. If we try to attack that group alone, we'll be massacred."

Just then we saw the lights of a second boat appear and this development galvanized us into action. Pulu let out a loud cry of alarm and the Indians retreated, leaving me alone on the wall with Melowa and Pulu. Pulu said, "I will get you aboard the boat, then you must stay still, hidden inside until your chance comes to escape."

We then crept on our bellies down across the short open area to the harbor and slid into the water. Diving down, we arrived at the underside of the catamaran and surfaced, listening carefully for any sign that we had been seen.

After about a minute I was satisfied and said to Pulu, "There is nothing more you can do here. Take Melowa and try to escape. I will do the best I can to get away if I see a chance."

Pulu looked at me with cold, dark eyes and said, "No, you will take Melowa with you and I will go back and kill every last one of these vermin. They are all dead in my eyes already and I will make sure they never bother my people again."

Before I could say anything more, he dipped under the water and was gone. Melowa started to follow him and I grabbed her arm saying, "No, Melowa, I need you to stay here and help me!"

◆◆◆

Less than five minutes after the initial explosion was observed by the infrared sensors on the satellite that had been allocated to observe the compound deep in the Colombian jungle, the CIA had notified the White House, and the general had Commander Bruske on the line.

Five minutes after that Bruske had his men boarding the V-22 Osprey long range helicopter which had its engines starting as they took their places inside the cargo area.

"Now listen up," he said as the men continued to wake themselves and gather their senses. "Intel says there was a big explosion on the ground and it is likely that the attack with the indigenous forces is now underway. It is our primary objective to rescue our citizens and the highest priority is the daughter of a U.S. senator. She is blonde, blue eyed, about twenty-four years old and probably a knockout. Maybe one of you can be her Prince Charming."

The men chuckled at this as the aircraft started to lift off from the carrier deck.

As they settled onto their route, Bruske went on. "Meteorology says it's still raining down there and we have only sketchy knowledge of the drop zone. We'll have them get us as close to the compound as they can and then it will be up to us to take out the uglies and we're going to have to be careful not to get into a friendly fire situation. It's our belief that there may be as many as a hundred indigenous fighters on the ground and we must not attack them by accident or we'll be fighting two sides at the same time. Rodriguez, Callwood, you're both fluent in Spanish. You take the bullhorns and alert the immediate perimeter of our identities and also demand the surrender of the hostages. This will help establish that we're there to help and may also cause the other side to cave early once they know they're up against a superior force."

"Johnson, Alberts, you will take your teams up the left and right flanks and try to get inside. I'll lead the center thrust. From what I'm going to show you here," he said as a large computer monitor in the aircraft came on, "Is that there are two distinct areas of this compound. The outer area has the majority of the soldiers as seen here in these satellite photos, but this may have changed since the attack is already underway. It's entirely possible that the enemy could be anywhere. All I can say is be sure to identify yourselves before engaging and stay sharp."

He looked at his watch and added, "It's thirty-five minutes till we are meeting the KC130 for refueling, and then our deployment will not be long after that. Get some rest and get focused."

◆◆◆

I was still treading water with Melowa when I heard the shouting and firing increase. Then we listened carefully as the gunfire began to shift farther away, being led by the Indians trying to create a diversion. I thought about Alex Peterson and hoped he hadn't done a suicidal crash through the walls of the inner compound and realized that even if he had, there was no way we could get the boat underway while two gunboats were tied up in the outer harbor. We'd have to go right by them and even if we managed to get past them in one piece, they would easily be able to outrun us on the river.

Suddenly I had an idea.

With the diversion underway, Melowa and I climbed up the middle of the boat by grabbing on to the dinghy davits, and slipped across the cockpit and inside. Jenny was right next to the door looking terrified and she visibly relaxed when she saw it was us.

"Oh my God, what are we going to do, Brice?"

She was clearly shaken but seemed to be thinking clearly and I said, "You keep everybody quiet. You and Bridget calm the people. Melowa and I are going to try to disable the gunboats. I need those spare dock lines from up forward."

By now Bridget had crawled over to us and I looked at her and said, "Can you get in though the access locker and get two dock lines for me? Now?" Jenny quickly translated what I had said into French.

Bridget quickly shuffled away and as my eyes adjusted to the gloom of the inside of the darkened boat, I realize that about ten people were on the floor with us in the main cabin.

I said to Jenny, "And after we leave, get all those people hidden in the cabins below decks and make sure they don't try to look out the windows! If someone comes down to search the boat they'll probably only scan the main salon. If they do come down below, at least there's a better chance you can take them out," and with that I motioned to Melowa to hand her the machine gun. I went on, "Do you know how to fire one of these?"

Jenny nodded doubtfully saying, "My dad's a gun freak. I've fired a lot of guns, but never one of these. Is this the safety?"

She thumbed one of the levers and I showed her where the safety and the fully automatic position was, adding, "Good girl! Now, wish us luck!"

I tucked the handgun, which now only had four shots left, into my pants and grabbed the two ropes from Bridget who had just returned from down below. I reminded Jenny to get everybody down into the hulls and to remain hidden, and Melowa and I crawled back out to the cockpit and slipped over the side off the back.

I gave Melowa one of the ropes and said, "Follow me. We'll swim underwater to the far side to the shadows there and surface." I pointed at a dark area over near the inner fence. And then I said, "Once we're there, we'll make a quick dash underwater to the outside of the first gunboat. Surface quietly and we'll do our business from there."

I took a deep breath and went under. Five minutes later we were next to the big black gunboat and I whispered to her my plan. "I'm going to go down and tie their props up, then I'll swim to the next one and do the same. Keep a watch for me!"

I slipped under the water and carefully felt my way along the bottom of the boat until I came to the prop shaft and followed it down 'till I got to the big four-bladed prop. I quickly wrapped the rope around the prop and tied it to the strut and then dipped under the short keel and did the same to the other side. Then I retraced my moves back to the surface next to Melowa. By the time I reached the surface, my lungs were on fire and it was all I could do not to make a sound as I fought to control my gasps for breath. Melowa grabbed my shoulder and put her finger to her mouth, then pointed up on deck. Just above us was a soldier with his zipper open and starting to pee. There was nothing I could do but make myself as small as possible under the flare of the bow while urine trickled down my face.

After a minute he shook himself and walked away. I took the other line from Melowa and whispered in her ear, "You stay here, I'm going to swim to the other boat and do the same thing. I'll surface over there and then once you see me, we can both swim back and meet in the shadows like before, OK?"

She nodded and I took a measured breath and sank beneath the surface.

This time it was a lot harder. I had over a hundred feet to swim before I got to the other boat's props and then still had to tie the ropes, so by the time I surfaced next to the far boat's hull, I was almost unconscious. It had taken every bit of willpower to hold my breath and not suck in water, but I'd made it. Now all we had to do was get back to the catamaran and wait for an opportunity to make our escape.

Melowa saw me the moment I surfaced and I held up my hand, signaling her to wait for a moment until I had regained my breath. A minute later I was ready and I shook my head and we both dipped under for the long swim back.

Miraculously, we had accomplished it all in about fifteen minutes and as we climbed back aboard the aft deck of the catamaran, we both smiled at each other while lying flat on our backs, our chests heaving as we regained our strength.

A couple minutes later we both crawled across the cockpit and took shelter down below. I realized that the wet trail we had left across the cockpit would be a dead giveaway if a guard were to come looking and was glad when the rains started to fall more heavily again.

Jenny peeked around the corner from the starboard stairway and smiled at me. As I gave her a thumbs up I said, "Any developments here? What have you been hearing?"

She told me that since that initial gunfire that she hadn't heard much of anything, and I commented that maybe the guard troops had pulled back. I crawled carefully across the salon floor and through to where I could look ahead. It was absolutely quiet and no-one was in sight.

◆◆◆

Pulu had found Alex just as he was about to finish hot-wiring a big truck and the reporter almost shot the Indian until they recognized each other. Pulu quickly filled him in with the change in plans and they left the truck. Alex told Pulu to wait a second and quickly retrieved a large bundle he had made up from behind the truck. He winked at Pulu and they both quickly made their way towards the back of the pool house compound. It was then that Pulu heard the call of the jaguar. He paused before answering with this own jaguar call and he looked over at Peterson and said, "This is the signal to fall back and regroup. We have agreed that if the first thrust is not successful, that we will fall back to the top of the hill across the basin. We can get there this way."

Pulu started off towards the edge of the jungle as Alex said, "But what about Brice and the prisoners? What if they're discovered?"

The Indian said, "All we can do is hope, unless of course you want to finish this attack by yourself, I think it is a good time to regroup and think. We still have plenty of night to work with."

Alex and the three Indians then slunk away into the shadows and climbed the hill behind the compound. Pulu knew the way through a small hole in the fence behind some bushes that he had made during his observations over the previous weeks and within five minutes they were at the crest of the low hill overlooking the lit compound. They could hear shouting and saw movement below and realized that the soldiers had figured out that the attack had ceased and were regrouping themselves, and it looked like they were moving back to a defensive perimeter down in the outer fenced area. With the two gunboats and the hundred or so extra soldiers, the area near the outer docks looked much more defensible and safer to the frightened and poorly trained guards.

Within twenty minutes the seventy or so remaining Indian survivors of the initial attack were all gathered at the top of the hill and began to discuss what to do next. Peterson brought up an important point. "I saw them take two prisoners into the caves, I'd like to try to get in there and pull them out. I'll need three men to go with me."

Pulu quickly agreed to go, as did two of the other Indians that had been helping Peterson for the last half hour. A plan was devised to create a diversion and within minutes the Indians moved to disperse. The rain began to come down harder and as soon as Alex and his companions were on the base of the hill and making their way to the cave entrance, the rain came down in a torrential downpour, effectively hiding them from the rest of the enemy across the lagoon.

Peterson was taking up the lead and as they approached the guardhouse at the entrance, they were challenged. "Who's there?" a frightened sounding man asked in Spanish.

Pulu said in excellent Spanish that he was there to relieve him and that Carlos himself had sent him.

The man opened the door a crack and that was enough. Peterson yanked the door open and grabbed the man, throwing him heavily down in the dirt in front of the shack. Pulu and one of the Indians jumped on him and Pulu killed him nearly instantly with his knife, thrusting it through the man's throat and severing his brain stem. Within minutes they had pulled the guard back into the shack and propped him up in a chair. Alex found the key to the door and quietly opened it. Leaving one of the Indians behind to guard the entrance, he put down his heavy package and the three remaining men slipped inside and shut the door behind them.

The two Indians looked with apprehension at the dark tunnel leading off into the mountain and Peterson told Pulu, "I've scouted out this entire system. I know where most of the tunnels go. Just follow me."

He took off at a half run down the long sparsely lit passageway and the two Indians padded along behind him, looking from right to left as they passed offshoots and side passages leading off into the gloom.

Soon they saw brighter lights up ahead and slowed down to a quiet, stealthy pace as they approached the brightly lit lower room Peterson had been in earlier that had the passageway to the treasure chamber leading up from it. They heard loud men's voices and the sounds of a woman sobbing.

Taking shelter in a side tunnel not far from the room, Peterson whispered to Pulu, "I'll go ahead and surprise them, then you guys attack and kill them. Just be careful to not hurt the girl or the young captain."

Pulu nodded and Peterson stepped out and boldly walked down the passageway to the makeshift torture chamber. What he saw was shocking and sickening and he felt his hands and arms tense in anger.

The young woman was strapped down to a crude wooden table and had been cut hideously across her breasts and stomach. She was sobbing and crying for mercy as Santiago stood over her, his sharp knife at her left nipple as he raped her, thrusting so heavily that she was shaking violently with each angry thrust while he sliced her breast, drawing blood.

Peterson said, "Am I interrupting anything?"

Santiago whirled around and reached for his sidearm, which he realized was down around his ankles. His companion, an older guard, brought his gun up to bear but an arrow pierced his left eye and went through his skull, pinning him to the wooden shoring of the cavern side. The life slipped out of his body as he slumped and Santiago threw himself to the left to try to get away as Alex lunged for him. Santiago held his knife out as he fumbled on the ground for his gun but Peterson kicked him hard in the arm which sent his knife flying across the room, up against the rock wall. The man tried to get back up but the angry reporter was too quick for him and kicked him in the face, sending teeth flying and twisting his head violently to the right as he went unconscious.

The younger Indian jumped on top of the fallen man and brought his knife up for a death thrust but Alex stopped him.

"I have a better plan for his death. Just tie him up, and make it quick!"

He then went over to the girl and began to gently untie her. She was sobbing as he told her he was there to rescue her and her brother. A quick inspection of her body revealed that most of the cuts were superficial and although undoubtedly painful, they did not appear to be immediately life threatening. Provided he could get her to a hospital, she'd probably live.

As soon as she was freed, he helped Pulu who was trying to get Toby untied from his chair. Alex grabbed Santiago's knife from the floor and quickly cut the remaining bindings and the young man struggled to his feet. He thanked Alex and the two Indians for saving them, then his legs gave out and he collapsed.

Peterson picked up the girl from the table and carried her down the passageway and the two Indians each picked up one of Toby's arms and helped him down the corridor towards the outer door.

"What about the evil one? Why not kill him now?" Pulu asked.

Peterson answered, "As I said, I have plans for him."

Within two minutes they were at the front door to the cavern and they exited into the small guard shack. The Indian guard reported that while there had been quite a bit of noise across the lagoon, that there was nothing coming from the inner compound. The rain sounded as if it was coming down as hard as ever. Alex placed the girl on a small cot in the guardhouse and told the others to make a run for the boat. "I've got a little something to do here first. I'll be there in just a few minutes. Now, GO!"

The two Indians lifted Toby's arms again and with Pulu they exited the shack and wasted no time in making a run for the boat, half dragging the delirious young man with them.

It took Peterson only a few minutes to make his preparations and he then picked the girl up again. She gasped with pain as he exited the doorway.

Once outside, the pounding rain made the girl's painful cuts excruciating and she began to cry out. Peterson put his large hand over her mouth saying, "I'm so sorry, but if you want to live, it's really important that you keep quiet. I'll get you outta here, but you've gotta help me, OK?"

She relaxed and pursed her mouth at the pain and nodded her head. Peterson hefted her with a new grip and thundered down the sidewalk towards the docks and in less than a minute they were scrambling down the finger pier to the catamaran. Jenny had seen them coming down the dock and I went out to help them aboard.

As soon as everyone was on the boat, I said to Alex, "I can get us underway any time, but the problem is, now all the men are down at the entrance. It would be impossible to get out unless there was some sort of diversion."

Peterson smiled at me and put his hand on my shoulder. Leaning towards me he said, "Have I ever got one of those in the works! But before I tell you about that, what about those gunboats? We'll never outrun them, even if we do get past them!"

I smiled and looked him in the eyes saying, "Have I got a surprise for *you*!"

He laughed a quiet chuckle and said, "I like your attitude, Cannon. Let's cause some trouble."

Peterson reeled about and took off down the dock with Pulu in hot pursuit while I helped the Indians get the injured siblings below decks.

Jenny helped Toby below and sent his sister Camila in Bridget's care to the other forward cabin. People moved aside for them and despite the crowded space, made room for the injured girl on the bed and Bridget immediately set about tending to her cuts. I checked on the other two and found that Jenny was nursing Toby which seemed to make them both immensely happy. Jenny leaned over and kissed Toby and he put his arms out to hold her. I hadn't seen that coming.

As soon as they were safely in the side cabins, and room had been made for them, I went up to the bridge and started the engines. The big Lagoon catamaran had quiet engines and so I doubted they could be heard, and in this driving rain it was still impossible to see across the basin.

Peterson returned to the guardhouse and worked quickly. He bent over and lifted the bundled package he had brought up with him from the store room and opened the door to the cavern one last time, carefully placing the package inside the heavy door and then bent over the bundle again, working quickly, while the puzzled Indian looked on.

"What are you doing, my friend?" Pulu asked.

Alex answered, "Just making sure your evil man never sees the light of day again and that he suffers a horrible, long death." Pulu smiled at this and just then, a fuse sputtered and Peterson said, "Let's go!"

The two men returned to the back side of the pool compound at a full run. No-one challenged them, so they thought they were home free when they ran into the motor pool. They practically ran right into four soldiers with machine guns who were checking the area out.

For a moment they stared dumbly at each other when Peterson grabbed the Indian and put him in a full nelson, screaming at the soldiers in Spanish, "Help me, you idiots, this guy almost had me! We need to tie him up, he's the chief's son and we can ransom him, get me some rope!"

The leader looked puzzled but saw the intensity and lack of fear in Peterson's eyes so he gave the order and the three others went searching for some rope. Peterson asked angrily, "What took you so long to get here? Carlos called you over an hour ago!"

The leader said, "I am sorry but we only heard of this less than an hour ago and we came as fast as we could. Just be glad we were not far away on the river or it could have been longer! I believe that General Alverado and Carlos have already left. We will have this place secure for you very soon, amigo, so relax, OK?"

One of the soldiers came up with a length of rope and set about tying up the struggling Indian. As he bent over to secure the man's feet, Peterson looked up behind the leader and said, "What is that? More Indians are coming!"

The leader looked away just long enough for Alex to grab the other soldier's gun and bring it to bear. He mowed down the four soldiers in less than five seconds and threw the gun aside as he worked to untie Pulu.

"We have to work fast. More soldiers will come after that bit of antics!"

"What is 'antics'?" the Indian asked as he got up, rubbing his wrists.

Peterson shook his head as he set about getting the truck hot-wired again and as soon as it was started he fiddled with something he had left on the seat next to him. Once it was done he put the truck in gear, threw a rock on the gas pedal and popped the clutch, throwing himself out of the truck door as it leapt forward towards the rear compound wall. "Run!"

The two men ran as fast they could, but not fast enough. The truck plowed through the wall and came to a shuddering stop inside the back wall of the guest complex and seconds later a devastating explosion rocked the entire compound. Both men had been knocked flat by the blast and had the wind knocked out of them, but within a few seconds were up and running again, down past the cell block and onto the pier just as the big catamaran began to strain against her dock lines.

◆◆◆

I had put the engines in gear when I heard the explosion and watched anxiously as Alex and Pulu emerged from the darkness, running towards us down the dock. They jumped aboard and I slammed the boat into full reverse. At first, nothing happened but then the power cord and the forward docking cleats tore free of the hulls and we surged out into the basin. I spun the boat around and lined up for where I believed was the opening for the inner fence and put the engines in full throttle forward. By the time we passed the inner fence we were already doing ten knots and as we approached the dock where the gunboats were tied up, we were doing close to fifteen. Small arms fire began to erupt from shore and we ducked down as I lined up for the gate in the outer fence. As we approached it we saw two men frantically trying to slide the gate closed, but Alex stepped out onto the foredeck and fired two rounds from his handgun. Both men dropped.

Then the cave entrance blew. The explosion shook the entire compound and in the bright light behind us we saw the entire hillside collapse.

By now Peterson had run back up to the helm area so that he could cover the shore better with gunfire.

"Holy shit, Alex! Did you do that?" I asked.

He smiled and said, "Just wanted to make sure that treasure stayed buried and I left that creep Santiago inside to guard it. Should keep him busy for the rest of his life."

The remaining Indians had taken the two explosions as their signal to renew their attack and in a matter of seconds the chaos on shore to our left brought an end to the enemy fire we were taking as the soldiers brought their weapons to bear on the attack from their rear. Ten more seconds passed and only a single soldier on land fired at us, raking the bridge deck and hitting my left shoulder with some fiberglass shrapnel. Peterson fired at the guy and he fell. And then we were through the outer fence and free! I turned by instinct to the port as I recalled the river had made a turn there and then carefully reduced speed to a more manageable level. I had made a GPS chart plot of our course on the way in and I followed it like it was a lifeline in the near zero visibility with the pitch-dark night and driving rain. We heard the big gunboats start their engines and could hear shouting in the distance as they prepared to follow us. A few minutes later the sounds faded and Alex, who had come up to join me at the helm asked, "Now why do you suppose they aren't following us?"

I answered nonchalantly, "I can't imagine. Maybe they got something caught in their props."

"Pretty good for an old man," Peterson jibed and then he said, "Of course, they'll probably clear the props soon enough. What's our plan?"

I realized I hadn't thought that part out carefully enough and then I remembered the river where the Indian village was. Could I find it in the dark? I hadn't marked it on the chart plotter and as I edged the throttles back up to where we were doing twelve knots, I started to worry about what might happen next.

◆◆◆

"How long 'til we reach the engagement area?"

Bruske was up behind the pilots and peering into the complete darkness ahead as if he might be able to help them go faster.

"Sir, we see seven minutes to engagement area. Drop will likely be in nine minutes. We'll have to find a safe place to put you guys down."

Bruske said, "Keep a full infrared scan going. I want to see what's out there. This rain is fucking my night up!"

He turned and went back to his company and announced, "We'll be in the engagement area in eight point five minutes. Satellite is picking up more explosions and small arms fire. This is a hot zone, gentlemen, and so be prepared to hit the ground running."

He sat down in his seat heavily and brooded for the next several minutes as they approached their landing area.

◆◆◆

I heard it first and then Melowa did too. She was at my side and grabbed my forearm as she said, "I think I hear those boats, Capitan Brites!"

I listened carefully and realized the sound was getting closer. It was the gunboats. At least one of them anyway. The more I listened as the droning became louder, the more certain I was that it was just one boat. What the hell difference did it make? One was plenty to finish us off!

I started scanning the sides of the river to see if there was a place to hide but the same driving rain that had aided our escape was now making it almost impossible to make out any details of the shoreline that was going by so dangerously fast. One short moment of indecision and we'd go aground or hit an overhanging tree and it would all be over. We'd be sitting ducks for the pursuing gunboat. I could only hope that our pursuers would have to travel slower because they probably didn't have a GPS and so I slammed the throttles back up to full speed. The big catamaran surged ahead into the blackness and I realized my hands were trembling. Melowa must have noticed this and she hugged me around my middle and pressed her head against my side saying, "It is OK, Capitan Brites. Even if we die tonight, you have done more for us than anyone could ever hope. I am in love with you, Capitan," and she went onto her tiptoes and kissed me on my cheek and hugged me again as we surged on into the night.

◆◆◆

"Drop zone in five, four, three, two, one! GO, GO, GO!" Bruske watched as all of his men tumbled out at five hundred feet towards the dense canopy below. The pilot had chosen what looked like a small clearing but it was damn small indeed. Bruske followed his last man out and within seconds was slammed into the ground and rolling up his chute. He gathered his things and met the platoon to make their move into the hot zone.

The men began their short march through the underbrush towards the sporadic gunfire they heard up ahead.

The pilot pulled up and began to bear off towards the carrier when his copilot said, "We've got a couple infrareds just up ahead. And the back one is moving up on the front one. Could be a pursuing craft on the river, awful close to the area of engagement. Want to check it out?"

The pilot thought for a second and said, "Oh what the hell, yes, let's check it out, I would never hear the end of it if we missed out on some of the action."

The heavily armed V-22 Osprey with is huge rotating wings bore off to follow the infrared traces and came up on the back one fairly quickly. "You want me to turn on the spotlight?"

The pilot said, "Arm the surface to ground missiles and stand by on the light. We don't want to give them too much warning, just in case they're the bad guys."

◆◆◆

I was out of options. We could hear the gunboat coming up on us now and it was only a matter of another minute or two at the most before we'd come under their fire. Our time was up. Then I heard another louder sound.

Oh great, I thought, *there's the other boat.*

We came around a bend and, looking down at my chart plotter track from when were on our way in, I saw that we had entered a straight stretch of the river and, looking over our shoulders, we could now see the bow wake of the gunboat behind us. We saw a flash and a huge splash erupted next to the boat on our left, drenching us all in spray.

A megaphone shattered our hope for escape. "Stop your vessel immediately! We will fire on you! Stop your vessel!"

Just then the entire night sky was flooded in light from above.

The gunboat crew stared at the bright light above them and were unsure of how to respond. Then the captain ordered, "Open fire on that helicopter. Shoot it down!"

The two deck machine guns swung up and both began to fire simultaneously as the aircraft surged suddenly up to the left and turned out its lights.

The captain said, "You see, it was nothing, they are cowards," and he turned back towards the fleeing catamaran and said, "Shoot them out of the water!"

The pilot swung the Osprey in a tight circle and made an approach to bring the target in line as he said to his copilot, "Engage as she bears."

Eight seconds later the gunboat erupted in a fiery ball.

I could barely believe what had just happened. One moment we were in dire peril with only seconds to live and the next we were running along an empty river with a burning patch of oil behind us quickly receding into the distance. I slowed the boat to eight knots and began to watch for the small river that led to the village which I knew had to be somewhere off to the left. By now Pulu had come up on deck and thankfully he knew the river like the back of his own hand, even in the dark, and so shortly we made a turn and were safely off the main river where pursuit would be unlikely, even if they did get the other gunboat running.

The Osprey made another pass and this time put us into their spotlight. I told everybody to wave and shout which the people did enthusiastically. I called the aircraft on VHF ch. 16 and was surprised when they answered.

"This is U.S. Navy aircraft A6071, come in, sailboat, and identify yourselves."

I spoke slowly into the mic. "This is the sailing yacht Lady of the Woods out of Tortola, BVI with approximately forty persons onboard requesting immediate assistance! We have two badly injured persons on board and are in imminent danger from pursuing forces. Please acknowledge!"

The chopper pilot responded with, "We copy. A support aircraft will be at your position within an hour. We will stay with you as long as possible. Please make your vessel secure and stopped so that a transfer can be made."

I responded, "There is a place up ahead where we will stop. I copy and will be standing by. Lady of the Woods, out."

Eighteen

The Marines worked their way into the battle zone in three separate groups. With full body armor and night vision, the men, who were all crack shots, picked off the enemy soldiers and guards as easily as if they were at a county fair shooting metal targets. Within fifteen minutes of engagement over half the enemy force was down and the remaining soldiers threw down their arms, surrendering. The Indians streamed into the area and began to systematically eliminate the remaining men until Rodriguez and Callwood convinced them to stop killing the prisoners and to place them in the cell block which was now under the full control of the Marines.

With the giant V-22 escorting us up the small side river under full illumination of their powerful searchlight, we made the final bend to the Indian village and I anchored the boat by dropping our bow anchor mid-stream and backed up towards the shore.

I noticed there was a small motor launch pulled up on the bank, but the village appeared deserted. I guessed that the villagers had all run up into the forest under the assumption that all the noise and bright light was from the enemy, and so Jenny and Alex got a stern line ready and Pulu jumped into the water, swimming the short distance to shore where he secured the line to a tree. We then centered ourselves off the riverbank and finally shut down the engines. I felt like we were pretty safe, but still wanted to get the injured girl and Toby off the boat as soon as possible, so as soon as we were secured I radioed the chopper pilot and told them that we were going to get the two people ready to be transferred up and that I would be sending one additional person along to help.

I turned to Jenny and said, "Look, you need to go with Toby and his sister. Can you organize some people to help us get them up here and we'll take them over to the shore where the helicopter can send a basket down for them?"

Jenny protested, saying that she wanted to stay behind, but I insisted that she accompany the two wounded and reminded her that her parents were probably sick with worry.

So after a brief conversation with the crew of the Osprey, we had the dinghy launched and the two wounded people were transferred ashore.

By now Pulu had gone back into the nearby forest and retrieved some of his people. So, by the time we got ashore, there were eager hands to assist in picking up the badly injured girl, and Jenny and Pulu helped Toby ashore as well. Fifteen minutes later, after a few nerve-racking moments when the basket that had been lowered to bring up the wounded had swung too close to some nearby trees, all three were aboard and the pilot radioed me on my handheld on the shore.

"We're going to proceed back to our ship. Another support aircraft will be with you within twenty minutes, so stay safe. We're outta here!"

The huge aircraft wheeled around and disappeared into the night and within a minute, silence closed in around us.

That's when we heard it.

Melowa was the first to say something. She grabbed my arm and said, "Listen! I think I hear another boat!"

I heard it too and realized she was right. It sounded like the other gunboat. Pulu turned and ran away into the village and as the sound grew louder we realized that the second gunboat had probably gotten its props cleared and had taken off in our pursuit. I knew that with all the light and sound of the huge V-22 Osprey hovering over us that our hiding spot up the small tributary had been discovered and so I shouted to Alex, who was still on the boat "We need to get all those people off the boat and hidden in the forest. Get everybody ready and I'll bring the dinghy back. We've gotta make this quick! That gunboat will be here any minute!"

I then pushed the dinghy off the shore and started the engine, quickly returning to the stern of the big cat, and Peterson helped ten of the people into the dinghy.

After two more runs to shore with a full boat, I was making my final trip back for the remaining people when the gunboat hove into sight. It rounded the bend just as I was bringing the dinghy alongside and a search light hit the catamaran, throwing a blinding stream of light across the water. The gunboat opened fire immediately with its portside machine gun. All around me the water exploded as the frenzy of bullets ripped the surface.

I screamed in Spanish, "Jump! Swim to the shore! Get off the boat!"

Within seconds the remaining ten people and Alex all dove into the water and swam for the shore and I whipped the dinghy in a tight circle away from the sweeping arc of bullets that was tearing up the water as it came towards me. It all seemed to happen in slow motion as the stern of the inflatable dinghy was overtaken by a hail of bullets and one of the bullets must have struck the engine block which then disintegrated with hot aluminum shavings, hitting my already injured arm and side of my torso, throwing me into the water.

As soon as I was in the water I made for the bottom of the river to get away from the bullets that were ripping up the dinghy above me and thankfully I was not hit again. A few seconds went by and then I saw the faint outline of the gunboat come alongside the cat just above me and crash heavily alongside. The light from a fire in the water in what I guessed was the remains of the dinghy off to my left illuminated the scene and I made my way up on the far side for some air, carefully listening for sounds of the soldiers who I knew were only a few feet away from me, thundering aboard the abandoned catamaran. That's when I heard the first screams.

After Pulu had run off into the village, it had not taken him long to gather the few remaining men, all older warriors, and a few of the teenagers who had been deemed too young to take place in the attack on the compound. He had then deployed them along the riverbank in the bushes and underbrush and so by the time the gunboat had made the final turn and opened fire, a hail of arrows and poison darts had covered the deck of the gunboat. By the time it was alongside the catamaran, over half the crew had been killed outright and the remaining soldiers had poured over onto the catamaran to get away from the attack from shore. Both machine guns had been silenced with the operators hanging over the side of the guns, a dozen or more arrows protruding from their bodies.

Within minutes the remaining solders had begun to return fire but by now they were badly outnumbered. As I continued to feebly tread water, I retreated to under the main hull and listened as some of the Indians swam out from shore and boarded the cat, finishing off the last of the solders in a bloody but nearly silent struggle barely twenty feet from my hiding place. With only the grunts and screams of the dying to break the quiet, finally, complete silence came back over the river and I shouted out in Spanish, "Alex, Pulu, I'm in the water. Please, tell the men to stop killing! I need to get out of the river. I've been hit!"

I heard a voice I thought was Peterson's shouting from shore and then heard a small motorboat coming my way. A few minutes later a head popped down from the afterdeck, looking for me under the bridge area. I could see from the light from the gunboat's searchlight, which was now pointed haphazardly into the river behind the two boats, that it was Pulu. He had led the attack on the cat and he reached out his arm saying, "Take my hand. I'll pull you out!"

I swam the short distance over and within a moment was hefted by three men onto the afterdeck. The pain was excruciating as the two injuries in my left arm and side were stretched, and I passed out.

Nineteen

While I was still unconscious, my friends transferred me into the small launch and I came to again as we were bumping up onto the riverbank next to the village. Many hands pulled me onto the shore and within a few minutes, Melowa was cleaning and bandaging my wounds as Alex and Pulu crouched next to me speaking in hushed tones.

I said, "Was that a motor boat? Where'd it come from?"

Peterson said, "It's the ferry boat I hired from the town up river. I'd arranged for him to pick me up."

I struggled to my feet amidst complaints and admonishments from Melowa and said, "If he took me up river now, I might just catch up to Carlos and catch him with his pants down."

Pulu said, "I'm going too," and he and Peterson both started to stand.

I turned to walk back towards the water and winced with pain. Melowa grabbed my good arm, imploring me to stay, but I said, "I'm going, and don't try to stop me! That creep's brother has my wife held captive and I need to learn where they are. Just help me get down to the boat." And looking at Peterson and Pulu I said, "Let's get moving!"

Fifteen minutes later we were out in the main river and heading upstream at a good twenty-five knots. The rain had finally stopped and as we heard a large helicopter go by overhead in the direction of the Indian village I said, "Maybe we should have waited for the Marines, but my best guess is that it's better to come in quiet and sneak up on these guys rather than come in from the air with guns blazing."

Peterson nodded and said, "My feelings too. I've just spoken to our captain here and he says he has a pretty good idea where they might have been headed."

Alex motioned with this head to the captain who was steering the big launch with his foot while leaning out over the side, peering off into the darkness and then added, "He says he hates these guys too and wants us to succeed in killing them."

Two hours went by and it was nearly 2 a.m. when, with the sky clearing and starlight showing imperceptibly, the lights of the small town and wharf hove into view.

The boatman slowed the launch down and leaned over to say something to Peterson who then came back over to the side I was sitting on and said, "He says we should land on the bank here. It's only about a half a kilometer and he thinks Carlos and the general will be in the same hotel I stayed at. He said he's called his brother on the VHF who'll pick us up in his taxi a short distance from the landing. I know the guy. I think it's OK."

A few minutes later we were off the boat and making our way up through the trees to the small road just as two car headlights shone at us. A small taxi bounced down the lane and came to a stop beside us.

"Señor Alex. Welcome back."

I was introduced to the taxi driver and he looked on with some disapproval when Pulu piled into the back seat along with me. Alex took a seat next to the driver in the front and said, "The Indian's my friend. He's got a score to settle with one of the men we're looking for."

The driver nodded reluctantly and we slammed the doors and bumped on down the rutty road towards the town.

Five minutes later we pulled up a block away from the hotel where Alex said he had stayed and we all got out. I heard Alex speak to the taxi driver saying, "Give us ten minutes, and if we don't come out, best you'd go be somewhere else, cause it won't be good!"

We closed the doors and now, with the moon beginning to show behind some the disbursing clouds, we ran around the back of the hotel and up the back steps. A minute later we were inside and quietly making our way along the corridor, listening carefully. Pulu had his knife drawn and Peterson had his 9mm in his hand. I had one of the submachine guns I'd picked up back on the shoreline in the village, a gun likely pulled off the gunboat after the attack.

As we reached the end of the corridor, Alex put his hand up and then his finger over his mouth, shushing us, and he then motioned me to listen.

Placing my ear near the door, I heard Carlos pleading.

"General, I have no idea how this attack came about! You cannot blame me! It is I who have lost everything! My compound has been destroyed, my slaves are now all gone, I have no idea who was behind it all!"

General Alverado spoke angrily. "Your incompetence has cost me not only over a hundred of my best men, but two of my gunboats and has possibly undermined my authority as well! This is not forgivable!"

A gunshot rang out and at that instant, on an impulse, I kicked the door in.

Peterson lunged inside and I followed. Just as the general's arm came up to fire at him, I cut him down with a short burst from my submachine gun. Peterson shot two more of the general's men and then silence overcame us. I looked at Carlos and realized that he was not dead. The general had only fired to scare him, a bullet having grazed his temple. He was reeling in shock and pain, but very much alive.

"You are stupid, Capitan, to have shot the general. You will never make it out of this town alive!" Carlos spat.

I threw the machine gun over my shoulder and then punched Carlos in the face as hard as I could, knocking him off his chair and he sprawled on the ground, motionless.

I looked at Pulu and Alex and said, "Let's get him out of here!"

The two men grabbed Carlos up off the floor and he came to, struggling. I hit him again hard in his gut and he doubled halfway over. The fight having been taken out of him, we managed to get him out of the room and down the hall. We were half dragging, half carrying him across the back lawn and down behind one of the other houses, and we cut out across a vacant lot when a bright light hit us. We froze.

Above us what appeared to be a large helicopter flew toward us and descended. Holding my hand up to block the glare of the light, I saw a gunner who had a large machine gun aimed at us. I told Alex and Pulu to drop Carlos and we put our hands up, dropping our weapons.

A loudspeaker announced, "Down on the ground. This is the U.S. Marines, do it now! Move!"

We all threw our weapons aside.

Just then Carlos, having played at being more badly hurt that he was, lunged to his right and grabbed the gun Pulu had dropped and turned it towards me. I tried to jump out of the way but felt my side get hit just as a burst of fire from the helicopter cut the man in half.

I grimaced at Peterson as I slowly got to my knees and held my hands out in front of me, finally lying flat. A few moments later we're surrounded by camouflaged men and one of them spoke to me.

"Who are you, and what are you doing with this man?"

Fifteen minutes later we were on our way to the aircraft carrier and I was on the phone with a man named Winters from the CIA.

♦♦♦

It was eight-thirty in the morning by the time the schooner My World had rounded the corner and was making its way into the bay Juliet had told Sarah about. As they rounded the final headland, a beautiful wooden motor yacht came into view.

"There she is," Juliet said, pointing at the yacht anchored about two miles farther up in the bay.

"I guess it's show time then," Sarah said.

Jamison, one of the Marines said, "Just get us alongside. We'll do the rest. And as soon as you hear any gunfire? Get down below!"

Valerie said, "You want me to do it now?"

Sarah responded, "Yeah, pour the oil in now."

In the engine room, Ben took a quart of motor oil and gradually began to pour it into the intake manifold of the Ford diesel. He poured it gradually so it didn't kill the engine, and the effect was immediate.

Captain Mack had crammed a large lobster boil pot full of newspaper and soaked it with lighter fluid and balanced it at the top of the companionway steps just under the main hatch, then set it on fire.

Ramon and Javier were sitting on the afterdeck enjoying a leisurely breakfast when one of the crew came aft to alert them. "Sorry, Señor, but there is a boat coming towards us that looks like it might be on fire!"

Ramon jumped up from the breakfast table and Javier followed him out to the side deck.

About a quarter mile away, a schooner they recognized from Cartagena was making straight at them with black smoke pouring from its exhaust. More smoke was coming from the main hatch and Ramon shouted for his captain to grab his binoculars.

Focusing on the rapidly approaching boat, he heard the VHF radio in the salon come to life. "Mayday, mayday. This is the schooner My World. We are on fire and need to get our people off. Powerboat in the bay with us. We are going to come alongside!"

By now the schooner was only a few hundred feet away and it looked like about eight or nine frightened young hippies were all lined up on the side deck, waving their arms and shouting, "Help, help!"

Javier grabbed the mic and said, "Do not approach. Stay away!" but the boat kept on coming.

Hastily the crew of the Inca Gold threw fenders over the side to ward off a collision and then the big schooner hit them, coming to a stop alongside. The confused crew of the Inca Gold didn't manage to stop any of the hippies who came onboard and then, in an instant, the boarders turned machine guns on the crew and took over. Ramon dodged down below out of sight just as a giant of a man ran after him. The giant caught up with him as he had reached a cabin door and the man yanked him off his feet with one hand, throwing him to the floor.

"Not so fast, man," the giant said and a moment later two more armed hippies came down the hall and grabbed Ramon. Ben wrenched him back to his feet and slammed him against the side of the passageway. "Where's the girl?" Tell me! Now!"

Ramon pursed his lips but the giant mashed them flat with a huge fist and the Colombian crumbled. The two other men pulled him back up and Ben demanded again, "Tell us! Now!"

Ramon motioned with his head, now dizzy from being hit so hard and the giant man slammed him back against the hallway again, punched him in his gut and then pushed past and went down to the last door, nearly wrenching it off its hinges while the two Marines pushed Ramon down on to the floor. With one man covering him with his gun, the other Marine went down past the giant, and entered the small cabin.

Ramon rolled suddenly to his side and pulled a small handgun out, talking aim at Ben. Two quicks shots rang out as one of the Marines shot him. Behind them in the passageway Javier threw himself out through one of the side doors and dodged down the deck, turning to open fire with a handgun, but he was quickly cut down from the deck of My World by Captain Mack who had been standing amidships, covering the Marines' advance.

Frederica, AKA Cynthia, was tied up in a chair. She'd heard all the commotion and was straining against her bindings when the door was suddenly flung open. She looked up in terror at the two large men, one with a submachine gun, who entered the room.

Juliet had come aboard the moment she saw Javier fall on the side deck and she rushed past the Marines and entered the door to the main salon. She quickly crossed the cabin where four of the crew were being held at gunpoint on the floor and scrambled down the steps to the hallway below. Running past the body of Ramon, she sidestepped around him and entered the small cabin just as Frederica was looking at the two men in terror.

Suddenly, the reality of the situation dawned on the Interpol agent and she slumped over in her chair in relief.

Juliet ran to her and held her as Ben quickly undid her bindings.

The entire operation had taken less than five minutes.

By noon, a Panamanian gunboat had arrived and the prisoners were taken off. A relief crew was assembled aboard the Inca Gold which was being seized by the Panamanian Government, and the crew of My World reassembled in the main salon of the schooner, now safely anchored a short distance away.

Captain Sarah went over to the refrigerator and pulled out three beers, then returned to the table where Juliet and Captain Mack sat. "That was a hell of a last two days!"

Juliet and Mack clicked their bottles with Sarah, and Juliet said in a somewhat worried tone, "Now all we've gotta do is go save my husband."

The sat phone on My World rang from the aft cabin and Valerie went back to answer it while Juliet and Mack talked about how to get down to southern Colombia to mount a search for her husband.

Valerie called from the doorway in the walk-through to the aft cabin; "Juliet? It's for you. Somebody named Brice."

Twenty

Sixteen months later

Juliet called out the soundings from the helm as I stood on the bow, carefully piloting Captain Olivier's tug around the final bend in the river, and we dropped anchor in nearly the same spot I had anchored the catamaran Lady of the Woods in what seemed almost like another lifetime.

Alex Peterson and the French girl Bridget were in the cockpit with Juliet and Toby and Jenny were up on the bow with me, watching as a canoe pushed off from the shoreline in our direction. Within minutes, Pulu and Melowa were aboard and we all shared hugs and tearful embraces.

Our crew of six had made the trip up the Amazon from Manaus onto the Putumayo in less than six days, enjoying visiting some of the places we had been to under such different circumstance nearly a year and a half earlier.

We were here on a mission...

After the Colombian military had relieved the Marines at the compound in the jungle, the buildings were destroyed and the fuel depot and prison block, which had been partially destroyed, had been allowed to deteriorate further. Within a year the jungle had already begun to take back over.

The rumors of treasure that some of the surviving guards had spoken of had been dismissed as crazy talk and in any case, the collapsed hillside where the old entrance to the cave had been, made any access impossible. Within a few weeks the idle speculation had been forgotten and any talk of treasure was dismissed with laughter and ridicule.

So, when Alex had gotten in contact with me about making an expedition up the Putumayo to visit Melowa and Pulu, I had agreed immediately. Juliet had been harder to convince, but in the end agreed because she said she thought that maybe revisiting some of the places would help me to stop having the terrible nightmares that still sometimes plagued my nights.

After the ordeal of being kidnapped and held prisoner in Colombia, Jenny Tatterson had returned to her parents' home in Maryland. Her father

Roger had insisted that she undergo a complete psychiatric evaluation to make sure that there were no lasting effects from her ordeal, but within a few weeks, she had convinced everyone that she was OK. Her main concern had been about Toby, and her and Bridget's testimonies in the investigation into his involvement in the theft of the charter cat and subsequent piracy of the yacht off Brazil, which had finally absolved him of any undue responsibility. Because he had been blackmailed into helping the criminals, and because of his subsequent assistance in gaining the freedom of the senator's daughter, he was eventually cleared of all charges.

Within a few months of the incident, Jenny and Toby had become a couple and were hired by Sunshine Charters in the BVI to run one of the big catamarans for the next charter season. They had just finished a successful first season and had recently made an announcement that they were going to be married.

Alex Peterson had won a Pulitzer Prize for his intriguing and meticulously written series on the drug cartel which had been destroyed and the human trafficking, enslavement of the indigenous tribes and corruption in the government which had allowed the whole scenario to exist. Arrests had been made and largely due to the revelations in his articles, the formerly lawless area of southern Colombia began to be safe again for the law-abiding citizens. Many who had fled the area over the years to seek asylum in the more settled north of the country began to return and with this, were bringing a new prosperity to the ecologically and agriculturally rich region.

After the reuniting of the freed prisoners of the indigenous tribes with their respective villages, Peterson and Bridget had stayed on for a few weeks while they helped Melowa and her brother Pulu open a school at the village where the attack on the compound had been started. By the time they left, Alex had asked Bridget to accompany him to New York and together they made a trip around the country to see some of America. Alex had also been instrumental in introducing her to some top people in New York's fashion industry and within a year she had become one of the most popular new models in the international modeling community.

When he had emailed her to suggest a reunion on the Putumayo, she had agreed immediately. While Alex had at one point considered strongly the idea of asking Bridget to marry him, his pledge to remain single had won out. But now, at least to me, the reunited pair seemed like a happy couple.

Pulu and Melowa's school was a huge success with families from the entire region bringing in their more motivated children to learn English and Spanish and about the larger world outside their borders. Because of the New Times articles, tens of thousands of dollars in aid had poured into an account that Alex had set up to help support their efforts.

Rudy Bellows had gotten the three catamarans back, and Ainsley and Dunbar had been thrilled with us. They even recovered the Beneteau 47 Alex Peterson had seen in Cartagena. The cats were all a bit banged up, but after the delivery crews, escorted by Captain Olivier's old tugboat, had convoyed them down to the port of Manaus on the Amazon, the boats had been loaded on a ship and taken to a repair facility in the Mediterranean where they were reconditioned for charter.

After being reunited aboard the carrier off the Colombian coast, Jules and I had been flown to Cartagena and went to retrieve Mahalo. It had been a bit dicey going aboard, but the Marines had provided us with two demolitions and explosives experts who checked the boat over prior to our going inside. It was a lucky thing too. The boat had been wired with enough C4 to destroy half the marina. I guess Ramon hadn't been planning to pay us our fee after all. But once we had the boat secure, we left immediately for the BVI where we arrived ten days later, a bit beat up from the windward trip across the Caribbean, but happy to be back in safe and familiar waters.

Rudy Bellows had taken us out to a great dinner and he had made sure we were paid a substantial bonus by the insurance company for our work. The Colombians who planted the bomb had never found our secret hiding place onboard Mahalo either, so we still had the money we had gotten from Ramon.

All in all, we had come out of the whole affair pretty well set for a while. But always nagging in the back of my mind was some unfinished business back in the Amazon jungle.

So as Captain Olivier's tug finally came to rest, and after our reunion exuberance had calmed a bit, we began to unload some of the school supplies we had shipped in from the States. Along with several crates which Peterson had insisted were for research were box after box of books, a few computers and two small gas generators, as well as fuel for them which was transferred to the shore and after several hours, we had transported it all up to a new hut that had been built which housed the 'Putumayo School of Colombia'.

Since our experiences in the horrendous tunnels under the hills behind the compound sixteen months earlier, I'd tried to bring up talking about the buried Inca treasure a few times with Alex, but he'd been evasive about the subject.

One evening, while on our way up the river from Manaus I'd finally cornered him and had asked flat out, "Why not try to get back inside the treasure chamber?'

He'd answered, "Maybe keeping that treasure hidden for a few hundred more years, or until a truly stable government can oversee its retrieval is for the best. Don't you think?"

So, as we gazed at the dense jungle shoreline slipping by, I looked over at Peterson, thinking about what he had just said. "Maybe you're right, Alex. Maybe you're right."

Then Alex had smiled at me and with his right hand in his pocket, he fingered the key he had taken from the dead guard inside the treasure chamber and pulled it out of his pocket as he answered. "On the other hand, what would I do with this key and all that diving and spelunking gear I brought along if we didn't at least try to get back in there? And besides, I've always dreamed of writing an epic piece for *National Geographic*. I've even got a title for it: '*The Lost Treasure of El Dorado*'!"

Author's Note;

Although this story is a complete work of fiction, and any resemblance of the characters in this story to real people is entirely coincidental and unintentional, there are some aspects of this novel that are based on real events that have occurred in the not too distant past.

Boats do occasionally go missing from the charter fleets in the Caribbean and at least some of these have later been recovered while running drugs.

A catamaran was stolen several years back from a Caribbean charter fleet and was eventually recovered from up on a tributary of the Amazon where it was serving as a brothel with indigenous Indian girls being used as sex slaves. A boat stolen from the BVI was found sunken on a reef in the San Blas after a failed backpacker run and an American yacht with a single-handed captain was stolen from the San Blas. The captain was murdered and the boat was found abandoned in mainland Panama.

Human trafficking and sex slavery is an ongoing problem even today, and not enough time or money is spent in combating this vile trade.

And lastly, although there are people who would scoff at the stories of the existence of the fabled lost city of El Dorado, the treasures of this legendary city are believed by many to still exist, hidden somewhere out there in the trackless jungles of Amazonia in South America.

About the Author

Todd Duff leads an adventurous life not unlike that of his lead character in this series. He began sailing at an early age, became a sailplane pilot at age 16, has been involved in mountain climbing, scuba diving and spelunking and his interests include anthropology and archaeology. He is a former professional musician, and has been involved in the yachting industry since 1982 where he has worked as a marine contractor, and a yacht broker. He holds current credentials as an accredited marine surveyor, and is a well-known writer for many of the popular sailing magazines.

Todd has sailed extensively with his children as crew and while homeschooling them in various countries, teaching them to be lovers of the sea. He is a passionate adventurer, and has been involved in long distance sailing for the past three decades. Since 1987 he has spent twelve out of the last thirty years sailing full-time, traveling to and exploring thirty-one countries.

After recently completing a six-year sailing adventure through the Caribbean, Central and South America, and the North and South Pacific, Todd has returned to the Caribbean. Currently living aboard his sailboat in the British Virgin Islands, he is completing the next installment in the Cannon and Sparks series, and is already planning his next great adventure.